EARLY THIRTIES

— A NOVEL —

JOSH DUBOFF

SCOUT PRESS

New York Amsterdam/Antwerp London Toronto Sydney New Delhi

Scout Press
An Imprint of Simon & Schuster, LLC
1230 Avenue of the Americas
New York, NY 10020

First Scout Press hardcover edition March 2025

SCOUT PRESS and colophon are registered trademarks of Simon & Schuster, LLC

For information about special discounts for bulk purchases, please contact Simon & Schuster Special Sales at 1-866-506-1949 or business@simonandschuster.com.

The Simon & Schuster Speakers Bureau can bring authors to your live event. For more information or to book an event, contact the Simon & Schuster Speakers Bureau at 1-866-248-3049 or visit our website at www.simonspeakers.com.

Interior design by Jaime Putorti

Manufactured in the United States of America

10 9 8 7 6 5 4 3 2 1

Library of Congress Cataloging-in-Publication Data

Names: Duboff, Josh, author.
Title: Early thirties : a novel / Josh Duboff.
Description: New York : Scout Press Books, 2025. |
Identifiers: LCCN 2024024415 (print) | LCCN 2024024416 (ebook) |
ISBN 9781668059937 (hardcover) | ISBN 9781668059951 (ebook)
Subjects: LCGFT: Bildungsromans. | Novels.
Classification: LCC PS3604.U257 E27 2025 (print) | LCC PS3604.U257 (ebook) |
DDC 813/.6—dc23/eng/20240607
LC record available at https://lccn.loc.gov/2024024415
LC ebook record available at https://lccn.loc.gov/2024024416

ISBN 978-1-6680-5993-7
ISBN 978-1-6680-5995-1 (ebook)

For my mom, Janet L. Berkeley, my best friend

EARLY
THIRTIES

1

I woke up in a hospital bed. The last thing I remembered seeing was a blurry image of Cameron Diaz in a magazine . . . she was wearing dark sunglasses and a fedora. The taste of raspberry lime hard seltzer in my mouth was overwhelming.

A nurse entered the room. Her NYU Langone name tag said ROSE.

"You've been out cold for a few hours," she said.

"What happened?" I asked, though I only knew I had said words out loud because she responded, not because I could hear myself say them.

"You swallowed a lot of pills."

When she said it, I knew she was telling the truth. I knew what the pills were. I knew where in my apartment I must have been standing. I knew which glass I would have used for the water to swallow them. I could envision the entire scene, but I didn't remember living in it.

"You're lucky," she said, holding on to the foot of the bed I was in. "All things considered." I saw that I was wearing fuzzy green socks that weren't mine.

"Whose socks are these?"

"Oh, we put them on you."

"Just . . . communal hospital socks?"

She appeared troubled by something, maybe my temperament, or my line of questioning.

"We called your mom," Rose said. "And someone named Zoey is outside. You might not be alive right now if it wasn't for her. She brought you in."

I felt suddenly like I was in an "inspirational" Oscar-bait movie (September release; a lot of buzz and a starry cast, but ends up garnering no nominations).

When the door opened a few moments later, Zoey moved silently to the folding chair next to the bed. She fixed her gaze at me and whispered, "What the fuck is *wrong* with you?" She had never looked more beautiful to me. No makeup, her light brown hair an absolutely chaotic mop, but she was *glowing*.

"I'm sorry. I didn't actually want to die."

"Is that so?"

"I have never been serious . . . when I would say, you know . . . anything like that."

"That's not true. You're always serious, even when you're being 'facetious.'" She made dramatic air quotes with her fingers, which I found deeply comforting. "You swallowed ten Xanax."

"That's it?"

"It was more than enough to knock you out."

"Ten Xanax is like—in L.A., that's a normal breakfast."

She didn't like this. "Victor, you were extremely fucked up, and then you swallowed a bunch of pills on top of that."

I had enough self-awareness to know that I was trying to keep the banter light so that I didn't have to reflect on what had happened.

"Okay, this isn't the time or the place to have this discussion," she continued. It occurred to me that this hospital room and this moment probably *were* the exact right time and place, but I was happy at the concession.

I reached for her hand. "Thank you for saving my life, ma'am."

"This *really* isn't funny," she said. "There is nothing funny about texting you and calling you, repeatedly, trying to make sure you were back home safe, and then *coming to your apartment* at 2 a.m. and finding you passed out on the floor. I truly thought you had died. So, you know, please take some accountability."

"I take accountability." I didn't know what to say. I loved her so much it was overwhelming.

"So you went to hook up with some guy?"

"I don't really want to do a, you know, minute-by-minute recap. I don't really remember things very well, anyway."

"Did the guy drug you?"

"No, he didn't *drug me.*"

She stood up and walked to the other side of the room, stopping to lean against the wall, next to a poster of a smiling middle-aged woman promoting flu shots.

I tried to remember the exchange I had with the guy before leaving his apartment in the Financial District.

"Can I give you a piece of advice?" he'd said, standing in his doorway, mere minutes after he'd been nibbling on my ear while we were entwined in bed together, our legs interlocked. All my one-off hookups followed a similar trajectory—it was shocking the clockwork of that transition, from supreme vulnerability to sudden paranoia once I was clothed and standing in front of their door.

I looked away from his face, his patchy beard, and fixed my gaze on the hallway behind him. "Sure, why not," I said. "Bring it on."

"Don't be so hard on yourself," he said, gripping my elbow. "Everything you were doing tonight was . . . you know."

"Everything I was doing was *what?*"

"Everything you were doing was fine."

I forced a smile at that. My right arm was shaking a bit, which he noticed, but I could sense he wasn't going to mention it. I was, after all, about to leave.

"Should I give you my number?" I asked, though I knew that even if he said yes, we would never see each other again.

"I don't know," he said. "Do you want to give it to me?" I guess he was trying to be coquettish, but he delivered the line in a monotone.

"Oh, please," I said, taking his phone and entering my number. "This isn't fucking *Bridgerton*. I met you on Grindr."

Zoey was on her phone now, texting. I looked up at the muted television screen in the hospital room. "God, you know I'm really messed up when I don't even notice there's a *Friends* rerun happening right in front of me." Monica and Rachel were preparing a turkey. "Did you tell Tom what happened?" I asked.

"What do you think? I had to tell him where I was going in the middle of the night."

"You could have tried to make him jealous. *I just have a quick errand, Tommy.*" She wasn't listening. My head was throbbing, and now that I was readjusting to being alive, I realized I was sore all over my body. My lower back felt like it had been dug into with a scalpel. "This is going to make Tom hate me even more."

"Tom doesn't hate you," she said, not looking up. "If anything, you hate him, and you just say the reverse because you're projecting."

"Wow, all the truths are coming out now that I tried to kill myself."

She stared at me gravely. "So you *did* try to kill yourself."

"No, I was just being *facetious*." I couldn't raise my hands for the air quotes. "Actually facetious."

"Do you realize how clichéd it is to try to kill yourself because your boyfriend dumped you?"

I let that marinate.

"Sorry," she said. "Was that too far?"

"No," I said. "You could never go too far. Because even if you did, it's you saying it, which makes it okay."

"The nurse called your mom."

"Yeah, she said."

"She texted me asking if she should come to New York. I told her it was all right and I was handling it. But you should call her."

"I will."

"She said Warren was anxious, too."

"Fuck Warren."

"I thought you liked your stepdad."

"I don't like anyone."

"Okay."

I looked away from her. "Dare I ask—does Oliver . . . know what happened?"

I could sense her disappointment without even looking at her. "Victor. No."

"I mean, we did date for two and a half years, Zoey. We broke up *yesterday*. I think he might be interested to know I almost *died*." My head was really pounding. "I think I need food."

"You need a lot of things." She paused. "A therapist, maybe?"

"Yeah, I mean, I should have been doing that anyway."

After I left the Financial District suitor's apartment, I stood for a while at the corner of Fulton and William. Probably for five minutes. The intersection was empty at that time of night. I took my phone out and saw a text from Zoey. I'd sent her a street address with no context, and she had responded with an eyes-rolling emoji. I wrote her back: All clear—I just left the guy's place.

I then pulled up my text thread with Oliver from earlier that day.

Oliver: are you sure you're okay?

Victor: I don't get why you care

Oliver: Victor please

Victor: yah I'm fine

I marched up Broadway, toward Tribeca, wielding my phone in my fist like it was a weapon.

It was March and just under 40 degrees and I was wearing a loose T-shirt without a jacket. But I was drunk and nothing mattered anymore. I entered the Duane Reade on Broadway and Park Place. I could throw myself down the escalator and perish . . . or I could quietly and carefully examine the snack options. Either way, it would be fine.

My right arm was still shaking as I walked down an aisle and picked up a box of Wheat Thins, "reduced fat" (I might try to kill myself in an hour, but god forbid I ingest a *full-fat* Wheat Thin even once!). Then I grabbed a jar of Skippy peanut butter and moved to the alcohol.

The guy behind the counter made eye contact and sauntered over. His arms were covered in tattoos, and he was wearing a tight blue polo.

"Hey man," I said, instinctively lowering my voice and then immediately undermining it by pointing at a raspberry lime spiked seltzer. "That one."

"You sure?"

"I'm never sure," I said. He took out the key.

I had already consumed a bottle and a half of wine and two shots of vodka that evening, as well as a "martini" at my FiDi entanglement.

I picked up an *Us Weekly* while the guy rang me up.

Paparazzi photos of Cameron Diaz now depressed me. They made me think about what once was, the passage of time. Leave the woman alone! She did what we wanted for decades; now she just wants to hang out with her Good Charlotte husband and do some gardening and enjoy a glass of sauvignon blanc. Why couldn't we all just agree to stop taking pictures of her "entering a doctor's appointment in West Hollywood" or "meeting gal pals for brunch in Montecito"? Why were we all so disgusting?

That train of thought was the last memory I had from the night.

Zoey moved to my hospital bed and sat down on the end of it.

"Do you want to know something funny?" I said. "The guy I hooked up with last night . . . he made this whole show, when I was leaving, of stopping me—all serious—and being like, 'Hey man, don't be so hard on yourself.' Like he was Gay Obi-Wan Kenobi. And then I left his apartment and literally overdosed on pills an hour later."

"I don't know if I would categorize that as *funny*," she said.

She grabbed my ankle with her hand. "You're a special person, Victor."

"You don't have to do this."

Zoey looked right at me and there were tears forming in her eyes, and I felt like I had to let her talk.

"I know you have your shtick—you have to rely on the shtick. It's what you do. I love the shtick. We all do. But it's okay to let it fall away sometimes. You want all of us to be great. *All your people*. You keep the focus on us. But it's not a crime to say, *Hey, I'm not okay. Hey, I need some attention on me*."

She held on tighter to my ankle. "Remember in college when I had that whole thing with James?" She sighed. "You didn't leave my room."

"We watched the entire first season of *Gossip Girl* in three days."

"You didn't force me to recount the whole story, like everyone else tried to do. You didn't, you know, make me cry or jam pastries down my throat. You were just there."

I felt a wave of melancholy. Everything she was describing felt familiar and close—the pink comforter, the walls of her dorm room, the sweatshirts—but also difficult to access. A year after we graduated

I wrote a short story based on Zoey in college that I published on Tumblr—it actually led to my first writing job. I changed a few key details. In the story, Zoey went to James's dorm the next day and spit in his face and humiliated him in front of his friends. In real life, they never spoke to each other again.

"You have so much to offer," Zoey was saying.

"Really, you can stop."

"You're so good at crafting all these narratives for other people. I feel like every text message you send me is a fucking novella. It's why you do what you do. But—I've been wanting to say this to you for a long time—I feel like whenever someone asks *you* a question, something real, you skirt the issue. I don't think that's, you know—ultimately, that isn't sustainable."

"Is this, like, a roast? A roast of the patient on suicide watch?"

"This is exactly what I mean."

I smiled. "I like observing other people," I said. "I'm good at it. Is that so bad? It's how I—I don't know. So do you. It's why we love each other."

She let go of my ankle.

"Do you have my phone?" I asked.

I had about seventeen texts and missed calls from my mom, a text from Warren (Just heard the news—hope you're holding up OK.), and a slew of emails, including one from the HR department at *Corridor*. I opened it immediately.

"Zoey . . ." I croaked. "Jesus Christ. I got it."

"Got what?"

"The writer job."

She shook her head. "Really? *Corridor*? Now?"

"Yeah. They want me to start on Monday—70K a year. I'm going to be writing for *Corridor* magazine . . . Fuck." I looked around my drab surroundings. "I feel like if they knew where I was opening this email, they would be rescinding the offer."

Zoey looked up at the ceiling, so I looked up, too. There was a large beige stain across the tiling.

"Well, good thing they'll never find out," she said.

The stain on the ceiling, I knew, was there to remind me of my bullshit. As always, I was lying to myself. *Everything's just fine, Zoey!* She was right: I was already making my accidental overdose into a *bit*, stripping it of any gravity. I didn't want to consider the ramifications. And this glam job had just conveniently presented itself as a new identity I could slip on. A distraction.

I watched Zoey, still sitting on my bed, checking texts on her phone, and she felt very far away. She had saved my life hours earlier, but now, when I looked in her eyes, I saw the not-so-distant future: a woman who would be married, living in some renovated farmhouse in Connecticut. Meanwhile, I'd be drunk somewhere and scrolling on Instagram and wondering if I should get Botox. She'd have two kids and send me Paperless Post invites to their birthday parties. I'd be crafting messages on Hinge to 43-year-old guys who list their favorite musicals under a selfie taken on a hiking trail.

Of course, none of this had happened yet, but I could see it so clearly, it was as if it already had.

As I walked out of the hospital building three hours later, I momentarily considered taking the subway home. *Fuck it, I just almost killed myself—let's splurge for the Uber.*

I sat silently, stiffly, in the back seat of the red Toyota, neck craned so that my head wouldn't hit the top of the car. Natalie Imbruglia's voice on the radio soothed me. "I don't think there's anyone that doesn't like this song," I offered weakly. The driver swiveled his head to look at me, as if required to do so, and then turned it back.

Now, in the Uber, I cycled through the familiar wheel of misfortunes in my head (Oliver had always been the one who could stop that wheel from spinning). If I had really *actually* hurt myself last night,

I reasoned, the only people who would truly care were Zoey and my mom. Though Zoey, on some level, probably expected it would happen eventually.

When I was wasted one night in college, I told her, "When you get married and have kids, I'm going to kill myself." It was a joke; she laughed. She would sometimes repeat the anecdote to other friends now, with the kicker: "He's such a little drama queen." But I thought about that moment a lot. She was engaged now. To Tom.

When Oliver broke up with me—when he said the words—a numbness had enveloped me. I don't know if I said anything to him in response (at most "Okay, I'm going") before leaving the room, the apartment, his orbit.

It's shocking how quickly humans can just recalibrate. It struck me as completely terrifying that Oliver was going to just go on *living*, acting out the daily minutiae of his life, as if the two years we'd dated were file folders that had been dragged to the bottom-right-hand corner of the desktop.

I closed my eyes in the back of the Uber. I tried to think about Cameron Diaz as she appeared in *The Holiday*. It was hard to do it, but I really tried. *I could do it.* I saw pristine snow and a comically massive fireplace and off-white cashmere blankets—and when my eyes opened, we were stopped in front of my apartment.

2

"If you could be any animal, what would you be?" Zoey asked.

"Is that a joke?"

"No. Why would that be a joke? It's not funny."

I was slouched in the window seat, with the scratchy blue airplane blanket wrapped around my head. Zoey was in the middle, even though the aisle seat was empty. We were flying to her friend Celeste's wedding in Miami. I hadn't been planning to go—it was only six weeks since I left the hospital, and I "wasn't drinking," and it seemed a little bit soon to be jostled among throngs of millennials in ill-fitting suits jumping in unison to "Mr. Brightside." Alas, Zoey convinced me. (Tom couldn't make it because of a work conference.)

"I don't know," I said. "Maybe a turtle. Is that weird? Turtles just kind of do their own thing, you know? I like that."

Zoey rolled her eyes. She readjusted herself in her seat—she looked uncomfortable—and stretched her spandexed legs out.

"What are you? Flamingo? Main character lion?"

"Yeah, I'm *main character lion*." She was flipping through the options on the digital screen. "All these movies sound like fake movies."

"What's the latest with Perri?" I asked. "I haven't heard you complain about her in weeks, I feel like." Zoey did communications for a small start-up that was developing a fashion-related app; honestly I only half understood what she did every day or what the app was meant to achieve. ("You enter your favorite celebrity into the app and then it gives you recommendations of things you might like," I had explained to my mom recently when she asked about Zoey. "Sounds interesting," she'd replied with a slight scowl.)

"Well, you've been dealing with . . . other stuff lately," Zoey said.

Even though I nodded when she said this, the truth was, after leaving the hospital, I had not dwelled on what led to my ending up there. Yes, I wasn't technically drinking for the moment, but I had not yet emailed any therapists. I had distracted myself with television and Instagram and, thankfully, the new job. Zoey texted me constantly, but mostly with links to E! Online articles or screenshots of our friends posting embarrassing content on their Stories. In fact, we hadn't talked directly about Oliver or the overdose since I left. Which is how I wanted it.

"Perri's the same, I guess," she said. "I do appreciate that she leaves a lot up to me." Depending on when you asked her and what the most recent Slack DM exchange may have been, her boss Perri was either a conniving tyrant or a benevolent protector.

"I was watching a video Perri posted the other day," I said. "It was her morning routine or something. It was incredible. It started with footage of her getting out of bed, which means she must have *actually* woken up and set up her phone to record herself, and then 'gone back to sleep' and *pretended to wake up again* for the camera."

"I don't think it's that calculated," Zoey said. She was allowed to criticize Perri, but I had to tread a bit more carefully, apparently.

"I actually told her that you started at *Corridor*," Zoey continued. "And that you might occasionally dip into some fashion coverage. I hope that's okay."

"I don't think I'm going to be writing about fashion. It's mostly, you know, celebrity, pop culture." I had noticed in the month since

I started at *Corridor*, I'd received a slew of texts and emails from people I hadn't talked to in a very long time: Congrats!; Let me know what you're working on!; Does this mean you're going to go to, like, the Met Ball?

"Do you think this job is going to make you—?"

"Make me what?"

"I don't know. End up hating celebrities?"

"What do you mean?"

"I don't know. You're such a fanatic—pop stars, award shows, gossip blogs—your love is so *pure* now. It's kind of like how I can't just enjoy coverage of fashion shows anymore. I'm thinking about everything through the PR lens."

"Well, I just started. I guess we will see."

"I'm so proud of you. I want to . . . Can I throw you a party?"

"A party for what?"

"Just being you."

"You are never this earnest; I hate it. I told you I don't want any special treatment." Zoey remained the only person—other than my mom and Warren—who knew I had spent the night in the hospital.

"Is your mom excited about *Corridor*? She loves this stuff."

"Yeah, she keeps forwarding me, like, tweets she sees about Harry Styles, and saying, 'This could be fun to write about!' I get the sense she is refreshing the *Corridor* homepage every hour to see what I write."

"That's sweet."

"Yeah. You know, as ever, I'm on my eternal quest to make her proud."

"You said that like it's a joke, but it's not a joke."

"It's *not* a joke!"

My parents divorced when I was nine and my dad promptly moved to Santa Fe. I talked to him infrequently now. The last time we spoke he asked me how my mom was doing and if I needed money, and he said he'd see me the "next time work brought him to New York." It all felt a little trite and pathetic, too pathetic to talk to anyone about. I never told my dad about Oliver the entire time we were dating.

Zoey reached out and held my hand.

"What are you doing?"

She let go.

"Tom hates when I touch him, too."

"Your hand is actually cold."

"It's not cold. Your *heart* is cold."

I took the blue blanket off my head and smoothed out my hair. I was wearing a zip-up hoodie and baggy corduroys. I felt like a 14-year-old.

"What's going on with wedding planning?"

"It's fine. I don't really want a—Tom is very, *here's what the wedding is going to be*. I weirdly . . . just don't care about any of the details that much?"

"Yeah, I always saw you more, I don't know, getting married in a restaurant one afternoon, impromptu, wearing a smock."

"A *smock*?"

"Yeah, like a chic smock, with a tasteful heel."

She laughed, showing her teeth. I loved it. She didn't laugh like that all that often anymore, since college.

The flight attendant walked by, pushing the drinks cart past us to the other end of the plane.

"I can't believe I am marrying Tom. Is it weird I'm marrying Tom?"

I decided to not answer this truthfully. Sometimes, that's what friendship is.

"No, it's great."

She looked back at the screen and resumed blithely scrolling.

"All I really care about is that no speeches last for more than three minutes, and that I look hot."

I felt deeply happy that this was going to be a weekend without Tom. I rested my head on Zoey's shoulder.

"Well, look at that," she said, glancing down at me.

"Shut the fuck up."

I looked up at her screen. Owen Wilson's face was guffawing next to a dissatisfied Reese Witherspoon's.

"Do you think that will be me and Tom in ten years?"

"No. Tom is cuter than Owen Wilson."

"It's funny to me your job now is to write about these people."

"I like it. I can make them into characters."

"I guess that's true. But they're real people."

I had always enjoyed controlling and distributing information. I liked the idea that I was a hub for *intel*. People fed me their opinions and secrets and I interpreted them, made sense of their value, determined how to redeploy and narrativize them. A year or two after my parents divorced, I started writing a family newsletter. I would interview my mom and my neighbors and my friends at school, and then write up articles about what was going on in their lives. I would print it out and sit cross-legged on the floor and watch my mom read the whole thing. Sometimes she'd take a pen out and correct my spelling or grammar on the page. Usually, she'd smile. I'd watch her smile. Sometimes she'd say, "I don't remember telling you that."

Zoey closed her eyes briefly.

"Tired?"

"No," she said, eyes still closed.

"Is it weird I'm going to Celeste's wedding?" Celeste was Zoey's good friend from high school, who had become my friend in our first few years in New York. But I had never hung out with her one-on-one, never without Zoey.

"Yeah, it is weird, kind of." She paused. "When we get to the hotel, can we nap and then order French fries?"

"I wouldn't have it any other way."

"But you can only let me have like three fries. I have to fit into my fucking dress."

Her eyes were still closed. It was hard to explain what it was about the specific moment, but I wanted to capture it and place it in a glass jar, to be able to return to it whenever I wanted, at all times.

3

Before I left work for the day, I typed out a list of fifteen questions I was going to ask Kate Hudson.

I had been working at *Corridor* for about three months. At this point, a typical assignment involved my being asked to produce two paragraphs of text—which it seemed doubtful anybody would actually read—to sit underneath a Miley Cyrus music video in a blog post titled, "Watch Miley Cyrus's Shocking New Music Video." Everything was "shocking."

There was a lot about my new daily routine I loved. I woke up at 7:30 a.m. and, from bed, I would scroll the headlines of the *Daily Mail*, the *New York Post*, *People*. I was meant to drop a few pertinent links into our office Slack. I enjoyed the ability to set the Slack conversation—if I wanted to pretend Page Six *hadn't* written a disparaging, thinly sourced piece about a pop singer's behavior at Fashion Week, I just *wouldn't drop it into the Slack channel* and hope no one else cared enough to drop it in themselves. A semblance of power in this one facet of the job went a long way.

Then I would shower and shave. I dressed with intention now; I wore tighter clothes than I ever had before. I attempted a sweater vest one morning—not one person at work commented on it, either positively or negatively, which was enough to make me determine never to attempt it again. I didn't look like any of the other boys in the office, who ranged in appearance—in their chiseled jawlines and lithe comportment—from Matt Damon in *The Talented Mr. Ripley* to Jude Law in *The Talented Mr. Ripley*. But nevertheless, I felt a slight air of confidence as I strutted into the office every day at 10:15 a.m., clutching a large hot coffee. My aunt had gifted me a shiny Coach messenger bag when I started the job—carrying it made me feel like a walrus dressed up in a glitter bow tie, but it remained draped on my shoulder nonetheless.

I would then take my place at my desk and write up posts for the website. The magazine housed a digital operation separate from the print arm—us digital folks were occasionally handed assignments from the print editors, which we received as greedily as if it were magazine manna from magazine heaven.

And on this afternoon, just as I was starting to churn out a post about Prince Harry, a Slack came in from Leon Marcus, my editor: Just forwarded you an email, Victor. Let me know your thoughts. Considering Leon's affectless manner, this could mean he was forwarding anything from an announcement that I'd been promoted to an alert that someone I loved had been murdered. My heart rate quickened as I double-clicked. It was an email from a publicist: Kate Hudson had a new fragrance coming out, and they were offering the magazine a ten-minute interview slot. There was a note at the bottom of the email, in bold, added by the publicist: **NO QUESTIONS ABOUT POLITICS**. Leon had added above the email that the *Corridor* beauty editor wanted the interview to take up a page in the next issue.

I was—maybe it was embarrassing to admit this—*thrilled*.

Kate Hudson was going to be my first interview, my first stab at publishing something I'd get to *craft*, my first print byline for the magazine, a piece of content I would be able to promote on my social-media feeds with a faux self-deprecating caption: Had a little chat with a dear friend! Link in bio!!

I was also thrilled because now I could *tell people* I was interviewing Kate Hudson.

At this point, I was still receiving consistent *Just checking in!* texts from my mom (and similar texts from Zoey, though they'd tapered off). They wanted to make sure I was "fine," seeking assurance that everything was "back to normal." Despite my best attempts, I had not demonstrated to them that I was no longer in need of a near-daily *How are you feeling?* or *What are you up to?* or *Do you have enough food in the apartment?* inquiry.

But now I would be able to tell my mom I was interviewing Kate Hudson for work: "Could a person who is in serious jeopardy of committing suicide interview KATE HUDSON?? *I don't think so.*"

Taking the job at *Corridor* had—and this was not an outcome I'd expected—managed to distance Zoey and me slightly. I had desperately been trying to make sure that didn't happen. I would regularly iMessage Zoey from my desk, taking pains to convey the vicissitudes of the daily dramas, narrating inside jokes and grievances and micro-feuds. I felt myself trying to synthesize the events of my work life into a soap opera tailored just for her—the right details emphasized that I knew she'd latch on to, certain elements played down, others drawn out. I had picked out my work ally (a photo assistant named Maya), my work antagonist (Leon), and my work unattainable crush (a straight senior editor). I couldn't have the ally come off as *too* appealing in my retelling, though. And I could always amp up the antagonist's villainous behavior if I wasn't getting enough of a reaction. I transcribed for her every elevator exchange between the crush and me.

When things were slow for Zoey at work, or if she was working from home, she would be present and engaged, active and quippy (Did you write back to his Slack, or are you just gonna leave it???). But, more often, particularly over the past month, she wouldn't respond for a few hours, sometimes not even until the next day. Rita Ora just came into the office for a meet and greet! I'd write her; she'd respond with a cool! thirty-six hours later.

Meanwhile, she had settled in to living with Tom. It was hard for me to remember there was a time *I* had been the one living with Zoey in New York, when I hardly responded to a Tinder message or ate a slice of pizza without getting her approval first.

Is this what getting older was? I felt like an emo teenager writing an online screed, shouting into a void. Everyone else around me was evolving, changing, taking risks, maturing. Meanwhile, in much of my life, I felt like I was treading water. At least I had Kate Hudson.

I got off the train and, despite the lingering Hudson high, anxiety had reached the back of my neck. I was twelve minutes late for dinner. I had almost canceled that morning when Zoey texted, Tom wants to join tonight!

In the past, I could have responded *how about he comes next time, and tonight is just us??!* and it would have been fine. But the plates underneath us had shifted—particularly, I felt, since the hospital.

Zoey and Tom were getting married in two months. Not to be melodramatic about it, but the thought—the reality of their engagement—made me feel nauseous. Did this mean for the rest of our time on this planet, Tom would be an implicit plus-one for Zoey, a male corporeal form conjoined to hers? It did mean that, I thought. *Would the agony of having to make small talk with him become a lifelong toll fee for my friendship with her?* Okay, yeah, I was probably being melodramatic.

―――

I entered the restaurant and looked around. The lighting was dim, and I noticed two different groups of friends Storying the same "oyster tower" starter at their respective tables. It felt like I had just walked into a *New Yorker* cartoon. I spotted Zoey in the back corner of the restaurant. And there was Tom, next to her, fixed on his phone. Zoey was waving at me.

They were both surprisingly dressed up: Tom in a . . . was that a Prada blazer? No, Hugo Boss. But still. Zoey was in a printed dress, probably Reformation. Meanwhile, I was wearing J.Crew khakis that were starting to fit too tightly (I had gained nine pounds since the Oliver break-up) and an untucked button-down shirt. It was always funny when I told people now that I wrote for *Corridor*. They'd give me this quick up-and-down—most people probably didn't even realize they were doing it—and chirp, "Oh!" or "The magazine?!" while their brain grappled with the dissonance of a decidedly unstylish person having scored an extremely stylish job.

"This place is cool," I said, looking up from the menu to Tom, then Zoey. I hated everything that came out of my mouth when I was with the two of them together.

"Yeah, isn't it?" Tom said. He was wearing a Rolex. I'd noticed that once they began seriously dating, Zoey started wearing more jewelry. Tonight, a new gold bracelet.

"Zoey and I were actually just talking about—we watched some *Drag Race* the other night." Tom looked at me after saying this as if that were the equivalent of donating money to a charity on my behalf. "Really wild! It's a lot of fun." Zoey smiled at him adoringly while he said this. She knew I'd never seen an episode of *Drag Race*.

In college, Zoey would always ask me for detailed feedback about every guy that so much as handed her a beer at a frat party. ("You don't think Sam is too *egotistical*, do you? Tell me the truth!!!") And for the first few months after Tom and Zoey met (at a Midtown bar), she had shared concerns and complaints with me regularly.

"He's, like, freakishly close with his mom."

"He legit texts like a Neanderthal. There are no verbs."

"He has this one friend, Justine, *from high school I guess*, who fucking knows . . . They, like, get drinks all the time, just the two of them? Justine has a boyfriend, but—that's *weird*, isn't it? It's weird."

Soon, though, the stream of concerns dried up—and now, on the rare occasion she did express a reservation, it seemed rote, like she felt obligated to do so for my sake but had zero interest in knowing what I actually thought about the specific grievance. Sometimes I wondered if she was wholly faking her Tom annoyances at this point for my benefit, to align with the established Victor-Zoey dynamic, in the same way I was drawing out the intra-office work conflicts to make her feel a part of the fabric of my life.

The first time I met Tom was at Zoey's friend Celeste's holiday party. He arrived in a Barbour fleece vest. Katy Perry's "Dark Horse" came on, and I said, "Finally, some good music," and he said, "Is this a famous song?"

Now Tom was here. At this dinner. At a lot of the dinners. Of course, there was nothing inherently strange about that—people brought their significant others to meals with their friends all the time—but it was the first time any of Zoey's boyfriends had ever qualified to this round.

Tom ordered for both Zoey and himself ("We'll share the calamari, and then the fish tacos"), which made me want to flip the table over. I ordered a salad with shrimp.

Zoey leaned across the table. "That shirt is so *good*!"

"It's the one I texted you the picture of. From the dressing room."

"I know! It's great."

I finished my wine in a single gulp and shifted my weight on the small metallic stool. I still wasn't supposed to be drinking—by which I mean, I had been told not to drink—but here I was, drinking. I wondered if Zoey was thinking about my night in the hospital as she watched me. We still had not discussed any of it much, and I would feel myself panicking if the conversation ever inched its way even close. I wanted to pretend that none of it had happened, so it was inconvenient, and also upsetting, to consider that Zoey was in possession of her own experience of that night, which she was still no doubt processing herself. I wondered what sort of conversations Tom and Zoey might have had about that night; it made my skin crawl to think about it.

I watched as Tom finished his glass of water, glanced around the room, and then checked his phone discreetly. I often wondered what Tom *liked* about Zoey, wondered what he *knew* about her. *Did he know the details?!* Did he fully grasp her obsession with Mandy Patinkin? (*Did he know who Mandy Patinkin was?!*) Did he know about the year in London? Did the two of them talk about her uncle, and the funeral, and what her mom said to her after? Did he know about James and her college years? It concerned me that I felt unsure if Zoey actually cared whether he knew about any of it in any meaningful way.

Zoey reached out and put her hand on Tom's shoulder. "So we had a fun day."

I noticed Zoey was wearing more makeup than she usually did. Her freckles were almost completely hidden.

"What did you do?"

"Oh man, it was an odyssey," Tom said. "She decided she wanted a new light *fixture* for our place."

"What about that orange lamp?" I looked at Zoey. "You've had that forever. Since sophomore year!"

"The orange lamp outstayed its welcome," she said. "It's fucking ugly! Come *on*. Right? Beyond ugly. It was really, really bad." It seemed imperative to Zoey that we all agree just how ugly it was.

Tom continued, "I borrowed my sister's car and we drove to Red Hook so she could pick up this—it's hard to even explain what it is. I guess it's technically a lamp—right, babe? But it does like eight other things, too."

"I found it on Facebook Marketplace," she said.

"Oh, wow," I said. "That's funny."

Somehow, the story of the Lamp Retrieved From Red Hook took Tom another four minutes or so to recount, blissfully cut off by the arrival of our food.

I guess maybe it was the wine, maybe it was my unease with the dynamic, maybe it was my baseline volatile state, but I decided now was a great time to bring up Kate Hudson.

"So I got a big assignment today!" I shouted across the table. I felt like a carnival barker. A woman at the table to our left turned and glanced at me, before resuming conversation with the man she was eating with; she looked both perturbed and bored. Was *everyone* completely miserable and on edge at all times?

"What is it?"

"I'm interviewing Kate Hudson tomorrow," I said. "Just for a short thing in the magazine. I'm supposed to ask her about her 'inspirations.'"

I noticed Tom was looking down at his phone. I picked up my wine glass and tried to take a sip even though it was empty. Zoey smiled, her brown eyes gleaming. "That's so fun," she said. "Is she still—what does she do now?"

"She's still acting. And she posts a lot on Instagram and, you know, has a bunch of random brands, like they all do . . ." I trailed off.

Tom looked back up. "Sorry, work thing."

The waitress came by and, before she even said a word, we each asked for another glass of wine.

"How goes the lawyer world?" I asked Tom, now wanting the focus off me.

"The lawyer world keeps me very busy," he said.

"It's actually insane," Zoey said. "Now that we live together, I really see it." She glanced at him. "You just—it's all the time." She shifted back to me: "He is answering emails, like, in his sleep."

"Well, you work a lot too," I said to her.

"Yeah, but law firms are another level—he goes in most *Saturdays*."

"It's true!" Tom said, raising his hands. "It's very unchill."

Our next round of drinks arrived.

Zoey took her phone out to look at an email, so I took mine out. I pulled up a Bella Hadid Instagram post and thrust it in her face. I was slightly drunk and slightly desperate.

"Did you see this?"

She shook her head. "No, I don't really look at that stuff anymore. I'm sort of out of the loop, weirdly." She then grabbed my phone and zoomed in on the picture. "Her legs look bizarre. Like, legs don't look like that. What happened?"

Tom was ripping off a piece of bread from the basket.

"You guys should start a podcast or something. You could talk about all this Instagram nonsense. People would love it."

Zoey looked up at me. "Didn't they say you might get to have your own podcast at *Corridor*?"

"Yeah, we're talking about it."

Tom stared at me as he bit into the piece of bread. "About . . . celebrities?"

I restrained myself from replying too snidely. "Yeah, pop culture. Celebrity culture. That's *what we cover*, so—"

I felt something brush against the back of my chair, and I snapped my head around.

A curly-haired man wearing an oversized coat was shimmying past our table. His coat brushed up close against the calamari bowl and—I watched this as if in slow motion—the entire bowl went tumbling off the table and clanged to the ground, calamari debris splayed out by my feet.

A waiter appeared suddenly, as Tom jumped up from his seat. "What the fuck, man?" Tom yelled at the curly-haired guy with such ferocity that I truly felt as though my head had floated up like a child's escaped balloon, through the ceiling and into the Brooklyn sky. Everyone else in the restaurant had turned around and was staring at us.

The man stepped back gingerly. "Sorry, it was an accident, dude," he grunted at Tom. "I'm—" He looked down at the calamari crime scene. "The bowl didn't even break." As another waiter arrived with a broom, the man shrugged and shuffled off to the bathroom.

Tom unclenched his jaw. Zoey had her face in her hands, as if she'd just witnessed a stabbing.

"Jesus," Zoey whispered.

Tom sat back down, shaking slightly. He reached out for my shoulder. "You okay, Victor?"

"Yeah, of course," I said. "He didn't *do anything* to me, or . . . obviously it's not a big deal. It was just—"

Tom nodded, breathing heavily.

"Thank you, though, for . . . I appreciate it." The words sounded deeply silly even as I said them. *What was I thanking him for?*

Zoey came around to sit on the empty chair next to me. She wrapped her arms around me.

"This is the dumbest thing ever," I said. "I don't know why we're, like, so shaken up—a guy knocked a dish off the table. It's not a big deal."

"No, it's not," Zoey said. "It was just—surprising."

Zoey pulled herself upright but kept her arms around my neck. I nuzzled my head on her shoulder. It felt nice. Now having processed the series of events and registered the fact that we were acting as though there had just been an actual murder in this overpriced seafood joint, I broke out into a giant smirk. I couldn't see Zoey's face but knew she was smiling now, too.

"Something just snapped in me," I heard Tom saying. "You just don't know, with people these days, you know, what's going to happen—what they're going to do. At first I wasn't sure what had happened since I didn't see the guy walk by and all I heard was a loud noise—"

His continued solemnity about this was now deeply hilarious to me; I was stifling a full-fledged fit of giggles.

Zoey was maintaining composure, however. "I know, Tom," she said. "It's fine. Everything's fine." She started gently stroking my head.

A waiter came over to apologize and tell us the appetizer was going to be comped. He put his hand on my shoulder as he talked. "People are clumsy—it happens more than you'd think," the waiter said. "We'll bring you an olive oil cake on us, too."

He looked at me before walking away. "I'm really sorry, sir."

I turned to Zoey and Tom. "I'm 'sir,' I guess," I said, smiling widely, and then excused myself for the bathroom.

Standing in front of the sink, I flashed back to the hospital room, to the moments after I received the email from *Corridor*, when Zoey was sitting on the edge of my bed.

We had never been big on "touch," on physical contact. Even then, in the hospital bed, maybe amplified by the strangeness and sterility of our surroundings, it felt uncomfortable when she held my hand, when she grabbed my ankle.

"It's funny when something like this happens, when you end up someplace like . . . here," I'd said to her then. "All the meaningless shit becomes blurry, and what's crystal clear is the, you know, the few people who you actually care about."

"Yeah, well, it's a good thing I didn't go to Celeste's bachelorette this weekend," she said. "I'm here."

We sat there in silence for a few minutes. Eventually, right before she left the hospital and went back to her apartment, she said, "Hey, try to focus on this amazing new job. I'm really—I'm so proud of you. You're going to write cover stories one day and, you know, I bet you'll be having lunch with, like, Jennifer Aniston soon. You'll be—you're such a funny writer. You're such a good friend to so many people."

"Zoey, truly, you don't have to do this," I said to her. "And I know I'm a funny writer."

Now, I stared at my reflection in the bathroom mirror at this sea-food restaurant, water running. I wanted to remain where I was stand-ing for as long as I could.

For Zoey, for all of us, there came a point, approaching your thir-ties, when it felt like there was no longer a plethora of options, no longer the luxury of *let's wait and see*. Time did not feel like an endless resource anymore. You either moved in with a Tom or risked falling behind, even missing out entirely.

When I got back to the table, I reached out my hand, holding a single lilac I had stolen from the vase in the bathroom.

Zoey had returned to the other side of the table, next to Tom again. "What is this?" she said, reaching out to take the flower from me.

"I don't know," I said. "But it's for you."

After we'd paid the check, Zoey and I lingered on the street outside the restaurant, waiting for Tom. I checked my phone and saw I had a few notifications on Twitter from Lady Gaga fans who were upset with a blog post I'd written that morning about the outfit she wore to the VMAs. I hadn't criticized the outfit, I was sure of it, but I pulled up the post anyway to double-check that I hadn't inadvertently writ-ten something incendiary. I'd described it as a "particularly daring" look; I decided to leave it alone. (A few weeks ago I had gone back into an already-published post about a Hugh Jackman late-night show interview and changed the adjective "questionable" to "intriguing"—I hoped no one at work had noticed.)

There was also an email from Leon, my editor: *Just FYI your Kate Hudson story is actually going to run online only. No room in print any-more.*

"Anything interesting?" Zoey asked me, and I looked up from my phone.

"No, all good. My editor's excited about the Kate piece."

"The editor you can't stand?"

"I—yeah, the editor I can't stand."

"Maybe you should be the editor," she said.

"No, I'm not—"

"Not what?"

"Not an editor."

"If you ever want to talk to Caroline, by the way, let me know. We haven't talked in forever, but I'm sure she'd get coffee with you."

Caroline Stevens was Zoey's friend from a summer arts program. Caroline was a freelance writer now, and even though I'd never met her, I felt oddly bothered whenever Zoey brought her up, or compared the two of us. I knew Caroline wrote articles on occasion, but they were usually esoteric, on niche topics—Zoey had recently texted me a link to a *W* magazine profile Caroline wrote about a 77-year-old woman who made sculptures of medieval pets.

"Thanks, yeah, I'll let you know."

She looked down the street for a few moments, then back at me.

"Are you . . . Is everything okay?"

"Yeah," I said. "I actually have been feeling really good. I just— I feel like I am finally doing what I'm supposed to be doing— career-wise. I have two movie premieres coming up that I'm going to. And this cocktail party for a swimwear line one of the Real House-wives is doing."

She didn't say anything. I felt like she was assessing if she could believe me, if she could take anything I said at face value anymore. Eventually she said, "I wish I felt that way. About my job."

"I thought you were loving everything at your thing."

"No, I—I am. I love Louisa. And the, you know, I like what we're doing. I believe in it and I believe in Perri. It's just weird sometimes working for someone else's start-up, you know? Someone else's passion project. Sometimes it's like, why can't we be doing what *I* want us to be doing!?"

I felt an urge to lean in and hug her—nothing could hurt me if I was close to her—but just then, the door opened and Tom emerged, his wavy brown hair curiously wet.

"Well, an interesting night," Tom said.

"Hey, we got a free dessert out of it," Zoey said.

He leaned in and kissed her on the lips, and, I had to admit, it looked nice. They looked good together. His pronounced chin. Her hair up in a tight bun. I watched them kiss, and it made me feel strangely serene.

Zoey pulled out of it and turned to me. "Do you want to come in our Uber? We can drop you off?" I should probably have felt an immediate surge of warmth at the gesture, but really what I felt was relief that they were leaving, and guilt that I felt that relief, and resentment toward Tom for being the one who kissed her and who took her home in a car and who wouldn't listen to any of her stories the way that I would have. I missed Oliver.

"No, it's okay," I said. "I'm just going to walk a little bit, I think."

Their blue Honda arrived, and Zoey waved. "See you guys soon," I said, as I watched them get into the vehicle.

I floated, aimlessly, in the direction of the subway. I took out my phone to text Zoey a few emoji hearts, but then decided not to; I'd text her in the morning. I had this vision in my head of her gazing out the window in the Uber, dissatisfied, while Tom absentmindedly took his Rolex off, placed it on his lap, sighed, and then scrolled through memes on his feed. But it was impossible to know if this was what I wanted to imagine their time together, alone, was like, or if it was the reality.

I walked down into the subway and saw the waiter from the restaurant—the one who'd put his hand on my shoulder and called me "sir"—was standing by a pillar. He smiled when he noticed me and took his earbuds out.

"Hey dude—recovered from the Calamari Incident up there?"

I laughed. "Yeah, the FBI is on it." The FBI is on it?! *What?!*

"That friend of yours was ready to throw down."

"Yeah, he's not really my friend. Or, well, yeah, he's dating my friend. They're engaged. Him and the girl who was—the woman. Zoey."

He nodded. "Got it." He looked around the subway platform. I glanced up at the monitor. The train was still three minutes away. He shifted his weight and then leaned back against the pillar.

"Where are you heading?" he asked.

"I—just home." I kept talking, not thinking about what I was saying. "I'm a writer. An *entertainment journalist*. I have a big story coming up, actually. It's for *Corridor*. The magazine. I'm profiling . . . I'm interviewing Jennifer Lawrence tomorrow." This embellishment came naturally.

"Oh, that's sick," he said. "I love her."

"Yeah, I have to ask about her different inspirations."

"That's awesome. She's super funny. I watched a clip of her on Fallon a while back. She was riding him hard. It was amazing."

He took a step closer to me. Engaged. He slipped the earbuds he'd been holding back into his pocket.

"Who else have you interviewed?" he asked. "Do you ever talk to pro golfers?"

"No golfers, no," I said. For some reason, I really didn't want the conversation to end. I felt a compulsion for it to continue, for the evening to not be over, for a thrilling next location. "Do you—do you like golfers?" I added feebly. "I think there's one that dates a model who I was just reading about."

"Yeah, man. Dustin Johnson. You should look him up. He'd be a fun interview."

I leaned my head back a bit, extending my neck. "That's a great idea." I felt like a theater actor. I was on a stage. My mind was blank.

"Have you been working at the restaurant a long time?" The train was pulling into the station.

"Yeah, not too long. Just a few months."

Why did I take every interaction so personally? Why did interpersonal stakes always feel high?

The doors of the train opened, and he smiled. He had great teeth, a faint mustache. "Nice to meet you, man. See you around."

"You too," I said, and even though I could have taken that train, I decided to wait for the next one.

Half an hour later, I emerged from the subway, back onto the street. I walked half a block, almost walked right into a mailbox. I steadied myself and then took my phone out. I texted Zoey: I can't wait to come over and see the new lamp!!

4

Zoey

"This doesn't feel very *wedding*."

"What would make it more wedding?" Victor was on his phone, gazing intently. It was impossible to know what was holding his interest.

"Victor."

He looked up at her in a strained, almost agitated, manner, his lips pursed.

"You can't be on your phone. I'm getting married in *two hours*."

Zoey fell back on the bed in her hotel suite; the bedspread had a garish yellow-and-purple floral pattern to it and a musty smell. Zoey was wearing purple spandex shorts—brighter than the bedspread purple—and Victor's faded U.S. Open T-shirt.

Zoey's wedding was taking place at a beachside resort in Cape Cod; Tom's family had been coming here regularly since Tom was in high school. Zoey was not a fan of tchotchkes or the sand, and there were tchotchkes and sand everywhere.

"Unfortunately, we don't have a choice," Tom had mumbled when they were discussing their wedding venue months ago.

"We don't?" she'd asked.

"My mom won't come to the wedding if we don't have it there," he said.

Zoey had restrained herself from reminding Tom that *her* parents were paying for the wedding. But since her parents lived in the city and they saw them all the time (or at least, she saw them all the time—Tom invariably had a "conflict"), it went unspoken that, for their wedding, they'd let Tom's mom have this one. When Zoey told her mom that they were having their wedding on Cape Cod, her first question was, "Can you get taxis there?"

Victor got up from the bed in Zoey's room and placed his hands on the Nespresso machine, unmotivated to try to figure out how to turn it on. "I should just sleep in here with you tonight," he said with a sigh. "I don't like my room."

"You can't stay with me on my wedding night."

Victor turned to look at her. "Why not? Because you want to fuck your husband?"

Zoey couldn't help but grin. "Enough. We should be *proper* today."

"No, we shouldn't."

Victor moved back to the bed and lay down next to her. He was in flannel pants and a black hoodie. It was mid-August and 85 degrees outside, but if Victor hadn't been in a hoodie, Zoey would have known he wasn't okay. In the midst of all her wedding planning, she'd occasionally had the thought that she wasn't being present enough for Victor. But she felt less worried about him knowing he had his job at *Corridor* now. He had his new friends, like his co-worker Maya, who was now regularly featured on his Instagram Story.

Victor was trying to keep her in the loop, she knew that, but she often found herself zoning out when he would tell her his work stories. The other week he'd recounted a long narrative about a conflict with his editor, and she realized she'd mistakenly thought for months that his editor's name was Liam (it was "Leon"—she'd been close). None of this mattered so much to the core underpinning of their friendship, she felt—it's not like Victor asked her anything so detailed about her job, really. She could sense his losing focus whenever she spoke about Perri or Louisa or Kiki.

"You're right," Victor said. "Today really doesn't feel very wedding."

"Remember how I always said I was going to go the Carolyn Bessette route for my dress," she said.

"Yeah, you didn't come through on that one."

Zoey's wedding dress was frilly, with big fabric-heavy shoulders. She wasn't totally sure how she had ended up with it. The truth was, she hadn't wanted to spend much time on any one item related to her wedding—once she had a dress that seemed satisfactory, she moved on to the flowers.

"I talked to Tom's cousin for a weirdly long time last night," Victor said. "I feel like he's . . ."

"Don't say it."

"What?"

"He's not gay, Victor."

Victor opened his mouth in mock outrage. "I was *not* going to say that."

"What were you going to say, then?"

"Not that."

"He's like 23."

"He's 26, actually. He's applying to law schools now."

Zoey stood up and moved to her dresser. She'd already had her hair done—she was going for "simple, easy waves" (she'd used a picture of Elizabeth Olsen she found on her Explore page as inspiration). She'd opted for low-key hair since her dress was . . . ornate. That was how she was approaching much of her life at the moment. She felt a great need for balance. If she was overcome with stress when leaving her office—Perri asking unreasonable questions, Kiki throwing her under the bus—she would get off the subway and immediately head to Van Leeuwen for ice cream. If this approach to living felt simplistic, Zoey felt confident that many solutions really were usually that simple. Most people overcomplicated things.

"Be honest," Victor was saying. "No joking or bullshitting or anything else. Is this—are you *happy* today? Is this what you always dreamed of? Do you feel like, you know, the princess, the Julia Roberts or whatever?"

"I don't feel like the Julia Roberts or whatever, no. I guess I—" Something about the way Victor had asked the question felt grating, but she tried to move past it. Did anyone really want to be asked a tough question ninety minutes before her wedding? And she knew Victor actually wasn't sure, that he really did want to know the answer.

"I think it's too hard to assess while I'm actually—I mean, *it's the day of.*" He did not look at all satisfied by this response. "But yeah, of course. *Of course I'm happy.*"

She didn't like the feeling that Victor imagined she was in her own version of *Jackie*, or another art-house film about a fragile woman on the verge of a grand collapse.

The rehearsal dinner the night before had been surprisingly fun. Her mom wasn't annoying her. Her half-sister left early with her one-year-old. She felt like she was gliding through it all—interactions that would usually bother her were barely penetrating the surface. That was a good thing, *wasn't it?*

"Hey, do you think—?"

Victor was back on his phone. "Did you see these photos Louisa posted from last night?" he asked. "They're weird of me."

"Victor, do you think—"

She couldn't get herself to say the words.

She knew she loved Tom. She was still deeply attracted to him. He was the only guy she'd ever enjoyed giving a blow job. She really liked how when he was driving and waiting to make a turn, his eyes would get all beady and his expression became super serious—he'd barely be able to keep up conversation. Actually, that was the same way his face contorted when she was going down on him, too.

Tom was a *big guy*, tall, brawny. She had never imagined that for herself; she always thought she'd end up with a *wispy fellow*—more diminutive. But Tom was a much larger presence. Tom took up space.

Victor and Zoey never really talked about Tom anymore. She was aware of this, and it actually felt nice, maybe, on some level—their friendship was enclosed in a bubble where Tom wasn't a direct concern. It wasn't that Tom didn't exist, per se, but more that he was oddly irrelevant to most of their daily conversations. Though, at the same time, Zoey felt that her not talking to Victor about Tom was eventually going to lead to friction—that someone was going to end up feeling left out.

There was a knock on the door.

"*Zoey?*" It was Tom's mother's rasp. "Do you want us to bring you anything back from the restaurant? Danielle and I are going down."

Victor and Zoey made eye contact and both pursed their lips in unison, holding their breath. These were the moments when Victor was perfect.

"I'm good, Lynn. Thank you, though!"

After a few seconds, Victor looked up. "She's really always got—she's always doing it her way."

"That is for sure."

"You look so good," Victor said. "You're crazy skinny." He was eyeing Zoey as if appraising a piece of art. In college, she sometimes felt like she was aspiring to "look hot" for Victor as much as she was for the straight men (or for herself). It didn't make much sense—*Victor would love her no matter her size or what she put on her body!*—but it remained the case.

"Thank you," she said, as if imitating Maria Menounos introducing a segment. "I haven't eaten since June."

"I know that to be basically true," Victor said. He was looking at his phone again. "Did I tell you about this guy Ryan I matched with on Hinge? Who weirdly used to work at *Corridor*? I feel like every gay guy on Hinge is named Ryan."

"Oh my god, Victor—we can't talk about your *Hinge* right now."

"*My Hinge?!* Why can't we talk about my Hinge?" He pulled at a brown staticky blanket on the floor and wrapped himself up in it. "You make 'Hinge' sound like it's a skin condition."

"It is." Zoey reached into a plastic container of fruit that Victor had brought her and picked at a piece of melon. "Did you see last night when Lynn came up to me and adjusted the straps of my dress? Unsolicited? That is not normal mother-in-law behavior. She thinks I'm one of her employees."

"I didn't see that happen, but I believe it. You're not going to be able to get away from her now."

Zoey decided she wasn't ready to actually start getting ready, to face the reality of her wedding. She sat cross-legged on the bed. "So you're really liking work, right?"

Victor laughed and picked at his ear. "I'm sorry? You never ask me such direct . . . I don't know."

"I always ask you direct questions!"

"Right, no, I know. I just—I thought you didn't want to talk about me right now."

"I changed my mind. I have *wedding day jitters*. I don't actually. I just want to be distracted."

"Did I tell you I get to do a quick phone interview with Emma Stone's stylist?"

"Oh, for a second I thought you were gonna say—"

"Yeah, not actual Emma Stone. But her stylist is really cool and up-and-coming. He does a bunch of people." He paused, his bearing a bit more serious. "Yeah, I guess I . . . I'm shocked at how much I feel different. Like a different person. I feel *sleeker*. Since I started at *Cor-ridor*. Does that make sense? I know I don't look physically different, but like . . ."

"No, I get it. You like how the job makes you feel."

"Yeah, I just think I have a *narrative* right now. Stuff to look for-ward to each week, you know? I mean, we don't have to talk about what—where I was at in my life not too long ago. But—"

"Yeah, we don't have to talk about that." Zoey didn't want to talk about it. It made the sides of her head hurt when she thought about it, actually: sitting next to Victor in the hospital, trying to act breezy and sardonic while he looked like a decimated version of himself, ghostly white and sweating. "Do you remember in college when we both got the flu at the same time but then you got better before I did and you sent me all the pictures from that weird crew team party?"

"Yeah. All the pictures of me inside that giant canoe with the foam in it?"

"That wasn't a canoe, but yeah, yes, those."

"What made you think of that?"

"I just remember being in bed, like, curled up and snotty and dis-gusting and thinking about you at the party pretending to be, I don't know—doing your whatever—and it made me feel better."

Victor smiled. "You're getting soft and maudlin on your wedding day. I don't like it."

"We can drink now, right? I want to drink. Is that . . . I know brides are *allowed to*, but I don't know. Is it weird?"

"No, we have to have a legit glass of champagne before the cere-mony. Maybe a glass and a half." Zoey was aware that her relief that Vic-tor was drinking again was potentially problematic—but she decided to wait until after her wedding to examine it further.

There was a knock on the door. "Z?" It was Tom.

"Tom!" Victor was shouting in a British accent. "You know you're not allowed to see your virginal bride before the two of you are bound for life."

"I have something I need to give Zoey."

"Leave it outside the door, weirdo!" Zoey shrieked, a little louder than she'd intended. She felt for an instant like she was in elementary school, outside at recess, chasing after boys and then being chased by them.

"It's an important item. I'm not leaving it."

Victor sighed dramatically. "Hold on." He galloped to the door and opened it slightly. "Do not come in!" He took an envelope from Tom. "Thank you, good sir." He closed the door and sat back down.

"It's a letter," Victor said.

"Read it."

"Really?"

"Sure."

"It's short."

"Okay."

"He doesn't have good handwriting."

"Just read it."

"'Z—I love you so much. I can't wait to marry you. This is everything I've dreamed of and—'"

"And what?"

Victor handed the letter to Zoey. "That's it."

"It stops halfway through a sentence?" She took the note from Victor. The end of the sentence read: *—and I can't believe I tricked you into saying yes to a life with me. Yours forever, T.*

Zoey put the note down on the dresser. She felt like she might cry—she should cry—but she didn't. She couldn't decide if it was a good sign or a bad one that she didn't feel much of anything.

"Do you want to have kids, you and Tom?"

"I mean, probably, yeah. I haven't thought about it, really."

"You haven't thought about it?"

"Not, like, seriously. No. I haven't." Zoey sat down on the armchair in the corner of the room. The material was scratchy and uncomfortable. "I think we both just kind of assume it will happen."

"I would have thought that was something a straight couple would—"

"Or a gay couple."

Victor laughed. "Right—*or a gay couple*—might have wanted to figure out before committing to each other for life."

Zoey slid down slightly in the armchair. "I think you just like to stir up shit. That's why you're good at your job."

"Oh my god. I think that's my cue to leave."

Victor moved off the bed and accidently knocked over a paper cup that was filled with coffee. "Fuck!" he shouted. He crouched down to pick it up from the carpet. "It got on your jacket. The one you wore last night. Fuck, I'm so sorry, Zoey." He jogged into the bathroom and returned with wet tissues.

"It's fine, Victor. I'm not wearing that jacket again. It was just for last night." She was still slumped in the chair. "Really, it's fine. You're stressing me out more jabbing at it like that."

Victor went back to the bathroom and reemerged with more wet tissues. "I don't know how I did that." He dabbed at the sleeve of her jacket for about thirty more seconds and then he stood up—Zoey just watched him in silence—and gingerly draped the jacket on the back of the desk chair by the wall.

"I don't know how that happened," he said, gently brushing the back of her jacket with his fingers.

"It's fine. It happens. It's coffee."

Victor looked upset, like he was on the verge of delivering a monologue. Instead he took out his phone and took a picture of Zoey. She grinned without opening her mouth.

"I'm gonna send this to Oliver."

"Victor, don't. That's not a good idea. He doesn't need to see that."

"He loves you. He'd want to see you on your wedding day."

"You're looking for excuses to text him."

Victor shook his head.

"I know you're not going to listen to me," she said. "Do what you want."

He was smiling, but he looked strange to her. Distant. For some reason his expression made her want to eat the croissant wrapped in a blue napkin on the tray on the dresser. The entire thing.

"Okay, well, I am going to go shower and get into my beautiful tuxedo and then I will be back."

"I'll be here."

"Will you? No runaway bride on our hands?"

Zoey thought about it for a second. She decided to take this question seriously. "I'm not running anywhere. But ask me again in an hour."

"We'll accept that as an answer," Victor said. He ripped off a piece of the croissant himself and walked out of the room, slamming the door behind him.

Zoey knew she should start getting ready right away—she was already technically running late—but all she felt like doing was remaining in the armchair. She could smell the coffee from Victor's spill. She felt serene in the chair, in her spandex shorts and T-shirt, hair made up, no makeup on. She could sit in that chair all day if she was allowed. Of course, she would have to get up and go get married. Of course. There was no choice but to go and do that. But there was a world in which she sat in the chair and didn't get up, and right now that was the one she wanted to imagine she lived in.

5

Zoey

Tom never responded to texts during workday hours. Zoey knew this. He told her it was because his job was "all-consuming" and "no one in our office does that." Once he even added, "There *isn't time,*" as if he worked for NASA rather than a corporate law firm. Truthfully, it didn't really make sense to her. If he was at his desk, slouched at his computer, which she knew that he was, and if he was responding to Slacks and emails and whatever other electronic correspondence all day, which she also knew that he was, then he was seeing her iMessages—and he could take the ten seconds to shoot back a "yes" or a "not sure."

Knowing all of this didn't stop her from texting him during work hours anyway. I'm gonna kill Kiki, Zoey wrote him, a few minutes after finishing off her Sweetgreen at her desk, adding, she never does her work. She then turned her phone over and checked her email.

Her cubicle was sparse: she had a few photos pinned up, and a small glass apple her uncle gave her a few months before he died, and that was about it for personal effects. She didn't like to "make herself at home" in professional settings; in fact, she thought people who did suffered from some kind of personality disorder.

A few minutes later she picked her phone up and sent Tom another text: lets do clarks for dinner tonight? im craving an egg sandwich

Yes, Tom wasn't going to respond to her texts, and yes, it was going to annoy her that he wasn't, and yes, she was still going to text him. If it ever occurred to her that this might in any way suggest friction (or potential future friction) in their relationship, it was easy to ignore it. He was her husband now; this was a minor concern.

Louisa turned the corner in front of Zoey and then slid into her cubicle, nursing her Hydro Flask. She sat down on Zoey's desk with a sigh. Even though they worked for what was essentially a start-up, consisting of twelve employees, Perri—founder and CEO—ruled with an ethos of formality and order. Perri had worked at a large fashion PR firm for fifteen years and she brought that level of intensity with her when she launched this new venture, Selah. Perri was unmarried; a few months prior, though, they learned she was in some version of a relationship with a venture capitalist (she liked to keep the current status mysterious—they didn't even know the guy's name). Her outfits were immaculate, always topped off with a gold chain necklace. She commanded the room.

Perri had a 23-year-old assistant, Cherry, who scheduled all her meetings. Once, Zoey had made a joke to Cherry about how her name rhymed with Perri's ("I feel like a 'Who's on First?'-esque mix-up is a very serious possibility"), and Cherry did not so much as flinch.

Louisa and Zoey both reported directly to Perri. As such, the two of them had quickly become confidants, the crux of their friendship a sort of ongoing strategizing session to figure out how to best "handle" her. They had learned together that you should never text Perri after 10 p.m., wear patterns in her presence, or sign off an email to her with "XO."

"How was that thing you went to with Tom?" Louisa asked.

"So, so boring. Tom was miserable. He hates that kind of event. He left the dinner halfway through and he was just, like, standing outside smoking cigarettes?"

"I didn't realize he smoked."

"Only when he's trying to make a point," Zoey said, turning her chair slightly away from Louisa. "It was fine, though. We left and watched *Frasier* at home. And there was peace."

"Your relationship is so different from mine," Louisa said, barely hiding her actual feelings on the matter.

Kiki, who worked in sales, slid up to Zoey's cubicle. "Hey, bitches." Kiki was 5'10", with long chestnut hair; today she was wearing what appeared to be a silk handkerchief around her chest. If Louisa and Zoey didn't have to work with Kiki, they would have been entertained by her—she conducted herself at all times like she was filming an episode of *Real Housewives.*

"I am *famished*," Kiki continued. "I haven't eaten since *yesterday.*"

"I have protein bars at my desk if you want one?" Louisa asked, even though she already knew Kiki's answer.

"Oh *god*—a bar? I'm not that desperate." She crouched down and continued, in a conspiratorial whisper, "Perri's in a mood today. She, like, scowled at me in the elevator." At this she spun around and glided to her desk. "I'm going to find Stephanie." Stephanie was the most patient and kindhearted of their co-workers; her wedding was coming up, and all of them were planning to attend. Zoey hadn't invited Kiki to her own wedding.

Zoey looked at her phone; Cherry was pinging to see if she was available. "Well, Perri wants to meet with me now," she told Louisa. "What a delight."

Zoey spent about three minutes in the bathroom en route to Perri's office. She unbuttoned and then rebuttoned the top button of her shirt. She straightened out her skirt. She looked youthful in a way she didn't like. She wiped off her lip gloss and added a touch of concealer.

"Take a Fiji Water," Perri said as Zoey entered her spacious office. Perri gestured toward the stack of bottles against the wall, which was painted a pastel yellow.

Perri had a way of handling her laptop that made it seem as if the item were a small and delicate jewelry box. When she closed it as you entered her office, it was an entirely elegant procedure.

Perri had recruited Zoey from her assistant communications job at Thom Browne. Their first meeting had been brief, but Zoey was taken with Perri's directness, awed by her years of experience. Perri never seemed to doubt herself. And she didn't dawdle or equivocate. She said what she meant.

Zoey picked up a Fiji water and sat down in the imposing silver chair. She felt sheepish about all the metallic bracelets and rings she had on; Perri's single chain necklace held a great power.

"How did the call with Maddie Brooks go?" Perri asked. Maddie Brooks was an influencer with a new Netflix deal (and 80,000 Instagram followers) whom they were courting for an eventual collaboration.

"Her rep said they don't want to do it," Zoey said. "I guess she might be starting a podcast or something. She has other stuff going on."

"Okay," Perri said. "So I wanted to float something by you."

Zoey admired the way Perri generally avoided small talk.

"As you know, I've been hesitant to give anyone a real *title* around here. I feel like that just leads to jealousy and competition and infighting. You know fashion people." She said this as if she herself hadn't worked in fashion for decades. "But I've been impressed by how you handle situations. You're levelheaded."

Zoey recoiled slightly at this. She wouldn't have described herself that way, really. When she was with Tom, or with her parents, she always felt like she was on the verge of a breakdown. Though she then thought about Victor—he would probably agree with "levelheaded."

"I want to give you a 'Head of Comms' title. We can finesse the specific language later."

"Oh, wow. Thank you. I mean, that's awesome."

Perri frowned, running her hand through her jet-black hair, and

Zoey immediately regretted the "awesome." She almost followed up to ask if there would be a corresponding bump in her equity or compensation, but she figured that could be dealt with in a follow-up email. *Let this be a nice moment.*

"I think our first order of business should be placing a big 'here's what we're doing' piece in a major publication," Perri said. "I think, six months in, we're ready for that."

"Definitely."

"You have that contact at *Corridor*, right?"

Zoey was somewhat surprised that Perri had filed that nugget away, apparently sitting on this thinly veiled request.

"Yeah, my—well, yeah."

"Perfect. That would be a dream fit."

Perri opened her laptop—truly, the way she did it was like she was spritzing perfume. "Why don't we see how it goes with *Corridor* before we make this official."

"So it's like a . . . test?"

"Who said anything about a test? Just let me know when you have it all secured and then we'll go from there. One other thing—can you go to a lunch tomorrow with Wiles Cooke? At the Lambs Club. He's a potential investor, lots of resources. He's in town tomorrow only, and I have that flight to Bozeman so I can't do it."

"Of course."

"He's a character. You'll be fine."

Perri started typing, and Zoey left the room without another word.

Zoey texted Victor as soon as she got back to her cubicle: This is so random but

She paused momentarily before crafting any subsequent texts. She didn't think Victor would necessarily *mind* helping to facilitate coverage of her start-up, but it felt a little tricky. She had never asked him for a "work favor" before, and while she could imagine him responding nonchalantly ("omg of course"), she also knew how often he complained lately about aggravating requests from friends of theirs ("Brooke asked if I can help her get Post Malone tickets??? *Why would I be able to do that?*"). Maybe it was better to reach out to the *Corridor* PR office, to leave Victor out of it. She fired off an email to an address she found in their database for a *Corridor* publicist.

Victor texted her a "?" and she wrote back, nothing sry

There was a brief period, after he got out of the hospital, where Zoey felt a chasm developing between herself and Victor. She didn't know quite how to communicate with him. She felt like the light, inside-joke texts weren't landing in the way they used to. And when she did try to get "serious" and actually check in on him, he didn't hide his irritation, or he just didn't respond. And at the same time, Tom had become the center of gravity in her life. It was a shift.

But that uncomfortable phase with Victor had come to an end—at her wedding, she felt they found their rhythm again. And now that Victor was more enmeshed at *Corridor*, he really did seem calmer to her. She felt like she had seen her child off to college. He had these new characters to talk about and busy himself with and, yes, post on Instagram (characters whom she honestly didn't care much about and couldn't really keep track of, but he seemed happy and that's all that mattered and she was happy to pretend to remember them all).

She picked up her phone again to text him.

Zoey: perri says i MIGHT be promoted

Victor: !!!!!!!

Victor: I thought you wanted to leave
and start your own thing?

Zoey: at SOME point! not like, today

Victor: okay well congrats!!

Victor: I'm proud of you baby

Victor: (what do you mean "might"?)

Zoey put down her phone.
She'd wait to tell Tom the news in person.

———

Zoey entered the Lambs Club in an oversized navy blazer and flared jeans. She realized she might have completely misunderstood the nature of this meeting when a man in his late forties leapt up from the table in a black Zegna suit. At least he wasn't wearing a tie.

"So you're Wiles?"

"As charged." He was British. Zoey usually came very prepared to these sorts of meetings, but there was scant information about him online—and when she Slacked Cherry to see if Perri might be able to pass along more information, Cherry said Perri was "in transit and not reachable."

"Oh, I didn't realize . . . your accent," she said, fumbling slightly into the chair that had been pulled out for her.

"I love to surprise," he said. He had a dark beard and broad shoulders, and the hint of wrinkles around his eyes. His hair was full and thick and slicked back. She wondered if there had ever been a steamy night in Milan or Taos between Perri and him.

"I spent a year in London when I was in tenth grade," she said. "My dad had to go for work."

"How cosmopolitan." She noticed he was drinking a martini. It was one o'clock. After Victor's overdose, she noticed she was drinking less regularly. (It confused her that Victor seemed to be drinking all the time again.) For now, Zoey preferred the occasional edible.

"Yeah, you could catch me with my fake ID out in Shoreditch," she said. "You know the drill."

He appeared to be doing arithmetic in his head. "So how did Perri manage to reel someone like you into the operation?"

"She didn't have to sell that hard. I was looking to make a move."

"Thom Browne, right?"

"Very good."

The waiter came by, and Wiles nodded.

"We'll both have the bass," he said to the waiter, smiling. He looked at Zoey and whispered, "I promise you'll like it."

Victor would have a field day with this whole situation, Zoey thought. He would probably tell her to try and sleep with him. "Why the fuck not, Zoey?!" he'd squeal. "Tom never has to find out. *This guy looks like Dominic West!*" Of course, she wasn't going to sleep with Wiles, but it made her feel good that she could sense that Wiles probably would if given the opportunity. *Right?* Why was she even thinking about it? This was supposed to be a business lunch.

She told him about the product they were developing: "You input the celebrity or influencer you like into the app, and we produce a list of clothes for you," Zoey explained. "Simple. It might be items your favorite singer or whoever was actually wearing, or just really good dupes—and then we take a cut."

He seemed interested, but also a touch bored, as she expanded on SKU counts and the "Fashion Nova model." After they finished their fish and he polished off his martini—she had demurred when he asked if she wanted to join him in drinking—he traced the face of his Hublot with his finger.

"So what do you want to *do*?"

"In my career? Today? You're going to have to be more specific."

He smiled. "Do you have a boyfriend?"

She had instinctively taken off her wedding ring before entering the restaurant, but now didn't know if that was a good idea. She laughed, though, and replied, "Not really." She wasn't sure why that's what she answered, but it's what she said, and now she had said it.

"Not *really*. Okay. You women and your 'not reallys.'"

"*You women!* It's like you're referring to a new subspecies of rodent found on the Australian coast."

"You're funny. Perri's girls are usually so *dull*."

"Perri's girls—you make it sound like she's operating a different kind of business."

Zoey suddenly felt a desire to entertain Wiles. After a short lull, she continued, "So what's *your* deal?" It wasn't her best effort.

Wiles didn't appear to be particularly moved. "My *deal*?"

Her hands felt sweaty, and she felt the age difference for the first time—it made her anxious.

"I'm just a friendly man who likes to meet interesting people," he said.

He reached into his pocket and took out his phone. Zoey stared at him for a few moments.

"So are you going to invest in Selah? Perri really seems to think you're going to."

"Very direct of you," he said, stroking his beard. "I like it. You're like Perri in that way." He paused. "Maybe. Yeah. I have to talk to some of my advisers. But I'd love to get into business with you guys." He looked right at Zoey. "I'm all about relationships, though. That's what really excites me. At some point, maybe you'll have an idea, your own idea, and I'll decide I want to help you out."

"What makes you think I have an idea of my own?"

"I don't know. You were lying just now about not having a boy-friend. You're clearly quick on your feet."

"What? No. *I didn't lie*. What are you talking about? Are you accusing me of being a liar?" She tried to smile.

"Of course not." He reached out and tapped her hand with his, the first physical contact they'd shared the entire meal.

"Okay, you're a little bit right. I do have—technically I do have . . . someone. I'm not sure why I didn't just say that earlier. I was trying to keep things *professional*—I don't want to talk about my romantic life, you weirdo."

Wiles laughed hard at this. "I appreciate the honesty."

Somehow she walked five blocks with Wiles after they left The Lambs Club. They were standing now outside his hotel.

"I'll let Perri know we had a fantastic meeting," he said. "And please, next time I'm in town and see you, I hope you have an idea. I want you to surprise me." There was something patronizing about this, but at the same time Zoey felt like a life raft had been nudged in her direction. People like Wiles didn't just *show up*, all debonair and nonchalant, handing out money like Kleenex—and also outfitted with perfect hair and a disarming British accent.

"There is something about you I can't get a read on," she said. She had wanted this to sound confident and enigmatic, but instead it sounded like she was in a high school play. She'd said it too loudly.

"I appreciate the compliment," he said, and he leaned in and kissed her on the cheek. Their lips touched briefly as they moved away from each other, and she tried to play it off as a chic accident, like Perri closing a laptop. Later she would decide it was a consensual, centripetal force sort of thing, but in the moment she felt like she alone had willed it to happen.

She turned around before she could catch his expression. "Have a good flight back!"

That night, Zoey walked into her apartment to find Tom making a beef stew. It was confusing that, as much as he went on about how overwhelming his job was and how it afforded him no time to pick up a prescription for her or watch a three-hour movie, he could spend hours cooking a (frankly, extremely bland) stew that she would have to pretend was completely revolutionary. "It's . . . so flavorful," she'd said the first time she tasted it. He received this as legitimate praise. "I feel like I'm really on to something with my measurements," he said. "Alison Roman, watch out."

After work that day, before taking the subway from Flatiron home to Cobble Hill, Zoey had spent twenty minutes walking aimlessly around a Zara. She had tried on a strappy, revealing top that she didn't buy—but she liked how it made her feel. She took a picture of herself in it to meditate on later. A year or two ago, she would have sent it to Victor; now, she just kept those pictures for herself.

"How was the day?" Tom asked from the stove.

Zoey sat down at the kitchen table and took her shoes off. "It was good, actually. Perri is out of town, so we can kind of just fuck around. Louisa and I took an hour-long coffee break—it was so nice."

"That sounds . . . chill."

Zoey opened the mystery novel on the table that Tom had bought a few months ago and still hadn't started. She leafed through a few pages and closed it absentmindedly.

"I also had lunch with this potential investor," she said.

Tom turned to look at her. "Without Perri?"

"Without Perri."

"How'd *that* go?"

"I am perfectly capable of entertaining a dude for an hour over some bass."

"Fish for lunch?"

Zoey glanced at her phone. She decided to say, "He actually implied I could start my own thing someday."

"Your own company? Do you even want to do that? You have a marketing background."

"I mean, potentially. At some point. Maybe with a friend or something. Who knows?"

"Who is this guy? Do you have a picture?"

"A picture? No. This wasn't, like, speed dating."

Tom walked over to the table and rubbed Zoey's shoulders. "Are you going to leave me for some d-bag 'investor'?"

Zoey swiveled away from his touch. "Who said he was a douche?"

Tom went back to the countertop and started dicing some carrots. Zoey watched him at the cutting board and felt an unexpected surge of warmth toward him. She was hard on him, she knew that, and in that moment she didn't really know why.

She looked down at her phone and saw she had a few texts from Victor:

Victor: IM GOING TO A PREMIERE
OF THIS RANDOM KATIE HOLMES
MOVIE???

Victor: OMG SHE LOOKS SO GOOD.
HER HAIR IS REALLY GOOD. DID WE
KNOW THAT??

She dropped her phone on the floor. "I'm going to take a shower," she said, and left the room.

That night in bed, Zoey received an email from Perri with the subject line: "Where are we on the Corridor placement?" (there was nothing written in the actual email). Zoey refreshed her Gmail, again and again, reflexively, and felt a tinge of panic. She'd followed up with the *Corridor* publicist that afternoon and still had not received a response— she was being ignored.

She looked up Wiles again and found his name cited in an article about Soho Farmhouse from three years ago: "Wiles Cooke is often spotted on the property, as well." She highlighted the text with her cursor and then swiped out of Safari.

She dashed off a response to Perri: *We're all set. It's happening!* She threw her phone onto the carpet and rolled over and closed her eyes.

The next Monday, Zoey received a text from Cherry at 8 a.m.: Perri's back in today and wants to see you.

When Zoey entered her office, a few minutes after she'd arrived at 9:30, Perri was lifting a small hot-pink dumbbell. She had her AirPods in her ears, but she ushered Zoey in.

"That's fine, Georgia. I just don't want to launch without, you know, *everyone* on it. I don't want someone searching for 'Emma Chamberlain,' but then . . . Right. You get me?" She looked disappointed, silent for a few beats. Then she said, "No, our whole thing is that we aren't trying to be—this is for women with real money to spend . . . I have to go. I'll call you later." She took the AirPods out.

"So Wiles said he really enjoyed lunch," she said to Zoey.

"That's good to hear," Zoey said. "We had a nice time." She felt guilty, as if Perri held information about her that she was going to try to suss out. She was going to make Zoey say it.

"I'm sure you did. He's a fun hang." She looked right at Zoey. "And he says he wants to invest. He's going to come by the office when he's back in town in a few weeks. You should join."

"That's so great. Incredible."

"And that's excellent news about *Corridor*. Is your friend going to write the piece or is someone else doing it?"

Zoey reached her hand to the back of her neck and dug her nail in.

"Yeah, he's doing it. I think. I have to iron out the details."

"Online only, I'm assuming?"

"Yeah, yeah. Just dot-com, it looks like. But I'll push for print."

"Well, that's great," Perri said. "You know, Cherry resurfaced a memo you wrote for me when you started. It was really funny and sharp. Once we get you settled in your new role, I'd love to get you on some morning shows, some podcasts, do some Q&As—have you get the word out about us."

"That sounds great."

"And I am going to draft a press release about your promotion, and we'll push that out this week."

"Great," Zoey said again, after a pause. It was the only word she felt like she could get herself to say.

After the meeting, Zoey walked out of the office building, onto the street, and called Victor.

"What's up? I'm at work."

"I know. But don't you just fuck around and scroll through the *Daily Mail* when you're at your office?"

"No."

"I got the promotion. Officially."

"Incredible. Did you find out—are you getting more money?"

"I assume? I actually haven't clarified that yet."

"You haven't?"

"Perri said she wants me to start doing press soon—kind of like a spokeswoman, I guess?"

"You are going to go on TV?"

"Don't be a bitch."

"No, are you kidding? I love it. We'll have a watch party—I'm going to make GIFs out of your appearances."

"Okay, relax."

"I have very big news, too, actually."

"Yeah?"

"I got a cover story, Zoey. On Valentina Lack. I am freaking out."

"Are you serious?"

"Yes. I just found out. *Valentina Lack*. And it's an actual cover story. Not, you know, five hundred words online about Kate Hudson's fragrance that no one clicks on. I'm not sure when the interview's gonna happen yet, but . . . I can't believe it."

Zoey felt a slight pang of distress at this news for some reason; she didn't feel like investigating it. "Victor, that's amazing. Oh my god. We need to—we are going to celebrate. That's amazing. I need to, like, process this." She paused. "Valentina is British, right? She seems sort of unexpected to get a cover story, no?"

"I mean, she got an Oscar nomination for *The Detour*."

Zoey knew that this timing wasn't ideal, but she couldn't delay any longer on her ask or she might never do it.

"Oh, one other random thing . . . This is so random. You know how Perri is insane?"

Victor laughed. "Yeah?"

"She said she—well, she basically was hoping maybe—I told you that I told her you were working at *Corridor*?"

"Yeah, you told me on the plane to Miami."

"Do you think maybe you'd be able to write something about what we're doing? Like tied to the launch? Or maybe someone else at *Corridor* could write it and you could just connect me?"

There was a long pause. "Oh. I wasn't expecting that."

"Is it that wild of a request? If you can't do it, that's totally fine. Obviously. I just thought I would ask. Since she asked me."

"No, no, of course. Oh my god. Of course. Just—yeah, I don't have that much power really, as you know. Since I basically just started. Even though—I mean, I can definitely bring it up to Leon and see what he says. I feel like if I wrote it myself, that would be—isn't that a conflict of interest?"

Zoey had never thought of Victor as someone particularly concerned with "conflicts of interest."

"Didn't you just write some gushing thing about that flower designer?" Zoey said.

"Yeah, but I wasn't *best friends* with him."

"I didn't realize this was such a big ask. Really. It's fine."

"It's not a big thing. It's totally not. I don't know why we're even—Let me talk to them and I'll let you know. This—it isn't weird at all. Of course. I'm so happy to ask."

"Perfect. Thank you."

Zoey felt her forehead burning. She knew it was not directly relevant, but she couldn't help it—her thoughts drifted to the fact that she had (somewhat recently!) saved Victor's life. The two situations were not connected to each other. She knew that. She didn't like that this was where her mind had led her.

A couple of weeks later, Zoey arrived at Rockefeller Center at 7 a.m. and was in hair and makeup ten minutes later. Perri had called in a favor to get this booking on the *Today* show, and Zoey was frankly shocked that Perri wanted Zoey to take the appearance instead of herself. "It's good to get you out in front of people. I've done enough of these," she said.

Zoey looked at her phone. Victor had sent her a series of texts:

Victor: You're going to kill it!!!!!!!

Victor: I can't wait

Victor: I am legit working from home today just so that I can watch you live on my TV

Zoey had a text from her mom, too: Remember to sit upright. You have a tendency to slouch.

Tom had prepared her an elaborate stuffed eggplant dinner the night before—it was really sweet, she had to admit. "It's just a quick

TV hit," she'd told him. "It's not such a major . . . whatever. Hopefully I'll do a lot of these."

"I know, I know," he said. "But you have to appreciate the good things when they happen. What else is there?"

The PA came into the room to tell Zoey it was time to head out into the studio. She looked in the mirror and examined the face reflected back at her. The makeup was caked on. Her hair was in ringlets. She felt a sinking sensation in her stomach as she stood up from the chair and moved out of the bright light.

6

Erica

"**H**is name is Max."

Erica said it again.

"His name is Max."

Valentina Lack looked up from her phone and stared at her publicist. "What?"

"*Max*. His name is Max." Erica held her phone up. "This is Max."

"What's happening with his sideburns?"

"Could not tell you."

Valentina was like a cat, the way she curled and uncurled on the sofa, unconcerned, comprising her own contained, small universe. "Can you—" She pulled down a strap of her yellow sundress. "Is this—like, is my left shoulder not weirdly so *shiny*? Does it not look shiny to you?"

"It does not look shiny to me," Erica said. "It looks great." Erica, at this point, felt like she could teach a MasterClass on how to convince an actress—or anyone, really—that she didn't look "oily" or "chunky" or "bitchy" or any other dreaded "-y."

It was raining in New York, and the blinding white-gray outside seemed appropriate, a mood ring. The hotel room the studio had put them in was ostentatiously lush. There were nine more pillows in the room than necessary—on the sofa, chairs, countertops—each a different shade of light purple or pink. They had arranged a spread of fruit on the coffee table.

"How many interviews do I have after this Mark guy?"

"*Max*." Erica sometimes wondered if she should just start making flash cards for press junkets.

"How many do we have after *Max*?"

"Just one. Someone from *Glamour*."

Valentina sighed, emphatically and drawn out, in a manner no one would ever sigh unless they were performing a sigh. Unfortunately, this was the only way she could sigh, and she did it all the time.

"I have nothing else to say about this movie."

Erica said, "I know." Though what she wanted to say was: *You were paid $3 million to film for four weeks in Morocco—and you're going to complain to me about having to do six ten-minute interviews on a Saturday afternoon?!* And then Erica picked a pomegranate seed off Valentina's shoulder.

Valentina had received a best-actress Oscar nomination for her first movie, *The Detour*, a trademark *quirky indie* about a woman who ends up on the wrong flight and decides to stay in the Midwest and start a new life there, rather than return to New York to her fiancé and family. Erica watched it On Demand a few months after it came out—she wasn't sure if anyone had actually seen it in theaters.

Reviews called Valentina's performance "a comic marvel" and "jarringly authentic." In one scene, the clip that got played over and over again in the commercials and at the award shows, Valentina stripped off her shirt and ran into a cornfield, in a purple bra and jeans, while *wailing* at the sky, a cathartic release. Of course, she looked offensively gorgeous in her bra and jeans, like no woman in a bra and jeans who has ever existed in the real world.

She was born in London but had an almost Grecian quality about her. Even after Erica's monthly spray tan, existing in Valentina's presence made her feel like she was a discarded piece of gauze. The *Daily Mail* once ran photos of Valentina with the headline "Valentina Lack Glistens as She Lunches with a Gal Pal at Malibu Sushi Joint," and, even in the long-lens paparazzi photos documenting this lunch, Valentina's hair up in a messy bun, dark sunglasses hanging off her nose, she really did—Erica had to admit—*glisten*.

It had been a year since Erica started working for Valentina. After the Oscars (where Val lost to a 67-year-old actress who'd been nominated three times prior: *it was her time*), Valentina reached out for a meeting. Valentina arrived at the coffee shop twenty-five minutes late, in a jean jacket and aviators, with an unmarked juice in hand. She sat down and asked, before any pleasantries had been exchanged, "So what do you think I should do next?"

Erica didn't even pause: "I'd go on a long vacation and then come back and do an A24 thriller or a Wes Anderson—a choice that people can *understand*, but that also surprises them. Something accessible, but that still says, 'I am a step ahead of all of you.'"

Valentina grinned—a huge, monstrous, absurd grin. "I like you."

She hired Erica on the spot. Of course, she did not actually take any of the advice Erica gave her. Valentina's manager—a slick, curly-haired British man named Mick, who once reached his hand uncomfortably low on Erica's back at a party—had felt strongly that she pick a movie for her first post-*Detour* project that was "right down the middle." (The way Mick looked at Valentina whenever he was talking to her made Erica shiver; he called her "Baby V.")

To Mick's delight, she signed on for *Whirlwind*, an action film that would be out in a month, in which she was playing what amounted to the "love interest," opposite Spencer Craft. Sure, Spencer Craft was popular and Chris Evans–hot, with four-quadrant appeal (he just played a double-agent in a blockbuster summer release and would be filming the sequel next year). And sure, it was a lot of money. Erica could understand and appreciate an argument for it. But it just didn't have any zest to it. You can palpably feel it when a project is a dud from the beginning: it's awful, Erica had learned, to have to go through the whole yearslong process with the client, both knowing it the whole time (the publicist knowing it more than the actor does). It's like getting to an online date and realizing immediately he's awful, but having to sit there for an hour and a half anyway talking about how long it takes both of you to get to work.

Erica was used to this by now—telling her client one thing about their career or image, and then watching as they did the exact opposite. Once, a pop-star client had texted her, I AM OVER MEN, ERICA!!!! I'm SERIOUS! OVER ALL THE TABLOID BULLSHIT!!! I WANT MY MUSIC TO SPEAK FOR ITSELF. EVERYTHING ELSE IS GETTING IN THE WAY. And then that very same night—Erica was in bed, face mask on, *New Girl* streaming—she saw that the pop-star client had posted a string of seven Instagram Stories of her snuggling with Jack Harlow.

Erica had learned—and she repeated this to herself on many occasions—that she just had to be a sounding board. The best publicists are the ones that their clients forget are even there. Valentina was going to do and say as she pleased; Erica just had to make her feel comforted and, more importantly, emboldened in her choices.

"This *Max* is going to ask if Spencer and I are dating, isn't he?" Valentina asked.

"No, this is Vogue.com. They won't. *Glamour* might."

Valentina scowled and then exhaled and drew a breath, as if blowing and popping an imaginary bubble.

"Just give the usual answer, you know."

Valentina flung off her strappy sandals. "*Should* I just date Spencer Craft?"

"No, Val."

"He would date me, like, if I wanted to."

"Of course. I'm sure he would."

"He's *wholesome*, you know?" She stared at Erica, and her eyes were right on her, but it was also as if they were looking around her at the same time—it was unsettling. "I feel like it could be good for me? No one really knows what to *make of me*. That's my problem right now. I feel like if I were dating Spencer Craft, people would get it. *Oh, she's going to be dating movie stars*. She's here. She's arrived. She's famous. She's an actual *thing*."

"Val, you don't have a *problem* right now. You don't need to date a movie star. You're a movie star all on your own."

"I've done two movies."

"And one got you nominated *for an Oscar*. And this one's projected to have a $24 million opening weekend. You've already done *Vanity Fair* and *Harper's Bazaar* covers only two years in. *Corridor* just reached out. You don't need Spencer Craft."

"That's true," she said, before trailing off in a whimper. "I don't know . . ."

When they were filming *Whirlwind*, Spencer Craft and Valentina were photographed out to dinner together once or twice, and *Us Weekly* ran a two-page spread with the headline: "*Whirlwind* Romance for Valentina and Spencer?" which the studio was obviously thrilled about. Erica texted her just to let her know the spread was running, and Valentina texted back LOL. Erica knew enough to know that meant she definitely didn't mind being linked to Spencer—and that they probably had already slept together.

Erica looked back down at her phone: her mom, her mom again, her sister, the studio. Ugh.

Once, on the phone with her mother, after a particularly trying day at the Toronto Film Festival, shuttling back and forth between two clients, Erica said that it felt like her job was to serve as a coat rack. She just had to withstand the weight of all the "fucking coats." Her mom responded, "Isn't that what you *wanted*, honey?" And in that moment, when it was put like that, she couldn't answer her.

Valentina's life was the television show, and Erica's was the television show within the show that you see the main character watching in a living-room scene for a few seconds before the camera pans.

The door opened and a lanky man with unruly sideburns peered in. "Hi? Is this—is this—am I early?"

"We actually need a few minutes," Erica said. "Just wait outside."

"Of course, of course. Oh god, I'm so sorry." He closed the door.

"We need a few minutes?" Valentina asked.

"No, that's just what you say."

After the Vogue.com interview, Valentina spread out on the sofa, rummaging through her bag. "Do you think someone could get me, like, an avocado? Just a plain avocado, unpeeled, with a knife."

There was an open container of baby carrots nestled next to her, and three jars of liquids (iced coffee, sparkling water, non-sparkling water). She was wearing a sweater now over the yellow sundress, and she had pulled her hair up into a loose topknot that, yes, *did* look chic in a fanciful, Sienna Miller "Oh, me? How silly!" way. If Erica wore her hair like that, she thought, someone would try to hand her loose change on the street.

"Sure, let me text someone."

Erica was wearing a baggy black cardigan and dark bootcut jeans, like always. "Good luck finding your George Clooney in that outfit," her mom liked to say.

"Eriiiiica," Valentina drawled.

"Yes?"

"Do you think this is all, you know, bullshit?"

Erica put her phone down. *Here she goes.* "Is—what do you mean?"

"Just the whole fucking charade of all of this." Valentina applied lip gloss, and then continued. "Like, let's say I do thirty movies over my career?"

"Yeah?"

"And maybe three of them are great films, movies where I get a, I don't know, Independent Spirit Award and like, Sundance bullshit, and an *Elle* cover or whatever—and I tell everyone how *amazing* and *fulfilling* the work is, and everyone sort of thinks I'm ridiculous but they all have to be nice to me, so it's fine. But then for the rest of the movies, it's all just . . . filler. The movie's fine, it comes out and does okay, people watch it on a plane—I become so numb to the whole routine that I just tell everyone I *really believe in the vision* of each film, or whatever, but I'm just saying the words, like this . . . robot." She paused. "Did you hear me just tell *Max* that I 'learned a lot about perseverance' while making an action movie where I fight CGI aliens with Spencer Craft??? Did you hear me compare my character to *Hamlet*?! *Where did that come from?*"

"I mean, that was a weird question he asked," Erica said. "You handled it well." Valentina frowned. "I don't know, Val, isn't it like any-thing? People start going through the motions when they have any job for long enough. There are good moments, here and there, hopefully a lot of them, but it's basically monotonous."

Valentina picked up a carrot and gnawed on it. "I don't know. I think I'm exhausted."

"Listen, we only have one more interview left and it's on the phone so you don't have to worry about, you know, whatever—and I'll make sure we don't go longer than eight minutes."

She was pouting. "Can *you* just do it?"

"Do what?"

"Do the interview. It's on the phone."

"No, I can't do your interview, Valentina. They'd recognize it wasn't your voice."

"These people are all totally starstruck and demented, Erica. There is *no way* they'd know. Even if they did have a hunch, what are they going to say? 'That's not Valentina Lack!' They'd be *petrified* to say that. Just say you have a cold and your voice sounds weird."

People often asked Erica what it was like to work with movie stars ("Is Valentina Lack *awful*? She must be a bitch, right?"). She always responded the same way: "They're just *people*, you know. It's like any job." She said it so often that she had nearly convinced herself it was actually how she felt.

"You know what? Why the hell not."

Valentina burst to life, clapping and hooting. Erica honestly didn't know Valentina could physically muster this level of enthusiasm. "Oh my god, *yes*. This is going to be so fun. Finally, some amusement."

"This is clearly not a good idea, and you can never tell anyone we did this."

"Who am I going to tell?" Valentina said, like an actress.

They sat at the table, on either side of the speakerphone module. Erica felt like she was about to take a standardized test. The situation was obviously ridiculous and her participation ill-advised, but at the same time, it felt completely meaningless. *Who would ever care about a ten-minute junket interview for this action movie?* They could have had Erica's 13-year-old cousin do the interview and it would be totally fine and no one would ever know.

The phone rang a few times.

"Oh, uh, hi? This is Chip from Glamour.com."

"Hello, Chip from Glamour.com," Erica said, finding an affected accent she did not know she had in her, adjacent to Madonna's back when she was "British," or a drunk American doing a *Downton Abbey* impression.

"Oh, *awesome*. It's such an honor to speak with you. I'm *obsessed* with *The Detour*. It's such an important film for me. I saw it, like, twice."

Erica didn't even look at Valentina as she leaned in extremely close to the speakerphone, as if she were about to softly kiss it. She could hardly believe she was thinking this, but she felt, honestly, famous.

"Thank you *so much*, sweetheart. It was such *a joy* to help create such an impactful piece of art. The team was so dedicated and passionate, and that film always will hold such a special place in my heart. In my *soul*, really."

Valentina held back a laugh and grabbed Erica's shoulder. She had never touched her before like that.

"Anyway, I'm really excited to discuss *Whirlwind*."

"Are you now?" Erica said.

Valentina at this point was covering her mouth with her hand, convulsing with stifled laugher.

"Oh, uh, is that—sorry, that's the name of the film, right?"

"No, it is, it is the name of the film—indeed, Chip. Sorry, just—there's a lot going on over here." Erica threw a packet of papers on the ground, though this didn't actually make any sound. "I'm distracted by all the commotion. The hubbub!"

Erica realized she was doing this entire one-woman performance for Valentina—this sort of strange, light parody of her—and it was exhilarating.

"Well, first, I just wanted to ask what it was like to work with Spencer Craft."

"Oh god, *Spencer*. Spencer, Spencer, Spencer. Where to even begin! So *hard* to look at that man, am I right? Isn't it a pity?! They *pay* me to look at Spencer Craft's face all day! Can you imagine that?"

Chip laughed as if this was the funniest bit he had ever heard. He must have laughed for twenty-five seconds. "It really is a pity! That's so funny." It occurred to Erica that this is how everyone would respond to all of her jokes if she were Valentina. No famous actors were actually funny: Erica was suddenly very sure of this.

"Seriously though, he's just so *talented*. He doesn't get enough credit for his talent, I think. And he's so gentle." (Valentina mouthed, *Gentle?!*) "With someone like Spencer, it's just, you know, everyone on set kind of looks to him as an example of how to conduct themselves. A north star, if you will. He oozes 'icon.' It drips from his pores."

She felt herself straining a bit. And Valentina was starting to lose interest, Erica could tell. Chip said something, but it came through staticky and unintelligible.

"Chip! I think you're breaking up!" Erica shouted, wondering if maybe she could just hang up on him.

"Oh, I was just saying"—they could hear him now—"that Spencer really does seem so—" There was a loud noise on the line; it sounded like a growl.

"Chip?"

"Where do you see yourself in five years?" he asked, his voice clear again.

"Well, it'll be interesting to see, won't it?" Erica said, speaking extremely slowly into the speakerphone. "I guess the most important thing to me is working with great directors, like I got to on *Whirlwind.* There are just so many—" It was all so *silly*, Erica thought. She was straight-up impersonating someone else, and no one was going to ever know. *No one would know!* How many times had she heard an actor say that all that mattered was working with a great director? She might as well have responded to Chip with a long groan. It would mean as much.

Valentina's hair pulled up, as it was now, made her face look particularly heart-shaped, cherubic. She had an impossibly small nose ("She had it *done*, right?" Erica's sister asked regularly) and jarringly large lips. Her face was completely preposterous. Erica almost—she had to strain herself but she could do it—felt pity for her. When your face is a heart, people don't bother trying to see beyond it.

"You know, Chip," Erica said, dropping the accent entirely. "In five years, I hope I'm living in a lighthouse. Or on a beach. In a shack.

Completely anonymous. No one will be able to find me. I won't wear makeup anymore. I won't be worrying about any of this bullshit. Maybe I won't even shave my armpits. In five years, I'll read books and fucking meditate and take walks. I'll never know what time it is. I won't use my phone. *No phones.* In five years, I will barely remember filming *Whirlwind* or sitting through the fucking Chanel and Gucci dinners or the daily workouts or the goddamn whole avocados. *Rise and grind!* All of that, forgotten. None of it will matter. I will be *happy*, though, *healthy*, and—"

Valentina reached over and grabbed the receiver, slamming it down to end the call. She fluttered out of her chair—it was as if she had just witnessed an execution—and stalked to the other side of the room, facing the wall. Erica had never seen her glide so quickly. She couldn't tell if Valentina was crying or expressionless or doubling over in laughter.

"What the *fuck* was that? What the fuck was that, Erica?"

Erica couldn't respond. She was no longer in the room.

"Was that a *joke*?"

Strangely enough, Erica considered, if you asked her what she actually thought about Valentina, if she liked her, if she thought of her as a real *friend*, she didn't know if she would be able to formulate a coherent response. "Like" was such a stupid word, anyway. Somewhere along the way, Erica had stopped being able to identify any feelings of genuine affection. For anyone.

"I'll call back," Erica said. She dialed the number, while Valentina continued facing the wall. It almost looked like she was swaying slightly, a buoy in the water.

"What's happening?" Valentina asked, as the phone rang.

"I'm calling him. What do you mean?"

"Um, hi?" Chip's voice said.

"Hi, Chip." Erica tied her hair up in a ponytail—*that* would solve everything. "This is Valentina's publicist, Erica—we emailed this morning." She continued, speaking in a deeper pitch, "So—I'm so sorry, we had a truly weird moment here. This very strange, uh, assistant barged into the room, in the middle of Val's interview, and, as you could hear, it was a deeply disturbed woman. She took over and just started talking. We got her out of here, thankfully. Security came in and everything. But—I think you still got good stuff from Valentina, right? Before the interruption?"

"Oh. Yeah. Uh—so that was . . . someone else answering the question at the end? It sounded just like her. But maybe less British."

"Yeah, it was someone else, yes. We're not sure—we're going to look into it."

After Erica hung up, Valentina finally turned back to face her. Her eyes looked red, though not teary, exactly. Had she been rubbing them?

"It's all dealt with," Erica said. "And I don't think—I didn't say anything bad, Val. Really. Honestly. I just got swept away in something. The whole impersonation and, like—"

"It was so *weird*, Erica. I don't know how else to put it. It was like I didn't know who you were."

"Yeah, I guess it was weird. I was due for some weirdness one of these days."

Erica stood up and pushed in the office chair. She walked toward Valentina, though she wasn't entirely sure what she was going to do when she got to her. All bets were off now.

"Don't come near me," Valentina said firmly. And then, in a thicker accent than she normally employed: "You're fired."

"Really?"

"You're *fired*."

"Okay."

Valentina moved to the sofa and lay down. "That was just . . . it was too far, Erica. Too much."

Erica wanted to say that it was Valentina's idea to begin with, letting her take over the interview. She wanted to tell her she hadn't listened to a single piece of advice she'd given her since she started, so firing her was effectively the same thing as keeping her on.

"You know, the 'Hollywood bullshit' line might have been a little much, and I shouldn't have sworn, but otherwise it wasn't *that* crazy, really, what I said. I've heard actresses say *way* more bizarre things, on the record." *Why was she even trying to fight this?*

Valentina looked at her. "It's been such a psychotic few years, and I really don't have that many people—you know, people I can *trust* trust, like *actually trust*. And you were one of them. You were one of the only ones, Erica. I felt that way from the moment I met you."

"Hey, listen, I'm really sorry. You don't have to—"

"No, you're not sorry!"

"You know I love you, Valentina. I think you're a really good actress."

"You don't love me!"

She was a good actress, Erica thought, it's true. She wasn't lying about that.

"And you think I care at all what you think about my acting?!" Valentina shouted. "Who has ever *actually cared* what you think?"

Erica picked up her bag and put her coat on. She paused on her way out. "Okay. Well, I'm going."

Valentina sat up on the sofa and threw her hands up in the air. "*Where?!!?!?!?*" she shrieked, reminiscent of her wail in the purple bra and jeans in the cornfield. "Where are you going?!??!"

Erica looked back at Valentina's glistening face—it really was a gorgeous face—and didn't offer an answer.

———

Usually Erica used a fork to extract the turkey and tomato from her sandwich, leaving the bread to languish behind. But today she picked up a half with her hand, jamming it all into her mouth. It wasn't even good bread.

It was 4:30 p.m. and Subway was empty. She had never been in this Subway before, but, like every Subway, it was a place where all hope was extinguished. Has anyone ever left a Subway feeling energized about their future?

She had texted Valentina an apology, but it was half-hearted, rote. She hadn't received a response yet. Erica had been fired before by clients, and almost always hired back, whether in an hour or in three months. That's the funny thing about actors, she thought: as much as they know how to deliver a dramatic monologue, as real as it might feel in the moment, they're always overcome with doubt in the aftermath, alone and replaying it in their heads.

Or maybe Val would never text her back and that would be the end of it. Maybe Erica would be sitting on an airplane in a year next to someone watching *Whirlwind*, on their second Jack and Coke, and she'd feel wistful about their professional dalliance. Maybe Valentina would win an Oscar someday and thank someone else—some other publicist—in her speech.

The only other people in the Subway were two women, maybe in their early twenties, sitting across from each other in workout clothes. One was picking at a salad, the other protecting a Diet Coke.

"I'm telling you, there is only one way to handle this," one of them said.

"You're insane. You are so insane. I'm dying."

They were both laughing now, one pausing to take another salad bite.

"No, I'm dying too, obviously. But like, I'm telling you—if you send it, you will feel so much better, a thousand times better. No question."

"I mean, you're definitely right. I just, like, is it not *such* a messed-up situation?'

The other woman took a deep breath. "By your standards, it's like, *just another Saturday*. But yes, objectively, for anyone else it is!"

"Oh my god, I hate you so much."

Erica was staring at them at this point—the two women were glowing, relaxed, both clutching their phones.

There was some sick part of her that felt—*was it jealousy?*—yes, jealous of them, the meaningless drivel of their back-and-forth that made them both feel nourished and understood. They shared a language.

Erica crushed the paper sandwich wrapping in her hand, then let it unfurl, watching it painfully reanimate. There was still so much she wanted.

7

My therapist called what I had "success anxiety."

I was waiting for Valentina Lack to show up at a Midtown restaurant, which I would probably end up referring to as an "eatery" in the profile when I wrote it. We had a corner table in the back reserved for us. As I scanned my list of questions for the eleventh or twelfth time on my phone, I wondered if this success anxiety was the reason I felt incapable of forming a coherent thought at the moment.

The waiter came by and asked if I wanted anything, so I ordered a hot tea. I was wearing a dress shirt with a sweater over it, and I was already perspiring through the button-down, which meant I would definitely not be able to take off the sweater at any point during the interview. I immediately regretted the tea order when it arrived a minute later, steaming.

When I was given the Valentina assignment, it was impossible for me to process that it was really mine. It was a *cover story*. Up until this point, I wrote almost exclusively columns and reviews and riffs on pop culture for the magazine's website ("Three Conspiracy Theories about Ariana Grande's Pink Hat"). I hadn't conducted any "major" interviews, certainly nothing at this scale. While it was becoming an increasingly common occurrence that friends of friends at parties would say my name sounded "familiar" when I introduced myself, or an acquaintance's new boyfriend would reference an article I'd written at a group dinner without realizing it'd been one of mine, now, fueled by this cover story assignment, I was feeling a palpable sense of *momentum* in my career for the first time.

I watched Valentina's movies and TV appearances to prepare, and I read all the interviews she'd given previously. She was, basically as a rule, extremely cagey. She never shared much about her personal life. She gave short answers, or recited anecdotes she'd already told on late-night shows or elsewhere. She'd told the same story in three different interviews about her first meeting with a casting director when she was 17—he told her she was too short to ever make it in Hollywood. In two of them she finished the tale with the same joke: "I want to say to him, you know, the view from way down here doesn't seem so bad *right about now*!"

Leon told me that they were planning to scrap the cover story until Valentina's publicist assured them that Valentina would be willing to discuss the accusations she made about her director, Herman Mancini, a few weeks after her movie *Whirlwind* came out (she hadn't given an interview since the Twitter statement in which she accused him of verbally harassing her on set). "Frankly, she better give you something juicy about him," Leon said. "We were ready to switch to Dua Lipa."

We had forty-five minutes allotted for the interview, which didn't feel like nearly enough time—though I also simultaneously felt anxious about devising how to fill all of it. I decided I would wait to ask any questions about Mancini until we were at least halfway through the interview, after we were "warmed up."

Getting the assignment had been a combination of luck and persistence. The assigned writer, the magazine veteran Genevieve Jones, had to leave the country for a book she was working on, so they needed a fill-in on short notice. I'd been sitting in Leon's office for a meeting when he got word about Genevieve, and when he bemoaned to the other editor in the room that they would have to find a new writer for the piece, I, as if possessed by a spirit, rattled off that I'd do anything for the opportunity and that I had seen *The Detour* multiple times (a lie—I'd seen just thirty minutes of it, once) and that I felt like I could provide a "really fresh take" on her. It was as if this more ambitious, confident, assured version of myself had expunged the usual me and taken over. Leon frowned and just continued checking his email, and I assumed that some other "established" writer would get it.

But an hour later Leon emailed me that the story was mine: *You're going to have to turn it around in 72 hours post-interview—the timing is very tight.* He added, *Don't fuck this up.* After a recent restructuring, Leon was now covering digital and print stories, which meant he was much busier and, to my benefit, wanted to get decisions made as quickly as possible.

When I saw Valentina walk through the doors of the restaurant, I stood up, as if an officer rising to salute. She was wearing a yellow T-shirt and jeans, with large sunglasses on, carrying a leather bag. She moved to the table breezily, not bothering to look around the restaurant, and slid into the booth.

"How'd you know I was me?" I croaked, sitting back down. *Great* start, Victor.

She kept her sunglasses on as she situated herself. "You just start to have a sense for these things at a certain point," she said.

I laughed. She was petite, sure, but she also was overwhelmingly striking, and I felt confused about how someone this beautiful just *functioned* in the world, running a dishwasher and sweating at the gym and picking things out of her teeth. Was I so superficial that I was instantly infatuated with her simply because she was so beautiful? Would I be able to ask her serious questions? Basically, I realized, I wanted to be her friend, which felt like the opposite of what a journalist was meant to be thinking at this point at the start of an interview.

"I'm actually new to this, kind of," I said.

She took her sunglasses off. "Well, I'm honored to help break you in." There was a practiced remove to her tone—she let you feel as if you were being allowed to enter her orbit, to receive her light, without *really* actually letting you in.

"Are you—do you like going to restaurants, or is it annoying when people recognize you, or do you feel like—"

"Oh no, I love it," she said. "I love going out. I hate when things happen that make me feel like I'm a freak, or like I can't just live my life, you know?"

I decided right then that I wouldn't be asking any of the thirty-six questions I had prepared beforehand. I just wanted to *chat* with her. When would I have that chance again?

I wasn't recording any of this yet, so I reached into my pocket and took out the cumbersome recording device I'd purchased recently. I felt embarrassed as I set it on the table. "I feel like I work for the FBI, like I'm taking your deposition," I said as I pressed record. (I had delivered a version of this line several times now, but smiled as if I had just come up with it.)

She looked up at me, her eyes widening. "This is probably a weird request, but can we just talk for a bit, off the record, first? I've realized, doing this for a while now, I do better when we don't just jump right in."

"Oh, of course, sure."

I turned off the recorder. It was strange how—and I couldn't tell if this was a function of her being a skilled actress—I felt this need in that moment to protect her. I wanted to tell a story that would make her feel good, to write something she would like. I felt in command and present—there was still a stultifying, professional context that circled the entire table—but also like I had just met a mysterious woman at a party and was deeply intrigued and captivated by her. Was this her trick? Was it just an extension of her performances? Actresses weren't *always* acting, were they? Wasn't that just a lazy assessment jealous people bandied about? I was definitely overthinking it.

"So, uh, what did you do today?" I asked. "Before . . . coming here?"

She didn't exactly relax at the question, but she smiled.

"You're sweet," she said. "Let's see, I worked out on the bike for thirty minutes. Awful. Torture. The worst." I obviously knew she was British, but somehow—maybe because she had an American accent in the roles I'd seen—her natural accent now jarred me. She spoke softly in person, as if everything she said was a version of a secret.

Zoey had texted me that morning: I bet she is gonna be obsessed with you. And I guess the fact that this made me feel good was sort of pathetic, not only because of course the subject of an interview would probably pretend she liked me even if she didn't, but also because it was sad Zoey knew (rightfully) that Valentina's feelings about me would *matter to me*, as much as "getting good quotes" or how the story turned out.

"It's actually ridiculous I pay for the gym," I said. "I go maybe twice a month. And then when I'm there I mainly end up, like, sitting on the mat and texting for forty minutes. Or gawking at the hot people doing choreographed routines."

Why was I doing *riffs on the gym* for her? Either way, she generously laughed.

The waiter brought us two sparkling waters, and a ginger ale, which neither of us had ordered. "Oh, my publicist always calls ahead," Valentina said, as if that was not even the slightest bit unusual. As she squeezed a lime into the water, she looked up at me. "So tell me more about you."

I felt suddenly very clear—it was unquestionably evident—that she knew her own power. It was obvious to me she rarely asked people questions about themselves, as a general rule, and that she definitely understood the force it had when she deigned to do so. Who would deny her requests?

"I'm not sure there's a lot to tell," I said. "I—I've been working at the magazine about seven months now, and having a great time—" God. Having a *great time*?!

She nodded. "Yes, yes, amazing." What exactly was "amazing"? What was this back-and-forth we were having, this bizarre form of small talk? Why were we still off the record? This was cutting into my forty-five minutes.

I decided to sit up straight, to try to get *serious*. "Do you want to, uh—"

"You know, it's funny," she said, stirring the straw in her ginger ale (she still hadn't sipped the drink). I wasn't clear if she was consciously interrupting me—it was possible she hadn't heard me start to speak; maybe she couldn't even see me at all. "I was so anxious about, you know, doing any press after the Twitter post I put up."

I nodded gravely, as if at a funeral or something. Way too solemn.

"I didn't tell anyone about . . . *him* until, you know, a few weeks after the movie came out, when all my interviews and everything were over with. My publicist, Erica, thought I should do the *Today* show or *Good Morning America* after I posted about it, but that felt too . . . I don't know, phony? Intense? Just not the vibe."

I nodded again, forcefully, though I didn't know totally what that meant, what "vibe" she was hoping to achieve with . . . me.

"But then I felt like doing a print piece, with a journalist, where it's not so *in your face*, and where you, where the writer, can provide all the context about what I'm trying to communicate, and it's not just about, you know, what I'm wearing or if I look sad enough, or how I react when they say his name on camera—I just felt like this was safer. I hadn't been planning to ever talk about any of this, back when I was doing the junkets and everything."

It was hard for me to picture this director—or anyone, for that matter—treating Valentina Lack callously. She had just recently been linked in the press to an art dealer who was five years younger than her, Reggie Osterman. He wasn't exactly attractive—he had a long face and a slender frame—but he definitely exuded a certain charisma and confidence, evident even in candids of the two of them casually traipsing across a crosswalk, hand in hand.

She hailed a waiter, who appeared within seconds. "Can I actually— can I have a glass of rosé?"

The waiter smiled. "Right away, ma'am."

Valentina looked at me. "Do you want anything to drink?"

"I'm actually, uh, not—I'm trying not to drink, really," I said to her, even though I was back to drinking almost nightly at this point.

The waiter nodded and left. I felt like I owed her more of an explanation for some reason, even though she had just taken out her phone to check it, not even trying to be subtle.

"I had a pretty bad break-up," I offered, while she jabbed at her phone. "And I—I am trying to be good and healthy for a while and see how that goes."

She looked up from the device and I thought she was going to ask me to repeat myself, but instead she put on a frown.

"Oh, honey," she said. "The worst, isn't it?"

I must have looked confused, because she continued seamlessly: "I was dating the most awful guy in the world—truly—as I was first becoming . . . known. Back when *The Detour* came out. Just undermined me at every turn. He'd literally text me links to pictures of me on Just Jared and write things like, 'Maybe you should retire this outfit' or 'Stairmaster doesn't seem to be doing much.'"

"No!"

She sighed, then shook her head. We were still technically off the record—I wasn't recording her—and I had no idea how or when I was supposed to interject about that, as I felt pretty sure if I interrupted her to ask if we could "start" now, she would end this train of thought about her ex, and maybe it would even break the trust we had developed. Could I even call what we had here "trust"? Was that insane?!

"Anyway, one day he straight-up threw something at me. A book. Not exaggerating." She leaned in and touched my arm. "The day after the Golden Globes, just—yeah. We were on the balcony of my hotel room." I nodded vigorously as if I had ever been on a balcony of a hotel room the morning after a major awards show. "I knew it had to be over, but—and how absurd is this?—I decided I should probably stay with him, not rock the boat, because the Oscars were coming up and I didn't want there to be this whole big story about my messy break-up right when I was about to be up for the first Oscar nomination of my career. No one really knew who I was then and, if that came out, that would suddenly be *everywhere*, you know? I just couldn't risk that, couldn't have that."

I was riveted, but also kept returning to the upsetting thought that I couldn't use any of this material. My hand was shaking, and my entire back felt sweaty underneath my shirt and my sweater. The water and the tea and her ginger ale and her rosé—all of this untouched *liquid* in containers—was making me feel even more stressed. My inactive recorder was sinking into the table, mocking me. She clearly knew it wasn't turned on—*right?* Was this part of some malevolent game she was playing?

"Could I just—?" I moved my hand toward the device.

She completely changed her tenor. "So, please, tell me about your break-up! I've been rambling."

"Oh—he was, well—" I grabbed the recorder and held it up, way more aggressively than I'd meant to. "Do you mind if I turn this on, and then—I'll tell you my saga and we can—"

"Oh yes, of course, of course."

The waiter returned to ask if either of us needed anything else. I had never witnessed such attentive service in my life. I turned the recorder on, as Valentina shook her head at the waiter. "We're good—thank you, doll."

She turned back to me and rested her head on her pink-manicured hand, elbows up on the table. She was staring at me, waiting for a story.

"Oh, uh, well, yeah. My story. It's silly, I don't know why I even brought it up. But I met the guy in college. Oliver. We didn't start dating until much later, though—we ran into each other at an alumni event. He's a few years older and I always had a crush on him, I guess. And—god, I don't know why I'm starting at the very, very beginning."

"No, no, please, continue! I love hearing people's stories."

I decided to just roll with it. "Yeah, uh, we dated for two and a half years. He's—he's, like, the kind of guy who has an Android, not an iPhone—you know what I mean?"

Her face went blank.

"Just, he wasn't tuned in. He never knew who any celebrities were. He doesn't keep up on—like, he wouldn't know your movies."

She shot me a look of mock disgust. "Well, fuck him, then!"

I laughed. We were probably ten minutes into the forty-five, but, particularly now that the recorder was actually recording, I decided this was . . . fine? Nice? Maybe it was even a good "tactic"—I'd share something; she'd share something.

"Anyway, it ended kind of disastrously." I decided at this moment to take my first sip of the tea, which was *scalding* hot still, somehow. I recoiled, coughing.

She leaned in. "Are you all right?" I continued to cough. The rattling spread to my chest and my face felt hot.

"Sorry," I eked out. "I don't know what happened there."

"You wouldn't get very far in Britain."

I laughed. "Yeah, right." She looked bored now, maybe. Had this all just been a way for her to stall? To delay me? We were going to have to talk about Herman Mancini at some point—she knew that, right?

"Anyway, we're talking way too much about me, and I—"

"Right, right. Let's talk about the Aronofsky movie!"

She had a Darren Aronofsky movie coming out in a few months, in which she had a small part as the mother of a vampire. I'd found it a somewhat brutal, harrowing watch when they screened it early for me.

"Sure!" I said. "Let's start there. So, not to—just to clarify—we're on the record now?"

She flashed a billboard smile. "Buckle up."

8

Zoey

Zoey walked into the Bowery Hotel lobby and searched for Wiles. She spotted him, again in a suit, this time light gray. He appeared to be on a call. The tips of his fingers were resting on the edge of a small bowl of almonds.

Let's celebrate your promotion! he had texted, with an "xx" follow-up. She knew she probably should have responded by suggesting lunch or a coffee—daylight hours—and the fact that she hadn't even told Victor about this drinks meetup confirmed for her it wasn't wise. But she was here, it was happening, and she was wearing a black jumpsuit that she hadn't pulled out of her closet in two years.

"It's like I'm looking at a completely different person," Wiles said, after she sat down on the plush chaise across from him, rather than next to him on the couch. "Head of comms."

"My title is actually Communications Chair."

"Chair. How fancy. Chair is very Perri."

He raised his glass and took a sip. "I saw you on the *Today* show. Honestly, I'm surprised you have time for me now."

"It was the third hour. But yes. I'm a star."

"I like that you're prickly. Have I told you that yet? I really like it.

Not the usual fashion-world prickly I'm used to, either. You've got some warmth swirled in there."

"Thank you? It's like you're David Attenborough narrating a nature doc about me."

"Oh, you love it."

She asked for a glass of rosé. And then for another glass. She asked him about his other investments, about his upcoming travel. She liked that he never monologued for too long—he was pithy. He understood her. And she felt like he was actually *impressed* by her. Intimidated by her, even. She liked that he asked her questions, too.

"What do you do with your spare time?" he flung at her, at some point after his third drink.

"Are you seriously asking me that? That's beneath you. That very . . . that feels like a job interview question."

He moved closer to her. She noticed how thick his quads were; they were straining the fabric of his suit pants. "*That very?*" he said, taking a sip of his drink. "Good thing Hoda Kotb isn't here right now."

She rolled her eyes, but not in the way she rolled her eyes for Victor. This was a different thing.

"I never know how to answer this," she said. "*Hobbies.* I see my friends. I—online shop. TV? This is depressing to talk about."

"You're not single," he said flatly. "You said that."

"I—yes. Correct."

He raised his eyebrows. "Okay. How serious are we with this mystery man?"

"Can I tell you something?" She said it in a whisper.

"Oh, I like this." He leaned in toward her. "I can tell we're going to be in each other's lives for a long time."

"What a line," she said. She was enjoying the repartee. He really was so different from Tom, living each day as a citizen of such a different universe—comprised of satin and velvet and probably criminal activity and smoke, too—that it almost felt like none of this "counted." At least, that logic made sense to her in this moment. She felt decidedly adult. Independent. When she was working at Thom Browne, prominent stylists and models and editors were in and out of her periphery, but she had never shared meaningful face time with any of them—no one looked for her, sat down with her, wanted to delight her.

"I don't know why I'm even telling you this," she continued. "But do you know *Corridor* magazine?"

"Yeah, of course. They wrote a story I was mentioned in a few years ago—it was a fucking hit piece about my friend. Don't get me started."

"Well, when Perri gave me the promotion, she asked me to place a story with them, because she knew my close friend worked there. Victor. It was somewhat—well, she made it sound like it was contingent on me getting the role. It was a little unclear. Anyway, my friend said he would ask his editor about it, and I guess his editor said they would consider it, but basically he just pushed it off. He told me they wanted to wait until after we launched. Now, it's been . . . well, Selah is obviously up and running, and it's clear the piece is never going to happen. But I told Perri already it was a done deal."

"And Perri hasn't brought it up to you again?"

"No, she hasn't. Isn't that weird? It almost scares me more that she hasn't." Zoey paused. "I'm close to getting us coverage in *Time*, which hopefully will make her happy. But I don't know; it's a mess."

"Just tell her *Corridor* isn't a done deal anymore. It's magazines. She gets it."

"You think? I feel like this is different because this was kind of how I got the promotion."

"Zoey, if *this* is going to stress you out this much, I don't know if you are cut out for this industry. This should be a typical Thursday morning for you."

"No, I know. You're right. Usually I wouldn't—this isn't a big deal. Let's not talk about it anymore."

"This friend of yours sounds like kind of a shitty friend."

Zoey decided not to respond to this.

"Do you know Maddie Brooks, by the way?"

"The influencer? Yeah, we were trying to get in touch with her for Selah for a while. Perri was very excited about it, but we couldn't make it work."

"She's a family friend of mine, you could say. Her father and I go back. I'll connect you two at some point. She's a very entertaining girl. You'd do better with her than Perri would."

Zoey knew that she liked how Wiles saw her, but it was easier to not think about his potential motives for seeing her this way. She didn't want to think about the reasons why.

The truth was—and she had been repressing this—she actually *did* feel angry at Victor. His follow-up to her request had been in an overly formal text message, with more punctuation than he ever used with her: I'm really sorry. I tried everything, Z. Leon just isn't going for it. He said maybe we can move forward when it's more clear that Selah is going to be a "thing"? Does that make sense? We'll try again then. XOXOXO.

The weirdness of the text almost made her wonder if he had even talked to Leon. Of course, she hadn't told Victor that she'd already told Perri it was officially happening. She wrote back: fuck, that's annoying, and Victor "!"-reacted the text.

"You know," Zoey said now, as she watched Wiles sign for the bill, "Maybe I should just follow up with Victor. I'm being kind of—"

"Immature?"

"No," she said. "If anyone's being immature, it's him."

"How good of a friend is he? Do you want me to send him an anonymous email?"

"*What the fuck are you talking about? Anonymous email?*" She playfully slapped his knee, but he didn't react to the physical contact, and she immediately regretted it. "Victor knows me better than anyone."

Wiles felt slightly removed to her now. The lights in the room were brighter to her; the energy had shifted. She didn't want him to think of her as immature, incompetent, sloppy. She wanted to leave.

She looked at her phone and saw a text from Tom: Hope drinks with Louisa are fun. Tell her I say hi.

"Why did you want to get drinks with me, by the way?" she asked Wiles. "We could have—you could have just sent me flowers to congratulate me on the job. A bottle of champagne."

"I don't know. You strike me as someone on the verge of something."

9

My first appointment with Dr. Beckman took place about two months after Oliver broke up with me. But I didn't tell him until maybe our sixth or seventh meeting about that night. Those first sessions, I just rambled about work and my mother and my friends, as if any of those things had caused me actual strife. I delivered my rehearsed lines about my parents' divorce. I told him I had a perfectly decent relationship with my stepdad ("It's like the dynamic you have with the nice math teacher in middle school"). I told him I was insecure about how I looked, my body, but also understood, rationally, that I could be worse off. I was essentially doing a performance for him, hitting what I imagined to be the therapy *talking points*, stealing furtive glances at the clock to see how much time was left—there was always more time left than I expected there to be.

"Well . . . I'm glad to see you're okay now," Dr. Beckman said, affectless, when I finally told him about the break-up and the overdose. His reaction was upsetting; I could sense I wanted him to make more of it. He did not appear to think there was anything special about me or my situation.

I told Dr. Beckman I hadn't consumed alcohol since that night— which of course wasn't true—and he just nodded, silent.

"I figured it was probably a good—I don't know, just given how intense things got that night, and the position I put Zoey in . . . It felt like a good idea to try to do something tangible, to make a change."

"Yes."

"I'm not, like, an alcoholic."

"Why is that an important distinction for you to make?" he asked. He was wearing a dark blue blazer over a white collared shirt. Every time we met, he'd get a call at the same time—6:45 p.m.—and he would always pick up and mutter "Yes" twice before hanging up the phone. I never asked him who was calling, and he never offered an explanation. Sometimes, I was convinced there was no one actually on the line, and that this was some kind of psychological test he was conducting to see how I reacted.

"I don't know why it's an important distinction," I said to him. "I just . . . I guess for my *sense of self*, or whatever. And my mom was worried, understandably, and I had to explain to her I didn't have a *problem*. So I told her I just wouldn't drink for a while." I made a point of making eye contact with Dr. Beckman here. "It felt like a concrete action."

"It is a concrete action."

Maybe because my job consisted of interviewing other people, I found the conversational flow of therapy extremely irritating.

We were both silent for another ten seconds, and then I continued. "I'm trying, at least. *Therapy and sobriety*." I paused, to see if he'd respond. "That sounds like the name of an awful play."

He didn't laugh at this, and in fact appeared annoyed.

"I do keep looking at pictures of me and him, though. That still happens a lot."

"Him?"

"Of me and Oliver, the boyfriend . . . my ex-boyfriend. I'm not going to delete them. Even though I know it would make sense to. And we still talk. We text. So maybe that means I'm not doing as great as I think I am. We're supposed to get coffee when he's in New York in a few weeks."

I was still worrying, even in my most lucid moments with Dr. Beckman, about how I was coming across, how this 56-year-old Upper East Side doctor might be perceiving me. I still had the urge to filter or temper thoughts that felt perhaps too vulnerable.

"It's perfectly okay to not be doing great," he said finally, and even though I nodded, I wasn't sure I believed him.

I had thought, now that I'd recounted the Oliver break-up tale to him and explained that I had been rushed to *the fucking hospital*, that that would be the focal point of our work together moving forward. But a few sessions later, when I gave him a brief summary of my interview with Valentina Lack, it became clear that what he was most excited about was discussing my job.

"So you'll be turning in the Valentina story—when?—next week?" he asked.

"Yeah, I—I actually had to get it done in seventy-two hours, so it's already been turned in. We're doing edits now."

He looked visibly upset—perhaps more distraught than he had about anything I'd told him in the office up to this point.

"Hmm." He paused. "You know, you could have pushed back on them, when they gave you that edict."

"That's not—you can't really do that. I'm not just going to, like, storm into the editor in chief's office and go, '*Hey.*'"

"Why not?"

On some level I was annoyed that we were using my therapy session to dissect office dynamics, to discuss the particulars of my latest writing assignment . . . but on the other hand, when I considered it further, this was much less emotionally intense than discussing Oliver or anything actually real. And that did feel like a relief.

"Yeah, well, I don't know. I don't feel like I am at a level in my career where—I just don't think it's normal for a 29-year-old to respond that way. I'm just a staff writer, still. I don't really have *leverage*, you know?"

He didn't say anything, but he slowly, deliberately crossed his legs, which—based on what I now knew to be his gestural language—felt like the equivalent of his throwing a clock at my head. Usually I tried to fill these silences in our sessions quickly, but I didn't really know what to say here.

"It's a big deal you were asked to write a cover story," he said eventually. "You were entrusted with an important assignment. Because you're talented. And that means you have power here. You don't need to agree right away to everything they ask. This just means the next time you get an assignment like this, they'll expect you to turn it around in the same amount of time."

This was the most I had heard him expand on any topic in the months I'd been seeing him. I could have reiterated the genesis of the assignment to him—explained that I had been handed the story last-minute when Genevieve Jones backed out, and that this sort of time crunch for a draft was standard practice (I assumed?) for these high-pressure magazine-world scenarios. He didn't know anything about how any of this worked; he had never even read anything I'd written—*how did he know if I was "talented" or not?!* But rather than dig in, I just scratched my scalp and crossed my legs myself. Was this an animal-reflex response, to mimic your interlocutor? It felt weird, but I had already done it and I couldn't now uncross them.

"Yeah, uh, I guess maybe I could have done that," I said.

The phone rang—it was 6:45—and he picked it up. "Yes . . . Yes . . ." He hung up and cleared his throat, as if there had not been any interruption. "You have to be your own advocate," he said.

"Yes."

"This is a really major event, in the arc of your career."

I looked away, shifting in my seat.

"Do you think you got good material from her?"

I wasn't supposed to talk about the content of my interview until the story was out in print. I felt like it was implicit that if I discussed any of it with Dr. Beckman, he would understand that—this was a therapy session, after all—but nevertheless, I said, "Yeah, I mean, I'm not really supposed to—obviously this stays between us . . ."

He didn't nod at this so much as flinch in the affirmative.

"But yeah, I think I got some good stuff. I don't know. I'm nervous about it. I'm not sure if she's going to like the story, and . . . I mean, obviously my job isn't to write something that she *likes*. Necessarily. But, uh, we talked about things that are touchy, and she *said them*, so . . ."

"Yes, that's the job. But, you know, you could maybe reach out to her after the story comes out and see if she wants to get lunch or coffee. You could stay in touch."

I was annoyed that he did not understand any of the protocol, and also annoyed that on some level he was right that I would *love* to find a way to get lunch and stay in touch with her, not that I would ever admit that to him.

"Yeah, well, maybe. I—she said all the right things, about the director. And I feel like—I mean, obviously she knew I was there to write about her, so she's going to act in a certain way, but she was really great. Articulate and open and nice."

It's true. She was articulate and open and nice. I didn't add to Dr. Beckman that I only ended up with twenty-seven minutes of recorded interview material to work with, because we didn't "start" until ten minutes in, and then she "had to run out" a few minutes early. We hit all the major points though, and the quote I'd received back from the director Herman Mancini's representative was indignant and ridiculous, sure to get a reaction on Twitter. Leon hadn't said much about the draft; when I looked in the system, I saw that about a third of what I'd turned in had been cut.

"Well, I am excited to read the story when it's out," Dr. Beckman said.

"Yeah, I—I mean, it's an important story, and I'm obviously a small part of it. People want to hear what she has to say. I'm just—the vessel."

"Vessel?"

"Yeah, I mean . . . I didn't think too hard about that word choice, but, yeah."

Dr. Beckman wrote something down on a piece of paper. I found this deeply irritating.

"I'm—I kind of find myself wanting to . . . drink again," I said.

He didn't look up from his writing, but nodded.

"Is that okay?"

"Sure," he said. "It's your choice."

"Right. But I mean, I feel like I wanted—I wanted to try to be sober for a while longer, just to—it's not really about the break-up or anything at this point. I just want to prove to myself I can do it."

"Well, just be careful—if you stick with it, or even if you don't— that you don't transfer your obsessive ways of thinking, that you may have imputed on aspects of your relationship with Oliver, onto other behaviors."

I stared at the ground for a few moments. "If I'm being honest," I blurted out, "I actually—I've had some drinks . . . on a few occasions, maybe on more than a few occasions, since—since the hospital."

He nodded. "That's fine."

I couldn't believe that this was all he had to say on the topic. Next week, I would quit. I was going to tell him that I no longer required his services. That therapy was a waste of my time. I wouldn't quit *now*. I'd think about it for a week. But I would do it next week.

When I left the building, I called my mom back. "I'm just leaving my therapist's office," I said.

"And how was that?"

"I don't like him."

"What a shock."

I smiled. "What?"

"You just—you never like anyone. Especially, you know, people in authority."

"Well, that's part of what's annoying. A therapist shouldn't really be an *authority figure*, right? I'm paying him—he works for me."

"I don't know, Victor." As I walked in a circle around the entrance to the subway, she kept talking. "I just ran into my friend Margaret Randall, by the way. She's about to leave for Arizona for one of her ridiculous trips. Some spa that costs nine hundred dollars a night, maybe even more. Her husband represents this major hotel chain—I'll look up the name for you later. Anyway, I told her you had a big cover story coming out. She was thrilled. Beyond excited. She loves Valentina Lack. She said she'll buy a bunch of copies. I told her you might be on TV when it comes out."

"Mom, you're really not supposed to tell people who the story is about. And you know the issue doesn't actually come out for seven more weeks?"

"I know, I know! I'm your street team. And don't worry—who would Margaret possibly tell? Also, I'm going to send you . . . I saw Valentina did an interview with some, maybe it was *Entertainment Tonight*, but it's about the vampire teeth she had to wear in a movie that's coming out. Or something like that. I'll send it to you."

I drifted away from the subway entrance, in the opposite direction.

"Do you have enough food for the rest of the week?" my mom asked. "Things to eat?"

"Yeah, I think so."

"Good. I'm making a salmon tonight. You know, the one with olives. Warren is out at some lecture. So I'm not sure if he'll actually be back in time to eat it. But if he's not, I'll just wrap up a piece for him. Then we'll probably watch another *Broadchurch*."

I missed being home, and missed being with my mom, though I'd learned that this was just sort of my resting state in New York, and that when I was actually back home in Chicago, I felt uncomfortable, unlike myself, a sea creature out of water.

"That sounds nice," I said. "I miss the salmon with olives."

"Warren's so excited about your story, too. We decided to watch that movie she got the Oscar for this weekend. We never saw it."

"She didn't win. Just nominated."

I got off the phone and circled back toward the subway.

I'd seen the proposed cover mock-up for the first time that morning in the office. The cover was going to feature a portrait of Valentina in a white blouse, unbuttoned about halfway down her chest. She was sitting in a regal wooden armchair, looking out a window, it appeared, with light streaming onto her face. It was the sort of picture you'd associate with a presidential memoir, or an ad for migraine medication. The coverline read: "VALENTINA LACK TAKES BACK HER NARRATIVE." ("Lack" and "Back" were both in a larger slanted font.) There was a pull-quote on the cover, too: "It's important to hold men accountable." (In the actual piece, that quote read, "I feel like it's so important that we hold people—well, men—accountable, for what they inflict on others—since so many of them don't give it a second thought, and get to walk away consequence-free.")

In those first few moments after seeing the cover mock-up for the first time, I had to admit, my entire body felt electrified: it was real, it was happening, *everyone was going to be reading my words.*

And when I spotted my byline—my name positioned a few inches from Valentina's elegant leg—I'd almost taken a picture and sent it to my mom. But I decided I'd wait and let her be surprised when it came out. That millions of people would see my name as they stood in line to check out at the grocery store, or as they loitered in the airport before heading to their gate—it made my skin tingle. It was comforting some-how that all my gripes and insecurities—the sleepless nights, the great anxiety—wouldn't be visible to any of these people, glancing at the cover. (*"Victor Harris . . . who is that?"*) That they might wonder what I looked like, how old I was, what my voice sounded like . . . it made me feel gigantic—like I might burst.

I would be *read*. I would be clicked on. It was terrifying, too—of course I wanted to scream—but I felt the potential for real satisfaction, somewhere ahead of me on the horizon.

As I moved through the turnstile, though, and descended into the subway, I was struck by a vision—it was vivid—of an alternate Victor tumbling down the stairs, limbs dislocated, his body finally striking the cement column at the bottom. As disconcerting as the specifics of this imagery was, there was something about it that drew me in and felt safe. Maybe *this* was a manifestation of success anxiety. Or was it something completely different? If I fell into a coma at the 72nd Street subway stop, would they still run the cover story? Would they put an asterisk under my byline? Would Valentina find out? Would she post something on her Twitter account? *My heart goes out to Victor Harris and his family*, it would say. *I only spent 45 minutes with him at a restaurant for lunch, but I could sense he was a really special person.*

For now, I held on to the railing going down.

10

Caroline

Perched on her fire escape, Caroline rested her Diet Coke on her knee—she was trying to stop drinking so much caffeine, but something about the can (the noise it makes when you indent it with your finger?) was just so soothing. She picked up her phone and glanced at her texts. The usual. Her mom had sent her three full paragraphs from a Wyoming senior citizens center's website about vitamin D deficiency (Caroline's mother had recently learned how to text from her laptop, a stressful development). Her friend Willow was asking if she was free on Tuesday for coffee; she was free on Tuesday, but not for that—Willow always had some sort of convoluted romantic dilemma to discuss at length . . . and then Caroline would text her to follow up a few days later and Willow would just write back, Oh everything's good now! or sometimes not even respond.

And there was the text from Ben: Going for a bike ride—I'll pick you up a croissant and an iced tea on my way back!

He was always doing this—going out and bringing her something back. Sometimes he'd bring her flowers ("You love this color, right?"). Sometimes a latte ("It's not super hot anymore, but . . ."). Other times he'd crawl onto the couch next to her, kiss her cheek (his still sweaty), and pull a book seemingly out of his earlobe ("Weren't you saying you wanted to read this?"). There was nothing *wrong* about any of this—in fact, at first, Caroline quite liked it, even came to expect it from him—but there was something, at this point, having lived with him for thirteen months, that chafed. If she wanted a croissant and iced tea, she could walk down the street and buy both for herself, from one of nine different cafés on their East Village block.

"You're so lucky," people always told her. And she knew that, technically, sure, she probably was. Ben was in his first year of business school, yet rarely mentioned his work—if he ever started talking about a "case" for too long, Caroline would just pointedly look away or down at her phone, and he would immediately change the subject. He was extremely handsome, the sort of handsome that older family members just can't help but remark upon ("The *jawline* on that boyfriend of yours, Caroline"). When he hadn't shaved for a few days, people would lean over from their nearby table and ask if anyone had ever told him he looks like a famous actor ("*No one* has said you look like a skinnier Jake Gyllenhaal?!?"). Caroline would roll her eyes, but she enjoyed it. "I wish!" he'd always say with a grin. And as anyone who had been around them for more than seven minutes would later remark to Caroline (either aggressively, passive-aggressively, or sweetly, depending on who it was), he *really, really loved her*.

Caroline had met Ben at a bar, at the birthday party of a man named Otto Young. At that point, she'd been hooking up with Otto Young on and off for about two years. Otto was a curator at the Guggenheim, and he had slept with dozens of women in the arts and literary scenes. Caroline—a pretty freelance writer who, at the time, lived in Greenpoint—knew there were at least five other pretty freelance writers from Greenpoint Otto could text any given night instead of her. Otto didn't drink, and he smoked what Caroline always estimated to be at least eleven cigarettes a night (but was probably more like three). He liked to say things to Caroline like, "I'm taking you to Europe," as if it were a threat. "Please, you couldn't even take me to *Penn Station!*" she shouted once in response, a line she often recalled, with a grimace or a smile, when she would scroll through Otto's Twitter feed at 1:17 a.m.

At Otto Young's birthday party, Ben had emerged out of the darkness and approached Caroline with an air of tequila-fueled confidence undercut by earnestness. "I really like your shirt" was the first thing he said to Caroline. And if he hadn't looked, if you squinted, a bit like Jake Gyllenhaal, and if she hadn't been on her third vodka soda, and if Otto hadn't been deep in conversation with a girl who had just written a *GQ* cover story, Caroline probably would have just smiled politely and turned away. But instead she looked Ben right in the eyes and said, "Thanks, it's actually a men's shirt."

Caroline had never lived with a boyfriend before Ben. On occasion, she'd watch as Ben completed an egregiously mundane task—cleaned out the blender, cut his fingernails—and she'd feel overcome with a desire to throw his cherished rhododendron against the wall and run out the door and keep running along Second Avenue, *Frances Ha*–style, until she got to Central Park (for some reason the vision always ended in Central Park, as if everything would be resolved there). When she started to feel this way, she'd usually retreat into the bedroom and watch whatever video autoplayed first when she opened her browser. Or she'd tell Ben she was "heading to a meeting," and walk around her neighborhood for eighty minutes. Once or twice—okay, several times—she had ambled all the way up to the Guggenheim, just in case Otto might be smoking a cigarette outside. He never was.

Caroline's career had actually been going quite well since she and Ben had moved in together. While she didn't exactly make it "known," the bulk of her income came from writing copy for ad agencies or brands (she once had to write about twenty pages of dialogue from the perspective of a piece of quinoa for a salad brand). The book reviews and magazine pieces she was assigned came about regularly enough that her acquaintances might have believed they provided enough for her to sustain herself. Once, she had found herself telling one of Ben's friends that she just "tried to write stories that had a personal meaning" for her. The friend had nodded skeptically.

Caroline had never expected that Instagram—which she mostly thought of as a mild annoyance, a distraction—would lead to so much work, but she was finding a great number of her jobs via incoming DMs. Caroline didn't post very often, but she had developed a following of more than 24,000. Her content was generally enigmatic, glimpses of her surroundings: a shadow of herself on the sidewalk, a violent-looking branch, a Boomerang of sunflower seeds falling out of a bag. When she did put up a selfie, it was always penetrating, vibrant in a manner atypical for digital material. It wasn't that her selfies were particularly well-lit, or that her angular face was so much more angular than anyone else's, but her expression suggested she was comfortable, and serene, in a way people rarely appear to be on Instagram. Her face wasn't asking anything of you. It didn't care if you liked it or not.

"Oh god, are you *putting up an Instagram?*" Otto used to say, whenever Caroline was on her phone for more than thirty seconds around him. (Otto, of course, didn't have an account. Ben had a private one, with 237 followers, and posted mostly shots of food he had prepared or vacation vistas.)

Sometimes Caroline would be asked to model—usually for a streetwear "online store" with no money to offer, or a makeup brand with a lot of money to offer. Caroline's beauty was so understated that it was as if each new person who met her felt like they were discovering it for themselves. If anything, she tried to play against it, wearing an ugly visor to a party, or a shade of distracting purple lipstick to an important interview. Her hair was smooth and dark, and her smile barely perceptible. Once she asked Ben if he liked her hair better up or down and he said, "I like it however you like it," and she had decided to never ask him any questions like that again. These days, she didn't wear much makeup at all and kept her hair down.

Caroline opened Instagram and, instinctively, tapped to look at her direct messages. She hadn't responded to a message from a girl named "Liv," sent three days earlier: Hi Caroline! :) I promise I'm not a stalker lol—I just wanted to tell you that I really love your whole vibe. Your style is so chic !! and sophisticated. Can i ask what kind of camera do you use to take your pics?? Hope you're having a sparkling day! —Liv

That's so sweet of you! xx, Caroline wrote back, pressing send and returning to her feed.

She quickly double-tapped a photo of her sister, posted from a wedding in Austin. A childhood friend of hers had put up a video from a runway show in Paris (it was unclear to Caroline who paid for these trips to fashion shows she always seemed to be going on). Her friend Zoey—they knew each other from art camp and hadn't spoken in about three years—was smiling in a photo next to a bland-looking guy in a wine orchard (the caption: Tom and I had a terrible time upstate); Caroline was pretty sure they had just gotten married. She liked a photo posted by *Vogue* in honor of Sarah Jessica Parker's birthday, then un-liked it.

Caroline could hear the door open inside the apartment.

"Babe?"

Ben always announced his arrival with "Babe?"

"I'm out here," she whispered through the window from the fire escape. She wasn't sure if she had even said it out loud.

About thirty seconds later, Ben stuck his head out through the window. "Hey." He leaned in to kiss her, and she configured herself so he could.

"I got you an iced tea. And a croissant."

"Yeah, you . . . said . . . that you were going to." Ben squinted—the sun was directly in his eyes—and Caroline felt herself soften a bit. "Thank you."

"I ran into Bobby on my bike ride. Remember him?"

"Bobby?"

"He came over that time, when I was in the SoHo apartment. He was the one who kept asking if anyone watched *Westworld* so he could talk about the finale."

"Oh. *God.*"

"He's a nice guy, actually."

Caroline put her sunglasses on and leaned back against the building wall. Sometimes she wondered if she'd survive the jump to the sidewalk—if there were an emergency, and she'd needed to jump—from their third-floor apartment. At this moment, she felt sure that she would.

"I was thinking maybe we could go to a movie or something," Ben said.

"I thought you had to study . . ."

"I do, but I'm not gonna study from now until—you know, the whole weekend."

"I don't know what I want to do."

He tapped the frame of the window a few times.

"You look beautiful," he said.

"I want to take a nap."

Caroline looked down at her phone. She had a new message from Liv: I'm actually releasing a line of lockets!!! Any chance I could convince you to put one on for a few photos for our Instagram account? I'll give you a bunch of free lockets, in exchange! I'll be in Chelsea all day.

Caroline peered in through the window. Ben was now sitting on the couch, scrolling on his phone. "I actually have to go to Chelsea," she said.

"For what?"

"Just a thing."

———

In line for a coffee by their apartment, Caroline studied the barista: she was wearing a fedora, and her nose was pierced. She was speaking to a man at the register, but it was clear to Caroline her mind was elsewhere. Caroline wondered about her, what music she listened to, who her "people" were.

In high school, Caroline contributed to the literary journal. When she was a junior, she wrote a short story about a student with a pristine image—editor of the yearbook, scores of friends, a hockey-player boyfriend—who was clandestinely wreaking havoc, sleeping with a history teacher and cheating on tests. The surface details about the character bore so many similarities to Caroline's real-life best friend Kristen—well-liked on campus, lacrosse-player boyfriend—that people started whispering about whether Kristen might be secretly sleeping with Mr. Miller. Caroline hadn't even realized her protagonist was so similar to her best friend.

New York had taught Caroline that friendships were primarily transactions—there was something being sought out and something being acquired, by both parties. Or maybe this was just Caroline's way of justifying why so many of her friendships had fallen apart.

She walked out of the coffee shop and right into Otto Young. He was wearing a beanie and a sweater, and Caroline didn't recoil or even try to adjust her hair or anything like that. She felt completely calm, as if running into him on the street in the middle of the day was the sort of thing that happened all the time.

"Well, well, well."

"Hey," she said, distractedly. She took a sip of her latte.

"I had a weird feeling I might see you today," he said.

"Yeah? What's with the beanie?"

"Keeps my head warm," he said.

"I'm walking, if you want to walk with me."

He didn't answer, but as Caroline started down the sidewalk, he floated next to her. He put his arm around her, and she pushed it off.

"Have you been writing?" he asked.

"Fuck you."

"What? I'm serious."

"Yes, I've been writing." She paused. "I actually have a piece in *T* coming out in a few weeks." She immediately regretted saying this. She felt like she had just held up a piece of deformed wood in front of her parents and announced, "I made this in shop class."

"Sweet," he said.

It wasn't that Otto made her feel *good*, she considered. In fact, he didn't make her feel comforted in the slightest. But it never really felt much like she had a choice in the matter. He showed up whether or not she wanted him to—in her daydreams, in resurfaced photos on her phone, outside coffee shops.

Otto stopped walking in front of a bodega on 2nd Street.

"Hey, so . . . I actually have something to tell you."

Embarrassingly, Caroline's first, immediate thought was that Otto was going to propose to her.

"What is it? This is . . . it's like we're on a reality show."

"What?"

"You know, how the people on reality shows are always announcing that they're about to say something important before they actually say it? 'Can we *sit down for a second*, Lauren?'"

"I do *not* know," Otto said, smiling, "but okay." Otto's *okay*s were devastating.

"I'm moving to Berlin," he continued.

Caroline felt faint, and then furiously angry. "What? *Why?*"

"I'm going to write a book there. And then just stay for a while and hang."

"Do you even know anyone there?"

"Not really, no."

She knew she had no right to be angry—the last time they had seen each other was about seven months ago at a *Document Journal* party . . . not to mention she was currently living with a different man, a man she was in a relationship with—but she felt suddenly, very palpably, like she was trapped in an elevator stuck between floors.

"Well, if that's what's good for you," was all she could say.

"You know, you can come visit me."

"Did you—did you come down to my block today, just hoping you'd run into me? You know this is where I live." It felt like there was something in her eye, but when she tried to pick it out, there didn't seem to be anything there. "You didn't text me to see if I was home. I could have been out of town. Or somewhere."

"I was in the area and, uh, I don't know."

She decided to leave it at that.

"Are you still dating that guy?" he asked.

"Why are you asking me that?"

He lit a cigarette.

"Do you remember when we ordered all that fried rice and—"

"Yes, I remember, Otto."

"I have to go meet someone," she continued, tilting her head almost parallel to the sidewalk so that her hair fell down to the side. "Have the best time in Berlin."

"That's it?"

"I guess so."

He kicked at some leaves on the ground and seemed to take an hour before saying anything.

Caroline knocked twice on the door, and a short girl with red-framed glasses opened it. She had pronounced, unflattering bangs, and her skin was noticeably pale.

"Ohmigod, thank you *so much* for coming over."

"Of course," Caroline said.

"You are, like, the dream person I envisioned when I started this jewelry line. I just want you to wear *all of them*. Your hair is—I *can't*."

Caroline smiled. You'd think she might feel uncomfortable in the presence of this sort of frighteningly earnest, fawning praise, but she didn't. It concerned her a little that she didn't, actually. She looked at her phone quickly and saw she had a text from Ben—Do you care if I watch an Ozark?—and tucked her phone back in her pocket.

"You're really sweet."

"This is actually my boyfriend's apartment," Liv said. "But I run the operation out of here." It looked like a college boy's apartment: a nondescript couch, a sad television, a framed *Eternal Sunshine* poster. There were five large boxes of plastic-wrapped jewelry taking up most of the "living room" space. There was something vaguely spooky about the apartment, but Caroline did not feel unnerved.

She thought about Otto hugging her goodbye, thanking her "for everything" before they parted ways, as if she were a family friend who had agreed to get a networking coffee with him.

She remembered once, a few years ago, when her mom had been visiting the city, they ran into Otto during intermission of a Broadway show. Otto was there with a different girl, and they had only chatted for about a minute. Caroline's mom had turned to her after and said, "Well, *he's* got a presence, doesn't he?"

Liv was holding two lockets out in front of her. "Do you like the silver or the bronze?"

"Oh, these are really nice." Caroline took both in her hands and held them up against her body. Now that she was holding the products, she felt curious about Liv. "How did you meet your boyfriend?"

"What? Oh, we went to college together. He's really helpful with the business. He designed my website and everything." Liv looked right at Caroline; her gaze was a little terrifying, as if she was trying to memorize everything about Caroline's face.

"So you're a . . . model, right?" Liv asked.

"A model?" Caroline said brusquely. "No, no, not at all. I'm a writer."

"Oh, sorry, I just sort of . . . I don't know, I assumed from your social media and everything. I don't know. Sorry. I'm such an idiot—I don't really—"

"No, it's totally fine. It's funny. I don't really post much about my writing, I guess." Caroline suddenly felt ridiculous—in some dude's apartment, surrounded by cardboard boxes, observed by Liv.

"Do you mind putting one on now?" Liv asked. "I'll snap a few options for the post."

Caroline looked over at the kitchen counter. Three cases of La Croix cans were congregated next to a large Duane Reade shopping bag.

"Yeah, that works," Caroline said. She turned around and slid one over her head. She ran her hand through her hair a few times and turned back.

"Wow," Liv said.

"I like the weight of it" was all Caroline felt like saying.

Liv took about twenty photos of her. Caroline didn't smile. She wondered what Liv would tell her friends about her later, when she held her phone up over drinks and scrolled through the pictures. She wondered what Otto would say if she sent him whatever shot Liv ended up posting. Probably "Gotta take the jobs you can get!" or something like that. Never the response she wanted. Ben read all of Caroline's pieces and he always said the same thing when he finished reading one: "Babe, I'm so impressed." Then he would kiss her on the head or rest his hand on her waist.

Liv scanned the photos on her phone, wide-eyed, as if examining religious texts. Eventually she looked up, with an almost mischievous expression. "Can I ask you something kind of weird?"

Caroline smiled, assuming she was going to have to explain that her mom was Brazilian and her dad was Canadian, when Liv continued: "This is, uh—would you mind taking one with me?"

Caroline instinctively took a small step toward the door, but nodded. "Oh, of course."

Liv laughed in sharp, mildly violent, fashion. "Do you mind taking it?" she said, handing Caroline her phone. "You'll do a better job."

About a foot separated the two women, as Caroline extended her arm to take a few selfies. Liv's face was exuberant, joyful, all teeth. When Caroline handed Liv her phone back, Liv bowed her head, solemnly; the service had concluded.

Caroline had nothing else to say. She gave Liv a hug goodbye.

"Thank you so much, for everything," Liv said, as Caroline opened the door to leave. "You're really incredible."

Caroline scrunched her face up. What to say to that?

"And don't worry," Liv added. "I'll make sure to tag you in all the photos."

Caroline felt a chill as she waited for the elevator. She was holding eight tangled lockets and felt a strange compulsion to just leave them on the carpeted floor right there, to walk out of the building with no sign any transaction had taken place inside. The elevator door opened and a man walked out, quickly coming to a stop when he saw Caroline. He was short, with a wan complexion, and Caroline felt positive he was associated with Liv.

"Oh, are you Liv's boyfriend?" she asked, caught off guard by her own directness, perhaps encouraged by the way he was grinning at her.

"Boyfriend?" he said. "I'm her brother." He didn't seem all that perplexed by her question. "How do you know Liv?"

"I—I was here to shoot some Instagrams for her jewelry line?"

Liv's brother—if he was even her brother, who could know anything for sure at this point—laughed heartily. "Oh Jesus."

Caroline felt like a possession had been snatched away from her. Her throat felt dry. "I'm confused."

"She's just—my sister is fucking weird. It's nothing serious. Don't worry. She found all these cheap necklaces on the street the other week and brought them up. There's no *business* or whatever. She isn't selling anything."

It occurred to Caroline that she hadn't even looked through Liv's account before coming over. She had just blindly believed a stranger who complimented her on social media, and then traveled across town to an apartment to be photographed by her, obtaining no further information.

"I'm sorry," the brother said, his demeanor shifting. "Imagine living with her."

"So that's not her boyfriend's apartment?"

He laughed and shook his head. "Let's just say, if Liv had a boyfriend, there would be a lot of people with a lot of questions right now."

"But if she isn't actually selling products, why did she want to take photos of me?"

"You think I fucking know what goes on in her head? She's probably going to get off to the pictures later." He laughed again, this one different, high-pitched. He was sweating slightly at his temples. It's ridiculous that anyone trusts anyone else, Caroline thought. We all hide so much, keep so many demented thoughts closed off and obscured from

the outside world—why wasn't it more obvious to us, factored into the
equations of our daily interactions, that everyone else was the exact
same?

"Why don't we ask her what's up?" he said, starting toward the
apartment.

If Caroline were a different sort of person, she might have marched
behind him and confronted Liv, asked her to delete the photos, raised
her voice, made a fuss. But a few feet from her sniveling brother, the
reality of Liv's situation settling in, she decided she felt something closer
to pity for her.

"No, it's fine," she said. "Let her do what she wants." And then she
pressed the button for the elevator.

An hour later, she found herself outside of Otto's apartment.
He lived with his aunt in her townhouse on the Upper East Side, a
character detail that might have seemed odd if it belonged to anyone
else, but which he managed to not only pull off but render chic and
sensible. You felt, upon learning the fact, upon seeing the physical
structure, as if you were inadequate somehow, lacking any glamour
in your own living situation or the right sort of casual intimacy with
your extended family.

She had been to the apartment many times, and knew his aunt
quite well. They used to trade book recommendations.

She wasn't sure if Otto was inside. He might still be traipsing
around the city. Maybe he was visiting all his other New York flings,
making them aware of his imminent voyage across the Atlantic.

A young teenager and his dad were playing catch on the sidewalk
near Caroline. She wasn't sure how long she had been standing in front
of Otto's apartment. She wasn't entirely sure why she had ended up
there, either, but she felt a strong desire to see him, to recount what had
happened at Liv's, to tell him how she very well could have been skinned
and taxidermied by a sad twentysomething with a creepy brother. He'd

give her a hard time, he'd have a field day, he'd kiss her, they'd laugh, he'd play her a song by a French artist she'd never heard of that she didn't really like but appreciated anyway, loved anyway, because he was the one playing it for her.

She was tired of having to decide what she wanted every single day. Standing there, in front of Otto's apartment, she was ready to make a choice. She wanted to put it in writing.

After about twenty minutes, or two hours, of lingering, she looked at her phone and saw she had a message from Liv. do you mind calling me? it read, along with her number.

She knew she should ignore it, that her interactions with Liv and Liv's brother should not be revisited, but she couldn't shake the visual of Liv and her posing for that selfie together. Caroline was still holding on to the lockets. She decided to call her.

"Hello," Caroline said, after Liv picked up on the first ring.

"Caroline, oh my god. I'm just, I don't know what to say. I feel like such a—when R.J. got back from his softball game and told me he ran into you and, like, told you that my brand wasn't real or whatever, I just started crying. I feel so, so dumb. I would not want to do anything that would make you angry or upset. I reallyreallyreally like you, and you were so sweet to come over, and you're so pretty and—" Maybe she was still being pathetically gullible, but Caroline really believed she could hear Liv's tears.

"Liv, it's fine. Seriously. It's whatever. You took a few pictures of me in some stolen jewelry under false pretenses. It's not a big deal. Do whatever you want with them."

"I'm not a weirdo. I mean, I'm not going to post anything, obviously, and you should . . ."

"I should what?"

"I guess I was going to say you should feel free to tell everyone I'm a fraud."

"Liv, why would I do that? Who would I even tell?"

"Well, you said you're a writer, right?"

Caroline smiled. After she hung up the call, she looked up across the street and then to the right, hoping she'd see Otto returning, floating to her. Isn't it more fun to believe the thing you most want to happen might just happen, in spite of all other evidence? What else compels us to go outside each day?

A few hours later—it felt like it was a new year—she entered her apartment in the East Village. All the lights were on, and she walked in to find Ben in their bed, half under the covers, shirtless, his laptop positioned by his head. His eyes were closed.

She sat down on the edge of the bed for a few minutes. She had thought she'd slip off her jeans and get in bed next to him. But instead she walked out of their bedroom, out the door, back outside, back into the dark.

11

—————

I was lying on top of the comforter, in my boxer briefs and a button-down shirt. My gut hung gently over the band of the underwear.

My phone was plugged in on the side table. I'd deleted Twitter and Instagram that afternoon, but I still didn't want to look. Who *ever* wants to look, even in regular, everyday circumstances? I had four Slack messages from Leon.

> victor call me
>
> I got your email
>
> we have your back
>
> but let's just talk through everything

I finished my room service—a hamburger and an endive salad, a $74.39 bill—and was now two glasses of cabernet sauvignon in. Now that I'd published a *cover story*, I felt permitted to expense freely.

In hotel rooms, of course, we get to operate as an alternate self. Not so much our fantasy self, or even our least inhibited self, but rather our basest, grossest self. I wished I could have a Snickers bar and a handful of salty trail mix every night, polished off with two half-bottles of bitter wine and a fun-size bourbon. It doesn't work like this at home: no one comes by the next morning to pretty everything up so you can pretend none of it happened.

I called Oliver.

"Hey," he said.

"What are you doing?"

"Uh, playing this VR game. Basically you try to make it through different parts of this forest while you collect stones."

"It continues to completely confound me that I dated someone who plays video games."

"Well, there are a lot of things about you that confound *me*," he said.

"Do you want to come by my hotel? We could get high? Order room service?"

"I thought we were hanging out tomorrow during the day?"

His specifying the amount of light that would be shining deeply annoyed me.

"Yeah, I know. But I just feel like seeing you now. I've had a really intense day."

"Well, I am pretty busy," he said. "Clearly."

"I can expense everything to the magazine, so, you know—"

"Are you drunk?" he asked.

"*No.* I'm about to call my *boss.* I am not drunk. Are you *stoned*?"

"I mean, yeah—just, you know, standard post-work high."

"Okay, well shut the fuck up then, cop."

When we engaged in this sort of banter now, at this point, I felt disgusting and pathetic, like I was standing naked in the middle of the street pleading for the cars to run me over. I was still prodding him along, forcing him to see me and respond to me—and to what end? He was simply abiding. I'd reached out to him when I was in D.C. a few months ago (and now I was contriving reasons to be in D.C. . . .). He contacted me the one time he came up to New York, but it felt politely reciprocal, like he knew if he didn't, there was a chance I might find out and get upset, and it would be an inconvenience to him were I to get upset.

The two times we had seen each other since the break-up, we'd had some coffee, "caught up." It was all very *cordial*. I couldn't exactly see what I was getting out of it, what I even wanted. I felt anxious before seeing him, phony while we were together, and then, naturally, empty afterward. It never occurred to me that I had the option to just cease contact with him, though.

He said he'd be over in thirty minutes. I slid into some dark jeans and switched out the button-down for a loose, long-sleeved gray shirt. I put on some cologne and moisturized my face. I felt like I was getting an apartment ready for an open house, as if a bit of moisturizer on my forehead would detract from the deficiencies in other rooms.

I decided I should call Leon before Oliver got to the hotel.

At this point it was very clear to me that my existence made Leon uncomfortable. I wasn't sure if it was because I was gay, or because I was on the rise at the magazine, or if it was unrelated to either, if it was just that he was this way—unfeeling, stilted, strange—with everyone. At a recent staff meeting, I had volunteered to travel to Miami to cover a black-tie auction during Art Basel. He said, avoiding eye contact with me, "Well, that's an interesting thought, Victor"; he ended up giving the assignment to Charles Cowell, a (straight) part-time staffer who played with him on the magazine's rec soccer team. (I'd never been to a game.)

Whenever I had to speak to Leon one-on-one, I felt like we were taking part in two different conversations, the conversation we were having and then the one that was playing out in my head. "There is way too much 'you' in here," he said recently, after reviewing a draft of a profile I'd written. "I would cut everything that isn't a direct quote or description."

I did not have the confidence to respond the way I wanted to ("What's the point of having me write anything, then?! Do you just want to run a transcript?"); I offered a feeble, "That makes sense," instead. And then I fumed and vented to everyone else about it.

Maybe I didn't make him uncomfortable; maybe it was in my head. Maybe it made me feel better to imagine that I did. Sometimes I wondered if he didn't think about me at all, and if I thought about him far too much.

Leon picked up on the first ring.

"Hello, Victor."

"Hey Leon," I said, my voice pitched lower. "Another exciting day in the neighborhood, huh?" It was always this way when I spoke to editors, or those in power. I'd make a comment, even one as innocuous as this, and then repeat it back in my head with searing shame, immediate regret.

"Yeah, so, listen, we're not going to change the web headline. I saw your email. I know this is a rough situation. I understand your argument. But you're tough; you can handle this."

There was no empathy in his voice. And I felt like there was nothing I could say that was going to help my case. Not only did I lack the conviction of the email I'd sent him earlier, I felt entirely unrelated to the previous version of myself who had sent it, who had believed in something.

"Yeah, well, uh, it's not fun," I said, "but I just keep reminding myself that it's just the internet."

"Well, for us, the internet *is* it."

Why did it feel like *I* was the one trying to comfort *him* about this?

"You're not in New York, right?" he said.

"Right. I'm in D.C. I fly back on Friday."

"Okay, well, just hang in there."

"I will."

A few minutes later there was a knock on my door. When Oliver entered, I stared at him for a few seconds; I couldn't help it. He was always a surprise somehow. Oliver was tall and broad-shouldered, with deep-set eyes. I used to joke to people that my type was "could be a relative of Mitt Romney."

"You look like you're having a great time all on your own," Oliver said, glancing around the room. He was wearing white sneakers, which he slid off as he entered. He sat down on the wiry desk chair, a few yards from the bed. I sunk into the mattress, which now, just like that, felt cheap and uncomfortable.

Oliver, bouncing on the desk chair, was relaxed and gleaming and his light brown hair was resplendent and swept to the side and his teeth were straight and shining and I wanted to absorb all of him at once in a mouthful. I felt embarrassed and sweaty.

"Help yourself," I said, gesturing to the minibar. "I have everything a man could want."

"I don't actually need anything to drink yet." He eyed me warily. "So what's going on?"

"I got canceled," I said.

"You lost your job? I thought you were on top of the world now."

"No, no." I found it deeply charming, always had, that Oliver barely looked at social media, didn't keep up on "popular culture," was still listening to circa-2006 indie rock. "'Canceled' meaning that the Twitter mob has decided you're finished."

"But you still have your job?"

"Yeah, yes. But it's awful to deal with, even if you don't *lose your job*."

"What happened?"

"You know how my cover story came out last week?"

He smiled. "Yes, I do know. I haven't read it yet, but—I texted you. The cover looks really nice."

"Yeah, maybe . . . don't. Don't read it."

"What do you mean?" he asked.

He rolled his socks up and started spinning his chair back and forth. Even though I was younger than him by two years, I felt a generation older sometimes.

"It's so stupid," I said. "I talked to Valentina about this director that mistreated her on set."

"Oh yeah. I saw that. He told her she needed to lose weight for the role?"

"Yeah. Right. Well, her team was upset with the piece when it came out and they are disputing one of the quotes. I quoted her as saying she was 'traumatized' by the director and that she 'will never work with a male director again.' But she says she never said that last part."

"Don't you have it on the recording, or whatever?"

"I know this sounds crazy, but I guess it was loud in the restaurant, and there are these patches on the recording where our voices are sort of muffled. It goes in and out." I paused to make eye contact. "When it gets to this particular quote, you can just barely make out what she's saying, but it's tough. I had to send the file to our legal team after and they determined it was 'inconclusive.' Which is insane. Since you can hear it all. Basically. And *why* would I make up that she said it? I know she did." I added, as if it might not be clear, "I was there."

Oliver had this tic where he would push his tongue up against one of his cheeks and just kind of rest it there, protruding out: I used to find it inexplicably sexy, but right now, him doing it in the hotel room made me feel sharply irritated.

"So what's going to happen?"

"I am *sure* Valentina said it."

"I believe you."

"Do you?"

"Victor, we don't see each other that often. Don't make this into a fight."

"It's just . . . I worked so hard on this piece, and it's my first cover story, and there is so much good stuff in there, and now it's all ruined. All anyone at the magazine is talking to me about is this, and her team is writing all these nasty emails to my editor, demanding we take down the whole piece. Which is ridiculous since the magazine is already on newsstands. I had to meet with the managing editor, who I have only talked to once the entire time I've been working at *Corridor*, and she was asking me questions about my reporting methods and my 'ethics.'"

I stopped to see if Oliver was going to say something, but he didn't, so I kept going. "And part of the problem is that they excerpted that specific quote in the *headline* online, but Leon, my editor, is being a dick and not changing it. And then today Valentina tweeted about how disappointed she was by the story, and how her quotes were 'taken out of context,' so all her weird fans are coming after me. A few of them figured out I'm gay, which has nothing to do with anything, and they're tweeting, like, homophobic shit at me. It's deranged."

Oliver was still rotating back and forth in his chair. "Okay. Isn't this like when you wrote about—who was that Disney pop star? And all her fans came after you?"

This irritated me, too. "Yeah, I mean, it's kind of like that. But this is more, I don't know, *personal*. That was just a million teenage stans spamming my Instagram comments with emojis."

"Okay, well, you know, take a breath. It sounds like it's all going to be fine. With your job. You're getting a few tough tweets—you can handle it."

"You make it sound so joyous. Do you know what it's like looking at your phone and seeing yourself called truly every derogatory word you can imagine?"

"The thing I'll never understand about the comments," Oliver started. He was speaking slowly. "Is that they exist on a made-up app, in a virtual world. Typed-out phrases from people you don't know and will never meet . . . These people aren't real. Most of them have avatars of squirrels or orchids or whatever, right? Also, one out of every—what?—two hundred people is on Twitter? And would understand what anyone on Twitter is talking about when they talk about whatever everyone's talking about?"

"Yeah, but it's an important one in two hundred."

"I'm not on it."

"You're not important!" I was pouring myself more wine. I slid off the bed and poured him a glass too, which I thrust next to him.

"I'm just pointing out," he said, "you can just not look at your phone, and then it's not happening."

"That's not a good argument! That's like saying if I got an email that said I had committed fraud and was getting arrested tomorrow but just *turned off my phone* so that I couldn't see the email, I wouldn't get arrested."

"No one is arresting you." Oliver smiled, and he abruptly stood and moved to the window. When I looked at him, handsome and patient, I couldn't even feel upset that he had dumped me. It made sense. Of course he was going to end it at some point . . . how had it even started to begin with?

"Does anyone at *Corridor* have your back?" he asked from the window. "It sounds like basically what happened is Valentina is regretting what she said, and then got lucky that you don't have a good recording."

"I just talked to Leon on the phone before you got here," I said. "He was like, 'We're not taking down the piece. We're not changing the headline. Deal with it.' He sucks."

"You hate anyone who doesn't just blindly praise you, though."

"That's not true," I said, throwing a pillow feebly in his direction. A bleak half-hearted flirtation. Why did I do things like that?

"Maybe you can reframe this somehow. Post a PSA on your Instagram about the pitfalls of relying on recording devices."

"That's not funny."

"God, I forgot how *personally* you take everything. I barely know anything about the internet and even I know this is the sort of thing everyone is going to move on from in a few days." Oliver leaned against the window and then relaxed downward into a crouch. "Not that you've asked, but my job is going well."

"Okay."

"And I'm actually seeing someone now."

I had been all but sure of this—I had seen the tagged posts; I texted the one "Oliver friend" I kept in touch with to ask if he knew anything about it—but the confirmation still thudded against my chest.

"That's exciting. What's his story?"

"He's a computer programmer. We actually met playing the same online game."

"Gays playing games." I wanted to throw myself off the bed and onto the patterned carpet, to stuff his white sneakers down my throat and choke myself.

"He's actually from Chicago, too. Like you."

"Where'd he go to high school?"

"I don't know."

That I found the fact he didn't know the guy well enough yet to have learned that information to be a "victory" in any sense was perhaps my lowest point yet.

My phone buzzed. My co-worker Maya was texting me.

omg I just saw you're a trending topic!!!!

are you ok???

"A girl I work with is worried about me," I said.

"Show me some of these tweets," Oliver said. He got up and sat on the edge of the bed.

"I don't want to re-download the app, but I'll show you the ones I screenshotted before."

I handed Oliver my phone, and he looked up after a few seconds. "You met Neil Patrick Harris? He's an actor I actually know."

"What? Oh, is that in the thread about how I am a 'disgrace to gay people' or whatever? These people are actually mentally ill, Oliver."

Oliver stood up again, moving off the bed. He always had a kinetic energy coursing through him, unable to sit still. When he played his video games he'd take breaks to do jumping jacks or pull-ups in the doorway. It was hard for me to sit on a bed there, gazing at him, and not think about when I used to push him onto beds after stumbling in the darkness—when I would pull his black boxer briefs off and go down on him, gleefully, insatiable. I was desperate for him to feel pleasure. I hated when he would try to reciprocate—"*Don't*," I'd say, whimpering, as he would move his head down my torso; eventually he learned to stop trying.

"Those tweets make the whole thing sound like a way bigger deal than it even was," I said.

"I don't know," he said, chuckling. "I'm starting to think you deserved to get canceled."

"It's just blowing up because Valentina tweeted about it—so now it's kind of her word against mine. And she's a famous movie star . . . and I'm me. Her publicist probably wrote her tweet, by the way. Valentina told me she doesn't even look at her social media." I turned onto my side. "And Valentina loved me. In person. I know she did. We really hit it off."

Oliver rolled his eyes, smiling.

"*She did!*" I was revved up at this point. "Also, this piece got more page views than literally anything *Corridor* has run on its site the past month. That's why none of them want to change the headline or anything. They're loving this. They don't care about *me*. It's not their handles people are using."

"But why *would* they change the headline? Wouldn't that imply you *did* misquote her?"

"It would just take the heat off me. I don't know, Oliver! The headline literally says 'Why Valentina Lack Is *Swearing Off* Male Directors.'"

For the first time since he got to my hotel room, Oliver looked at me with what felt like contempt. He didn't want anything to do with me. He'd be happy when he was heading back to his apartment. He didn't want to listen to me mope, to watch me drink and eat and complain.

"Why are you in town again?" he asked.

"I'm working on a story about the young people who work in the White House—sort of like a D.C. Gen Z scene piece. What they do. Where they eat."

"That's cool. Why aren't you just focusing on that, then?"

"Because everyone on the internet is mad at me, Oliver."

"Okay, well, it sounds like maybe you should, you know, weed out the terrible people, and register the feedback from the people you care about, and then move on with your life."

I was quiet and wanted to be quiet.

"You love drama," he said, shaking his head, the closest I had felt to him all night. "There's a part of you that loves this."

"Jesus Christ, you think I *love* people sending me literal death threats?! I do *not* love this! I wasn't sure what Leon was going to say when I talked to him! I thought maybe I'd be fired!"

"*Right*. But the magazine is standing by you. It's all going to be okay." He took out his weed pen, which he handed to me. I was pleased to see he had finished his glass of wine. "I have an idea," he said. "Why don't you call Valentina directly? Hash it out with her like a normal, actual person. Or call her publicist. I don't know."

"Oh my god, *no*. Are you serious?"

Oliver was spinning in the chair again. "This is so you."

"What's so me?"

"To act like a lunatic about this, and complain and kvetch, but ultimately just do nothing about it. To complain to me and whoever else, but just sit around and drink while it happens."

I stared at him as he spun. He didn't love me—maybe he never had.

I figured I should change the subject. "Let's go to the swimming pool. Or somewhere else."

"There's a swimming pool here?"

"Yeah, on the roof."

———————

I remained fully dressed, sitting on the edge of the pool, while Oliver swam, shirtless, in his stretchy athleisure pants. I guess on some level this is why I had suggested the pool, right?

He submerged himself under the water and I felt, truly, like a beached whale. There was a young woman swimming on the other end of the pool, darting back and forth with a haunting, hypnotic precision.

Oliver came up for air and swam toward me. "Is this getting your mind off things?" he asked.

"No," I said, even though I hadn't thought about any of it for the past fifteen minutes.

"Hey," Oliver shouted at the woman across the pool, who was checking the phone that she had left resting on the edge. She turned to look at us, unnerved. "Uh, yes?"

"Do you have a Twitter account?"

"I—I think so. I don't, I haven't looked at it in a long time."

"See?" Oliver said, turning back to me. He returned to the woman. "My friend was canceled today on the internet. He's a pariah."

She smiled. "That's nice."

I couldn't help it. I knew I always would love Oliver, no matter what he said or did, and I knew, sitting on the edge of this pool with all my clothes on, that I would sink down to the bottom with weights on my ankles, if it meant being close to him forever. I saw him so rarely now that it was possible to forget that I felt like this, easy to spend all my time living in a world in which no real people exist.

He dried off and we went back down to my hotel room. I felt clear-headed, for all that I had drunk, for all that had happened.

"How's your family?" he asked.

"My mom is my mom. I can never really tell what's going on with her. We don't talk about anything real. And my dad, well . . . same old. He sent me an email a few weeks ago by accident—it was meant for some friend of his. What's sad is when I saw his name in my inbox and the subject line 'next weekend,' or whatever it was, I actually got excited."

"That all sounds about as healthy as I'd expect."

I didn't ask about Oliver's family. His parents had been married for thirty-nine years. When he came out in high school, they sent a mass email to everyone in his extended family with the subject line "Oliver's Big News!"

I decided to expand on the topic. "I think my family still doesn't think of me as . . . It's like I'm not gay or straight to them—I'm just an amorphous, nonhuman blob."

"A blob?"

"Even when I was dating you, it wasn't like—you know how it was."

"Your stepdad was nice. When I met him. Your mom was, you know—she was nice, too."

"That's true. They were nice to you."

Oliver's hair was still wet from the pool. "If you could go back in time, would you do anything differently?" he asked.

"What do you mean?"

"I don't know."

"Like, in terms of how I came out?"

"Sure."

"I think maybe I would have just written them a letter."

"A letter? And not said anything in person?"

"Yeah, I think I might have expressed it all more . . . clearly. In writing. And I wouldn't have in my head what their faces looked like in that moment."

Oliver, maybe for the first time since he'd walked into my hotel room, didn't seem to know what to say.

We watched two episodes of *Parks and Recreation*. We were both stoned at this point, and I really did forget how hot my blood had felt just hours earlier, how every time I'd picked up my phone I felt an actual pain in my chest.

As the credits rolled on the second episode, I let my hand graze against Oliver's side. I could never just let things be good. I always had to push them too far.

He turned away, imperceptibly at first and then completely, and moved off the bed.

"You know, I hesitate to bring this up, but if it ever feels too hard for you to hang out now, maybe we . . . shouldn't."

"Why would you think it's too hard for me?"

"Victor."

I rolled over under the covers, away from him, a toddler throwing a silent tantrum.

The party line on our break-up, what we told "the public," was that Oliver had taken a job in D.C. and we decided together that we couldn't sustain a long-distance relationship. But the truth is that my drinking and my neediness and my neuroses and my jealousies had become overwhelming and poisonous. I was too much. He had been looking for a way out, and I couldn't blame him and I couldn't stop him. We had never spoken about what took place the night of our break-up, after he left—the hospital. It was truly misguided—

dangerous, even—that I still texted him and called him and saw him. I knew that it was. Everyone told me I needed to move on with my life, which meant cutting Oliver out. But I didn't want to and physically couldn't and when I would nod to Zoey or whoever else and sigh, "I know, I'm going to stop," I always knew in my head I was a fucking liar and a sick person.

"Before you leave, can you just take my phone and look at the tweets and what people are saying and tell me if it's bad? I don't want to look."

"Sure."

I re-downloaded Twitter and flipped to my mentions—I had 78 notifications—and handed the phone to Oliver.

"Just scroll down."

I watched his face. He looked distressed, to an extent, but basically neutral. "It's more of the same," he said. "Really. It's nothing bad. It's petering out."

"Well, it's like 11:30 now. That's probably why."

"Someone called you, and I quote, 'an embarrassing hack' . . . and let's see, we've got, someone Photoshopped your head on . . . I honestly can't tell who that's supposed to be, but it's not good. . . . A lot of people are just saying, you know, 'Valentina Lack deserved better.'" He kept scrolling. "I am going to be honest though, it looks like there are some valid criticisms here, about journalism or methodology or clickbait or whatever. It's like 15 percent valid and smart, 85 percent useless. Though I still need to read the article."

"I don't know why I do this to myself," I muttered into my pillow. "I would have done so much better in the nineties, when there was no social media."

"Are you kidding?" Oliver said. "You would have hated it. You're way too much of a narcissist for that."

He slid his feet back into his sneakers.

"Well, say hi to the computer programmer," I said, not moving.

"Don't end it like this."

"End it like what? I am being courteous! I'm offering well wishes."

"You know like what."

I rolled over to look at him, even if it pained me to do so. Time could stop right then and I still wouldn't be satisfied.

"Okay, last thing."

"No."

"I promise. Tweet something from my account. Anything. Address the Twitter population on my behalf. I haven't tweeted anything today. You said I should engage. So can you do it for me?"

"I can't do that. I don't even get how this works."

"It's easy. Just type words where it says 'What's happening?'"

He started typing on my phone and, while he did, I pulled the comforter over my head and said "What's happening" over and over, in a whisper at first, and then audibly, and then louder.

He tossed my phone onto the bed. I pulled the comforter back down. I couldn't read his face. "Wait until I leave to look at it," he said.

This familiar feeling—this urge to cling desperately to a person, to take the smallest sign and project it onto a billboard—it made me want to pull Oliver toward me. To trap him. He had already been that person for me, though, and he was not that person any longer. And I knew, when it was 1:43 p.m. on a Thursday and I was on my way back to my apartment from Whole Foods, that this was how it was meant to be, and he wasn't supposed to be my person anymore. I knew it then. But I didn't know it *now*.

It was distressing that I still could so easily find myself in this position—vulnerable, struck with the belief I'd been shunned and left behind. Zoey couldn't fill that need for me. My mom couldn't. People I had crushes on who liked my Instagrams certainly couldn't.

"Listen, take care of yourself," Oliver said, standing at the door. "And don't—I don't know, I have no other advice." I didn't get out of the bed to say goodbye or give him a hug, as if making some grand point—some ineffectual and grand meaningless point. The door slammed behind him.

I picked up my phone and looked to see what he had tweeted from my account. It was just a sentence: *I'm happy to be here.*

12

I took my wet jacket off and, holding it pathetically in one hand, I scanned the lobby of the Loews Regency hotel for a—*oh, there it was.* I spotted a large brown-and-beige posterboard, affixed to a stand, the word "Ghirardelli" printed on it in a massive script. What had brought me to the corner of Park Avenue and 61st Street on this Wednesday afternoon? A meet and greet with Gerard Butler for Ghirardelli chocolate, naturally. What did the action star (he was an action star, right? I wasn't sure if I had actually seen him in a movie before) have to do with a grocery-store chocolate brand? At this point, when it came to these sorts of events, I asked as few questions as possible. That's the first thing they teach you in journalism school, right? *Ask as few questions as possible!*

The lobby was fairly empty, save for a few men in suits talking into headsets and a student with her laptop out. A man and a woman were stationed at the makeshift table set up by the Ghirardelli poster—both looked to be in their late twenties. The man was wearing a T-shirt that had ASK ME ABOUT MY CHOCOLATE ADDICTION emblazoned on the front in brown block letters.

"Hi! I'm Victor from *Corridor.*"

"Yes," the woman said, riffling through envelopes arranged on the table. "We are *so excited* you were able to join us today."

"I'm—so excited to be here." My hair was wet from the rain. I smoothed it out with my hand.

"So, we're running a little behind," the CHOCOLATE ADDIC-TION man said, somehow in a condescending manner. "But if you want to just wait in the room in the back, we'll come get you when we're ready to bring you to the suite."

The woman handed me an envelope. "This will fill you in on everything happening at Ghirardelli this year."

"*Amazing*," I said.

"And you'll get about eight to ten minutes with Gerard when we take you to the suite."

"Great," I said.

"And just one other thing: we can't *tell you what to ask*, of course, but we'd love it if you threw in a question or two about Gerard's upcoming collaboration with Ghirardelli for the launch of our new eco-friendly dark chocolate innovation."

There were about twenty folding chairs set up in the glum "room in the back," situated around a bowl of wrapped chocolates on a small glass table. There was only one other person in the room, and I recognized her immediately. "Oh, you're Maddie Brooks," I said. "I just saw you on *Deadline*."

"Oh. Right. I keep forgetting that's up now."

Maddie looked to be 25 or 26. She had cascading dark red hair and was wearing overalls over what appeared to be a tight black tank top. I'd seen a few viral Twitter threads about her recently, in the wake of her Netflix deal for a show "based on her life."

I situated myself a few seats away from Maddie, tossing my damp jacket to the side. A woman who I recognized as an *Esquire* editor walked through the door. She stared at me as she sat down on the opposite end of the room from us—apparently she and I weren't going to acknowledge each other, even though we had run into each other at about a dozen different press events and exchanged pleasantries a handful of times.

I turned to face Maddie and switched to a softer voice. "I'm really excited for your show. You're going to act in it? I didn't read the announcement carefully."

"No, no. I'm just writing it. It's based on my life." She said this as if I had great familiarity with the contours of her personal history. "I'm also starting a podcast soon. It's a super stressful time."

"So you're interviewing Gerard Butler, too?"

She laughed. "I'm sorry, what?"

"I'm waiting for—"

"Oh no, I'm not *interviewing* him. I'm just supposed to film some content with him for Ghirardelli's social. My day job is still influencing."

"Ghirardelli content? Are you guys going to, like, do a skit?"

"A skit?" She laughed. "You're cute."

"I wouldn't think—do you even know who he is? How old are you?"

"Listen, they pay me; I show up." She paused. "But yeah, I mean, not gonna lie—the first time I watched *300*, that was a moment for me."

Maddie had a sort of brusque confidence that I found both terrifying and alluring. I felt like she was either going to be an incredibly huge star someday, or fizzle out in dramatic fashion.

She was staring at me. "I feel like you're the kind of person who is constantly apologizing for things." She grinned at my look of confusion. "You don't know me yet. I show affection by reading people."

"I'm scared to know what you'd say to a stranger you *didn't* want to show affection to."

"Yeah, you don't want to find out."

I smiled and took my phone out.

"So what questions are you going to ask Gerard at your *big interview*?" she asked. "Do you think he actually eats chocolate?"

"I am sure he does not."

She rearranged herself to sit cross-legged on the chair. She pulled a notebook out of her bag and placed it on her lap. "Hey, do you mind if—while I'm up there, my friend Hannah might be coming by—do you mind giving her this book when she comes?"

For a moment I wondered if I was being recorded in this room by a hidden camera for some sort of prank show.

"Um, okay."

"Thank you so much. We're working on some ideas for our podcast, and this is our notebook."

"You write your ideas by hand in a notebook?"

"Yeah. I can't just, you know, stare at a monitor all day." She handed me the book, and I reluctantly took it from her. "Hannah's cute. Kind of mousy. I'm—" She looked at her phone. "Oh, never mind, she's not coming."

It was clear Maddie's life was one in which plans were continually in flux.

She looked back up. "So you just—you come to this hotel, ask Gerard Butler some random questions, eat some chocolate, and then go write it up for—"

"I write for *Corridor*."

"Oh, damn. *Corridor* cares about Gerard Butler hawking some chocolate?"

"I'm not going to ask him about the *chocolate*. I don't know. I'll ask him about his next movie, maybe his thoughts on the death of the old-school action star, his 'take' on social media . . . We'll see."

Maddie laughed. "Got it. Real *Frost/Nixon*."

I smiled. "And I'm not going to eat any of the chocolate."

"Good for you. Stay strong."

The *Esquire* editor looked up from her phone and eyed us.

"Hello," Maddie said to her, sharply.

The editor looked back down at her phone without acknowledgment.

"People are so weird," Maddie whispered to me, though not so quietly that it didn't expand to fill the room. I nodded in agreement.

"I actually just wrote a cover story," I announced. "For *Corridor*."

"That's sick!" Maddie said, now typing furiously on her phone. I assumed she was going to ask who the subject was, but she didn't.

In the weeks since the Valentina story had come out, I had tried to separate myself from the heat of the fallout; I could sense everyone else in the office had moved on, so I was trying to do so as well. I'd made my social-media accounts private. I had returned to my usual blend of fulfilling and unfulfilling assignments. The sense of deflation I had about it all was lingering, however—that the jubilation I'd been anticipating had been so short-lived was crushing. But I was forcing myself to remember what Oliver had advised and will myself to reframe the experience, to try and reclaim a sense of pride.

The male Ghirardelli rep entered the room. "Maddie, you ready to come up and make some content with Gerard?"

Maddie looked at me and grinned as she gathered her jacket and bag. "Follow me on Insta. Let's hang at some point."

I realized I hadn't even told her my name. "I'm Victor Harris, by the way."

"That's great," she said, as she linked her arm with the Ghirardelli man. "Hello again," she cooed to him as they left the room.

I looked up Maddie Brooks on my phone—she had almost 100,000 Instagram followers. Her bio was "Don't Talk To Me."

The *Esquire* editor looked up at me. "You know her dad is some famous cinematographer?" she said.

I nodded and smiled. Maddie's most recent grid post featured her riding a white horse with her tongue stuck out. The caption: HORSE GIRL, ya heard?

I felt like a wizened scientist in a lab as I clicked to follow her account.

13

Zoey

Zoey gave a cursory nod to the statuesque woman at The Odeon's hostess stand on her way in. Victor and Zoey were here often enough that the woman knew them by face, if not name (was she the manager? the maître d'? Zoey wasn't sure). She had porcelain skin and sleek blond hair and always wore a different floral print. Zoey wondered if she herself would ever be *known* for a distinctive look, like Perri with her jet-black hair and chain necklace.

Zoey was escorted to the back of the restaurant, and, as she slid into their usual booth, she saw Victor entering at the front. She watched him nod at the hostess. She found it oddly exhilarating to observe him before he saw her. His lanky frame was slouched a bit—his head was hanging low. He ran his hand through his thick brown hair, looking at himself in his phone's camera before he started texting. His features all appeared more exaggerated to her from this vantage point—his large forehead and high cheekbones, the mole by his mouth, the two-day stubble, his skinny legs. She felt like she was back in fourth grade science class hovering over the guinea pigs lurching about in their cage, everyone taking notes on their movements in their blue "observation notebooks."

He finally looked up toward the back of the restaurant, made eye contact with Zoey, and then walked toward her.

"I feel like I haven't seen you in years," he said, shifting in the seat across from her.

"Yeah, well . . ." She hadn't decided exactly what approach she was going to take yet.

"You know when you're overwhelmed by texts and emails and you just kind of throw your phone onto the bed and decide it's easier to ignore everyone instead of trying to keep up?"

"You sound like you're describing some kind of Gen Z meme."

Victor didn't smile at this.

"I'm not everyone," Zoey continued. For whatever reason, she felt like being slightly aggressive today.

"That's true. You're you."

"But everything is . . . fine?"

"Yeah, what do you mean? Of course."

"Why is that 'of course'?"

"What would be wrong?"

The waiter was standing at their table—they hadn't opened their menus. "We'll split a burger and the Caesar salad," Zoey said.

"And we'll each have a glass of sauvignon blanc."

Victor looked at his phone and then put it on the table, face up. Zoey's was on the table, face down.

"It's been almost two weeks since I've heard from you," Zoey said. "I get nervous. Especially when I know you're dealing with all this Valentina stuff."

Victor looked away from her. His hair appeared to be uncombed. There was gray starting to come in at his temples.

"I feel weirdly disassociated from it all. Honestly." He looked right at her. "*Honestly*." She didn't believe him, but she let it go.

"Okay, that's good."

"I'm very 'whatever happens, happens' these days. What's that Shakira song? Whenever, wherever . . ."

"You have literally never been 'whatever happens, happens' in your life, Victor. And that song is about a completely different thing."

Their salad arrived and they both reached for their forks.

"I hate when the food comes before the wine," Victor said.

Zoey bit into a crouton. She wanted to ask if he had talked to Leon again about the Selah article. Usually she felt so brazen and confident with Victor—anything was on the table. But it was impossible for her to ignore the strange energy around the topic—it felt prickly in a way that, even if it was all in her head, was palpable.

Tom had told her that morning she needed to bring it up to him. She had never liked talking to Tom about Victor. He always seemed disapproving, as if he'd somehow expected that Zoey wouldn't rely on Victor as much once they were married, and it was curious to him that she still seemed to. Tom waited for his moments to pounce, it felt to her, when he had an opportunity to make her feel badly about how Victor was treating her. Once when Victor put up a grid post of himself at a bar with three female *Corridor* co-workers—one was Maya and two she didn't recognize—Tom said, next to her in bed, "You've been replaced!" He was not one for subtlety.

"Well, I guess I should just tell you," Victor said, picking a piece of lettuce out of his teeth. "I saw Oliver."

Zoey continued chewing and then swallowed. She waited a beat and then said, "*What?*"

"Yeah, I was in D.C. for something else. A story for *Corridor*. I actually saw him the day things were really going wild with the Valentina fallout. He came by my hotel."

"He went to your hotel? Did you have sex?"

"What? Of course we didn't have sex. Why would we have had sex?"

Zoey let her fork fall into the salad. "In what world did it seem like a good idea to, you know, see him and—it's just not a good idea. Not

to be weird about it—it's your life—but I just think . . . it's just going
to set you back. You know that."

"You know I saw him for that coffee when he was in New York. We
talk on the phone. Well, we text."

"Okay. Listen, I'm not—I'm really not—I feel like it's not my place
to tell you what to be doing or who to see. I'm really not trying to be
annoying about this. You know I'm just looking out for you."

"No, I get it."

Their wine glasses arrived, and Victor immediately finished half his
glass. Zoey watched him, unsure what she wanted to say.

"I just—it's been a weird few months," Victor said.

"It has? I feel like you're *always* having a weird few months." She
hadn't meant this to sound mean, but it came out of her mouth with a
sour kick. She couldn't help it.

Victor did smile now. "Yeah, that is true. Listen, you don't deserve
at all for me to not keep you in the loop about things—so, I'm sorry
about that." He paused, staring at the remnants of the salad. "But let's
not . . . How's Tom? How are things at Selah since your promotion?"

Zoey laughed and took the first sip of her wine. "You're insane."

"I know."

"I don't really know where to start. Everything is fine with me."

"*Okay*," Victor said, frowning. "Well, I'm really proud of you."

Zoey tried to smile at this.

"Listen," Victor continued. "I think, if I'm being honest, when I
know I'm doing something quote-unquote *bad*, I don't want to tell you
about it, you know? Isn't that like Psych 101? Everyone does that. If
I'm inviting Oliver to my hotel room, I know that's not exactly what I
should be doing. Or that time I took acid with my cousin. So *when I do
those things*, I don't want to tell you."

"Because you think I'm going to judge your behavior?"

"No, no. It's not about that."

"I've never judged you."

"I know. That's not what I mean. I just—it's like you're my conscience or something. You've been inside my head for so long, and I always know what you're going to say. So—"

The waiter arrived with their hamburger. The Odeon always brought out food so quickly, and usually this was welcome, though at times it could feel like a nuisance. It was sometimes hard to predict which way you would feel.

Victor continued with his train of thought. "Anyway, sometimes I'd rather just pretend I'm invisible, you know? That way I don't have to actually confront the behavior, if no one knows what I did. Does that make sense?"

"I am not some fucking puritanical guardian angel, Victor." Unexpectedly, her voice was wavering and she was nearly shouting. "And you're not invisible. We are all real people."

"I know that. You don't have to—I obviously know that."

"I want to be here for you. But—" She paused. "How are you liking that therapist you're seeing?"

"He's annoying."

"Well, I just don't want you to—it was stressful for me knowing you were dealing with this work catastrophe, given we're still—" She paused. "It hasn't been so long from that night . . ." She never could quite get herself to say the words.

Victor nodded. He reached his hand out toward her and gently nudged her elbow.

"You don't have to worry about me. Truly." He finished his wine. "I have a fun new assignment they just gave me. They want me to go behind the scenes at New York Fashion Week to, like, figure out what 'actually goes on' with the models who aren't Hadid-level famous. I'm trying to figure out which two models to tail."

The burger sat between them, untouched.

14

Hannah

Hannah closed the door to Maddie's apartment behind her. Gently.

Maddie had given her a key about a week after they met, as if it were a shirt that didn't fit her anymore: "You want this?"

The lights in the apartment were on and Hannah could just make out a remix of a pop song.

"Maddie?!"

She left a plastic bag—two large raspberry seltzers, an Advil canister, a bottle of red wine—on the counter, where it rested near a box of tampons, assorted makeup, and take-out Thai cartons. She threw the cartons in the trash and tidied up the makeup. She took the Fantastik out from underneath Maddie's sink and wiped down the counter, rubbing the paper towel at a curiously hardened pad thai noodle affixed to the surface. Maybe it wasn't a noodle. She jabbed at it with her finger.

"Baby!"

Maddie had emerged. Maddie always emerged, never entered. She was topless, wearing black leather pants.

"Did you bring the seltzer?" she asked.

"Yeah. It's here."

"Perfection."

Maddie opened the refrigerator, which—Hannah didn't even have to look to know—was empty except for a carton of eggs, a half jar of mayonnaise, and two cases of Diet Coke.

"Fuck. Where's my granola?"

"Probably in a cabinet, right?"

"No, I like it cold. You know that."

She slammed the fridge shut and turned to the counter, removing the items from the bag. "This isn't the wine I wanted," she said. "This one tastes like cardboard."

Maddie's hair was reddish-brown, thick and voluminous. Her face was small, the features drawn precisely, which made her hair even more, almost cartoonishly, overwhelming. Hannah sometimes had the desire to lean in close and burrow her face in it. She felt like she could find all sorts of things in there: Pop Rocks, gold specks, some great turns of phrase.

Maddie popped four Advil and swallowed them without water.

"Did you bring your laptop?" she asked.

"No," Hannah said. "I thought—weren't we going to go to Marlon's show?" She said this even though she knew well that having a plan with Maddie meant little. Everything was subject to change.

"I don't want to go anymore. I'm exhausted. Did *not* sleep last night." Maddie picked up a purple towel from the floor and wrapped it around her shoulders. "It's okay—we'll use mine. Frank is here, by the way."

"He is?"

"Reading in my bed."

Hannah had not met Frank yet, but he had been prominently featured in Maddie's Instagram Stories over the past few days. The weeks before, it had been Homer. A month ago, Joe.

"Can you pour us some wine?" Maddie muttered, gazing intently at her phone. "Just use the mugs. I don't know where the wine glasses are."

Maddie owned more than a dozen wine glasses, yet such a notion—
all of Maddie's wine glasses are inexplicably missing in action—was unsur-
prising.

Hannah brought two wine-filled mugs from the kitchen out into
Maddie's spacious living room, where Maddie was now cross-legged on
the floor, the purple towel draped over her. She was texting furiously.

"It's Darren," she said. Darren was a 47-year-old artist whom Maddie called either her "mentor," her "soulmate," her "therapist," or her
"nemesis," depending on her mood. "He wants me to go to Tokyo with
him."

Hannah carved out a place for herself on the couch, which was covered in magazines and books. No one ever witnessed Maddie reading—
nor could anyone really picture it happening—but yet it became evident
during even a brief conversation with her that she had read, it seemed,
absolutely everything. At the beginning, Hannah mentally noted all the
references she made, and then would look them up later; now she just
absorbed them, as if Maddie saying the name of a film or book trans-
ferred its essence, everything within it, upon those around her.

Hannah was in her usual: dark pants, fuzzy socks. The word JEAN
was printed on her sweatshirt in a large font; she didn't know what the
JEAN referred to. On the couch, near Maddie, Hannah felt languid,
slow, like a glop of yogurt.

Maddie set her phone down, her signal. She reached across the
wooden floor and grabbed Hannah's foot. "*How are you*, cousin?"

Even though they were not related, Maddie often referred to Hannah as her cousin, and many people they met took this at face value.
In certain moments Hannah could let herself forget they *weren't* blood
related. It was so much more thrilling—imbued her life with a sense
of velocity—to imagine they actually did share DNA. It would be like
sharing DNA with an Olsen twin or a tasteful high heel or a smoky
cocktail.

"I'm fine. I got a lot done today, sort of. And I've been—actually, Matty sent me a really cute text."

Maddie jumped up, dropping the towel. Hannah tracked Maddie's breasts as they journeyed to the small desk set up against the wall and then swayed as Maddie leaned over to pick up her laptop. Hannah was well acquainted with them at this point, but yet still felt a heat underneath her skin when they were present.

"It's so fucking confusing you're dating a guy who basically has my name."

"I'm not dating Matty. We haven't even—nothing's really happened."

"Can I read you something?"

"Sure."

Maddie lit a cigarette before opening the laptop. "Hold on." She flung her hair around.

It was a short poem, a third of which was in French. Hannah admired Maddie's confidence, the deliberate way she recited it, the use of the words "sequester" and "ointment."

"It's great," Hannah said, after a pause. "What are you thinking you'll—?"

"I don't know . . . I think I'll send it to Ava and just have her publish it. Though I could almost see it being set to music, you know, with dancers."

When Maddie signed her Netflix deal, Hannah received a flurry of texts, which fell into a set of buckets, mostly overheated accusations of nepotism (Maddie's father was a semi-successful cinematographer) or rumormongering ("I thought Maddie was in rehab in New Mexico?????").

However she felt about Maddie at any given moment, Hannah would always instinctively defend her. "Her dad isn't like, Steven Spielberg," she'd write back. Or: "I mean yah, she has money . . . but she lives in a one-bedroom in Gramercy, not a penthouse."

Maddie closed her laptop and thrust it in Hannah's direction. "So do you want to just do the typing?"

Hannah was helping Maddie put together a proposal for a podcast, which Maddie would host and Hannah would produce. Maddie's agent had told her a podcast would be a good career step while they were waiting for the TV project to move forward, and that he could probably get her $100,000 for fifteen podcast episodes. (For all of Maddie's near-comical scatteredness, she was extremely involved in the crafting of her contracts and business agreements; the majority of her income at this point came from the brand deals she made as an influencer.)

The theme and structure of this podcast were in flux, and Hannah would often wake up to a string of texts that Maddie had sent over the course of the night with disjointed lists of ideas or inspirations.

"I think we should actually try to, you know, script the opening," Hannah said, opening the laptop. "I don't like it on podcasts when the beginning feels totally haphazard and unplanned, you know?"

Maddie was looking at her phone. "Yeah, totally."

Hannah picked at her chipped nail while she waited for the Google Doc on Maddie's laptop to load. "I can't get over that you did that video with Gerard Butler."

"I know. So random, right? He smelled really good." Maddie didn't look up. "I have no idea where my notebook is, by the way."

"Hey, ladies."

Frank was now standing, shirtless, at the end of the hallway, peering into the living room. He had shaggy dark hair and an excessively hairy chest that seemed to work as a complement to Maddie's confounding mane. He was wearing wire-frame glasses, skinny jeans, and Maddie's Ugg slippers.

"Loser! Come onto the floor with me."

Frank glanced at Hannah first. "Hey, I'm Frank."

"It's nice to meet you."

Frank then brushed up behind Maddie and placed his hands on her shoulders, massaging them slightly. It was as if Hannah wasn't there. And maybe she wasn't. He craned his neck around to look at Maddie's face. "Hi."

Hannah minimized the Google Doc and focused on Maddie's laptop screen. The wallpaper was a picture of Maddie's family's cat—which she had named Rihanna—perched on a porch in Nantucket. The cat was looking off into the distance, annoyed, bored.

"Hannah and I are making a podcast," Maddie said.

"That's cool," Frank said. "What about?"

"We don't know yet. It's probably going to be me, like, talking and interviewing cool people."

"So, like every other podcast?"

Maddie groaned. "Shut the fuck up, cretin. It will not be like any other podcast because there is *no one* like me, and there is no one like *Hannah*."

She crawled away from him on the floor, leaving the purple towel behind her. "If you're going to be an imposition to our creative process, then you have to leave."

"*Yeah*," Hannah added. She had finished her mug of wine.

She had basically whispered this, but Maddie raised her eyebrows, delighted. "Hannah, I love this side of you." These were the comments Maddie made that caused the adrenaline to course through Hannah.

"It's fine, I'm going to leave soon anyway," Frank said. "I have to get to work."

"Frank is a *bartender*," Maddie said. "We should go to his bar sometime, Hannah."

"What bar is it?"

"It's this place in Greenpoint," he said. "You probably wouldn't know it."

"Don't make assumptions about Hannah!" Maddie shouted, throwing a handful of almonds at him. Hannah wasn't sure where the almonds had come from. "Maybe she goes to *raves* every weekend and fucks strangers and eats beans and hot dogs. You don't *know* her."

"It's true," Hannah said. "I love beans."

Frank laughed. "You know, I think you guys should host the podcast together."

"Honestly, that is so insane," Maddie said. "I was *going to suggest the same thing*. Such a good call. Hannah, you can be my, you know— Howard Stern has Robin. Dax Shepard has that woman. It would be so good. You would chime in at the right places, like a little Tinkerbell, and rein me in." She reached out her arm. "Come back to me, Frank."

Frank shifted toward Maddie, creeping closer on the ground like a caterpillar. Having reached her, he rested his head on her thigh. She stroked his hair with her manicured fingers.

"What do you think, Han? It's not like you don't have the time."

Hannah picked at the skin on her arm. She was in her last year of grad school at NYU and was working part-time as a copywriter for an ad agency. Ever since meeting Maddie, she had harbored fantasies of quitting—school, the job, her friend group, everything. Maddie engendered that sort of feeling in everybody who knew her.

"I mean, I've never really hosted, or co-hosted, anything before."

"I vote yes," the back of Frank's head said. "God knows Maddie needs a counterbalancing presence."

"I'm going to put my cigarette out on your scalp, motherfucker."

"Go for it," Frank said.

Frank rolled over, off Maddie's lap, and got himself up. "Can I wear one of your shirts to work?"

"Do whatever you want," Maddie said. She turned over onto her back, immersed in her phone again. "Hey Hannah, do you want to come with me to buy a printer? I need a printer."

"Yeah, sure."

Frank hitched his pants up and walked out of the living room.

"Nice to meet you, Hannah."

As soon as Frank left the room, Hannah found herself shouting: "I really want to host with you, Maddie! I feel like that could actually be super good."

Maddie put out her cigarette and moved her hand to her bare stomach. "God, I'm ravenous," she said. She rolled over toward Hannah and put her phone down. Her hair was in her face, so Hannah couldn't see her eyes. "I think you'd be a fabulous co-host," Maddie said, and the adrenaline rushed through Hannah again.

Four days later, Hannah showed up at Maddie's apartment with two bags of mini pretzels, a bottle of steak sauce, and the latest issues of *In Touch*, *Life & Style*, and *Us Weekly*.

She could hear the shower running. It was Saturday, a little after 3 p.m., and Maddie had texted her that morning to come over so they could write the treatment for the first episode.

Hannah had told some of her friends about the podcast idea at dinner the night before, and the response was one of extreme skepticism. That she was friends with someone as chaotic and potentially harmful as Maddie to begin with was strange enough to all of them—the idea that she might actually "get into business" with her, to them sounded at best a foolish, and at worst a dangerous, proposition. It hadn't affected Hannah, though: if anything, when her friends or her sister tried to "warn" her about Maddie, it only made her feel closer to Maddie and more distant from them.

Maddie sauntered into the living room wearing a pink robe, drinking raspberry seltzer straight out of the large bottle. "*Cousin!*"

"I brought you the steak sauce."

"Oh, I actually don't need it anymore. Thank you, though."

Her hair, today, was wrapped up in a loose bun, enveloped on top of itself, as if at any instant it might come undone, a game of hair Jenga. Her hair that way made Hannah anxious.

"Is Frank here?"

"What?"

"*Frank*, from the other day."

"Oh. No. I don't know where he is. He could be anywhere. Maybe at his bar."

Maddie picked up the three tabloids on the counter, as if she had just wandered into a dentist's waiting room and of course magazines would be there for one's perusal. She flipped through *Us Weekly* in grave silence. Eventually, she turned to look at Hannah. "I feel like I could look *just* like Valentina Lack with just one or two procedures."

"Sure."

Maddie moved to the couch, positioning herself like origami. "I'm craving some pineapple. Or a peach. Are you ever in that mood?"

"No, not really," Hannah said. The couch occupied, she decided to take over the swivel chair at Maddie's desk.

"You're so *controlled*," Maddie said. "It's really incredible. That's why I love you."

"I'm not that controlled," Hannah said. "I'm just, you know, enigmatic."

Maddie cackled. "Maybe we should call the podcast 'Two Enigmas.'" Hannah couldn't help it: over the past few days, she had started to visualize the Instagram account they would make for the podcast . . . the understated pastel-pink logo . . . the write-up on Vogue.com . . . the link she would send to all her friends, to people she hadn't talked to in years ("Hiii! Long time no talk! Wanted to let you all know about my exciting new project!"). The content of the podcast was irrelevant, barely even a component of these fantasies. She was visualizing the professional photo of the two of them—maybe in black-and-white—that Maddie would have one of her friends take for the press release.

Maddie pointed at her laptop on the ground. "Can you put on that song I like?" She then looked back at her phone. "Darren sent me a bunch of ideas for the podcast, by the way. I'll forward them to you. I feel like he wants to be a co-host, too."

Hannah spent the next two hours working on the treatment, while Maddie napped, ate a bowl of granola, called her mom, and watched five Britney Spears music videos on her phone.

At one point she asked Hannah to read her what she "had so far," but Hannah didn't want her to hear it yet. Hannah had become more assured in her writing since meeting Maddie—a result of her approval, presumably—but she was terrified of blowing it all up, terrified that if she ever presented something at all off base, Maddie would question the entirety of their friendship, why she had even let her in to begin with. It was safer to present as little material as possible.

"I feel like this is going to be so good," Maddie said.

"How do you know? I haven't read any of it to you yet."

"I can just tell. I fucking know these things! I am a prophet." She stood up and walked to her bedroom.

The first time Maddie invited Hannah over to her apartment, there were two other women on the couch, Nina and Cassie, both luminescent and striking. Hannah felt deeply inadequate, and had finished two gin and tonics within ten minutes. Nina was a Korean fashion designer whom Maddie had met "on a plane." Cassie looked like a shinier version of Hannah, a put-together brunette white girl. Cassie had eyed her suspiciously, as Hannah hovered in the kitchen.

"What do you do?" Cassie had asked her.

"I'm in school," Hannah said. "But I do a bunch of other stuff on the side." She figured the vaguer she was, the better.

"Don't we all," Cassie said.

It didn't feel to Hannah as if she was in competition with Cassie and Nina at the time—they were in a different league—but rather that each of them was out of their own depth, struggling to stay above water, grappling with their own self and self-image, all while Maddie remained oblivious, tanning on dry land.

It was now close to 6 p.m. and it was getting dark and Hannah had four pages of dialogue finished. She got up and looked in Maddie's fridge. There was a piece of birthday cake inside, wrapped in plastic. Whose birthday had it been? Who had eaten the rest of the cake? It was simply not possible that Maddie had carefully wrapped up a last piece of cake. Who had done the wrapping? To know Maddie was to become a sort of detective, but one who could never quite solve the case.

The buzzer rang, startling Hannah. She opened the door to find a young guy—he couldn't have been older than 22 or 23—at the entrance. He looked Italian or French. In a leather jacket. Stubble that appeared way too effortful to be seductive.

"Is this—are—I'm looking for Maddie?"

"Hi, hi, hi—" Maddie's voice floated softly from inside the apartment. Hannah turned, and Maddie was shuffling toward the door, in light-blue fuzzy slippers and a long blue T-shirt that cut off at her bare upper thigh.

"Hey Han—I've got it. This is Ricky."

"Ricky! It's *so* nice to see you," Hannah said. "*Enchanted.* What a pleasure." She felt high even though she clearly wasn't.

Ricky was confounded by the situation—perhaps he was even mulling turning around and leaving. But Maddie pushed past Hannah and reached for his hand. She led Ricky into her bedroom, while Hannah remained at the doorway. Maddie's bedroom door slammed shut, and Hannah could hear muffled laughter. She closed the front door with her side; instead of returning to the living room though, she walked down the hall, stopping herself outside of Maddie's bedroom.

She stood as still as she could, as Maddie put on a Lorde song. She heard Maddie say, "No, no, *stop*—she's cool. She just has, you know, her own way of going about things. She's from Pittsburgh. I don't know."

Hannah focused on holding her breath. Ricky said something she couldn't make out through the door, but she could hear Maddie laughing in response. "She's really smart. Seriously. She, like, really pays attention to things. She's funny."

A few moments later, she heard the shower in Maddie's bathroom start running. Hannah let herself exhale. She picked a pair of Maddie's shorts off the ground—they were light orange, cotton—and held them to her chest.

Hannah walked back to the living room, and sank into the couch cushions, where Maddie's body had imprinted earlier. She decided to text Matty: hey what are you up to. The most recent text in their thread was a link to an article about black holes she'd sent him a few nights ago; he hadn't responded.

Hannah took off her pants and swung her bare legs up onto the couch, resting them atop a few *New Yorker*s and a copy of Gwyneth Paltrow's cookbook.

She had never been clear as to why she was allowed to remain for all these months, for more than a year now, while the conveyor belt of Maddie's friends and lovers and allies had churned on. She learned quickly that you could never be sure of your standing in Maddie's world. A few months after meeting Cassie and Nina, Hannah turned to Maddie while they watched an episode of *Riverdale* on Maddie's laptop, and she murmured, "I saw Cassie and Nina posted they're in Spain?"

"Oh," Maddie said. "I haven't been keeping up." And that was the last time they had been spoken about.

The orange shorts Hannah had snatched were now balled up by her legs. She slid them on, leaving them by her knees, not pulling them all the way up. She picked up Maddie's laptop from the floor and reread the beginning of the treatment, but after a few minutes, she realized she was just staring blankly at the screen. The words she had chosen were flavorless and simple, the sentences obvious. She felt embarrassed at the prospect of showing it to Maddie for feedback, felt silly about the entire endeavor.

She closed the document and dragged the cursor down Rihanna the cat's face to a Word doc saved on the desktop titled "understanding." She had been curious to click on it at various points prior, but now felt like the destined time.

All she found in the doc was a short list:

Orlando Bloom!!!! He would be PERFECT for "BART"

Email Telly and Roger !! SOON!

Devise a new plan for bedroom walls!!!!!!!!

And then underneath:

YES IT'S YOU – It's only YOU

THERE IS ONLy ONE PATH FORWARD. THIS is a breakthrough.

Hannah hadn't realized she was doing this, but she was holding her breath again. Her hands had crept under her back and her arms felt numb now underneath her weight. She shifted her body, and Maddie's laptop went tumbling off her stomach onto the ground, making a loud thud.

Maddie's bedroom door opened—Hannah could hear it distinctly—and then an instant later, Maddie was in the living room.

"What the fuck is going on? What are you doing out here?"

Hannah attempted to slide off Maddie's shorts, but they were now caught around her ankles. She closed her eyes and said gravely, "I'm working."

"What are you doing? Why are you—? Are you fingering yourself on my couch?"

Her eyes still closed, Hannah could hear Maddie crouch down and pick up her laptop.

"What the fuck? I think you broke it. It's not turning on. *Hannah.*"

"Everyone okay?!" Ricky yelled from the bedroom.

"Everything is fine, Ricky," Maddie shouted. After a pause, she addressed Hannah: "I thought you were working on the podcast stuff."

"I was. I am."

"Okay." Even with her eyes closed, Hannah could sense Maddie's focus shifting. "I'm just—I'll be done with him in like half an hour," Maddie said.

"No problem. Take your time."

"*Hey?* Hannah?"

Hannah finally opened her eyes. "Yeah?" Maddie was leaning against the counter, staring at the wall. She didn't look angry, as Hannah had expected she would.

"Is everything all right? Are you all right?"

Hannah felt like someone had just pierced her heart with a butter knife.

"Sure. Yeah. Yes," Hannah said, sitting up. "Definitely." She wished she hadn't taken off her pants. *What was she thinking?* She wanted to hug Maddie, to smother her.

That morning, just a few hours earlier, Hannah emailed the ad agency to tell them she was quitting. She wanted to have more time. Time for the podcast. For Maddie. She hadn't told anyone yet that she'd quit. Not her friends. Not her sister. Her mom wouldn't care; she probably didn't even remember Hannah had a job outside of grad school.

"Everything's going to be fine," Maddie said breezily, and Hannah wasn't exactly sure what she was referring to, what was going to be fine, but she felt comforted nevertheless. Maddie looked down the couch.

"Do you have my shorts on?" she asked.

"Um, yeah."

Maddie appeared unfazed. "Okay." Her slippers began their return to her bedroom.

Hannah shouted after her: "*Maddie?!*"

The shuffling stopped as Maddie turned back around. "Yeah?"

"I have a question."

"What?"

Hannah paused, locking eyes with Maddie. "Why is there birthday cake in your fridge?"

"Not all questions have answers, Hannah," Maddie said. She looked disappointed. And then she shuffled into her room.

Hannah stood up and put her pants on. She folded up Maddie's orange shorts and left them on the couch. She grabbed the steak sauce and a Diet Coke on her way out of the apartment. She wanted to go home and take a bath. Everyone was always telling her to quit Maddie. At times she could convince herself it would be the right decision, the healthiest choice. It never happened.

She opened the door to leave and found Frank the bartender was standing in the hall, texting. Hannah was so startled that she slammed the door shut, before opening it again.

"Frank?"

He was wearing a tattered tank top and bright yellow high-tops. He looked distressed, angry, scratching the back of his head.

"Oh, hey. Podcast girl."

"What are you—is Maddie expecting you?"

"I'm texting her and calling. She's not responding."

They stared at each other, a duel.

"Well," Hannah said. "I'm leaving, but—she's sleeping, so." She started to close the door behind her, but Frank moved to swerve around and push it open.

It was a reflex, all instinct: Hannah raised the steak sauce bottle and whacked Frank's shoulder as hard as she could. It struck cleanly and made a deep, loud thud. She was surprised at how easy it was to hit him, knowing it would cause him pain.

He groaned loudly, wilting into a crouch, grabbing his shoulder. "What the fuck is wrong with you?" he screamed.

She grabbed the handle of Maddie's door behind her and slammed it shut. Then she shuttled past him, barreling down the hall.

"You're a lunatic, you ugly bitch," he yelled after her. She could barely hear him.

"You don't even *know her*," Hannah yelled, getting further and further away.

―――――

Hannah didn't usually drink by herself. She found that when she did, she just became paranoid and tired. She would scroll through old text message threads and wonder where things had gone wrong.

But she was now on her fourth glass of wine, at a nondescript, over-priced Gramercy bar, by herself. The steak sauce—the weapon—was in her bag. She hadn't heard from Maddie, and she hadn't reached out yet. But she felt liberated. She had an urge to shave her head or to send a really bitchy text to her mom. Instead, gargling a large acidic sauvignon blanc sip, she sent Matty a text, even though he hadn't responded to any of her recent ones: hey, do you wanna meet up . . . ?

He responded immediately. He was at his apartment for another few hours if she wanted to stop by.

She finished off her glass, and forty-five minutes later she was at his apartment. He lived in Park Slope and had two roommates, but neither was home when she got there. He muttered something when she arrived about "finishing up some work," but as soon as they were in his bedroom, they were on his bed.

Hannah, cheeks flushed, her clothes collected on his IKEA desk chair, paused after a few minutes. "Do you mind if I put on music?"

Matty grunted. "Sure."

She turned on the same Lorde song Maddie had been playing earlier.

15

I sat down toward the bottom of the stairwell and unbuttoned my pants. I was wearing the one pair of dress pants I owned that weren't wrinkled—it had been a while since I'd worn them.

I had a bunch of notifications on my phone that I was ignoring. I enjoyed that feeling, the not responding; it made me feel some imagined strain of power. When I'd gone private on Instagram in the wake of the Valentina story, I'd found that electric for similar reasons. "What's this guy's deal?" I imagined a 23-year-old aspiring writer wondering, coming across my locked-up profile, tagged in someone else's Story.

"Are you ready?"

I hadn't even heard the door at the top of the stairwell open. I looked back and the woman's face was just visible behind the railing.

"Oh, yeah. It's time?"

"In like twenty minutes. But we thought you might want to meet the guy interviewing you?"

I rebuttoned my pants and stood up. "Sure, yeah. Great."

She waited, holding the door open as I moved up the stairwell. She looked mildly annoyed with me, but I may have just been imagining it—it was probably just indifference.

They'd constructed a makeshift "green room" that looked to be a rehearsal space of some sort. There were a bunch of empty music stands in one corner, with assorted folding chairs and end tables arranged in clusters. When we entered the room, I quipped, "Real *Mr. Holland's Opus* vibes in here," gesturing toward the music stands, and my guide did not smile or even acknowledge the remark. The word "transference" was written on the large whiteboard—in orange marker and circled twice.

"I can get you a water, if you want," she said. "We have coffee, too."

"I'm good. Coffee right now will ruin my stomach."

"I'll come back and get you when it's time to go out."

She handed me a few sheets of blank computer paper.

"What's this for?" I asked.

"I don't know. They told me you might want to write down your thoughts."

She left, closing the door behind her. But then it almost immediately reopened.

"Sorry, I forgot. They wanted me to make sure you knew that, after all the panels are over, there's gonna be a little reception with the students and the other panelists."

"Yeah, right. They mentioned that. Schmoozing hour."

"I'm sorry?"

"Schmoozing . . . Like, wine in plastic cups. Fake smiles."

"I don't think there will be wine. It's 11 a.m. And they're students."

"Right."

She looked at me as if everything happening in the school building today was part of an elaborate experiment, and I was a test subject, and all my responses were going to be dissected and mocked later by a group of researchers in lab coats. She closed the door again and she was gone.

A gross part of me, looking around the drab room, felt like I deserved better accommodations. A few days ago, one of the *New Yorker* music critics had posted a photo from a banquet hall that looked like it could be a set for *Succession*, where he was—per his caption—going to be giving "a little talk."

A few minutes after I'd been left alone in this haunted purgatory of a room, the door opened again. A man about my age entered—his hair was slicked back, and he had a thin moustache. He looked vaguely European. He was very skinny and he was dressed in an extremely well-tailored burgundy suit: he looked like a British actor being photographed for the *Hollywood Reporter*.

He ran his hand through his slicked hair, seemingly unperturbed by our drab surroundings. "Otto Young. You're Victor?"

I nodded. "I am. Welcome to the 'green room.' Help yourself to this bounty of charcuterie and champagne." I waved my hand around.

He grinned politely and pulled out a folding chair to sit on. "I'm a fellow alum. I think maybe I was a few years ahead of you?"

I was shocked that I didn't know this handsome, debonair male with incredible hair who may have traversed the same college campus as me at the same time.

"And you're doing the—?"

"Yeah, I'm moderating a few of the panels today—including yours. I used to work at the Guggenheim. I'm actually living overseas now—working on a book—but I'm back for a few weeks."

"Oh god—well, I'm sorry," I said. It was a gut-reflex apology, and he looked confused. "Just that you have to deal with engaging with me onstage."

He was looking at his phone now. "No, I'm excited. It'll be fun."

I felt sweat forming in my crotch and thighs. This was my worst possible interlocutor: an effortlessly cool, stylish, slightly older straight man.

"I hope you didn't look at my social media," I said. "It's kind of embarrassing. I'm supposed to, you know, promote my shit. So it's all sort of . . . overly earnest."

I was making things worse.

"I'm not really on social media," he said. *Of course.*

"But I read a bunch of your articles," he continued. "I like your POV. I can tell you're skeptical of a lot of the celebrities you write about, but I appreciate that you're not overtly judgmental. There's something generous about your approach."

"I don't know. I think some people would say that's just tentative writing."

The door opened, and the guide from before reappeared. She was holding a paper cup, which she handed to Otto. "Your espresso." She turned to me, scowling. "Eight minutes till you guys are up. The panel before yours is almost done." She closed the door.

"You're braver than me," I said.

"Asking for an espresso is brave?"

"To me, yes."

There were maybe thirty-five students in the theater. It was hard to make out their faces from our position on the stage—there was a bright light on Otto and me. We were sitting on two stools, and the clash between the dark brown of my dress pants and the light gray of my blazer looked particularly ugly under the light, particularly ugly next to Otto—I knew this would be all I'd be able to focus on later when I saw pictures of the talk.

I flipped into a sort of autopilot for these kinds of events. I told stories with a certain frothiness, hyperbolizing, name-dropping and embellishing, but also strategically underplaying at points, too. ("I interviewed Greta Gerwig at an arcade once," I'd say, waiting for the approving nods, before adding, "This was before *Lady Bird*, though, when it was more just like, 'Oh yeah, she seems cool!'") I actually felt a surprisingly comfortable rapport with Otto—after he'd ask a question, he'd fix his gaze intently on me. Whether he was putting it on or not, he made me feel like he was genuinely interested.

"Who's the most famous person in your phone?" one of the students asked during the question-and-answer portion.

"Oh, I don't know, maybe Alison Brie—do you guys know her?" I took a long pause. "Or wait, I guess Chrissy Teigen." There was a collective gasp at this. I'd answered similar questions before in similar fashion—I'd start with an Alison Brie, and then pretend I had forgotten about Chrissy Teigen. I wasn't proud of this.

One of the students asked what advice I would give to someone who wanted to "enter the field."

"It's a combination of luck and hard work," I started. Embarrassingly, I greatly enjoyed offering up platitudes like this, on a visceral level, as if I were imitating Maggie Gyllenhaal at a Cannes press conference. I wasn't famous, of course. But whatever I was doing in my career, it was enough to be asked by one of my college English professors to speak to thirty-five undergraduates. I'd be able to post a seven-photo slideshow on Instagram tomorrow expressing my *gratitude*. And wasn't that the lamest, most minor version of a Cannes fantasy come true: a seven-slide Instagram post expressing gratitude for an achievement no one else cared about.

At one point Otto asked me what story was the toughest for me to write, to get my head around. "Well, I wouldn't say 'toughest to write,' necessarily, but I got some blowback for this profile—it was a cover story—I wrote maybe nine months ago. It was about an actress who—well, she disputed some quotes in the piece. And ultimately, you know, these things are complicated, but I learned a lot from the whole experience. I kind of stopped looking at social media for a bit there." I glanced at the students, grimacing almost comically, but the fact that I couldn't see their expressions in the light really drew out my feelings of disingenuousness.

"What would you say you learned from it?"

"I think—" *Had I learned anything from the experience?* After their initial outcry, Valentina and her team left it alone. The story was never taken down from the site or altered at all. As Oliver predicted, the internet moved on in a matter of days. Every once in a while a Valentina stan would send me a cruel message or death threat, but they were few and far between at this point.

But when I was reminded of the incident now—even though it felt like it happened in a different era of my life—I would feel a sharp sting of discomfort, even culpability. Maybe Valentina had a point? Maybe her quote should have been removed, with a correction, since I didn't have the conclusive audio to back it up. *Had* I misquoted her? I was in such a twisted mental state during that interview, so fixated on the recording device, on the conversational flow, of wondering if she *liked me*—maybe I *had* imagined what she'd said!

Even though I had theoretically emerged "unscathed," still had my job, and was continuing to receive plum assignments from the magazine, I noticed I had stopped imbuing my stories with anything that even verged on the controversial. If I thought that a phrasing in a piece might get some "attention," of any nature, I deleted it. If a celebrity said something to me in an interview that I imagined they might end up regretting when they saw it in print, I'd delete that from my draft, too. I tweeted less. I Storied less. This had all happened without my actively contemplating it—really, a valve inside me had been shut off.

I smiled at Otto and continued speaking: "I think I just learned that you can't let what people say get to you. And to trust your instincts."

Otto nodded and moved on to the next question, but I could tell he didn't believe me.

The last question came from a student who—I could see by twisting my head down to my knees, basically—appeared to be prepubes-

cent. *Is this what college students had always looked like?* "If you didn't
have this job, what do you think you'd be doing now?" he asked.

Otto turned to me. "A classic."

I answered without even thinking about it. "Whatever it was, I'd
actually be happy. Maybe I'd have a dog."

No one laughed at this or made a sound—the theater was silent—
and Otto shook his head at me. "Nice to end on a positive note!"
The students laughed at that. I wished that it had been the other way
around, that I had been interviewing Otto on the stage. About his life.
About his burgundy suit. About anything.

After the interview, they turned the bright house lights up, and a
few of the more industrious students came up onto the stage to speak
with me. One of the students was clearly gay, and I felt a mixture of
affection and envy as he announced, with confidence, "I'm going to
move to New York after graduation!"

"That's great," I said.

"The only *thing* is that it's hard for me to know exactly how I'm
gonna make that *work*, since I want a job in media. And not just, you
know, *any* job."

"Yeah, it's definitely tough, but you'll be able to figure it out," I
said. "I can tell just by the way you're going to something like this in
the middle of the summer, and then coming up after the panel to ask
a question."

He said he was going to follow me on Instagram and asked—with
no self-consciousness—if I'd be willing to serve as a "reference" for a
hypothetical job he was going to be applying for in a year.

"Why don't you just message me then and we'll go from there," I
said.

Another student—wearing a maroon cardigan, her dark hair in
pigtails—announced, "I *really liked* your Valentina Lack profile, actually."
She added, "And I'm *a fan of hers*." She then asked for my email address.

Otto was standing nearby, talking to an older woman in a cropped trench coat. She smirked in my direction. After the last of the remaining students had shouted a question ("Do you have any advice for someone who wants to write about *fine art*?"), I returned to the "green room," where I'd left my bag. I had told my editors that I was going to be speaking at an event today and "wouldn't be online until the afternoon." Neither of them had responded to my Slack.

I texted my mom a photo of the event flyer posted on one of the walls. It was strange how I felt so dissociated from myself on these occasions—when I was being acknowledged for my career. My career was the one thing in my life that I actually felt confident about, that I took a sense of pride in, but when I was being celebrated for it, I felt uneasy, even sick. Maybe Dr. Beckman had some sort of hypothesis, an underlying theory, when he would regularly change the subject in our sessions to discuss my career. Maybe he knew something I didn't.

I opened the door to the green room—in typical Victor fashion, I now felt love for this depressing room and was thrilled to be returning to it—and found a woman sitting on one of the folding chairs. She looked like she was a few years younger than me. There was a certain remoteness about her that immediately drew me in. She looked familiar. She was wearing a loose satin blouse and faded black jeans. She had a great tan and extremely striking eyes. I immediately felt a desire to win her over.

"Oh, is it over?" she asked.

"I—well, my interview is done, yeah. I think there's another one going on now."

"Oh, right. I forgot there was a whole *lineup*."

I sat down on a folding chair across from her. "I'm Victor."

"Caroline," she said.

"What do you . . . what brings you to this fine establishment?"

"My friend is moderating the—I don't even know what all this is. He asked me to meet him here." She was talking very softly, and I realized I was leaning in close to her.

"Your friend's Otto Young?"

"Yes?"

"He just interviewed me."

"What do you do?"

"I'm a writer. An *entertainment journalist.*"

I couldn't read her expression. "I'm a writer too," she said. "Freelance. I mostly write features. A few book reviews. I'm making headway on a . . . longer-term project, too."

She carried herself with the air of Someone You Should Know. She looked like the sort of shiny-haired chic socialite whose wedding would end up on *Vogue*'s website and you'd spend twenty minutes trying to ascertain what her deal was and what she actually did for work, before giving up.

Caroline didn't seem like she wanted to chat, particularly, but I didn't feel like leaving the facility just yet. I took my phone out and scrolled through Twitter. Even though I rarely tweeted myself anymore, I still compulsively, hourly, checked the app. Nearly every tweet made me wince—either out of distress, jealousy, or anger. It was like I was microdosing poison every time I opened it—and I did it, willingly, all day long. Eventually I looked back up. Her eyes were on her phone, too, but she wasn't touching or swiping—just gazing at something.

"Do you like writing?" I asked, for god knows what reason.

"Does anyone *like* it?" Caroline said, looking up slightly. "But we don't have a choice, right?" She appeared to be a touch more engaged now. "How do you like your job?"

"I mean, it's technically *fun.* I'm full-time at *Corridor. An enjoyable job.* At least that's what people who don't understand what I do tell me about what I do." She struck me as someone who did not particularly appreciate these sorts of vacuous responses. "But yeah, I mean, I interview famous people for a living. Who wouldn't enjoy that?"

"I think everyone hates their job, no matter how much they act like they love it."

"Yeah, I think I probably agree with that." I looked around. "Do you want to step out for a cigarette?"

"I'm not going to smoke," she said. "But I'll get some fresh air."

We were now standing outside the building on a quiet block of 23rd Street. I had my scuffed shoe up on the banister. Caroline was leaning against the brick wall. It was somewhat breezy for July.

"Your name sounds so familiar," Caroline said. "Did you—no, never mind." She looked up at a noise down the street.

"Maybe we met at some media happy hour type thing?"

"I don't really go to those," she said. "I sometimes feel like I should be doing more . . . networking, or whatever. But it's just not me."

"Yeah, it's really draining, having to be so fake to so many people in such a condensed period of time." I looked at her and then continued, "You might know me because I wrote that Valentina Lack profile that got all that—" Normally I would avoid this subject at all costs, but I felt like confiding in her. She was really beautiful.

"Oh yeah, maybe that's it. I'm actually friendly with Erica, Valentina's publicist."

"I feel like Erica must hate me."

"No, no. She doesn't give a shit. Between us, Valentina is kind of a nightmare for her. I think Valentina even fired her at one point. Erica actually left PR for a bit—went to live in Vermont for a few months—but now she's back."

Now that we were discussing Valentina, it was clear the wound still felt disturbingly raw. I wondered what would happen if I were to have a few drinks with Erica, if I laid it all out and we both shared how we really felt.

Caroline studied me more carefully. "I'm sort of surprised you smoke."

"Yeah, it's sort of off-brand. I'm not, like, *cool.*"

"Smoking isn't cool to me."

"I agree." I thought about it. "I think it makes me feel gayer, for some reason. Smoking."

She stared at me, intrigued.

"Yeah, I don't know," I continued. "I feel like when I go onstage at events like this, I kind of act 'straight.' Does that make sense? Like I don't want to rock the boat."

"What does 'acting straight' entail for you?"

I laughed. "I lower my voice, I guess. And take on this sort of *gruff* persona. I'm not going to do it now because I feel stupid even explicating this to you as a *thing*. But, I don't know. Like, imagine me playing charades and getting 'Matt Damon' to act out—it's sort of like that."

"You can't say anything when you're doing charades."

"You know what I mean." I took another drag. "You shouldn't feel bad for me at all. It's all my own fault. Everything is."

"I didn't say I felt bad for you."

I watched an elderly couple make their way down the other side of the street. The wife was holding on to the husband's sleeve.

"God, I'm sorry," I said. "I was just onstage and spoke about myself, exclusively, for forty-five minutes, rambling and fielding questions. And *now* here I am talking about myself some more, complaining to a stranger I just met. It's really gross. I'm awful."

Caroline looked at me and smiled. "*So* awful."

It was bizarre how comfortable I'd felt today, engaging with Otto, and now with Caroline. More comfortable than I'd felt recently with my friends, my family, my co-workers. I'd stopped responding to texts from everyone except my closest friends. And when I did socialize, I never wanted to share anything about myself; I just asked whoever I was with a lot of questions about themselves.

"I might be overstepping," Caroline said, seemingly energized. "But when that story came out and—when Valentina 'clapped back' at you, or whatever, I don't even remember all the details . . . did you—did you want to go into hiding? Or was it more . . . was it liberating in some way?"

"I'm not sure if—honestly, I kind of blacked out that entire week," I said. "But I don't think I would say it was liberating."

"Just, I mean . . . writers—especially when you're profiling someone, I feel like—we're always so nervous about what the subject is going to think. Right? And we're trying to do this incredible job and reflect who they really, truly are. So maybe on some level, when something like this happens, it shows, you know . . . *No matter how hard you try, you can't guarantee you'll succeed.* You can't predict or control any of it. And maybe there's something freeing in that."

I felt myself wanting to agree, to keep things light. "Yeah, I think in the end it definitely made me tougher." I didn't really believe this, but it was an answer I gave people.

She looked forlorn again. "I should probably go in and check on Otto," she said. "He'll be mad if I never peek in." She reached out her hand and lightly touched my shoulder. "I'm really glad we met."

Maybe it was the way she made physical contact, sparking something in me, but all of a sudden it clicked how I knew her. "Wait, oh my god. You know Zoey Prince, right? From your art camp thing? It's just coming to me now. Zoey's my really close—she's told me a few different times that you and me should meet. I'm not sure how I didn't put this together earlier."

"Oh wow, Zoey Prince. *Yes.* I must have recognized you from her posts and stuff. I haven't talked to that girl in years. How is she?"

"She's good. Really good. She's still in fashion, working for a start-up."

"Weird. Small world. I can see you guys being friends."

"Yeah?"

"Yeah, you both come off like you're, I don't know, on the lookout for something."

"Isn't that everyone?"

"Yeah, maybe."

She quietly slipped back inside, and I wasn't sure if she was going to be returning, or if that was goodbye. I felt unsettled in her wake.

I momentarily considered waiting around for the "schmoozing" hour, but I felt like being dramatic and skipping it. They wouldn't care. I felt a slight pang of guilt as I walked down the street, away from the building, but I knew it wouldn't last long.

I stopped in a Starbucks and sat down at the wooden communal table. I now had a bunch of Slack notifications. Hey do you have an angle on this? one of my editors had written me, along with a link to a *New York Times* story about paparazzi tactics. What angles did I have anymore? Was I all out of angles? I felt like I had become a journalist robot. I was just writing the same stories everyone else was writing: we all covered the same fashion brand at the same time, the same singer after the same successful hit single, the same TV series, the same supermodel. We all made the same jokes on social media, used the same jargon, guested on the same podcasts. We alternated which magazines and websites we worked for—she goes here, I go there—but there was no way to tell us apart. We all hated each other but *loved* each other and posted each other's articles even though we didn't read them.

One of the students at the panel had already emailed me: *I found your talk super informative! You have my dream job! I have always loved celebrities (and celebrity culture). I am fascinated by Jennifer Lopez. I want to find a way to enter that world after graduation, and hearing you talk about your job made me feel even more confident that this is the right path for me.* I put my phone down before finishing reading the email.

Two weeks ago I went on a date with a 53-year-old I'd matched with on Hinge. I had never gone on a date with someone that much older than me, but when I entered the bar and saw him hovering by a stool in a windbreaker and khakis, I felt oddly relaxed. I'd had a glass of wine beforehand, but discovered within minutes that he was more nervous than I was. He had a daughter in college ("She's hilarious—she's going to write for Jimmy Fallon's show one day—*watch*") and at one point he referenced his daughter's mother—but when I asked if he'd been married, he just laughed and said, "It's a long story."

It turned out he had read a bunch of my articles before the date. "I could never do what you do," he said, after we'd been talking for about an hour. He was an economics professor at NYU and had written a few books. "I'd *love* to do what you do, don't get me wrong, but I just could never."

"Why is that?" I asked.

"I just—it would bother me too much, being so close to these gorgeous, talented, famous people, and having access to them, but still being *just* on the other side. I think I'd just feel jealous. I'd want what they have." He concluded, "I think I'd end up feeling a lot of rage."

I'd just nodded and smiled, trying to seem more enigmatic than I actually was. I wanted him to feel unsure about whether this had upset me.

In the Starbucks now, I slid my phone back into my pocket and looked up to see the woman in the trench coat who had been talking to Otto earlier, accompanied by one of the students. Maybe she was his mother? They both looked sullen and distracted: unhappy to be here, or anywhere.

The woman spotted me, and I watched her recognize me. She waved enthusiastically, and the two of them walked over. "We just watched your panel!" she shouted. The son looked resigned to the fact that this is what his mother did, this is how she was.

"Yes, I remember seeing you. It's—great to see you again. In this glamorous Starbucks."

"This is my son, Lucas," she shouted. "He's a senior in high school, actually. I'm close with Otto's aunt, and she told me Otto was doing this talk with you, so I decided to sneak him in. He wants to write about music." Lucas nodded almost imperceptibly.

"That's great," I said.

"Aren't you supposed to be at the mixer back there?"

"I had a work thing I had to deal with," I said.

"To deal with *here*?" The first words Lucas had spoken.

"I was just saying to Lucas how impressed I was with your talk," his mom continued, ignoring the low-grade disinterest her son was demonstrating. "I told Lucas that this kind of job requires a thick skin. There's a lot of rejection. Uphill battles. People saying no."

I nodded, and she continued: "And what you were saying about just keeping your head down and not being sensitive. All of it. It's very impressive, and it's not easy to do."

I turned to look at Lucas. "What kind of music do you like?" I asked.

"All kinds," he said. He glanced around the Starbucks and then looked back at me. Something had shifted in his mood. "Do you get to go to lots of cool parties and whatever?"

"I do," I said. "I do indeed."

"But that's not why you pursue this as a career," his mother said, looking at Lucas and then at me. "You don't put up with, I don't know, you don't put up with it all just for a nice cocktail and an autograph."

She was wearing leather boots and black leggings. Her brand of casual condescension actually felt soothing.

"That's true," I said to her, after a pause. "You don't."

I looked toward the door and took a few steps. But I stopped myself and turned back to them.

"But you want to know what's so fucked up about it? You *finally* get there. . . . You do all that 'hard work' you're talking about, over however many years—years of barely being able to make a living, constantly monitoring your bank account. And even when you quote-unquote 'get there,' when you 'make it,' you're never satisfied. Yes, you eventually might get paid a living wage, and, yeah, some writers become *New York Times* columnists or whatever, but it's not like you accrue power as you go. It's not like other jobs. You think you'll finally be fulfilled when you get your first big story. And then it comes out and goes away and maybe someone from high school writes you on Facebook about it, but then everyone moves on . . . and whenever your next story comes along, the cycle just repeats itself. You're at the whim of psychotic editors—but god forbid I tell someone that I think my editor is psychotic. . . . They tell me I'm just being sensitive, that I just don't like to hear criticism of my work." I took a breath.

"Everyone's competitive and cutthroat, but nice to your face. If you're interviewing famous people, you find yourself asking them the dumbest questions in the world, hoping they'll like you, or you ask them actual hard-hitting questions, which they don't answer honestly. And then you write something that either reads like a press release, and makes you hate yourself, or is actually interesting, in which case someone will have a problem with it."

I paused. "So yeah, considering all of that, it *is* nice to have a cocktail sometimes at a fancy party for a fashion blog you've never heard of, sponsored by Bounty paper towels and Tag Heuer, with a gaudy fountain and a performance by, like, two of the five Backstreet Boys. It doesn't change any of the other stuff, but at least the drink is free and you can feel, for a moment, like you have the same value in the world as, I don't know, *Anya Taylor-Joy standing thirty feet away from you.*"

They were both staring at me, unsure what to say. There really wasn't anything to say. I walked past them, out the door, but stopped as I pushed it open and whipped my head back. "Best of luck, Lucas!"

As I turned out of the Starbucks, I took my phone back out and put on Phoebe Bridgers's "I Know the End"—yes, sometimes all of us embrace cliché; it can feel fucking great. The unseasonably cold air—it was colder now—was lacerating and clarifying. It made me smile that I had chosen the song—it's stupid and amazing to play a melodramatic song when you're feeling melodramatic.

After the song was finished, I decided to call Erica, Valentina's publicist.

16

Erica picked up the phone on the first ring. "Hello?"

"Hi, Erica. It's, uh, Victor Harris."

I immediately regretted the call. I felt like I'd shrunk by a foot since leaving the Starbucks, since my outburst.

"Oh, hi," she said. "It's been a while."

"Yeah . . . How are things going?"

"Things are going . . . fine. What's going on?"

I pushed through. I envisioned Oliver encouraging me—*say what you want to say; don't do your usual equivocating thing.* "I was just wondering, and this might be a ridiculous thought . . . but for whatever reason, I've been thinking recently, a lot, about the Valentina cover story."

"Uh-huh."

"I feel like, maybe, if you wouldn't mind setting me up on a brief call with Valentina—the two of us could . . . I just feel like we really clicked actually, when we met at the restaurant, and then things got, maybe, *confused.* I think we could really easily resolve our issues and then we can both just move on with our lives and that will be that. You know, *carte blanche*, what have you. Is 'carte blanche' what I mean? You know what I'm trying to say. Maybe we could even do something really cool where we have a meta conversation about media coverage and journalism. We could record it, or go on a podcast, and we could, like, talk about what goes into crafting a cover story, how the sausage gets made."

For a few seconds after I stopped talking I wasn't sure if she was still on the line. I reminded myself that I had just learned Erica couldn't stand Valentina. Maybe she would be sympathetic.

"You're referring to the *Corridor* piece you wrote like a year ago?"

"Yes."

"Right. Right. Well, let me . . . why don't we—so *what exactly* are you asking for?"

"I just—I think it would be nice for me and her to chat."

"Oh. Well, she's so busy, as I'm sure you know. Her calendar, it's just . . . But let me—I'll check with the team and I'll get back to you."

"Okay, that sounds great. Thanks so much, Erica."

"Of course. Stay well, Victor."

I hung up and walked into a bodega on 14th Street. Even though it had clearly been a terrible idea to call Erica, and our conversation had been, well, humiliating, I still felt proud of myself for taking an action.

The reality was—now that I was letting myself really contemplate this—that whenever I saw Valentina Lack on a billboard or in one of those strange artsy Coach ads that played in the theater before the movie starts, I would viscerally tremble. I honestly felt like she was haunting me—is that ridiculous to say? But now I understood there was no way that any sort of conversation I would have with her would play out as I'd want it to. Clearly, she already had forgotten about the entire ordeal. No doubt she floated frictionless from sponsored event to dinner party to the set for her next project. *She didn't want to talk to me on the phone.* Why would she? Her publicity team might not even have looped her in when the "controversy" was going down with my article. My pleading to her publicist for a follow-up call this many months later was actually the darkest thing I'd ever done—*and I tried to kill myself.*

Erica was probably recounting our back-and-forth to her whole office right now ("It sounded like he'd been *crying*").

Recently I'd identified a desire to *go unnoticed*, is I guess the best way to describe it. To disappear. I wore clothes that wouldn't stand out. I didn't work out anymore. I ate in a way that would give a nutritionist a stroke, vacillating wildly between consuming every morsel I could get my hands on and totally starving myself. Never a happy medium. I increasingly felt . . . a nagging sense of existential dread during all waking hours? It just sort of ran present in the background, like that scrolling "BREAKING NEWS" banner that runs on the bottom of CNN.

I could imagine Dr. Beckman's grim facial expression if I told him all of this. *Dr. Beckman*—I'd vowed to quit therapy so many times but could never bring myself to actually stop seeing him.

I walked out of the bodega with a Diet Coke and a bag of pretzels I certainly didn't need to eat. I could picture myself slumping against the armrest in Dr. Beckman's office, on the leather chair next to his decaying plant, and recounting that a high school student had come up to me at a Starbucks after my talk and that this had unexpectedly triggered a meltdown. I'd probably try to frame it more generously, assuring him that I didn't feel any malice or ill will, toward the kid or his mom. I'd make a pop-culture reference, maybe compare my behavior to Alec Baldwin in a parking lot altercation. I'd create more distance between myself and my behavior, tell him that it felt like everything I used to love (my job, Oliver, my love for celebrity culture) had been made colorless. I'd tell him I felt waterlogged. I'd quickly change the subject.

It had started lightly drizzling. I was half finished with the pretzels already. I walked right past my subway stop. I loved walking through the West Village. All these years in New York and I still had no idea what any of the streets in the West Village were called or which connected to which. It still felt like I was entering a maze when I'd get off the subway at West 4th Street. It made me feel like a teenager—

where might I end up?! I liked that it still felt like I could come across uncharted terrain.

Lately I kept thinking about the obsession I'd had with Taylor Swift's "Forever and Always," the notion of a rainstorm in my bedroom. I used to have this ritual in my mid-twenties where I would roll around on my bed at night listening to that song on repeat and imagine that Oliver had broken up with me and that I was devastated. I would actually cry real tears to the song! Which was doubly absurd and pitiful because we weren't even officially dating at that point—we had maybe just started hooking up. I couldn't just enjoy that period of time that should have been so exciting—it was the beginning of something that had the potential to be wonderful; I should have been elated. But no. Not me. I was already imagining the despondent state I'd be in when it was all over. Are other people like that? How do you fix that behavior?

Maybe I was a genius though for approaching life in that deranged way—because things *did* end with Oliver and I was fucking ruined and it did rain in my bedroom, etc., etc., etc. So it was like my brain was trying to prepare me in advance to soften the blow when it came true.

A large man brushed past me on Barrow Street—*was this Barrow Street?*—and I lost balance for a second. I righted myself quickly, but I felt physical pleasure—it was visceral—at the sensation I might fall to the ground.

17

There's no good way to find out your ex-boyfriend is dead.

This was how my morning went: I woke up and turned to the side and retrieved my phone (nestled beside my cheek) and groggily took a screenshot of the photo from college my iPhone had resurfaced for me on the home screen. It was an image of Zoey and me tangled in a hammock. She was in a lavender sweatshirt, and I was wearing flannel pants and a sweater vest. I looked terrified; she looked mischievous; we both were deeply uncomfortable with ourselves at the time but trying to pretend we weren't. I loved the photo anyway and sent it to Zoey with a yellow heart.

I noticed I had a slight earache and decided if it was still bothering me in the afternoon, I would call my doctor. I jumped in the shower, and when I got out, I saw I had a missed call from an unknown number and a voicemail. I pressed play, on speakerphone, as I slipped on underwear.

"Victor, hi. This is Andrea. I'm just letting you know that Oliver . . . There's no easy way to say this—he died last night. A car hit him when he was biking home. I—we wanted to let you know, of course, and, uh, we are going to be—well, I'll keep you posted. There's going to be a funeral at—soon, I think. Anyway, we wanted you to know."

The message ended there, abruptly. I played it again immediately to make sure that I hadn't imagined it. Her voice was quiet, but, improbably, she said the same words the second time. My arm started shaking, which hadn't happened since the night he broke up with me.

I called Zoey.

"What is it? I just got to work. I saw your picture."

"What picture?"

"The one you texted me. The hammock. From college. I look fat."

"Zoey, Oliver *died*."

"I'm sorry?"

"He died. In a car accident. A car hit his bike."

There was a long, long pause.

"Do you want me to—? Where are you?"

"I don't feel anything yet."

"That's shock."

"I don't know what to say. I can't really believe it."

"Well, you don't have to say anything. Just . . . you should take the day off. Or—can you?"

"I don't know. Yeah. Maybe."

I was having a conversation with Zoey on the phone, yes, but I was elsewhere at the same time. I was inside a Dunkin' Donuts in a Maryland suburb, standing in line with Oliver, waiting for our order of forty-five munchkins. I was in a car with him and his mother, a few weeks after we started dating, when she told me about when Oliver played the role of "a kite" in an elementary school play.

My hair was still wet, uncombed. I lay down on my bed and got under the covers.

"The last time I saw him was in D.C., Zoey. At the hotel. I was such a bitch—dealing with all the Valentina bullshit. We went up to the swimming pool in the hotel. God, I was being *so* annoying."

"You can't—don't focus on that. He knew how much you cared about him. I promise you he did."

"I'm never going to hear his voice again. How is that possible? He had a perfect voice. I was so jealous of how deep his voice was." I stopped talking. "Is that a weird thing to say?"

"Nothing is weird right now. You're—it's all going to take some time."

I hung up the phone and got dressed and emailed Leon that I needed to take the day off. "My good friend died last night," I wrote.

I texted my mom, and she called me, but I let it go to voicemail.

I got back under the covers, now in my jeans and T-shirt, and wondered if this would be the point I was stuck at for the rest of my life. I would never evolve past this. I would never love anyone again the way I had loved Oliver, I was sure of that. I hadn't been sure of that up until this moment, but now I knew it for sure.

The last text I sent him—the last text he would ever get from me!—was a Spotify link (a Rosalía song). I had written underneath it: I think you'll be into this ! (sent at 1:09 a.m. on a Friday). He'd given it a thumbs-up reaction.

I texted Zoey: how is it possible OLIVER is dead and I am alive??? I regretted sending it. I switched my phone into Airplane Mode and closed my eyes.

I woke up three hours later and remembered what had happened. Was that how I would wake up every day from now on? My mind was straining to process the news, to devise coping mechanisms already, I could sense it; perverse thoughts were formulating in my head . . . *Well, I guess this means I won't have to deal with him marrying someone else someday!* . . . *Everyone is going to be really nice to me for the next year or so!* . . . etc., etc. I hated myself for having these thoughts, and hated that they did provide solace.

I strained to focus on him, the person, but I found my mind kept wandering to what I would say at his funeral, if I would even be asked to say something at his funeral, guessing who would be at the funeral. I kept refreshing his Instagram feed to see if there were any new comments on the last post he'd put up (a photo of a lobster roll with the caption hold my calls).

I took another shower, sat on my bed for about thirty minutes, and then left my apartment and walked into a nondescript sports bar. Even though the bar was about a block from my apartment, I'd never seen the inside of it before. In fact, I'd never noticed it until now. It was 2:03 p.m. on a Thursday.

Zoey still hadn't responded to my text from earlier. I'd received a long email from my mom with a link to a Brené Brown YouTube video. I opened Instagram and double-tapped a photo of a gay guy I'd met once who was standing shirtless in a pumpkin patch. I finished a vodka soda and then another vodka soda. The woman sitting next to me at the bar glanced over.

"Do you mind if I put on a different song?"

"What?"

I now saw she was holding an iPad. "I was going to pick a new song," she said.

"Go for it," I said.

She was about my age. Brown messy hair. She looked exhausted. I thought maybe she was a regular. It didn't feel like she wanted to be perceived, and, for a split second, I wasn't sure if she was even real. Maybe the bar itself wasn't real and I was still in bed, dreaming. I decided I wanted to talk to her.

"Are you a performer?" I asked. *Where did that come from?*

"Define *performer*."

"Do you . . . perform things? On a stage?"

"Uh, I work here. My shift hasn't started yet, though. So, no, I'm only a performer in the most . . . general sense. I used to be a copywriter. I dropped out of grad school."

She was drinking a beer. I asked the bartender for a glass of white wine.

"I'm Hannah," she said.

I looked at her and tried as hard as I could to come off as a serious person. "Hannah, would you guess I was gay or straight?"

She laughed. "I have no idea."

"Say whatever you want. You won't offend me."

A few months ago, an editor Slacked me to ask if I was available to profile a young male comedian who had recently come out as gay. This editor, whom I had talked to maybe once or twice since she started at *Corridor*, wrote: I thought you'd be PERFECT for this assignment.

I took a screenshot to send to Zoey: why is this woman I barely know saying I would be "PERFECT" for this?? Lol. It struck me then that maybe every straight person I met, or at least a large share of them, categorized me in their head as gay first, all other traits second. I'd wanted to discuss this with Oliver at the time and almost texted him, but thought better of it.

Hannah still hadn't answered me. "I don't like to make judgments about people," she said finally, cautiously.

"We can go somewhere and hook up," I said. "If you want."

She cackled, sharply. "Excuse me?"

"I live close."

"So . . . that was a pickup line? When you asked if I thought you were gay or straight?"

"I'm a little rusty. Fresh out of a long relationship."

She finished her beer. "I am *not* going to sleep with you."

"Of course."

She looked at me, smiling, in an almost maternal way. "You're . . . interesting," she said finally. "You remind me of someone I used to be close to."

I traced the rim of my wine glass with my finger. "I'm interesting?"

"That was not intended to be flirtatious. To be clear."

I finished my wine in a gulp. "When I was 16, in high school, my French teacher had one of those little Page-A-Day calendars on her desk . . . you know, the ones where you tear off the different days?"

I was picking up on a different energy from her now. I thought she looked frustrated, ready for the conversation to be over, like she had been down this road before with many a patron. But I continued my story regardless.

"Anyway," I said. "One morning this teacher marched over to my desk and presented me with the page for that day. It said 'C'est un drôle d'oiseau' on it. And underneath was the translation: 'He's an odd duck.' I asked her why she was giving it to me, and she went, 'Well *obviously* this one is meant for you,' and everyone in the class laughed."

Hannah raised her empty beer glass. She looked now like she was working out an equation in her head. She smiled. "All right. Sure."

"All right sure what?"

"It's been a weird day. I listened to an upsetting episode of a podcast this morning. My ex–best friend is the host." She added, as if it should be obvious: "So you can come over here and kiss me. If you want."

I realized my back was sweaty—the fabric of my shirt was stuck to my skin like a licked envelope. I hadn't kissed a woman since high school.

She was pretty, it turned out, up close. I hadn't even really looked at her until now. Even though her hair was in disarray, it smelled good, and I was surprised that I had an impulse to pull on it. Maybe I was going to be a different person after Oliver's death—like a guy you read about in a Reuters article on your phone who wakes up from a coma and all of a sudden knows how to speak Italian fluently.

I grabbed her thigh roughly, leaned in, and jammed my tongue into her mouth. Robotic. She was startled, for sure, but she didn't stop me. It was like I was learning to kiss again; all I thought to myself was: *her mouth is soft.*

I bit the tip of her tongue, and she moved her legs around my waist. I decided to really try on this "feral persona." I let my fingernails dig in around her shoulder blades, but then I balked and pulled them back. I swerved my head down and started nibbling her neck, biting softly.

I was getting hard—again, a surprise—and thrust my groin against her leg. Nothing elegant about it. Was the bartender still there? Was he watching us? Did it matter?

"Okay, that's enough," she said, as my tongue started to travel back to her lips.

I breathed into her ear. "You're sure?"

She laughed. "Yeah."

"I'm getting into this now," I said.

She pulled herself away from me. She looked down and took a sip of water. "I don't know why I do these things," she said.

"I'm sorry," I said. Maybe I was worried I'd violated her. Maybe I was saying sorry for something else, for everything else. I sat back down on my stool and watched her finish off the glass of water.

"Why did you stop being friends?" I asked. "With your 'ex–best friend.'"

"It wasn't really my choice," Hannah said. "She just decided one day she had moved on."

"Do you miss her?"

"I think I missed the idea of her for a long time," she said. "Now I mostly think I dodged a bullet, so to speak." She wasn't looking at me. "If someone is meant to be in your life and stay there, I think, they will. You know? You can't do much about it either way."

I nodded, even though I wasn't sure I agreed.

I left the bar and decided, walking back to my apartment, that it was imperative for me to have actual sex with a woman. I took my phone out and saw I had a missed call from my co-worker Maya. Maya was still the closest thing I had to an ally at work—during the height of the Valentina drama, she was the one who would stand up for me in the Slack trenches and keep me abreast of people tweeting in my defense. I called her back.

"Oh, hey. We were wondering where you were."

"Do you know any women—like, any friends of yours—who I could hook up with?" I asked. "It doesn't have to be tonight. Just, like, in general."

"Is this for a TikTok or something?"

"*Please.* Do I strike you as a *merry prankster*?"

"You sound weird."

"Yeah?"

"Where are you?"

"Leaving a bar."

"It's like four o'clock."

"*And what of it?* Like that Ariana Grande GIF. Where she goes, 'What of it?' You know the one?"

"What are you talking about? Where are you? You weren't at your desk this morning."

I hung up and entered my apartment. I got in the shower and I jerked off thinking about Oliver. All it usually took was remembering back to when he ordered me to "get down on the rug" one time when we were fooling around in my apartment watching a Hulu rom-com—it got me hard in an instant. It was that easy. It worked every time. But this time getting myself there felt different, like I was disobeying a law.

I got in my bed, back under the covers again, and texted Oliver: I was never going to be your guy and I have made peace with that.

———

For the next week, I felt like a character in a video game—completing task after task, showering, ingesting food, sleeping, drinking, charging my phone. I had no thoughts. When I talked to my mom or Zoey on the phone, I spoke monosyllabically.

Nine days after Oliver died, I went down to D.C. for his funeral. I waited at Union Station for Zoey's train to get in—she was on a later one. I sat on a bench outside a Hudson News, funneling the leftover sugar in a bag of Sour Patch Kids into my mouth.

"Hey," she said, when she eventually rolled up. She was wheeling a small suitcase behind her. In her black jacket and black capri pants, she looked like every woman I had stood in line in front of at a Midtown Chopt. She sat down next to me on the bench. "Ready for a funeral?"

I rested my head on her shoulder, the sort of physical affection I rarely displayed and that only she could elicit from me.

"Have you had anything to drink today?"

"Zoey, don't ruin the moment."

(I'd had one glass of wine with breakfast.)

As of the day before, I was eating on a semi-regular schedule again. I was sleeping in two-hour spurts, but that had actually pretty much been the case beforehand, too. I was working again, though I hadn't strung together more than a few sentences yet (and anything I had written was produced in an inebriated state—the next morning, reading back, I couldn't make sense of any of the transitions).

"I tried writing something about Oliver on the train down," I said.

"To say at the funeral?"

"Just for me. Not for public consumption—for once. I don't have a *take*."

Zoey was frowning.

"I don't want to forget anything about him," I said.

"You're not going to *forget* him."

"I'm so glad you came," I said. I really was thankful. "How's Tom?"

"I don't want to talk about Tom now. This is a good distraction for me."

"Nothing like a cheery funeral to get your mind off the shittiness of life!" She smiled at this. "I didn't tell you when it happened," I continued, "but the day I found out about Oliver, I hit on a girl at a bar."

"What do you mean?"

"I tried to pick up a girl."

"Pick up *how*?"

"Pick up to sleep with."

Zoey's entire face scrunched up into a rubber band ball. "*What!?*"

"I was in a fugue state. I don't know. I asked this lonely woman at a bar if she wanted to have sex with me. I don't know how to explain it."

I'd never seen Zoey grin wider. It happened in a flash. "*Stop.*"

"It's true."

"What did she *say*?"

"Why are you acting like it's such an out-of-this-world preposterous idea?!"

"I'm—what do you *mean*? It's just *funny*."

It was impossible for me to keep a straight face now. "I don't know what you think is so funny about it," I said, forcing a neutral expression. "She turned me down, but we made out first. She was into it. It could have happened."

"You're serious? A consenting adult woman made out with you?"

"*Consenting adult*, Zoey?" I nodded sheepishly. "I guess it was more *I* made out with her."

"Hey, listen, sleep with a chick, I don't care," Zoey said. "Maybe it would be good for you." She reached into her bag and took out a half-eaten bagel that she ripped off a piece of. "Have you been talking to your therapist about Oliver and . . . all of this?"

"No, actually."

"Very wise."

"I just—just the idea of having to *talk* about it, and what it *means*, and how I feel . . . is exhausting.

She nodded. "I get that."

"Knowing my fucking therapist, I'd tell him about Oliver, and he'd just want to change the subject to talk about work, anyway." I continued, "Also, I don't know . . . I had the thought today, *Am I making this all about me?*"

Zoey laughed, overdoing an eye roll for effect.

"Okay, shut up."

"Victor, I love you, but let's just say 'Am I making this all about me?' could be the tagline of the Victor Harris musical."

"I mean, Oliver and I weren't even dating anymore when he died. Obviously. We weren't speaking regularly. It's almost . . . do I *deserve* to be grieving? Is it weird I'm even at the funeral?"

"It's not weird."

We walked around Union Station for a few minutes, mostly in silence. I hadn't expected Zoey would come to the funeral, and the fact that she volunteered without my even asking her was almost overwhelming to me. I was such an inadequate friend to her. I had been so driven in my career, had felt so far away from my friends who had gotten married or moved to the suburbs (or both), that it sometimes felt like I had fashioned myself as a solo astronaut, chasing after things I didn't even want. I was going to rededicate myself to her, to our friendship.

Eventually, after walking in circles amid throngs of travelers, we got in an Uber to head to the funeral. When we were in the car, I held out my phone. "Do you want to read what I wrote about him? You're the only person I . . . want to see it."

She took the phone and scrolled solemnly. Eventually she looked back up and put her arm around me. We rode in silence the rest of the way.

18

Tom

"**D**id you see that email from my parents?" Zoey asked.

Tom knew that Zoey knew that Tom was going to be out of town that weekend for Nital's birthday.

"Oh. Yeah," Tom said. "I'll write back that I won't be here."

"You must be devastated."

"Zoey . . ."

She was standing at the bedroom door, holding her coffee mug. She had been growing out her light brown hair, and it was almost past her shoulders now. Her freckles were visible on either side of her nose.

Tom was still under the covers, half-heartedly scrolling through an *Atlantic* article about Elon Musk on his phone. Zoey and Tom lived in a one-bedroom in Cobble Hill that sometimes felt to Tom like a computer simulation of an adult apartment. They had nice candles, and nice curtains, and a wooden table in their living room that could comfortably sit four for dinner. Once, he watched Zoey take about thirty photos of the sunlight spilling through the window onto a sculpture they'd bought at a flea market—the sculpture involved two women, ecstatic, holding hands mid-dance—and he felt an overwhelming malaise (she posted it with the caption dancing queens). The plush beige comforter on their bed cost almost as much as a month of their rent, and that was the only thing he could think about whenever he made their bed.

"Tom, the last time we were at their place, you literally looked like you were being detained in a holding cell."

She sifted through a pile of laundry on the bedroom floor.

Why did it still bother Zoey so much that he wasn't entirely *himself* around her parents? He was perfectly genial! He had set up their Apple TV and he laughed at their convoluted stories about their relatives he had only met twice and he worked hard to display just the right amount of affection for Zoey in their presence.

"We already talked about this. I had just flown in from Kansas City." He paused. "I just, you know, was not operating with my normal energy levels or whatever."

Zoey consumed herself with clothes-folding. They'd had some version of this disagreement countless times, and generally Tom would apologize or deflect. This morning, he felt like engaging, though.

"I feel like I do a pretty decent job. Honestly, Zoey. I mean, considering how often we have to see them . . ."

"Jesus Christ. My parents live on the Upper West Side. I can't help that." She tossed a pair of pants into the closet for dramatic effect. "It's just . . . how it fucking worked out. I'm not going to *not* see my parents because you're an asshole."

"I'm an asshole now? When I go over there, I'm Action Figure Mr. Cufflinks Tom Brady." He had pulled down the covers and was sitting up in bed now; it wasn't ideal that he was wearing a faded Death Cab for Cutie T-shirt for this argument. "I play your fucking doormat *husband* when we go over there."

"Well, you're a shitty actor, then."

Zoey started to walk briskly out of the room, before turning around and retrieving her mug, down by the laundry pile. Then she marched out and seated herself at the dining table. Three years of arguments in a one-bedroom apartment had made them both experts in fortitude and discomfort management.

She returned to the bedroom about forty minutes later. He was finishing an oatmeal PowerBar, now watching an episode of *Frasier*.

"We have to leave in an hour," she said.

"Yep."

"Here," she said, tossing a ginger ale can to him on the bed. It landed with a thud by his knee. "And are you—if you talk to Louisa and Travis tonight, nothing about us trying to, *you know*."

"I won't."

"You almost slipped with Victor the other night."

"No, I didn't." He looked up at her. "Why haven't you told Victor, anyway?"

"I will. I just—I will when I'm ready."

"He'll probably be weird about it."

"Don't say that. I can say that, but you can't." She looked down at the crumbs accumulated on his chest. "You just have those bars stored in here? To eat?"

"Yeah. They're in the thing."

She refocused her gaze on their small metallic nightstand, located on his side of the bed, and she scowled, as if the nightstand could be blamed for all of her problems, all of his problems, the problems that plagued them as a unit.

———

They pulled up in front of Brooklyn Winery. Zoey turned to Tom and whispered, "Well, here we go," as if they were arriving for a medical procedure.

Tom had met Stephanie, the bride, a few times; she was one of Zoey and Louisa's co-workers at Selah. She was a bubbly, gregarious character; if she joined a conversation in which you were taking part, you were always relieved, knowing she was going to take hold of the conversational reins in a light, effective manner. She was marrying Seamus, a graying man in his early forties who had a six-year-old son from a previous relationship ("partners," never married). When Tom had once asked Stephanie if she had any qualms about marrying someone who already had a kid, Zoey had squeezed his leg sharply under the table. But Stephanie had laughed amiably and responded, "Oh, I love it. Are you kidding? Getting to skip over the awful toddler years? It's the ultimate life hack."

Zoey and Tom entered the venue, an airy Williamsburg winery that had been converted into an airy Williamsburg event space. The entire interior seemed to be constructed out of a variety of wood materials and looked like a generic Instagram Explore post come to life. One had the sense, walking around, that a knit beanie might fall out from a crevice in the ceiling at any given moment.

Tom pointed at a large chalkboard at the entrance that had "#MERRYSTEPHMUS" drawn on it in purple chalk bubble-letters. "*Stephmus*? Sounds like an infection."

Louisa and Travis—both wielding glasses of champagne—emerged from the throng of guests, assembled by the chairs arranged for the ceremony.

"Merry Stephmus, my man," Travis said, putting his arm around Tom and slapping his back.

"And a prosperous Stephmus to you, as well, my good sir."

"This may be the whitest wedding we've ever been to," Travis said. "Me and Louisa are bringing it from 100 percent down to 99."

Tom laughed. "Yeah, I feel like if you open the wrong door, Bon Iver is gonna come spilling out, just each of 'em stacked on top of each other."

Zoey was muttering something to Louisa, and Louisa was nodding forcefully as she finished off her champagne. Louisa looked up: "We're going to go save seats for the ceremony."

Zoey and Louisa turned around, in sync, and waded through the crowd.

"What'd you guys do today?" Travis asked. Even though Travis and Tom got along perfectly swimmingly, there was always a bit of uneasiness when their wives weren't present, an unspoken sense that anything they were discussing when Louisa and Zoey weren't there was, in some sense, filler.

"We—I caught up on some work," Tom said, lying plainly. "And uh, Zoey went out."

"Nice. We went on a bike ride down the West Side Highway this afternoon," Travis said. "It was gorgeous, man."

Travis was muscular, with wavy dark hair, and he was getting a master's degree in education at Columbia. Tom would sometimes catch Zoey looking at him, when the four of them were out at dinner, with what he interpreted as desire, though it seemed less lustful than it did covetous, more about wanting something that wasn't what she had.

"That's impressive," Tom said, now desperate to acquire a drink before the ceremony started. This was going to be a gin-and-soda night, not a beer and wine one.

Tom knew enough at this point about Zoey's job that he sometimes felt like he worked there, too. When Zoey returned from the office at night, she would monologue about the day's grievances—a comment in a meeting that got under her skin, an ostensibly supportive remark on Slack that rubbed her the wrong way. Most of the complaints were related to overlord Perri, whom Tom had still yet to meet. He'd checked out her Instagram a few times, though; Perri was the sort of public-facing founder who would post vistas of the Rhode Island beach on Instagram and would say things in interviews like, "A bad hair day should be the least of a successful woman's worries."

Generally, Tom's advice to Zoey was that she shouldn't be worrying at all about what this unfeeling robot CEO, who appeared to have been crafted in the passé "girlboss" model, thought about her. Or what she thought about anything, really. One night they fell into an argument about Perri in front of Zoey's parents, and Zoey's mom gave her daughter a look that seemed to say, Tom was quite sure, "Don't listen to him—*we'll* talk about this later."

Drink now in hand, Tom sat down next to Travis on one of the folding chairs set up for the ceremony; Zoey was boxed in by Louisa on one side and the brick wall on the other. She was holding up her phone to take a picture of the altar, which was oriented around a very Instagram-friendly quilt of purple and white flowers. A microphone stand was positioned in front, where the officiant—a short woman with dyed green hair—fidgeted with a sheet of paper, mouthing to herself.

Eventually she tapped the microphone: "Hello, comrades, lovers, citizens of the world and of Brooklyn, friends from the east, friends from the west. We are here today to crack open our hearts, to break down the walls and guardrails we have up, and to look around and *see*. Yes, we're here to see Stephanie and Seamus. We're here to see each other. We're here to swallow up love and accept love and digest love and say yes to love." She looked up at her congregation. "Despite everything in this world that makes us scared and terrified and want to give up on a daily basis, we're here today to say *yes* and pay tribute to this gorgeous thumping organ inside us that gives everything we do its purpose. It's that beat—coming from that speaker system installed within our chests—that we all must march to." She took a breath, and then waited a few moments to continue. "I'm now going to lead us in a meditation. Please join me in a brief chant as we cleanse ourselves of all other thoughts and distractions."

Tom turned his head to his left to make eye contact with Zoey, but she was determined to look straight ahead. He could discern, however, the slightest smirk in her dark-red lips.

During the cocktail hour, the four of them congregated by the bar. The ceremony had served as a reset of sorts for Zoey and Tom. Zoey was on her third glass of champagne. Tom had switched to the house cocktail, a Guinness-based drink called, disappointingly, "Seamus's Selection." Travis was sampling from a paper plate of assorted vegetables.

"Do you think after 'Merry Stephmus,' they just gave up on trying to come up with names for the drinks or anything else?" he asked Travis. "Da Vinci probably had trouble picking up the paintbrush after finishing the *Mona Lisa*, that sort of thing?"

Louisa was telling a story about how Kiki, one of their other co-workers, had RSVPed she was coming to the wedding, but then told Stephanie on Friday she couldn't make it anymore because she was "coming down with something."

"You *can't* do that," Louisa said. "A day before the wedding!"

Louisa, who had recently cut her long dark hair very short, was wearing a low-cut black dress, and Tom found his eyes scanning down her neck to her clavicles as she told the story. He had always found her attractive—Zoey knew this, and loved to make a thing of it—and on a night like this one, the temperature what it was, he knew that if he so much as pulled out Louisa's chair for her, or asked her what she wanted from the bar, Zoey would mentally make note of it, clocking it for later.

Zoey turned to Louisa. "It really is fucked up of her. I told Steph that she should ask Cherry to change around the desk assignments in the office. Steph shouldn't have to keep sitting next to Kiki every day."

Tom couldn't help himself. "Wait, babe," he said. "I really don't think it's that big of a deal. Flaking out on a wedding isn't . . . a criminal offense, or even, like, at all relevant to the workplace. They're co-workers, not sisters. It happens all the time."

"You don't even *know* Kiki, Tom," she said, snapping back to face Louisa. Zoey had taken her white cardigan off, and the taut straps of her navy-blue dress strangled Tom as she spoke.

"Isn't Kiki the one who lied about the Sweetgreen gift card?" Travis asked.

"*Oh yes she was,*" Louisa said.

"Oh my god, I *forgot about that,*" Zoey shouted. She turned to look at Tom. "That's funny, Tom and I actually were just having a discussion about my Sweetgreen consumption."

Tom recoiled, he hoped not too obviously. "What do you mean?" Louisa asked.

Zoey wrapped her arm around Tom, by far the most physical contact they'd engaged in all night. "Tom was a little concerned, looking over our most recent bills, that my regular $15.99 harvest bowl was—"

"I think it's more like $17.50," Tom said, immediately regretting it.

"Sorry, my *seventeen-dollars-and-fifty-cent* salad, let the record state—" Tom looked down as Zoey continued, "Tom's just trying to keep me, you know, frugal and vigilant. Frugal with those lunches! And I *love him* for it."

"What can I say?" Tom said, unclear what was going to come out of his mouth next. "I'm the roughage police."

Tom spun around and went to the bar to get another drink.

───────

Zoey watched Tom as he approached the bar. His pants didn't fit quite right, both too roomy and too long. Travis and Louisa were discussing a brunch plan.

Whenever she went to weddings now, she'd end up thinking back to her own: the pantsuit she changed into (a mistake), her father's long toast (mortifying at the time, sweet to her now), Victor's oddly short toast (capped with a joke about Mandy Patinkin's "sexy beard"), Tom getting sick (annoying at the time, somehow sweet now, too). She wasn't sure sometimes if her wedding memories were actually sequences she had witnessed and registered, or if they had been constructed via stories told after the fact and assorted social-media documentation. She probably shouldn't have had the glass and a half of champagne before the ceremony. One thing she did remember herself, for certain, was Tom bounding over to her at one point—there is a sort of adrenaline throughout one's wedding similar to the rush of receiving incredible news and wanting to text everyone at once—and his whispering in her ear, "This is fun!"

It was two parts an admission of surprise—he hadn't thought it would be this fun—and one part an earnest assessment. She had squeezed his arm and said, "Better than the alternative!" And at this, he'd leaned in and kissed her, an unselfconscious, wet kiss.

———

Seamus was standing at the bar by himself. It struck Tom as so odd to see the groom at the bar on his own—as uneventfully and gloomily as any other guest might be—that he was struck by a demented, outgoing spirit.

"Hey, congrats!" he said, reaching out to shake Seamus's hand. "We haven't met, but I'm married to Zoey, who works with Steph."

Seamus smiled and shook his hand. "Pleasure. And thank you. All somewhat mad, this whole shindig, isn't it?"

Tom looked around the room. A few people had started dancing—the D.J. was playing easy listening for the cocktail hour (currently: "Can't Feel My Face"). There was an odd mix of lively twentysomethings with forty-year-olds who looked like they spent their weekends chasing toddlers around Prospect Park.

"It's great," Tom said. "We're having a blast."

"What do you do?" Seamus asked, and Tom suddenly felt guilty for having positioned himself to take up any of a groom's time at his own wedding.

"Oh, I'm a lawyer. For the state. Boring. No one needs to hear about it, let alone *you!*"

"We love Zoey. She's a gem. Steph just adores her."

"Yeah, well, I'm just doing my best not to fuck it up! You know how it is. Or—you know, you will know how it is," he mumbled. "I don't think I'm very good at . . ."

He let this trail off; Seamus appeared to not have been listening anyway. He took his drink from the bartender and gave Tom a brief nod as he moved past him, back onto the dance floor.

Somewhere around 11 p.m., Tom watched from his table as Zoey danced with Lincoln—the only male employee at Selah—a strapping, high-octane gay man whom Tom had learned earlier that night had been an Olympic swimmer briefly after graduating college. Lincoln was grinding rhythmically behind Zoey as Ja Rule and Ashanti's "Always on Time" reverberated across the dance floor.

They looked good together. Lincoln was about 6'3" and had a Polo Ralph Lauren upper body. Zoey was wearing lavender socks—her black heels long since tossed off—and was shimmying her body, feline-like, against Lincoln. She was smiling ecstatically—she kept brushing her hair away from her eyes—and Tom liked the way her dress rode up her thighs when she crouched down in front of Lincoln. He felt, for a strange instant, like he was at one of his high school dances, sitting with his friends at a cafeteria table pushed toward the back of the room, whispering about whether some girl dancing on the raised platform might be down to give one of them a hand job if they invited her to Jonah's house later. . . .

Louisa sat down next to Tom, jolting Tom back to the present.

"Lincoln is so goddamn handsome, isn't he?" Louisa said. Tom was alone at their table, sipping on his whiskey—everyone else was dancing.

"Yeah, it's intense."

"Jealous?"

"No. He can have her. I'm *sure* he'd make her happier than I do."

Louisa was sweaty from dancing, her face flushed, which only made her more appealing to Tom. She shook her head, looking around the venue. "It's hot as hell in here."

"Yeah, I rolled up my pant legs," he said, raising one up onto the chair next to him. "Alert the press."

Louisa reached her hand over and tapped Tom's bare ankle with two of her fingers. "Very, very on trend of you."

Tom felt his pulse quickening, but he couldn't tell if it was due to this extremely minor flirting with Louisa or the fear of Zoey becoming aware of the extremely minor flirting with Louisa.

"So, Zoey . . . she told me you left your firm?"

It was rare Zoey did or said something that surprised Tom at this point, after three years of dating and a year of marriage. *She told Louisa that? Tonight?!*

"Oh. Yeah. I—uh—they *let me know*"—he was speaking in an affected voice, meant to be comedic, but he could tell it was coming off as something closer to aggrieved—"that I, they let me know I wouldn't be making partner, so I decided to get out, *hightail it*, and now I work for the state, yeah. My hours are way better now. I don't have to work Saturdays and Sundays. It's just all around so much healthier for, you know, quality of life, everything. I think Zoey's really—"

He stopped suddenly mid-sentence.

"Zoey's really what?" Louisa asked.

"I—actually don't know. You probably know better than me, what she really is."

Louisa picked up a glass of water from the table.

"You know Zoey," she said. "She only tells you as much as . . . I don't know, she feels like telling you."

Mandy Moore's "Candy" was playing now, and Tom glanced over at Lincoln and Zoey, who had come together in a sort of joyful, yet also elegiac, slow dance.

Tom was drunk.

"You know, Zoey and I are trying to get pregnant."

Louisa was scrolling through photos she had taken at the wedding. She was in the process of cropping one of Seamus giving Steph a piggyback ride on the dance floor.

She looked over at Tom, unfazed after his disclosure. "Yeah, I know." She continued to crop.

Tom watched Zoey writhing in the mass of bodies. She rarely looked this carefree—this side of her only usually emerged when she was with Victor.

Tom had always felt like Victor was a language Zoey could speak fluently that he was not conversant in. He'd tried various tactics: asking Victor an arsenal of questions at a brunch, or making a show of leaving immediately when Victor came over to give them space, or texting Victor and Zoey TMZ links with a line of commentary. None of it had forged a closer bond between the two of them. It didn't bother Tom, per se; in fact, he assumed Zoey preferred a separation. But when Victor came up in conversation, he felt at a loss—anything he said about him now, in any direction, seemed to annoy Zoey.

A few moments later, Tom propped himself up. He stumbled to the dance floor, where Lincoln was now linking arms with Zoey and another woman, whom Tom had met earlier but whose name he'd forgotten. She looked like a Lauren. Zoey couldn't see Tom approaching yet, and he came up behind her and palmed her lower back, moving in to kiss her neck as she throttled forward to the beat.

Her head snapped back. "Oh."

She relaxed her neck and let Tom kiss her. He bit her softly and moved his body gently against hers.

Lincoln bounced from Lauren back to Zoey. "You stole my woman!" he shouted over the music.

"Yeah, you did!" Zoey said, blissfully, and she spun away from Tom into Lincoln's arms.

Tom left the dance floor and moved outside, sitting himself down on a bench in front of the winery. It was a deep purple late-summer night, cooler outside the venue, and Tom stretched his legs out, nearly to the curb. A few teenagers biked down the street. "Don't you fucking dare!" one of them shouted at his friends. Tom couldn't make out what the other biker responded.

It was 11:34 p.m. Usually, on a Typical Night Out, this would be about the time that Zoey would lean her head on Tom's shoulder, rest her hand on his upper thigh, and announce she was ready to go home.

One of Stephanie's cousins was loitering by the bench. He looked college-age; he had a shaggy haircut that would have fit in great back when *The O.C.* reigned. He had untucked his white button-down and loosened his skinny green tie. His face was almost beet red. Tom had seen him earlier taking shots at the bar with the other cousins. Now he was vaping.

"Hey," Tom said.

"What's up?"

"Would you mind if—"

The cousin handed his pen to Tom.

"My wife would think this was very lame of me," Tom said, holding the pen to his mouth. The cousin gave Tom a look of casual pity.

"Not because vaping is lame," Tom added. "Because *I'm* lame."

"Right."

"It's cool you're Stephanie's cousin. I feel like she would be a fun cousin to have, like, at Thanksgiving. I bet she's always baking shit and coming up with weird games or whatever."

"Yeah, she's cool."

Tom handed him back the pen. The cousin scratched his face, studying Tom. "How long have you been married?"

Tom shot him an affected look of surprise, as if the cousin might be addressing someone else on the bench and he was just realizing the question was meant for him.

"A grand fourteen months."

"Do you like it?"

"Being married? Yeah. You know. It's nice to have someone to go to a wedding with."

A condensed sliver of smoke crept out of the cousin's mouth. His eyes drilled into Tom. "You don't really look like a husband."

The cousin emitted a low grunt and then stumbled back into the venue.

A few minutes later, the door opened and Zoey and Stephanie emerged outside. They were mid-conversation, Zoey gushing, "—*honestly*, you don't even *understand*. The absolute best. Truly."

"Can I just say," Steph shouted, "you look fucking incredible. Majestic. Like, I have been drooling over you all night on the dance floor. 'Call Me Maybe'?! *Stop!*"

They both became aware of Tom's presence on the bench at the same time.

"*Tom!*" Stephanie yelped. "I haven't seen you all night!" She was a consummate professional.

Tom jumped up and gave her a hug—her back was covered in sweat—and then took a step back. Stephanie, her yellow hair tied in a complex system of braids, had changed into a short, frilly, white lace dress; it looked all wrong, too ornate and complex for a party dress, but at the same time as if the designer hadn't quite completed it—a rough draft of a garment.

"It was such an awesome wedding, Stephanie. Really. I—" He looked at Zoey, who was gazing down the street, up where the teenage bikers had traveled. "We had such an awesome evening."

"I'm so glad. I am just—everyone told me before, you know, '*Steph*, make sure you don't drink too much, make sure you *eat*, make sure you *take it all in* and take mental photographs'—and you know what, I really feel like I aced the goddamn test. I took a fuck ton of mental photographs."

Tom, unsure what else to do, raised his hand in the air to give her a high five. "Nice work!" He felt stupid. He shouldn't have had so much to drink.

"Okay, I should probably—" Stephanie started to move back toward the door. "You guys are coming to Baby's All Right later, right?"

"Yeah, we'll definitely try and make it," Zoey said, now a few yards away from them.

And then Stephanie was gone. Tom sat back down on the bench, while Zoey paced down the street.

"Leaving?" Tom said, resting his head on the arm of the bench. "Have a hot date to get to?"

She stopped moving and then reached down, still facing away from Tom. She touched her toes.

"Nice ass, lady."

She maintained that position, arms dangling, for about thirty seconds. For those thirty seconds, Tom felt gleefully, disconcertingly content. There are tiny wars every day, and we forget them all.

Without any warning, Zoey's body realigned and she was standing up again. She screamed down the street, to the sky, a low, primal yell.

Tom remembered when he first met her. She had bought him a drink and introduced herself, and he didn't see his friends again for the rest of the night. The two of them hadn't kissed when they parted ways, to his surprise; she'd just said "goodnight, partner" and handed him a gum wrapper. As soon as they were walking in opposite directions, he realized he wanted to turn around and follow her. He wanted to track everywhere she went; or, more to the point, he didn't want her to go anywhere he didn't know about. It was a feeling he'd never had before, and it made him nervous. He couldn't understand what it was about him that had made her want to buy him a drink and pursue him in the first place—he had never elicited that response in anyone before. Maybe he still didn't understand, now. He was a shitty husband.

Zoey turned to face Tom, no expression on her face. She looked radiant. The streetlight was hitting her from almost directly overhead, and it was like she was making her entrance onstage in a Broadway musical; there should have been piano music. Tom could feel a breeze.

"Hey," she said.

"Hey to you, as well."

She crouched down into a squat, coming close to making the awkward stance look elegant.

"I have something to tell you," she said.

He stretched his arm but couldn't quite reach her knee. "Yeah?"

"I got an abortion two weeks ago."

Tom felt incapable of forming a coherent thought. The street was silent, his mind was blank, time fully stopped. "You—what?"

She stared at him, her lips trembling. Her hand might have been shaking.

"But we've been . . . ?"

"Yeah, I know." She remained in her crouch.

"Why didn't you tell—?"

"I didn't want it to be . . . It didn't feel like a discussion I wanted to have. I felt sure that I wanted to do it and I did it."

"But we're—we're married. So."

The "so" lingered, diffusing, taking up the expanse of the block.

"Yeah, we're married," she said. It felt to Tom that Zoey was *past* her, in a way that made sense when he closed his eyes.

"Well, I don't really know what to say, Zoey. I fully support you in—you know. And this is a weird fucking place and time to be having this conversation. At fucking Stephmus. But, you know, we'll get through this." He reached out again for her knee. This time she leaned in and took his hand with one of hers.

"I'm sorry, Tom. I made a decision that . . . it affects both of us, obviously—without telling you. I wanted to tell you." She looked right at him.

"We were trying to get pregnant."

"Right. I know. I can't explain it in rational or precise terms. You just sort of have to . . . understand."

Tom felt that there was nothing for him to say. His chest was heavy. He rolled up his sleeves and loosened his belt.

"Are you okay?" Zoey said.

He stood up and turned around, facing away from her.

"Yeah, I'm okay," he said. "Are you?"

He felt as he asked the question, unable to see her, that if he turned back around, she might not be there anymore.

———

When Zoey would think back later on this night—the "Stephmus wedding"—and she would think back on it often, there were a few details she returned to: the green hair of the officiant; glancing over at Tom from the dance floor and catching Louisa grazing his bare ankle with her fingers; Stephanie in tears in the bathroom ("I don't know why I'm crying, Z").

When she would think back on this night later, though, she had trouble remembering the actual conversation with Tom on the street. It was as if she could see the scene from above, playing out on mute. There were no words. But she knew she had told him what she needed to tell him. And she knew in the moment that it was all over between them. And she felt a great release, as if she had just caught her breath.

Even though she didn't remember what she said to him, she did remember watching Tom as he turned around on the street to look at her. She remembered searching his eyes for a sign. She was really looking for it. She had loved him at one point; she couldn't ignore that. But what she saw in his eyes was sadness and relief. And she knew everything would be okay. In fact, she was pretty sure this night marked a beginning for her.

19

I was a few minutes late to my appointment with Dr. Beckman. I almost canceled again, but I figured it was better to get the first appointment after Oliver's death over with. I felt resigned to my fate; I could manage for forty-five minutes. *Have your way with me, doc!*

I let him know in my email the previous week that Oliver had died, and he wrote back: *I'm so sorry to hear that. I'm available if you want to talk on the phone. Otherwise, I will see you next week at our scheduled time.*

I sat down in the office, on the solitary leather-cushioned chair, and fidgeted with my sleeve while Dr. Beckman finished typing on his laptop. He closed it and stared at me. His wrinkles were more pronounced than usual. Somehow this made him more attractive to me, which I decided not to contemplate.

"How was the funeral?" he asked.

"It was all right. It felt a little bit . . . like the Platonic ideal of a *funeral*, you know what I mean? Paint by numbers, kind of. Everyone said all the right things. Cried a lot. I don't know. It didn't feel like a particularly authentic experience."

"I think that's actually a pretty common feeling to have at a funeral. Especially when it's someone you know very well who died."

"There were a few people there who I know for a fact Oliver hated. So that was kind of amusing."

He nodded.

"I didn't speak, or anything like that."

"Were you asked to speak?"

"No. No, I wasn't. But that's fine. It made sense. I processed in my own way."

The cadence of our therapy sessions had picked up over time. I still didn't feel entirely comfortable around him, per se, but I appreciated that at this point we had a history and something of a shared vocabulary. I didn't have to remind him who characters were anymore. And there was a sense of relief in not feeling like I had to win him over. I spent so much of my time and so much energy trying to ensure that everyone I encountered liked me. *And for what?*

"How have you been in terms of drugs and alcohol?"

The clinical chill of the question disarmed me slightly. "I'm drinking . . . the normal amount. Maybe there's been a slight uptick." I paused. "I'm not about to jump out a window or anything."

"Glad to hear it."

We sat in silence again.

"I don't really *miss* him. Is that strange? I feel almost a sense of . . . calm about it. I feel awful saying that, but I think it's true. It's so odd, an ex-boyfriend dying. In a way, I had already buried him in my head. When he dumped me. The night I took the pills."

"Grief is a very complex beast. It can also shift day-to-day, as you know, so it's good to just let yourself really be present with each turn. Sit with it all."

I let these sorts of phrases of his ("complex beast," "sit with it") waft right by me at this point. They didn't even bother me.

"I think, if I've gleaned anything from this, it's that I am certain now that *nothing matters*. I knew that already, I guess. But now I understand it so fully that it's kind of painful. Why was I ever so worked up about the placement of a pointless Q&A on the *Corridor* website, or an annoying text from some person I don't even care about, or the fucking Valentina situation that you and I have wasted all this time talking about?"

"Again, these are very valid emotions to be having at a time like this."

I raised my voice slightly. "I know you know me, and I'm not one to be—I'm not *trying* to be difficult. But nothing anyone is saying to me lately feels very helpful. I just keep wanting to be alone."

"That's fair. And understandable."

I took a deep breath.

"Not to be rude, but you're kind of like an 'autocomplete therapist machine.' I could script your dialogue at this point." I said this with a smile, but I immediately felt bad about it. "Sorry. I've been acting like more of a dick since Oliver died, I think."

"You can't offend me, Victor."

"I had this moment—well, right after he died, I really wanted to sleep with a woman. Like, in a sexual sense."

"Have you ever slept with a woman before?"

"No."

"And where do you think that's coming from?"

"I'm not really sure. It feels a little on the nose almost, you know? I think I just really want to be something different. Someone different. I don't *like* who I am. You know that."

He paused and crossed his legs. He appeared mildly concerned, as if I'd just triggered some kind of response mechanism in his AI operating system with my sequence of words.

"How's work going?" he asked.

"I cannot believe you are asking me that. Work is the last thing I want to think about right now. Who *cares* about work? I hate work. I wish I didn't have to work."

"I think there are aspects of your job you like."

I hardly wanted to respond to this. This is why I hadn't wanted to come to this appointment in the first place.

"Why does it bother you so much when we talk about your job?" he said.

"Because it's all you ever want to talk about."

"That's interesting that you perceive it that way."

"There is nothing to say! It's the one aspect of my life where I'm doing well."

"Well, I don't know if I'd say that. The Valentina debacle. All the issues you have with your boss. There is a lot there."

"Oh my god. I just told you ten seconds ago that I want to have sex with a woman! Isn't that of interest to you? Doesn't that speak to some dark, twisted internal strife?! *My ex-boyfriend is dead.* My dad abandoned me. I am a *troubled person.*"

He smirked a bit, as if finally having gotten the reaction he was aiming for from me.

"Victor, you're very intelligent. I think you understand that humans are multifaceted. There are layers to these things. We can talk about your career in the same breath as we talk about Oliver or your dad. It doesn't mean we are saying all of these things are of equal weight, or comparable."

Surprisingly, this didn't annoy me as much as I'd have thought it might.

"Oliver was a great love of yours," he continued. "What happened to him is tragic. You will go on to have many other great loves."

"Many?"

"Perhaps. People, projects, places."

"I think there is also a part of me that wishes it was me who had died," I said. "Oliver was so *good* and handsome and successful, and he wasn't going around overdosing on pills or monologuing about his grievances or posting cryptic Instagram Stories to try to incite people to text him because they're concerned for his well-being."

"We all want explanations for the major, transformative events that happen in life. Sometimes there aren't any."

"That's very, you know, *Oprah Wrapping Up An Interview* of you."

He didn't smile at this.

"I don't actually mean that," I added. "That I wish it was me who had died."

"I know," he said. "Well, we're out of time."

———

I walked out of Dr. Beckman's office and, I couldn't believe it, I felt light on my feet for the first time since I'd found out about Oliver. I wasn't sure how long it was going to last, but it was a start.

I watched as a horse with a policeman in the saddle waltzed down the street. I hadn't realized that happened anymore, but apparently it did. Two teenagers skateboarded past the horse, and it felt like the setup for a joke. I was going to make a point of searching for absurdity wherever I looked. It was generally easy to find.

If this really was going to mark the start of a new chapter for me, I decided I didn't want to leave it to chance.

I called Leon and told him I was going to quit my job at *Corridor*.

20

Zoey

Zoey started going on walks after her marriage ended. She had never been a "walker" and would silently (or not so silently) scoff when friends would wax on about the "power of a good walk." She walked to get places, and that was all the walking she felt she needed in her life. She would sometimes come across influencers in her feed (usually outfitted in a matching spandex workout set—lime green, hot pink, it was always some egregious color) who would be preaching to their followers, "Guys, you *have* to start your morning with a walk! I don't care if it's just for five minutes, you won't *believe* what it does for your skin, your mood, your sex drive, your metabolism." Zoey felt like this kind of girl was essentially a different species from her, this girl who would (a) make a production of going on a walk, (b) dress for it in neon, (c) converse with their "followers" while on said walk, and (d) actively decide to share that footage with the world.

Now, though, now that her marriage was over, she walked. She woke up in the morning, slipped into a sweatshirt, and walked. At first she'd try to make the walk more "efficient" by calling her mom or her high school friend Clara. Clara lived in Ann Arbor now and had recently left her boyfriend for a woman; Zoey liked talking to someone else who had ended something, who was starting something else.

But eventually she stopped making phone calls. She wouldn't bring her AirPods on her walks, either. She'd get home from the walk and shower and eat half a bagel and scroll Instagram and check Slack and then she'd leave for work.

She never thought about anything too intently on the walks. *Should I watch another episode of* Sex and the City *tonight or try something else? What's Jack Nicholson up to these days? Should I head to Duane Reade during my lunch break or will it be too crowded?* Sometimes Tom-related thoughts or memories would drift into her periphery, like one of those floaters that emerges when you close your eyes.

She never cried. She didn't listen to sad music. She didn't scream. She walked.

She hadn't yet told Victor that the marriage with Tom was over. She wasn't sure entirely what she was waiting for. She'd told him about the abortion, and she'd texted him that things were a mess with Tom, but she stopped short of divulging the rest of it. They were getting a *divorce*. She didn't think she was delaying telling Victor because it was an admission of failure, though that would have made sense. She didn't feel like she had failed. And she didn't think it was because she couldn't handle what he was going to say in response. She knew he was only going to support her. He had never liked Tom anyway.

About a week after Tom moved out, she decided to invite Victor over to her apartment—it was now just her apartment—for drinks. He arrived with a box of five Billy's Bakery cupcakes. Five. Not an even six. Not two, one for each of them. It was very Victor to arrive with five.

He was wearing what looked like a shawl. He had recently started dressing, particularly since Oliver's death, in a way that Zoey could only describe as "like you're being styled by someone who's out to sabotage you." The shawl he was wearing was made out of what looked like gray sheep's wool. He was shedding.

"Well, hello, my little freelancer," Zoey greeted him.

Victor smiled. "Not officially. My last day at *Corridor* is on Thursday."

"You really should message Caroline Stevens—she's been freelancing for so long." Zoey moved to the sink to fill up a glass of water. "You never really told me what happened when you ran into her, by the way."

"Oh yeah. It was so weird. I truly didn't connect it was *your* Caroline until she was leaving. She's very . . . enigmatic? I don't even know how to describe it. Really pretty, though." Zoey didn't react to this. "She's a little scary? I wasn't expecting that from how you'd talked about her. It makes sense she's a writer. She makes me feel like—I don't know. You know how there are cool writers and then there are not-cool writers?"

"I never really thought of Caroline as *scary*."

"We did start following each other on Instagram." Victor looked around the apartment. "What's Tom up to tonight?" he asked, positioning himself on Zoey and Tom's couch, legs pretzeled uncomfortably under him.

"He's—out. He's not here right now."

"Out like *getting a pint with the boys* out?"

"No, like *he doesn't live here anymore* out."

From a young age, Zoey had tried to avoid drama and drawn-out theatrics. She used to write down pertinent information on Post-it notes and hand them to her mother instead of initiating a discussion ("Mom, I don't like going to school," one note read). In general, in her life, she liked getting things over with.

Victor stood up. The shawl fell to the couch. "I'm sorry—what?"

Zoey leaned against the kitchen counter and nodded.

"Like, you're divorcing? I'm having trouble . . . When did this *happen*?"

Victor's head was a spinning top. Weirdly, in this moment, his expression reminded Zoey of how he'd looked in the hospital, when he woke up and strained to put the pieces together of how he had ended up there.

In an alternate universe, Victor would give her a hug, envelop her in that sheep's fur shawl. But that's not how the two of them were. They didn't touch at moments like this.

Zoey moved to the dining table and sat down on the creaky wooden chair that Tom had come home with one day. "We are getting divorced. It happened maybe three weeks ago."

"Three weeks ago?" Victor was back on the couch. He was smiling now and had his hand in the open bag of Trader Joe's tortilla chips. Zoey felt a resistance to having the conversation with him. "God, I'm so happy for you," he said. "Are you happy?"

"Yeah, I'm really happy. I mean, I think it's going to take me a few beats. I don't think it's like . . . You know the meme of Nicole Kidman?"

"Yeah, of course, when she's all jubilant after her divorce."

"I'm not at that stage of things yet. I'm still—I'd say I'm at the stage of . . . like, the bill has passed the House and now the Senate is going to vote on it."

Victor put the bag of chips down and spread his legs out on the couch. "So what happened? I didn't realize we were at *this* point."

"I feel like I'm on a podcast right now," Zoey said. She felt her legs stiffen. She didn't know why she was having such a hard time diving into the conversation. She walked to the refrigerator and poured herself a glass of sauvignon blanc from a twist-off bottle she'd opened the night before. "It just became really obvious, I guess. You know how I am. Once I decide I'm over something, I'm *over it*. I don't really look back."

"Yeah, I'm the opposite of that."

"Yeah, you are. You'll be in the same apartment your whole life."

"That's not true. I want to move."

"Right."

"So there wasn't a big fight or anything? I know—I mean, you said he was actually really supportive when you told him about your . . ."

"Yeah, no, he ended up being great and understanding about the abortion. It's weird. Everything has actually been really nice and polite and drama-free between us. I just realized, I think, that—" Zoey was shocked to realize she was tearing up.

Victor reached his arm out from the couch, not standing up. "*Zoey!*"

"I'm fine. I'm not actually crying." She wasn't going to actually cry. "I think I just have a lot of pent-up emotion about it all."

"That makes sense. I'm sure it's—it's going to be a process."

"Yeah. I mean, Tom is just—he's a really solid sandwich. You know what I'm saying. He's solid. He's great. I could have it every day. I could be with him for however long. I could be with him forever, probably. Some people might even say I'm dumb for leaving."

"But you're ready for the steak salad."

Zoey smiled. "Something like that. I can't believe I just called Tom a 'sandwich.' Who am I?"

"So he just . . . put his clothes in a suitcase and called a Lyft?"

"He's staying at Tim's."

"Oh god. The worst."

"Tim isn't that bad. You just hate—"

"Hate what?"

"I don't know. Hate anyone who doesn't really pay attention to you?"

"I'm going to excuse that comment because you're getting divorced." Victor went to the refrigerator and poured himself a glass of the wine. "So does this mean you're going to date now? *Get on the apps?*"

"I'm not there quite yet, Victor."

Victor pulled off a paper towel to wipe up the wine he'd spilled on the counter. "You didn't—neither of you, like, cheated or anything?"

"Don't you think you'd know if I *cheated on him*?"

Victor lingered by the kitchen counter. "Is it okay for me to say I think this is going to be really good for you?"

Zoey now felt like being somewhat combative. "Sure. But I'm not going to be one of those people who, you know, throws some huge party in a bowling alley to celebrate my divorce. I'm not posting it on Instagram."

"You're not? You're going to be one of those cryptic people who, like, breadcrumbs their break-up?"

"I'm not going to *breadcrumb* my divorce. I just—I don't owe an explanation to anyone. No one needs information about me."

"But don't you want people to know you're single so they can set you up?"

"Victor, that's not—I'm not ready for that anyway. I think it's—we both need some time to grieve." She noticed Victor flinch. "How are you doing with—everything, by the way?"

"We don't need to talk about that now."

Zoey nodded. Victor's reaction to Oliver's death had initially struck her as somewhat callous—the day after Oliver died, Victor texted Zoey to ask if "people would think it was weird if he didn't post a carousel of Oliver photos on Instagram." And then, after the funeral, she felt like he'd swung dramatically in the other (equally concerning) direction—he seemed to be acting as if this death was going to define the rest of his life.

"I think I knew it was over between me and Tom a year ago, actually," Zoey said. "I came home from work and I was sitting right here, where I'm sitting now. And I didn't feel like making dinner or ordering anything and I was just kind of on my phone doing what I do." Victor nodded. "And Tom came out of the bedroom, and he looked totally fine, nothing was different. But I felt like there was a *big person* in the apartment with me. I suddenly felt like I was living with a giant. I didn't recognize him at all. That had only happened to me once before, early on when we were dating. I was pretty drunk one night, maybe our sixth or seventh date, and we were—did I ever tell you this?—we were making out in the back of the taxi and I had this flash of 'Wait, who is this guy again?' Like, I actually had to remind myself who he was. I know that doesn't make sense."

"No, it makes sense."

"Just these odd moments where I think my body—or some part of me—was trying to tell my mind, 'Get out. This is a stranger. He represents danger.' Or, well, not *danger* danger, but—"

Victor looked somewhat pained, like he was watching a torture scene in a movie.

"Anyway, yeah, I think after that night here, I just started seeing things differently. I didn't talk to anyone about it. Not my parents. Not you, obviously. But I just—it was like an emotional Chekhov's gun or something. I knew the end was coming. And then when I found out I was pregnant, I was like, 'Jesus Christ, Zoey, *wake up*.'"

"Have you told your parents yet that he moved out?"

"Yeah. I called them the other day. My mom doesn't seem too alarmed. I think she had a feeling this was coming."

Victor was staring at her. "I love you, Zoey. You know that, right?"

She felt like he needed something else from her in that moment; it was strange. She didn't know if she could give it. She wasn't sure what to say, or what it was he didn't have from her. So she just nodded her head and smiled and nodded some more and then went to get some more wine. She was already thinking about the walk she'd be going on the next morning. She was going to set her alarm thirty minutes early.

21

Erica

It was 11:42 p.m. on a Wednesday night and Erica was watching *The Proposal*. It was *almost* a parody. She was almost a parody. She was aware of this. If she hadn't been aware of it, she thought, then it *would* be full-on parody. She had a face mask on (she had ordered it off an Instagram ad). Her dark brown hair was tied up in a scrunchie.

Celia was already asleep. Celia went to sleep at 9 p.m. every night; she usually had to be up at 6 a.m. to get ready to go into the hospital. It felt like a bad joke to Erica sometimes: she was a publicist, and her girlfriend was an emergency room doctor. They had a bit they'd perform at parties sometimes: "We each show up at work when there's a crisis!" Once she overheard Celia tell someone on the phone: "Yes, our work is *equally important*—for sure," followed by giggles. Erica loved Celia, but she wasn't sure they were meant to be together for life. Working with as many movie stars as Erica had, she wasn't sure anyone was meant to be together with anyone for life.

She'd finished off two tequila sodas. She took out her phone to text Valentina Lack.

Erica: Hi

Erica: I thought you did really well on Colbert last night

Valentina: oh thank you

Valentina: he makes it easy!

Valentina: Im confused though. I thought
I deal with "monica" now for day-to-
day??

Erica smiled and sunk deeper into the couch. For all the fame and
money Valentina had now accumulated—she had just purchased a
$6.1 million four-bedroom in Laurel Canyon—Erica knew Valentina
was, pretty much at all times, deeply, deeply bored. Valentina was no
doubt at home with her dog right now, maybe with her boyfriend of
the month nearby playing video games (it could be the male model, or
maybe the "production exec"). Erica was sure Valentina was scrolling
through TikTok and online shopping.

Erica: you do deal with monica now!

Erica: but we can still text, can't we?

Erica: how are you?

Valentina: fine

Valentina: exhausted

It was, Erica knew this, *sick* that she still wanted to be in constant
contact with Valentina. When she started out as a publicist, she'd made
a point of telling her friends and family that she "didn't even care about
celebrities." She'd roll her eyes. She was *so* above it all. She'd tell disparaging stories; she'd share juicy gossip. But then when she left the business and took her break, she felt as if someone had shut off the power
in her house. It was way too quiet all of a sudden. She had thought
she wanted "time to read again, to recharge and think"—but it turned
out all she did during her break was search symptoms on WebMD and

watch *The Bachelor*. Though she had used her break for one creative endeavor—she was very pleased about that.

She fixed herself another tequila soda.

> *Erica*: listen, I know you still feel hurt about how everything played out
>
> *Erica*: I needed some time off
>
> *Erica*: it wasn't related to you

Valentina: I am not hurt!!!

Valentina: please

Valentina: I have too much going on to be worried about my publicist's mood swings

Valentina: am I even supposed to call you my publicist??? Are you officially back??

Valentina: I know about your play btw

Valentina: you thought I wouldn't find out about that????

Erica had spent four months in Vermont. When she returned and took her job back, she was "reassigned" to the events division of her agency. But she still was allowed to "consult" for her former clients, even if Monica had taken over day-to-day responsibilities.

And yes, there was the play. She had written a play. She hadn't told Celia about the play yet. She knew this was absurd; she had talked to her therapist at length about why she hadn't told Celia about it. She just knew Celia would find it distasteful somehow, writing a lightly fictionalized version of her life. And Celia would hate that it was about Valentina.

> *Erica*: the play is fictional valentina

> *Erica*: and I am officially back at the agency, just in a slightly different role

> *Erica*: we talked about this

Valentina: okay, but the play is about a publicist and her "lunatic" celebrity client, so I think people will put two and two together

> *Erica*: okay for one thing, it's written under a pseudonym!

> *Erica*: no one is going to know I wrote it!

> *Erica*: it was just a cathartic exercise for me when I was in Vermont

> *Erica*: it was an exercise my therapist suggested . . . and then I ended up deciding to send it to a few ppl

Valentina: well I am so glad you got your catharsis Erica

> *Erica*: you're being a little unfair I think

> *Erica*: I highly doubt the play will get produced anyway

Valentina: CAA has it!!! my agents know about it

Erica: valentina relax

Valentina: were you ever going to tell me
about it???

Erica: of course! you never want to see
me or talk to me since I got back!

She knew that this text message conversation was more than bordering on unprofessional. Of course she knew that. It was after midnight. She was slightly inebriated. They should really be having this discussion on the phone, not over text. But she couldn't help it—it was exhilarating. Wasn't that it? And she didn't want to admit this, but the pitter-patter with Valentina stimulated something in her. *Yikes*. Was that part of it? She needed to discuss this observation with her therapist, but she was slightly terrified to uncover what the root might be. It didn't feel like a *sexual* stimulation, per se—but . . .

Valentina: honestly I don't care what you
do or what happens to you

Erica: are you going to "fire" me again?

Valentina: potentially

Erica: well keep me posted

Valentina: you have a lot of nerve

Valentina: your career has benefited
wildly thanks to me

Valentina had "fired" Erica three times now, each time rehiring her a few days later.

Erica turned off the television and went to brush her teeth. She left her phone on the couch, certain there would be another text from

Valentina when she picked it back up. She could anticipate her patterns, like a parent might for their infant child.

Valentina: Erica?

> *Erica*: I don't feel like arguing V

> *Erica*: Celia's parents are in town right now and there's a lot going on

> *Erica*: I have a lot on my plate

Valentina: I would just like to be treated with respect

Valentina: and I'd appreciate it if you sent me a copy of the play

> *Erica*: of course

Valentina: and as for our working relationship . . . TBD

> *Erica*: understood

Valentina: I kind of liked not having a publicist when you were "in Vermont"

Valentina: so we'll see how this goes the next few months & I will come to a decision

Valentina: I know that technically "monica" is my publicist now and you're—what?—my fairy godmother??

Valentina: but I still have to assess what I want to do

Erica had seen, time and time again, that with increased fame came an increased sense of isolation. Of paranoia. Valentina had few real friends to begin with. At this point, she really had only two or three confidants left—and one of them was her hairdresser who had just left her for Jodie Comer.

Valentina: am I ever going to meet this Celia BTW?

> *Erica*: I think our client-publicist relationship is weird enough as is

Valentina: I don't think it's "weird"

Valentina: but fine

Valentina: I would have thought you'd want the points

> *Erica*: celia truly is not the type to be impressed by meeting a movie star

> *Erica*: she barely wants to hear about my job

Valentina: well that sounds bizarre

Valentina: okay I am going to try to get some sleep

Valentina: I have an early flight to New York tomorrow

> *Erica*: I know

> *Erica*: I am on all the emails

> *Erica*: we should talk tomorrow BTW

before you get on set with the Evian
people

Erica: I want to be careful about what
images they share on social before any
of the materials come out

Valentina: I thought MONICA was my
new point of contact!!!! WHY are you
talking to me about work

Valentina: this is such a clusterfuck

Erica: she is

Erica was reminded of the phone call she received recently from Victor Harris. He had sounded unhinged on the phone, but she also gleaned—it was obvious—that he was spellbound by Valentina. Wasn't that it? Wasn't that why he was so upset? In that sense, they were kindred spirits. She picked up her phone again.

Erica: old habits I guess . . .

Erica: I can't help myself

Valentina: what's the name of the
Valentina character in the play?

Erica: it's not based on you!

Erica: Lucia

Valentina: Lucia?!??!?!?

Valentina: wtf

Valentina: how did you come up with that!

Erica: and then the publicist is named
Bridget

Valentina: oh that name sort of fits for you

Erica: ok ok that's enough

Valentina: Well when I do finally read the
play, if I have any suggestions or edits, I
hope you will take them

Valentina: I read a lot of scripts, you
know

Erica was going to delay sending Valentina the script as long as she possibly could. She was going to have to call her friend at CAA to stall them from sending it to her, too. Fuck.

Valentina: you can't just not respond to me

Valentina: I'm your client

Erica: believe me I'm aware

Valentina: are you drinking? You're
awfully feisty tonight

Valentina: I think I may actually prefer it
to your usual though!!!!!

Erica: I am not drinking

Erica: have a good flight tomo

Valentina: xx

Erica grabbed her eye mask from the couch. She walked to her bedroom and opened the door slightly.

Celia was fast asleep, sprawled out in the middle of their bed. Erica decided to close the door and sleep on the couch tonight. She grabbed a blanket from the closet and nestled herself into the back of the couch. She closed her eyes for a few minutes and then opened them and picked up her phone, resting on the floor by her head.

Two texts from Valentina:

Valentina: lucia!!!

Valentina: I am going to start using that when I check into hotels

22

"I'm still technically grieving," I shouted. "I can have a fucking cigarette."

Zoey's head fell back and she cackled; I hadn't seen her this relaxed in a long time. Watching her brush her heel against the curb, nearly floating in front of the parked cars, it felt a bit like I was encountering her for the first time. It was almost like I didn't know her at all.

"That isn't a good reason," she said. "He died—what?—like seven, eight months ago. Or I mean, do whatever you want. You know how I feel about the smoking."

I looked around, hoping no one had seen us. We were on Celeste's block in Bed-Stuy, lingering by the bodega about thirty yards from her apartment. It was chilly, but I wasn't wearing a coat or anything: just tight black jeans and a Goop sweatshirt ("It's *ironic*," I explained, though no one ever believed me). Zoey was in a wool coat.

"You don't get to just *use* the Oliver thing like that now."

"What do you mean?"

"All of us deal with tough shit, Victor. I recently went through, you know, a significant *life event*. Horrible things are constantly happening all around us. You deal with it and do the work and then you move on."

"Nice, Zoey," I said. "Really sympathetic." I was grinning.

"I went to *his funeral* with you. You can't say I'm not sympathetic."

Celeste's baby shower started at 4 p.m. It was 4:35 now, but neither of us felt any urgency about traversing the last half block. I had not even seen Celeste since her wedding, but for some reason I made the cut for the shower, presumably considered an automatic add-on with Zoey.

"You're right," I said. "I cannot say that."

Zoey laughed, shifting back and forth. She had lost a fair amount of weight since her divorce. I hadn't brought up the weight loss, and neither had she, but I knew she knew I was aware of it. We had been friends long enough that subjects could be covered without actually ever being discussed.

I hated to admit this—actually, I didn't really hate to admit it—but I was thrilled that Zoey and Tom had separated. It wasn't even about Tom. Well, maybe it was a little bit about Tom. He was *fine*. I had grown accustomed to his presence, let's say—or, rather, I never thought I had an option for expunging him.

For the moment, I was just really enjoying the sense that I had Zoey *back*.

Now that Tom and Zoey weren't together, I was reminded, again, that there is so much we don't know about the people we feel the most closely connected to. That there was clearly so much going on in her life that she hadn't shared with me while it was happening—even if I might have intuited some of it. At first, it made me sad, even a bit angry, that she had kept so much from me, but now that ache had dissipated. Oliver always used to say I made everything—no matter whom it concerned or what was happening—into a referendum on myself. I told him I thought that's what everyone did, and he just laughed.

Now Zoey was casually dating a graphic designer named Thad. He told her recently he wanted to get a tattoo of her name on his thigh. She said if he did that, she would break up with him, but I could tell it turned her on. She kind of loved it.

Zoey was now leaning her back precariously against the window of the bodega, as if posing for a street-style Instagram account. "I still can't believe you wore a bow tie to Oliver's funeral."

"Yeah, that was weird. I wanted to make him laugh, I think."

"Okay, so now we are communing with the deceased?"

"Yes, we are."

Zoey turned her body to face me, though she avoided making direct eye contact.

"Do you ever miss—do you feel good about not being at *Corridor* anymore?" she asked. "I get worried."

"No, I love it. It's been really good. You know. I can go to Duane Reade in the middle of the afternoon now."

"*Please*. You were doing that before. You barely went into your office by the end of it!"

"That's not true," I said. I looked down the block before glancing back at Zoey. "I really don't want to go to this baby shower."

Zoey moaned at the three cars to our left, waiting in line for the light to turn green. "Not more than I don't want to, I promise!"

At one point, during our first years in the city post-college, Celeste, Zoey, and I had ended most nights out together, dancing in Williamsburg or sulking on the subway—or, often, the latter would follow the former. Celeste and Zoey had drifted apart, though, especially in recent years, and I only saw Celeste now at these formal functions. She posted a *lot* of Instagram Stories, and I muted her about a year ago. She was the sort of person who would definitely notice if I outright unfollowed.

When Zoey and I reached the door of Celeste's apartment, we could hear loud music coming from inside. It sounded like show tunes.

"I am going to have to get trashed in there," Zoey said.

"I am going to be the only guy here. How much do you want to bet?"

Zoey knocked, and Celeste greeted us. "Oh my god, hi!"

The shower, thankfully, was extremely casual, almost like a cocktail party. There was a table set up with food and drinks, a few pictures of Celeste as a baby plastered on the wall, and that was about it for pageantry. After twenty minutes or so, I looked up from texting and saw Zoey was talking to Celeste by the food. I walked over and leaned my head onto Zoey's shoulder. I was almost finished with my second glass of champagne.

"I just feel like it's time for, you know, a reset," Celeste was saying. "I'm almost 32. And I mean, what better reset than this?" She reached to pat her stomach. "I know I'm *privileged* though, to be able to go part-time. I can't *complain* at all. I'm lucky I have the opportunity and that . . . well, I don't know what I'm saying."

Zoey seemed faraway. Celeste turned to me. "Victor, oh my god," she said. "I love looking at your social media. It's like following an actual celebrity. You're always at *something*."

I smiled. "Well, I used to be, at least."

"Did I see—you posted they're making one of your articles into a movie, or something?"

"A limited series. Yeah, one of my old stories. But weirdly I don't really have anything to do with it—the magazine has all the rights." I added, "I actually left *Corridor* a few months ago."

"Oh, oh my god, *right*. I think I knew that. That's so cool. That's so brave of you."

"I don't know about brave, but it's something."

"I still tell people all the time about when you took us to that Adele concert, and we went backstage," Celeste said. She looked down again at her stomach, as if it were whispering to her. "Oh my god, Kev actually suggested the name Adele the other night. But we can't name her that, right? We *can't*, can we?"

Zoey looked up from wherever she'd been. "No, Celeste, you can't."

"It's so funny," Zoey was saying. The two of us were now on the sofa with a plate of sugar cookies. "No one brings up Tom. It's like he didn't exist."

"Well, I think people just don't want to—you know. People probably don't know if it's a kosher topic, or how it ended with you guys. I think most people are basically terrified all the time about saying the wrong thing to someone."

"You're not."

"Well, not when I'm talking to you."

"I guess I just feel like it'd be so much more real if people were like, 'Hey, I hated your ex-husband, too.' Or even if they liked him! You know, they could say that."

"*Hey Zoey, love that top you're wearing. By the way, that guy you were married to for two years was a dick.* No one is going to say that to you."

"He wasn't a dick. It was me. I was the dick."

"You were not a dick. You were you. You were a person. You had certain feelings about him, and feelings about the situation you were in—and those feelings shifted over time and you acted on them. That is not a criminal act. There are people who are doing *actual* sick things all the time."

"Right," she said. It wasn't convincing.

While Zoey caught up with her friends from high school, I ambled into Celeste's bathroom. I examined myself in the mirror, like no one actually does unless they're drunk or fully succumbing to self-pity. I wasn't the only guy at the shower, it had turned out. There was another gay guy, Cole, who of course I had waved at but not spoken to yet. We had met probably six times at various Celeste events, but we rarely actually communicated. There was a smattering of women there who I knew well enough to remember where they worked and which neighborhood they lived in, and with whom I had almost the exact same five-minute conversation every time I saw them.

There was a knock on the bathroom door, which was even more startling than it should have been.

"It's me."

I opened the door and let Zoey in. "What are you *doing*?" she said.

"I feel like I look gross. My face is—doesn't it look *fuller*? You know it does."

"No comment."

I stretched my cheeks out and then released them. "I think I look worse since I quit my job. Shouldn't it be the opposite? My skin, like, *breaks out* now. Like it did in high school."

Zoey squeezed past me and sat down on the edge of the bathtub. I had brought in a plastic cup filled with white wine, which I picked up from the sink.

"Do you remember when you tried to set me up with that guy you worked with? The tall swimmer guy?"

"Lincoln! Of course." She continued, "Did I tell you he just moved to Mexico City? He left Selah and totally pivoted and became a personal trainer. His body is *insane* now. Even more insane."

It was strange these fleeting moments when, so suddenly, I would feel intensely distant from her. Something as insignificant as her riff on a guy I'd gone on one date with.

I went to sit next to her on the bathtub. "I've been having dreams about Oliver."

"Here we go." She looked at my cup. "Are you sure you should be drinking?"

"Yes."

"Sexual dreams?"

"Yeah."

She looked amused. "You're going to be mad."

"What?"

"I had a sex dream about Tom the other night." The ends of her mouth curled a bit. But then she looked despondent. "It probably doesn't mean anything."

"Yeah, I don't think it does. Dreams don't always mean . . . things."

"Wise words."

"But I guess it's still interesting . . . that our subconscious isn't moving on."

"Well, it hasn't been that long. For either of us. It's a process."

She leaned back and turned on the faucet in the bathtub so that water started to trickle. She kicked her shoes off and swiveled on the edge of the tub so her feet were positioned underneath the stream.

"This isn't, like, Walden fucking Pond, Zoey."

She laughed. "No, it definitely isn't."

Since we'd arrived at the shower, it felt like she was in her own bubble that I couldn't quite penetrate.

"They're about to do a 'guess the baby's weight' game," she said. "Do you think we can sneak out without anyone noticing?"

She looked away from me and turned the faucet to let more water out. I reached out and touched her shoulder and she flinched.

"What are you doing?"

"I was just trying to be a gentle and sensitive friend!"

"When has that literally ever been—"

There was a knock on the door. "Hello?"

"Oh, it's just me and Victor!"

Celeste opened the door and peeked in. She glared at us. "What is going on?"

Zoey turned off the water. She slid back around on the edge of the tub, though without any urgency.

"We're doing nothing."

Celeste looked as if she might have reached a breaking point, as if years of minor resentments toward Zoey had culminated in this moment. Or maybe I was just imputing this onto her. "We're about to play the guessing game," she said. "So . . ."

Zoey nodded but didn't move from her perch. Celeste didn't seem to be addressing me at all. Maybe I was invisible. I was relieved that my presence at the guessing game was apparently not mandatory.

Celeste opened the door a little wider. "Hey, if this is all too much for you . . . I totally understand." She was still only addressing Zoey.

After a pause, Zoey erupted in laughter. It was unnerving, but I greatly enjoyed how it seemed to upset Celeste.

"Seriously," Celeste continued. "I know you hate stuff like this to begin with, and then coming off everything with Tom, I just . . ."

"I'm good, Celeste. I wouldn't be here if I wasn't!"

Celeste nodded tentatively and closed the door.

Zoey sighed and glanced at me, and we both smiled wearily.

The door immediately reopened, and Celeste was now joined by her friend Brooke, who had told me once I was "so rude, in a hilarious way" when I called a girl at a bar "Budget Angelina Jolie." Brooke had bleached blond hair and was wearing a tight fuchsia jumpsuit with a chunky white belt: the kind of woman who clearly engages with Hailey Bieber's social-media content.

Brooke looked deeply distressed. "Hey, *did either of you* see a small charm bracelet anywhere? It has a *B* and an *L* hanging off it."

For some reason I responded to this immediately and with great authority. "No, we haven't, Brooke. I'm really, really sorry."

Brooke stared at me, somewhat accusingly. "We can't find it anywhere."

"Well, we don't have it in the bathtub," Zoey said sharply.

Brooke cracked a slight grimace, which—it was shocking how quickly this happened—shifted into a pitying smile. "By the way, Zoey, I was *so* sorry to hear about you and Tom."

Zoey glanced at Celeste, and a charge passed between them that I couldn't quite parse. She then shifted her gaze to Brooke. "Thank you so much, Brooke. I'm doing great."

They closed the door, and Zoey wailed: "*Jesus!*"

"Well, you said you wished people would acknowledge it."

"Not *her*."

I stuck my finger in my plastic cup and lapped up the last few droplets of the cheap pinot grigio. There was a frightening compulsion to my drinking at events like this.

"We've both recently lost men who were important to us."

Zoey shifted her weight so she was basically straddling the edge of the tub now. I moved onto the bathroom floor and sat cross-legged, looking up at her.

"Victor, it's a little different," she said. "Yours is dead."

"But you were *married* to yours. So it evens out."

"This is really weird. I don't want to compare them."

I tried to laugh. "You know me. It always has to be a competition."

"Have you talked much with your parents about Oliver?"

"My mom wanted to discuss it a lot at the beginning. Or, well, she more just wanted to tell me how she reacted when my dad left us."

"At least it sounds like she's trying."

"And of course, Warren and I have not talked about it directly, but he forwarded me some article from Harvard Divinity School about grief."

"That's sweet."

"I guess. And then my dad . . . obviously I never even told him about Oliver to begin with."

I started to tear at the edge of the plastic cup, pulling off small pieces.

"This is so funny," Zoey said.

"What is?"

"I'm divorced. You're out of work. We're hiding in the bathroom."

"I'm not *out of work*."

"You know what I mean."

Zoey and I reentered the party and went to refill our cups. My head bobbed as I scanned the texts from Thad The Graphic Designer she was showing me. "Isn't he cute?" she said. "He isn't aloof and, you know, the kind of guy who sulks by himself in the corner at a party. You know? He's the guy buzzing around the room, telling stories, having fun, meeting people."

"Is that what *you're* like at parties?"

"I mean, no. Not always. But that's why I like that he's like that."

I had restrained myself from disparaging Tom since their split. It felt like it would be cruel, unnecessary. She knew how I felt about him. There had been an unspoken acknowledgment from the first time I met him.

Cole, the "other" gay guy, approached the drinks table. He tapped Zoey on the shoulder. "*Hey!*"

Zoey overdid a whole welcoming shimmy, which led to a hug. "Hi babe!"

He then looked at me, raising his cup of red wine. "What's up, Victor?"

With no explanation, Zoey stumbled away from the two of us toward Brooke and Celeste. Cole and I were silent for a few beats before he asked, "So, having fun?"

"Oh yeah—it's like we're in a *Fast and the Furious* movie up here."

He laughed way too forcefully at this, which I hated to admit made me feel good.

"I know, I know," he said. "These baby showers are always a little funny for . . . us."

"Yeah, I guess they are."

He looked down and then back up to make eye contact, and I felt self-conscious, ungainly. He was very handsome, and his hair was gelled in a way that seemed foreign to me, where the hair itself appeared immobile but also, I imagined, if I were to run my hand through it, it'd be smooth and wet. I never actively felt sexual interest in these attractive-and-they-know-it guys like Cole, but I was so desperate for any form of validation that I wanted to see if it was possible that they might be interested in me . . . which somehow manifested itself in my flirting, inelegantly, to see if they were . . . and then feeling badly when they clearly *weren't*, all when I hadn't even been into them in the first place. As ever, I was the manufacturer of my own distress.

I hadn't slept with anyone since Oliver died. And with each passing week that I didn't, I felt more and more like a grieving widow, the sort of elder celebrity who would appear in a *Daily Mail* article described with words like "stoic" and "wearied" and "beleaguered."

Cole was now detailing for me his feelings about Doja Cat, and how he justified listening to her music even though he found her to be problematic ("You write about, like, pop culture, right?" was all he had used as a transition to the topic). I nodded along and finished another glass of wine; I was churning through them. Now that I didn't actually work at *Corridor*, I felt somewhat phony, even pathetic, when I spoke in a "professional" manner, citing Spotify streaming numbers or expanding on Doja Cat's "personal brand," as if I were rambling to a cafeteria attendant in a senior center.

I rejoined Zoey, who was talking to Brooke alone now. There was a tension between them, and when I draped my arm around Zoey, jovially, she didn't acknowledge me.

"I had no idea," Brooke was saying. "Oh Jesus."

"Yeah, yeah." Zoey was nodding vigorously. "It's hard for me to process it all now, even, but—yeah."

"Did anyone go with you to—for the actual . . . ?"

"No, I just wanted to get it done."

I felt like I should back away, but it was too uncomfortable to do so at this point, my arm around her—plus, maybe Zoey would want me there? Unsure what to do, I nodded in a performative solemn manner, which I was immediately sure was the least helpful way I could have acted in the moment.

Zoey was swaying a bit, nervously I assumed, causing her dress to billow and then grow still again—she had been a dancer in college, and I always wondered why she had stopped after graduating. I took my arm off her shoulder.

"I'm so sorry for everything you've . . ." Brooke looked close to tearful. "Obviously, so many people we all know have dealt with—*I've* been in that situation, too. And to have the relationship issues on top of it . . . I feel for you, Zoey." Brooke glanced at me.

"I appreciate that, Brooke, thank you." Zoey spun to the right and then back again. "Anyway, we're at a baby shower. This definitely is not the time to be discussing this."

Brooke nodded. "So did—do you talk to Tom now?"

"No, no . . . I think he's dating some editor at the *New York Review of Books*. Something like that. She's—she's cute—right, Victor?"

"I mean, she's fine." What was I supposed to say?

"She's fine, quoth the journalist. But yeah, I do text with him actually, now and then. I texted him when I made the decision to leave Selah, since I knew he'd be surprised. And he commented on a random post of mine when I went to Italy. I don't know. It's all stupid." Zoey had told me she was planning to leave her job and "start her own thing," but we hadn't discussed it recently and this was the first time I had heard her put it in these terms.

Zoey finished off her drink, and continued, "Isn't it so fucking weird that you can *divorce* someone but then still see their Instagram posts of, like, the tree outside their dumb Airbnb in Maine?"

Brooke frowned. "Life these days can be very complicated," she said, pulling at her chunky white belt.

Both Zoey and I nodded with extreme seriousness at this.

"You two are lucky," Brooke continued, looking from Zoey to me. "It's so cute that, you know . . . I see the stuff you guys put up and I always think, like, *I'm happy they have each other*."

I wasn't sure how to take this entirely—it wasn't exactly delivered like a compliment—but Zoey responded by taking a step away from me and then fixing her gaze right at me like a laser. "Yes, I'm a lucky gal." For whatever reason, I still didn't feel like I knew what to say.

Zoey and I moved to the couch, where we positioned ourselves facing each other; the shower was winding down. Of course, despite our stated intentions, we were among the last ones there.

Zoey's neck had broken out in splotches of red. My head was throbbing slightly, as if happily drunk and also already hungover at the same time.

"Thad wants us to meet him at this bar, but it's so *far* from here."

"I can't deal with Thad right now."

"Oh my god, you *hate* Thad. How did I not realize that until now?"

"I do not hate him! I have only met him like twice."

"You hate everyone you meet, though. At the beginning."

"Yeah, that's true." I paused. "Though I didn't hate Oliver at the beginning."

"You did!" she said. "I distinctly remember you telling me after your first real date that you thought he was 'fake-smart' and 'boring' and that 'people only respected his opinions because they thought he was hot.'"

I jabbed her shoulder with my finger. "I never said any of that! Don't speak ill of the dead."

"Oh please. You're a lying motherfucker." I loved hearing Zoey swear. "You lie, lie, lie. All the time."

"Would you say—do you think of me as a good person?"

She brushed her hair out of her face.

"You're seriously asking me that?"

"Yes," I said. "I want to know."

"I don't know what I would say to that. Is anyone a good person?"

"Yes. There are definitely good people. *We* don't know any of them. But they exist."

"Okay. I guess I would say . . . you are a good person to me. Does that suffice?"

I liked that answer.

Over the past few years—the entirety of the Tom-and-Zoey era, I suppose—I had gradually stopped sharing as much with Zoey. I had closed myself off, sequestered myself. I could see that now. It just started to feel pointless, a waste of our time spent together, to explain convoluted plot developments in my life that would require necessary context. I didn't feel as eager to divulge. It was easier to just gossip about our friends and co-workers. Or ask her questions.

Zoey suddenly shifted in her seat, reaching under her leg. "Oh my god." She pulled out a shiny bracelet from the crack in the sofa. "Do you think—isn't this Brooke's?"

It was definitely Brooke's. There was a *B* and there was an *L*.

"Celeste!" Zoey shouted, and Celeste and her friend Molly looked up from the other end of the room. Celeste scurried over, and Zoey held up the bracelet with an outstretched hand. Zoey looked like she had tears in her eyes. I looked closer and she actually did; she had tears in her eyes.

Celeste took the bracelet from her. "I can't believe you found it. Brooke already left, but she is going to fucking die." She petted Zoey's head. "You're an angel."

I got up to get another drink from the makeshift bar, which at this point was comprised of just three already-used plastic cups and half a bottle of pinot grigio.

———

Zoey got in an Uber to meet up with Thad. I spotted Cole and Molly standing by the bodega at the end of the block, and I walked toward them. I felt like a ghost.

"Waiting for your *ride?*" I said to Cole, ignoring Molly.

He looked up at me, startled. "Oh, uh, yeah," he said, curt, before turning back to Molly. It was very cold now and I was shivering in my Goop sweatshirt and I felt incapable of desiring or being desired.

I thought I'd feel this great surge of confidence after I left the magazine—like a superhero leaping out of the building and taking flight. Instead, now I felt, well, like a ghost. A ghost who continued to stew and dwell, to yearn for things and to hold himself back—which, of course, had all been the case before, too. Now there was just more time to contemplate; there was less to distract. No Slack notifications, fewer parties, less drama. I'd told people I would travel, finally write the script I'd been talking about forever, take on "fun" freelance assignments, spend more time with friends and family. And to some extent, I'd done those things. So why did I feel distress, a tinge of panic, when I arrived at Celeste's baby shower, or a dinner party, or lunch with an acquaintance? Why did I still look up my former co-workers' Instagram posts late at night? Why *hadn't* I moved to the Irish countryside for six months? Maybe the distress would always be there, no matter where I was living or what answer I had when someone at a party asked what I did for work.

I realized now that, in the past, when I was working at *Corridor*, the one solace I had was that I was always in possession of a tale to tell. There were always things *happening to me*—plots for me to detail to others. It didn't matter whom I was talking to: I could provide them with entertainment. Now, I felt bereft.

I had hoped I would gain strength and power from my independence, from my lack of any affiliation. Maybe that would happen at some point—but for right now, it just felt like a loss.

Cole and Molly's car pulled up to the bodega, and they hopped in. I decided it was time to call one for myself. After a few minutes of waiting for a Tesla, I received a notification from Uber that my ride had been canceled.

But instead of reopening the app to order another one, I went into my contacts and texted Oliver, for the first time since the day after he'd died: My ride was canceled, Oliver. What am I supposed to do?

23

Zoey

Zoey checked her phone. She had three missed calls from Victor. Even now, at this point, that was enough to cause concern. She excused herself from Altro Paradiso; she was eating with a reporter from the *Washington Post* and the reporter's publicist friend, who was in the midst of telling them an involved story about Lauren Sánchez.

She leaned against a wall outside the restaurant and took a deep breath before calling Victor. "Hey, what's up? I'm at a dinner meeting. I just stepped out." It was warm out for early spring.

"You and your *dinner meetings*." She didn't like this as an opening line.

"Is everything okay?"

"Yeah, I'm just kind of drunk. And I was walking by that concert *hall* in the East Village where Oliver and I saw Modest Mouse. Remember when I was in that phase?"

That "phase" was very difficult for Zoey to recall. She was wearing wide-leg pants and a fitted blazer at the moment. In so many facets of her life, recently, she was feeling like a much more assured version of herself. She didn't like memories. When various apps on her phone resurfaced images from years ago, she felt viscerally uncomfortable. Often, these photos would feature Tom, but somehow that

bothered her even less than when she was confronted with old photos of herself.

"Hey, can I call you back later?" she asked.

"You don't have *time* for me anymore."

"Are you serious? You're the only person I *do* have time for. We were
just at Celeste's shower together."

"Which you immediately left to go see *Thad*."

It didn't make sense to argue when he was in this sort of state. She
and Victor had stayed until the very end of the shower; there was nothing immediate about her departure. She knew Victor knew this, too.

"Would you say I am *repressing* my feelings about Oliver's death?"

"God. Victor. I—no. I feel like you have been grieving and . . .
grappling with it. It seems close to what I would have expected."

"*An expected amount of grieving* . . . I feel like Betty Draper sometimes."

"So that means Oliver is Don now? Don Draper if he died?"

"Yeah, he's Don Draper if he was dead."

"How much did you have to drink? What did you even do tonight?"

It suddenly occurred to her she didn't know what Victor did most
weeknights, especially since he'd left his job. Or what he did with his
weekdays, either, really. She knew he was writing for a few different
outlets now, but she did not have any sense of his routine. Sometimes
she'd get a flurry of texts from him at 2:03 a.m. (I'm playing pool at this
guy's apartment!). One Wednesday morning he sent her a picture from
a diner in Hudson, New York: randomly in Hudson this week, he wrote.

"Are you still outside your work dinner?"

"It's fine. I can talk. It's with a potential COO for my new thing."
The meeting wasn't with a potential COO—though she was going to
be meeting with one later in the week. Zoey wasn't sure why she had
lied.

"Look at you—my little exec . . . Anyway, yeah, I had three vodka sodas. Maybe four. And then some wine. I was on a date. The guy came out when he was 34. He's 36 now. He kept scratching his elbow really intensely. Like, whenever I asked him a question, he would instinctively reach for his elbow, and scratch it really hard. It was tough to focus on anything else."

"That feels like a lot to drink on a first date."

"Thank you, headmaster! What happened to us being hot-mess best friends?"

"Victor, neither of us was ever a hot mess. At least not in the way you mean."

Zoey no longer had a strong urge to go back inside to her dinner. She sat down on a bench and watched as a pair of female best friends walked past her, arms linked, both in chic black coats.

"I will have to consider that point more thoroughly," Victor said. "You know what I was contemplating recently? Do you think—you're not going to *like* this question—but do you think we would be friends now—like, if we met now, for the first time, would we become friends?"

Zoey answered quickly. "I think so? I mean, we both hate basically everyone who isn't us. We still tolerate each other, which has to count for something."

"Isn't it weird neither of us really—we have co-workers and people we really like, but neither of us has another *person*."

"Well, I had Tom."

"That's different."

"You had Oliver."

"Same. Also different. And even your friends from high school like Celeste—you don't even like them even though they're your friends."

"I think we're both distrusting and generally sort of . . . we like to do our own thing." She paused. "Turtles, right?"

"You think we're distrusting?"

"I guess what I mean is it takes work to get to know us."

"I don't know, though. I feel like if you and I met now for the first time we'd both . . ." Victor trailed off.

"Both what?"

"I think there is a lot we both overlook. You kind of have to do that with your friends you've had forever."

"I don't know if I agree with that."

The *Washington Post* reporter was now peering out from the door of the restaurant. *Is everything okay?* she mouthed. Zoey almost responded, *It's impossible to answer that question!* But instead she just nodded, and the reporter went back inside.

"Are you still nervous I'm going to kill myself?" Victor asked. "Is that something you think about?"

"Oh my god, Victor. I'm exhausted."

"I know. I'm a mess. But can you answer?"

"I mean, I don't know . . . maybe in an abstract sense, I think about it sometimes. Every now and then you'll say something . . . But no, I'm not actually, palpably nervous. It's not an everyday concern for me."

"I think—after Oliver died, I can't do it . . . I'm going to *choose life*. If I killed myself now, it would be, like, Romeo-and-Juliet vibes."

"You're insane. Actually."

"Zoey, I'm sorry."

"For what specifically?"

"For what specifically! Funny."

"Okay, I'm going back inside. I'm being rude. And I—"

"Are you even really at a dinner?"

"Of course I'm really at a dinner!"

There was a long pause and she almost thought he had hung up.

"Do I annoy you? Be honest."

"You're annoying me now, yes. Victor, I have to go. My chicken is just sitting there."

"But *do I annoy you, Zoey?*"

"What are you getting at? Say what you mean."

"*I hate my life*, Zoey. That's the subtext of everything I am saying to you right now. My life has nothing in it. You know it's hard for me to say things outright. I never do it. It's worth trying, right?"

"Where are you? Do you need me to come to you?"

"No, no. No."

"What are you doing right now?"

"I am like . . . crouched down on the sidewalk. I took my shoes off. I'm outside a CAVA."

"You don't sound like yourself right now. Your voice sounds weird and gravelly. I'm gonna come find you . . . Victor? Are you there? *Your shoes off*?"

"Yeah. Yes."

"I think you need to get a real job again . . . Victor? Hello?"

"Fuck you!"

"Did you take anything tonight? Drugs, I mean."

"Fuck you again!"

"Victor, I feel like we're running into a wall here. If you're going to just wallow and feel sorry for yourself and not give me any information . . . At a certain point . . . I have to protect myself, too."

"What are you trying to say?"

"Listen, you're not giving me much to work with here. You can't just close yourself off and push everyone away. You have already pushed away so many—I mean, your family, your friends. Who's going to be left? You have to do something—to make some choice to, you know, actively make your life better. I can only do so much."

"Well maybe I *should* just kill myself, then."

"You don't mean that. Don't say that. You *just* told me you weren't going to do that. This is exactly what I'm talking about—this isn't productive. This is cruel. I can't support you on my own when you're—this just isn't fair."

"I agree. You're right. I'm really sorry, Zoey. I'm sorry."

"I can leave this dinner, Victor."

"No, it's okay. Please." He sounded more coherent to her now. "I wouldn't want to ruin your whole night. You've got your *professional obligations.*"

Later Zoey would feel like that was the turning point. The way he said "professional obligations." But in the moment, she somehow remained engaged and positive. "Have you thought about—I don't know—Lexapro?"

"Lexapro, Zoey? Why don't you go throw yourself at some boring bearded man and leave me alone?"

"What are you even talking about? I am hanging up now. I don't need to take this. I'm not *trained* in this. You're actually being mean. At a certain point, you know, I have to say *enough*. I have been astoundingly patient. I think we need some time just . . . not talking quite so . . . This conversation is deeply upsetting to me. I am sure you understand that on some level. I am sure when you wake up tomorrow morning you are going to understand that."

There was a long period of silence. It felt like minutes.

"You're right. I do understand. I don't know what I'm saying. I'm sorry. I love you."

"I'm hanging up. Text me when you get back to your place, okay?"

"Okay."

24

The Maddie Brooks Podcast—Transcript

Maddie: Hello, freaks! Surprise—it's Maddie Brooks. Once again. The one and only. Welcome to another episode of *The Maddie Brooks Show. We have fun here*. Darren, we still really need to figure out that slogan. It's been a placeholder for months now.

Darren: You say that about the slogan . . . every episode.

Maddie: Yes. And I mean it every time. Now, we've been telling you guys that it's important to us—we're making a very conscious effort to . . . branch out a bit with our guests on the podcast. We hear you. I read the comments. We know we've had one too many *influencers* on in a row.

Darren: I didn't mind it.

Maddie: Of course you didn't. They're all 23-year-old hotties who wear like two pieces of lettuce over their tits. Anyway, we are trying to get cultured over here—I'm a cultured woman—and I am proud to announce that this week we have a full-fledged *author* on the show. And I loved her book. I *related* to this book. It's rare I read something in this present climate that actually permeates my icy exterior and lodges itself in there and burns hot. I hate everything.

Darren: I did not read the book, for the record.

Maddie: Okay, that's fucking annoying to say, Darren. Don't say that right before we're about to start the interview. Riley, can we turn off his mic? Riley, our producer, you can't hear her—but let me tell you, she is nodding vigorously and agreeing with me right now. I am going to turn off your mic, Darren, if you don't shut the fuck up.

Darren: Don't worry. I will only speak when spoken to, madam.

Maddie: All right, then. Let's reset. I am so thrilled to have Caroline Stevens on with us today. Her debut novel, *Sparkling Day*, came out last week, and it's so immersive and bizarre and specific—and there is a crazy twist, which I absolutely adored. Caroline, thank you so much for being here. Also, before we even start, I have to say, I love your whole . . . you're dressed like a sexy corporate executive, kind of. It's, like, The Row meets sex worker somehow.

Caroline: Okay, can we stop the interview here? That is such a major compliment. And thank you so much for having me on. I am extremely honored. I love all of your content.

Maddie: Thank you! What are any of us defined by at this point if not our content?

Caroline: Exactly.

Maddie: Also, I'd like to state for the record, I am very into the way you're sitting. You're giving off an almost . . . I want to say, catlike energy. And also, listeners, yes, she's wearing this incredibly sharp, chic outfit—*she's rocking the loose blazer, honey*—but then she *also* has on . . . these adorable little purple frilly socks. I covet them.

Caroline: Oh my god, these socks . . . they're so dorky.

Maddie: You can pull it off. Oh my god, Darren is, like, getting turned on by this right now.

Darren: Can I say something?

Maddie: No. Okay, Caroline, so I devoured your book in an afternoon. Just could not put it down. It was like gorging on French fries.

Caroline: I am so glad to hear that. I . . . I guess I am still just getting used to the fact that anyone has read it. It's only been out a week. So just the idea that you have actually read it is crazy to me.

Maddie: Did you always—were you always like, *I am going to write a novel*?

Caroline: Well . . . I don't know. I don't think so, actually. I was freelancing for a while. I wrote for magazines and journals. And I was doing a lot of brand work and other jobs to pay the bills. I was . . . I don't know, I think on some subconscious level I felt like something was missing, like I wanted to dive into a really huge overwhelming creative project that I could lose myself in and just, like, find myself through that. So I think this is a circuitous way of answering your question: yes, on some level, maybe my *soul* always wanted to write a book, even if my head wasn't aware of that. This guy I'm—my friend, Otto Young, he mostly lives in Berlin now—but he always used to say to me, "You're going to write a real *story* someday, kid." Yes, he speaks like he's in an Old Hollywood movie, just in normal conversation. Anyway, so, I guess some people did. Did think I might.

Maddie: It's funny. When I was reading it I was trying to figure out . . . The main girl, the main character, she just reminds me of so many girls I have come across in the city. I used to have this, I wouldn't even call her a *friend*, I'm not going to use her real name . . . but she was someone very much in my life, let's say. And I was thinking about her a lot when

I was reading your book. Was your character—Ella, right? Was Ella based on a real person you know?

Caroline: It's so funny. I've noticed that—maybe because of what Ella in the book ends up doing, or turning into, I feel like people aren't—no one actually has asked me, really, point-blank, "Is this based on one specific person?" Even though it kind of is!

Maddie: Wait, let's back up. God, I'm always so chaotic with these interviews. I'm like, *we haven't even said what the book is about yet*! Super quick synopsis: the book follows this—would you call her depressed?

Caroline: Yes, I think so. Or maybe "chronically lonely"?

Maddie: Cool. Chronically lonely girl. In her mid-twenties. She lives with her freaky—really twisted, really creepy—brother. It turns out her brother is into some fucked up sexual stuff, too—I want to ask you about that later. But Ella and the brother are just sort of on their own— their parents died and left them this gorgeous apartment in Midtown. And then Ella kind of figures out all these ways to meet, well, hot people. Or, I guess, glamorous and interesting and quote-unquote famous people across the city . . .

Caroline: Yeah, she realizes it's easier than you'd think it'd be to trick interesting people into becoming friends with her. So she creates, essentially, all these different personas, until ultimately she loses track of them all and—god, I was about to fully just spoil the end of the book.

Maddie: Go for it. No one cares about spoilers anymore. We're all too jaded and impatient.

Caroline: Okay, she kills herself.

Maddie: And you know, I was expecting *something* demented to happen, but on some level her schemes were all sort of . . . going so smoothly that I—? I thought maybe you were making a point about how easy it is to fake being a completely different person nowadays? And never getting caught.

Caroline: That's really interesting. Let me think about that.

Maddie: I don't mean that as an insult or anything. Obviously. I really appreciated where you took it.

Caroline: Of course, of course. No, yeah. You know, it's funny. When I started writing the book, I think I actually did imagine it was going to end up somewhere closer to what you're saying, that she would end up on top. When I was first pitching this, people would bring up Anna Delvey or Elizabeth Holmes—obviously they were both operating at a completely different magnitude than Ella is—but I think, and maybe this is an unpopular opinion, but I feel like even though they both had their fall from grace . . . they were both still kind of folk heroes, or whatever, in this strange way.

Maddie: Oh yeah, totally. I mean, I have thirty different photos of each of them saved in my phone. And only semi-ironically.

Caroline: Right? I feel like there's this subset that was like "yas, queen!" about those two . . . Though I'm obviously not trying to say that *you're* saying "yas, queen!"

Maddie: You can say that. Say anything you want about me.

Caroline: You know what I mean . . . With some of these scam artists, I feel like there's this sentiment on social media of: "They took advantage of this corrupt system and scammed people, fuck yeah!" I guess with Ella, I wanted to create someone who maybe was never happy or satisfied in life and became this more . . . low-level, middling scammer, and then it just kind of crashed and burned and she lost her life and there is nothing "sexy" about her story.

Maddie: At certain points it felt to me like she was . . . *getting off* on the people she was coercing into these friendships or transactional relationships. In a sexual way almost? She had this sort of obsession with a lot of them that verged on the erotic—at least that's how I read it.

Caroline: Yeah. Maybe. Maybe.

Maddie: [*laughter*] It feels like you're judging me. Darren, Caroline's giving me a look, isn't she?

Caroline: Oh my god, not at all. No! I am so not.

Darren: I feel like you don't actually want me to weigh in here, Mad.

Maddie: You're right, I don't. So, Caroline, you're this, maybe this is a blunt way of putting it, but . . . you're very pretty, striking . . . I've known you for two seconds, but I can tell you're well-adjusted and basically normal.

Caroline: That's very kind of you, but actually I'm a true psychopath.

Maddie: Me too, by the way. I guess it's just intriguing to me: How did you get *here*, to writing this intense, dark story?

Caroline: Yeah, well, I was living with a boyfriend when I started writing this book, and now we are no longer dating, if that gives you a sense of what pouring this story out of me did to my psyche. But yeah, I think there were moments rereading it where I was like, "Damn, Caroline. This is fucked up." Especially some of the Franklin stuff, her brother. Does it make me sound totally terrifying if I tell you it was almost easier to write that stuff than some of the other sections?

Maddie: Only slightly! No, I'm kidding. I get it. But wait, I'm dying to know . . . I want the full download on who this girl is. The inspiration. Who gave you the idea for this?

Caroline: You know, I haven't really talked about this at all. This is—this feels weird. But uh—I won't say her name, but I got an Instagram message from a girl who said she had a line of necklaces, and she was, you know, reaching out to see if I wanted to model for her, wear a few lockets in some pictures. Just, you know, for free, as a favor. I was in kind of a weird headspace at the time. I don't know what compelled me to—maybe it was this guy I was living with—

Maddie: Wait, now that you're saying this, I feel like this girl might have messaged me too! Oh my god. When you said "line of necklaces," you hit a nerve.

Caroline: She probably did! That's hilarious. Anyway, I'm an idiot and I go there, to her apartment, and it turns out, I won't get into all the details of it, but it wasn't . . . she wasn't really selling the necklaces. I found out afterward that it was all a ruse, just for her to, like, meet me and take some pictures of me in the jewelry. I still don't really know what she *wanted*, what her motives were, deep down. I think I remember she was making little comments about my face and asking about my skin-care routine and style, and, I don't know, I guess maybe there were signs I was missing that something was up. My mom is Brazilian, and I think I thought at first maybe she was from Brazil and wanted to connect about that? She lied about having a husband, or boyfriend, who owned the apartment; I remember finding that out. I never saw the photos she took of me.

Maddie: This whole dynamic you're describing, that energy, it's reminding me so much of Hannah. My friend I was talking about before. Fuck, we're going to have to edit out her name later. Or I'll leave it in. We'll see.

Caroline: Wow, I guess this is a more . . . universal situation than I realized! But yeah. I—I am as confused about it now as I was then.

Maddie: So you walked out of her apartment and you were like, "This is going to be a *character* for me . . ."

Caroline: You know, I'm not sure it was so immediate or obvious as that, where it struck me that—that that would be something I would want to do. She did call me to apologize, which I found actually very sweet at the time. But, I—you know, Ella, in the book, is obviously way more . . . there's a lot more going on there, her as a character. It's darker. She is a way more extreme version than the real-life—than she was in real life. But I do think, for whatever reason, that whole series of events that happened, it really did stick with me.

Maddie: Have you spoken to her since?

Caroline: No, no, we haven't spoken. But I do feel like it is possible she'll read the book. I guess I almost feel like she definitely will? Especially when she sees what it's about.

Maddie: What do you hope is—as you may know, I've got a few writing projects in the works myself. I have a TV show that's been in development for a very long time.

Caroline: Oh, that's amazing. So cool. Yeah. I didn't know that.

Maddie: Oh, okay. Thank you. But anyway, I guess I am curious just, what do you want someone reading the book to . . . what do you hope they text their friend after finishing it? What's the takeaway?

Caroline: I love that question. Let me think.

Darren: Good question, Maddie.

Maddie: Oh my god, I *completely* forgot you were here. It was so nice.

Caroline: You two are so funny. Hm, you know, I feel like sometimes we, as humans, have sort of unexpected reactions to things. Oh god, I sound like the most idiotic—*Humans respond to things unexpectedly sometimes! Amazing insight, Caroline!* But after Otto—my friend—after he read a first draft of the novel, he texted me he thought the book was "a delight." I was like, "Excuse me? *Delight?* The girl kills herself." But I do feel like sometimes a story that supposedly ticks all the boxes and is marketed as "inspiring" or "hopeful" or whatever, ends up making me feel like shit when I actually consume it. And then vice versa. Am I making sense? Have you ever gone to an uplifting happy movie and just wanted to, like, hang yourself after? I feel like that happens to me all the time.

Maddie: Are you serious? One hundred percent. I remember as a kid watching some cheesy—oh, maybe it was *Rocky?*

Caroline: The boxing *Rocky?*

Maddie: Yeah, I made my parents turn it off halfway through because I found it disturbing. It bothered me that I could sense you were *supposed* to be inspired by it—I hated being told anything when I was kid. Told how to feel. My parents were like, "We're bringing her to a therapist *stat.*"

Darren: I call bullshit on that story.

Maddie: Darren, I'm going to actually ruin your life.

Caroline: Yeah, I mean . . . I think sometimes, for me, when I read or see or ingest things that are deeply troubling or messed up or *upsetting*— that's when I want to, I don't know, confess my love for someone or make a big important decision or go live in a new country.

Maddie: Wow, you're—*this* is like therapy right now. So what you're basically saying is—?

Caroline: Reading this weird little unhinged book of mine might make you feel numb and despondent . . . or feel euphoric and great. We're all impossible to predict.

Maddie: I love the chaos of this conversation we're having. All our episodes end up turning into this. I can't help it.

Caroline: You know, I've really been trying to embrace chaos lately. My life was really—I mean, it was maybe always chaotic to some small minor degree, that I was keeping repressed, basically. But now it's just full-blown chaotic, and it's great. And I guess on some level I have Ella to thank for that. So, you know, in the end, it all worked out as it was supposed to, and I have her to thank.

25

Zoey

Zoey closed her eyes in the back seat of the Uber from Heathrow to her hotel. She was meeting Wiles for a drink at 8 p.m., and she was cutting it close.

She was ostensibly in London for a *British Vogue*–sponsored fashion conference, scheduled to speak on a panel about the "intersection" of social media and fast fashion. But she probably would have turned down the invite if it wasn't for the opportunity it provided to see Wiles.

They had not seen each other in about a year and a half, but they emailed occasionally, and she would text him links now and then—sometimes with only the loosest pretense (an op-ed about the royal family, once, for example). She wasn't entirely clear why she still thought about him regularly, since she felt fairly certain she wasn't interested in him romantically. But she realized she must have deeper feelings about Wiles when it dawned on her how little she had shared about him with Victor.

She had never told Victor that Wiles asked if she had a boyfriend at their first meeting, or that he was the first person to push her to start her own company. And she definitely didn't tell him that Wiles once sent her a picture of himself, shirtless on a beach, with the caption Come to Portofino!

Since splitting from Tom, Zoey had embarked on a spree of flings—though, if she was being honest, it was not quite the anything-goes debauchery she had been anticipating. She immediately dated Thad, the graphic designer, who was sweet but obsessive. She then started seeing a 45-year-old former indie-band drummer for two months (they met on Raya). She slept with a college friend who texted to get drinks when he was in town (he told her he'd "always thought she was super intimidating"). And she went on a few dates with a family friend her mom had been championing ("he went to Princeton" seemed to be his only attribute).

She didn't really *want* to sleep with Wiles, she didn't think, but she also knew she never would have planned this London trip if she were still married to Tom.

She looked at her phone and saw that Perri had texted her: I see you're on the roster for the British Vogue panel.

Perri had taken the news that Zoey was leaving to pursue her own venture surprisingly well. Zoey had been bracing for the worst when she went in to tell her; she even took half a Valium beforehand. But Perri had barely looked up from her laptop when Zoey said the words.

"I knew this would happen one day" was the closest Perri came to offering congratulations. "You can't take Louisa with you, you know," she added. "Or anyone else. You signed an agreement." Zoey nodded: "I know."

Zoey looked down at her phone in the Uber and wrote back to Perri: yes—are you in town??

She didn't feel like she was close to being Perri's *equal* yet—it wasn't so much the age difference that made Zoey still feel beneath her, but rather the sense of calm Perri emanated.

Zoey's confidence was growing, though, and she was aware that the shift was largely mental: she *believed* she was a confident person now. She was appearing on CNN fairly regularly at this point, contributing whenever there was a fashion-world story to weigh in on. She liked appearing on television more than she ever imagined she would, the practice of talking in sound bites. She liked that, even though her name appeared in the chyron when she was on television, even though it was literally her face being beamed out worldwide, the woman talking on camera felt like she had a personality distinct from Zoey's actual personality—distinct from her actual self and personhood—and in this sense, she didn't feel nervous about it at all.

"I can't believe you *do TV now*," Victor said to her one night, grinning mischievously, a few glasses of wine in. "You're an *on-camera personality*. My mom keeps texting me when she sees you on." He looked at her, and she could sense a subtle uneasiness.

Zoey walked into the hotel lobby to meet Wiles. He had buzzed his hair off almost completely and dyed what was remaining a dirty-blond color. He had gained about ten or fifteen pounds since she last saw him, and his cheeks had a bit of a red coloring to them now that she hadn't remembered.

Yet, in spite of all this, she thought when he stood up and smiled at her that he still looked pretty good.

"Well if it isn't my little girlboss," he said with a sneer as she sat down next to him.

"You look terrible," she said.

He laughed. "I know. I don't sleep anymore. It's taking a toll on me." He called the waitress over and ordered Zoey a drink.

"I'm sober now, by the way," he said. "Well, as of a few months ago."

For whatever reason, this made Zoey feel self-conscious about having dressed up, having put effort into her makeup.

"It's a short-term experiment," he added.

"Good for you," she said.

"So, you're doing the damn thing," he said. It didn't sound like something he would say. The waitress brought over a Manhattan and Zoey took a long sip.

"Yep, *Zoey Inc.*—we're still trying to figure out the name. It's going to be me and this woman Irina who used to be a creative director at Hearst—and then I have two other junior go-getter types."

"Well, I'm really happy for you." He sounded sincere. "You know I've been wanting this for you."

"Yeah, it's exciting. I wanted to start something that felt more . . . human to me. You know, *fashion for the girl who doesn't want to actually think about fashion.* I'm sick of all the pretension and jargon and snooti-ness in fashion."

"You tell them what they want, and they think they're coming up with it themselves."

"I don't know if that's how I'd put it. Our subscribers are going to tell us how they get ready in the morning, their astrological sign, that kind of thing—and then we start sending them stuff. I did consult with an old psych professor of mine; some of this definitely verges on . . . manipulating people. You're right about that."

"How's Perri taking it?"

"You'd know better than me."

"We haven't talked about it, actually."

Zoey smiled and took another sip of her drink. "I don't believe that." She looked down at her phone. "Speaking of." She had a text from Perri: Call me ASAP, plz. Zoey quickly finished the drink. "I can't escape," she said, holding up her phone to Wiles.

"No, she won't let you." He paused. "I see you on TV all the time these days. Even over here."

"Yeah, it's fun . . . I wasn't planning . . . well, you know me. Or you kind of know me. It's funny—Victor, my friend—he used to do TV hits all the time. I always felt like it was so ridiculous. Not that I told him that. But when I saw him on TV, I couldn't help but think that this was the guy I spent the weekends getting wasted and stumbling around town with—pouring beer on our heads or whatever . . . and then he'd be on some morning show the next day talking about the Grammys. But now, I'm the one going on and polishing myself up and pretending I know what I'm talking about."

"Don't be self-effacing," he said. "It doesn't suit you."

"Yeah. I know. Sorry." She hailed the waitress for another drink.

"You really look great," he said.

"Thanks. I—I wasn't *trying* to lose weight or anything, but when you start seeing yourself on TV all the time, you . . . you know. It just kind of happens."

"You used to wear so much—" He patted his forearms.

"Yeah, I don't do the jewelry anymore."

"And you're single now."

"How did you know that?"

"I know people. I heard you divorced the husband you never once mentioned to me."

"I told you I was dating someone! I distinctly remember that. In New York."

"You didn't exactly spell it out."

She smiled. "I was actually dating a new guy for a bit. After my divorce. Thad the graphic designer. But that ended recently. I don't really have time for dating, anyway." She checked her phone again, as if to underline the point.

Wiles shifted his weight in his seat and he placed his hand on her knee. She noticed the sweat accumulating at his temples. "It appears the timing is finally right for us." His accent was thicker as he said this—it almost sounded put on.

Before she could say anything in response—she was holding her breath, she realized—he removed his hand. "I'm just joking," he said. "We could never. Obviously."

She laughed. "Yeah, maybe when you were drinking, it would have made sense, but—" She immediately felt this was a really strange thing to have said. "Sorry, you know what I mean. I'm—I'm jet-lagged." She stood up. "I feel like I should go out and call Perri. I can't really focus when I know she's waiting for me."

Zoey navigated her way back outside—it was a brisk night in London—and she waited for Perri to answer the phone. She was pacing back and forth on the sidewalk, picking at the straps of her dress.

"Zoey," Perri said finally.

"Hi Perri. What's up?"

"The *New York Times* is writing a piece about me."

"Oh, that's great. Congratulations."

"No, not that kind of piece."

Zoey felt her heart beating quicker. She was glad she'd had a strong drink.

"You know Kiki . . . your former colleague."

"Of course I know Kiki."

"Well, she apparently called the *Times* up and told them I was a tyrannical boss, that I have treated people unjustly. She gave them all these anecdotes. God knows what she made up. You know she hardly did any work for me."

"She canceled on Steph's wedding the day before. I'll never forget that."

"What?"

"Never mind."

"Anyway, you know this is not in my nature, and I don't like to be in a vulnerable position, let's put it that way. But if you could . . . I think they got a few other people I worked with in the past—from my old job—to say I'm some monster. And they're using it to make a point about the changing of the guard in fashion. You know how they love to make things up. But I just wanted to give you a heads-up that they might be calling you. And I can't ask you to defend me on the record—I know you're out on your own now and probably don't want to get wrapped up in all this. But I wanted to, well, apprise you of the situation."

Zoey had never heard Perri this flustered. Or flustered at all. She felt an instinctive pang of sympathy for her—ultimately, in spite of all of Zoey's gripes, Perri had been good to her. Maybe it was easier for her to see that now that she wasn't working for her. Sure, Zoey had witnessed a number of incidents that others might classify as "microaggressions." Perri still hadn't promoted Louisa, three years in, even though she definitely deserved it. Perri was ultra-demanding. She once threw a plastic salad bowl at the wall in front of her. She was aggressively humorless. She expected everyone to work obsessively, and without appropriately calibrated salaries. And she definitely had "favorites." But she was not an *abuser*. Right? Was a full-on *New York Times* takedown really in order?

"Thanks for letting me know, Perri," Zoey said. "Let's talk soon." Zoey sounded eerily like her mother to herself when she said this.

"And Zoey—I—I guess I just want to say, finally, that I hope you remember how much I've supported you. The connections I gave you."

She felt a chill down her spine. "Yes, Perri. I'm very grateful. You know that."

"Just something to consider. And I've never brought this up before, but remember, I still gave you the promotion even though you never came through with that *Corridor* placement."

"I do remember that."

Zoey went back inside the lobby and saw Wiles texting and she almost just turned around. Instead, she sat down in the seat across from him. "I should probably head up to my room," she said. "I'm exhausted."

He put his phone down. "You haven't asked me to invest in *Zoey Inc.* yet, though."

"I'm not going to. We don't need investors right now. You know we have our Series A already. Plus, we're friends. I don't want to ruin that."

"We're not friends." He shook his head and then smiled. "I can't believe it. You don't need me anymore."

"When did I ever need you?" She could have ended it here, but instead added, "I hardly know you." She could picture Victor nodding approvingly, watching from the empty seat to her right.

Zoey's various worlds were in the process of collapsing, the ones that had defined her past decade, and she felt like she was extracting herself, out from the ruins. This collapse had been happening around her for some time, but she hadn't let herself see it—now, it felt exhilarating.

"That hurts, I must say," Wiles said. His button-down shirt was a size too small, she could see clearly now. He needed new shirts. She stood up and they kissed each other goodbye on the cheek.

"Not to make too much of it, but you wouldn't be where you are right at this moment if it wasn't for me," he said. "I gave you the push. You were a little girl when I met you."

"Wiles, please don't."

"Say whatever you want," he said, starting to move out of the lobby. "I'll be keeping an eye on you."

"Wait," she said. He turned around and looked at her.

Her mind went blank. "*Fuck you*," she said. "Truly. Fuck you." It felt incredible to say it. When she got back to her hotel room she ordered a grilled cheese.

26

Zoey

Victor was waiting for Zoey in their booth at The Odeon.

They only saw each other about once a month now, and their texting rhythm had slowed dramatically. Zoey had identified, ever since leaving Tom, a great desire to "start over" in her life—it's partly why she left Selah, too. And while she didn't want to leave Victor completely behind—and in fact she was still, to some degree, scared how he would react if she ever did—it did sometimes cross her mind that Victor was deeply linked to the past she was hoping to move on from. The recent late-night phone call, his berating her and casually threatening to kill himself, didn't help either. Even though she'd told him at the end of that call that she needed some space, they resumed texting later that week as if nothing of note had happened. And of course they hadn't referenced it directly since.

When she took Victor to the hospital after his overdose, she felt in that moment that they were undoubtedly bonded for life. There was no world in which they wouldn't be in each other's lives. But their bond felt to her now more like that of siblings living on opposite coasts, even though their apartments were in fact a twenty-minute subway ride apart. That she could remember so clearly the purity of their friendship in college and through their twenties only made the distance she felt now more palpable.

Since Oliver died, and also since Victor had quit his job, she felt increasingly confused about how to approach him, unsure where his head was at on any given day. He shared less with her. And, as a result, she'd started sharing less with him. He had definitely been appreciative when she went to Oliver's funeral with him, but she sometimes wondered if he would be there for her, should the situation be reversed. She *thought* so, but she had a nagging uncertainty.

"One sec," Victor said, as Zoey slid into the booth. Zoey picked a French fry off his dish. After a few beats, he put his phone down and grinned. He looked a bit gaunt to Zoey, but she had passed the point where she would express such observations. As unbreakable as their connection may have been, the relationship now felt extremely fragile.

"You look great," he said, half-convincingly.

"I brushed my hair for you."

"Have you talked to Perri?"

Zoey shook her head.

"The *Times* story wasn't *that* bad," he said. "Could have been way worse."

"It wasn't good. I don't think she is going to hold on to Selah for much longer. Louisa texted me she hasn't come into the office in like a week. She has never gone MIA like that. Cherry doesn't even know how to get in touch with her, apparently."

"I'm surprised she hasn't put out a statement or anything."

"She doesn't do phony bullshit like that."

"Well, yeah, but . . . you kind of have to put a statement out. You just do."

"None of the statements mean anything. They're all, like, regurgitated meaningless drivel. You know that."

"Is that how you'd advise a client, though?"

Zoey paused. She was getting worked up, which was upsetting and somewhat surprising. Up until this lunch, she had felt pretty unaffected by the article. She hadn't told Victor—and wasn't going to tell him now—that the journalist had reached out to her twice, and she had declined to comment or even talk to her on background. Perri had texted her a few times to ask directly if she might consider publicly defending her ("Even if you just did an IG Story supporting me, that would mean so much"), but Zoey told her she couldn't.

"It's all just kind of depressing to me," Zoey said finally. "Where are the exposés about . . . you know, everyone? The people *really* doing the terrible things. Perri is a beautiful, competent, successful woman, so of course, you know, everyone's orgasming over this takedown."

"I guess. Yeah. I'm obviously never, like, *in favor* of going after someone who doesn't deserve it. But some people do deserve it, and . . ."

The waitress came by, and Zoey ordered a glass of rosé and a Caesar salad.

Victor looked up at her. "And I mean, you did hate her, right?"

"I didn't *hate* Perri."

"You would complain about her all the time, Zoey."

"We all complain about everyone. You used to scream about Leon Marcus literally 24/7."

Victor looked away from her.

"Also, I can't believe you of all people are thrilled to hear about someone being, you know, attacked online," she said.

"Well, this is a little bit of a . . . specific set of circumstances," he said. He looked at his phone and then back at Zoey. "So, any dating updates?"

This conversational shift was so abrupt as to almost make Zoey laugh. She could feel Victor's discomfort from across the table.

"I really haven't been focusing on it," she said. She felt some pity for Victor in the moment, a desire to calm the waters. "I did sleep with this guy I met at the airport, though."

"Seriously? Who was it?"

"He's actually a male fashion model. I know, it sounds like the punch line to a joke. Or a setup to—you know what I mean."

"You're really—you're a character on *Euphoria* now."

"Oh yes, exactly." She smiled. "He's a sweet guy. He's some kind of artist, too—he makes stuff out of sand."

"I don't even know what to say to that."

"I'm proud of myself. I've been in the mood for, you know, *brief and meaningless liaisons*. I think I still need to get some of that out of my system."

Zoey looked at her phone. Louisa had sent her a nymag.com link: "Is Perri Patrick's Once-Hot Start-up Selah in Its Final Days?"

"So your—it's going well? Your new thing?" Victor asked. "You never really answered my texts the other day."

Zoey looked back up. "Yeah, I mean . . . I am working nonstop."

"You're everywhere. I just saw the *Fast Company* article."

"Yeah, am I posting too much promo on Instagram? I feel like I should be posting as much as possible right now. You know?"

"I mean, I am the wrong person to ask. I just put my Twitter and Instagram back on private. This weird Valentina stan who used to harass me back in the day literally responds to everything I post *still*. I don't even work at *Corridor* anymore!"

"Can't you just block that one person?"

"Yeah, but that's not really the point. It's all just . . . it's not fun anymore."

"I feel weirdly removed from it. Even though I look at all the comments and see the engagement and everything. I don't know. You have to think of it as an alternate universe—you can't let it get to you."

"Yeah, well, that's easy for you when all your followers are, like, basic white girls who drink kombucha and do their Pilates, you know? Not to be . . . whatever."

This was the kind of callous comment Victor would never have made in the past. At a certain point, when she was married to Tom, Zoey noticed that many of the tossed-off aggressive comments Tom would make, usually delivered quite amiably, had in fact permeated her psyche. Sometimes she would argue back and offer a rebuttal, but if you get pricked enough times—and know that all replying will do is allow for more pricks—you eventually decide it isn't worth the effort. It's easier to bleed and not let anyone see it.

"Do you remember when I called you when I got the promotion?" she said. "And asked if you could help me get a story about Selah in *Corridor*?"

"Of course. Didn't you ask me to *write* the story?"

"No, I didn't say it like that," she said. "Well, Perri told me at the time that I needed to get that placement in *Corridor* to get promoted. A few days later, I told her I'd talked to you and that it was happening . . . and I got the promotion."

Victor leaned in toward her. He wasn't smiling. "But *Corridor* never did the story."

"No shit. I had to tell Perri that it fell through. It took me a few months, but eventually I traded in a favor to get us that write-up in *Time*. Which she said was better anyway. So it all worked out."

Zoey had wanted to bring this up to Victor so many times. It always felt too hot to excavate.

"You never told me how important it was to you," Victor said, after a few seconds. "You didn't explain it fully."

"I mean, wasn't it implicit, just in the fact that I asked you? I never asked you for work favors like that."

"That was a really long time ago. You've just been holding in how pissed off you are?"

"Do I seem pissed off?"

"Yes."

"I guess maybe I am. I expected you'd just do whatever you could to write it. You were writing fucking cover stories for the magazine. But you couldn't figure out a way to finagle a short write-up about a fashion start-up to help out your best friend? You probably could have churned it out in twenty minutes and published it on the site without anyone there even noticing."

"Zoey, you could have just *said all this to me then*. This is like how I never knew what was going on with you and Tom until it all exploded. You can't just expect everyone to know what's going on in your head. I can't help you if you don't ask for it."

"Well, not all of us just spill our guts to anyone who will listen because we're so desperate for validation. And I *did* ask you for help."

Victor took a bite of his burger, which he hadn't picked up since she'd sat down. "What made you want to bring this up now? You're on top of the world. Why do you possibly care? It didn't affect your career trajectory whatsoever."

"What? *Top of the world*?" She realized she had affected a slight accent and was speaking very loudly.

"I'm sorry," he said. "Ever since Oliver . . . I just. I'm more of an asshole, I think? I say things to people that surprise me. Like when I was wasted after the date and called you and—well, you know what I said to you. It's like I have no emotions about things that are happening to me. My tank is just—it's empty." He paused. "Not to sound depressive. I've been there, and it's not that. It's just a kind of pervading numbness." They both reflected on this for a few moments. Victor then continued, "I guess I just never thought you even wanted to be in the public eye. It's been a surprise."

"Aren't you proud of me? And excited for me? You act like I've wronged you or betrayed you or something, when you say it like that."

"No, I'm not saying that." He took a long pause. "Dr. Beckman says I should be dealing with things more directly, so I'll just say it: I feel like we're barely even real friends at this point. We see each other so much less frequently. All these . . . animosities have built up. I never thought this would happen to us, and now I feel like it's actually really happening. And I've had more time, obviously, without a full-time job, to *think about* how it's happening to us, you know? And I feel like it gets channeled through me in all these unexpected ways. It's exhausting; I feel beaten down. And then you come in here and bring up this incident from years ago."

"Oh my god."

"I guess the truth is, with the Selah thing, maybe I thought you were using me a little bit."

"*Using* you? In what world?"

"I was just getting so many weird requests and emails and texts when I started that job. And then there was the Valentina of it all. I was in a strange headspace, and everything was stressing me out. I just—I remember thinking it was uncomfortable, you putting me in that position."

"Victor, did you even ask your editor about the Selah story? Did you ask Leon if you could write it?"

Victor looked away from her. "I did."

"Are you lying?"

"I don't remember." He looked at her. "I might not have asked. *I didn't know it was such a big deal to you.*"

"You know, maybe the reason it feels to you like I'm not your friend anymore and you're lashing out is because you always think you're being persecuted. You think everything is *happening to you.* Stuff is happening to everyone. Not just to you."

"Is the idea that you really don't want to be friends anymore?"

She reached out across the booth and held his wrist. "Victor, this is exactly what I'm talking about. You saying *that*." She let go. "Listen, there's not a world in which we're not connected. I brought you to the fucking hospital."

He leaned back in the booth. "Sometimes I think, because of the history, we both feel obligated now to . . . just all of it. I think maybe you're worried if you leave me in the lurch, I won't be able to handle it."

He stopped momentarily. She wasn't sure what to say.

"I'm so appreciative of you," he continued. "Appreciative of every-thing. But, you know, people change. It sounds like maybe you don't want this friendship anymore. Maybe you don't need me, and we're not good for each other right now. Maybe it's not meant to be. And that's okay. Clearly there are things about me that really bother you."

On other days, in years past, Zoey would have sat there in the booth with him for as long as it took to hash this out and rectify things and smooth it over. She didn't feel like she had it in her at this moment.

"Victor, that's fucked up to say. Don't push this back on me and try to make me feel like I am somehow not a good person. I have been there for you again and again and again. I've put up with a *lot*. We're family. I think you clearly are . . . going through some things. And have a lot to think about. If you want to shove me away and cut me out, that's up to you. But that's not what I want."

She stood up, slid out of the booth, and left the restaurant.

Outside, on West Broadway, she called Perri. It went to voicemail, but then Perri called her right back.

"You don't have to check up on me," Perri said.

"I know. But I am. That's what I do."

There was a long pause.

"I'm doing just fine," Perri said.

"Great. I'm glad to hear that."

There was another pause.

"I hate to say this, but you're going to have a very successful career," Perri said.

"Are you sure? I'm not always so sure."

"You know yourself," Perri said. "You're present when it matters—you know when it matters. And you leave when it's time to leave. What's crucial is that you don't linger."

27

Liv

Liv turned off the podcast. It'd taken her about a week to finish it. She could only stomach five-to-ten-minute increments; breaks had been necessary.

She'd been sitting at the gate in the Denver airport for about an hour, and her flight still wasn't going to be boarding for another twenty minutes. She'd lived in Colorado for a year, and hadn't left the state until now. She hadn't had a reason to.

When she thought about it, and she didn't think about it as much as you'd imagine, her life was immeasurably better now. She cut her hair a few weeks after arriving in Colorado and had maintained a short, stylish pixie cut. She went to the gym three times a week. She cooked her own meals. The Wi-Fi hardly ever worked at her house, and she had no interest in getting it fixed. She spent most of her time outside, often lounging on a white lawn chair in her backyard that the previous tenant had left there. She was working remotely for a professor, spending about thirty hours a week doing research for him on European culinary customs. Her aunt and uncle lived about half an hour outside of Denver, and she went over to their place for dinner about once a month.

She went to sleep no later than 9 p.m. every night, a far cry from her years in New York, when she would regularly stay up until three or four in the morning, scrolling through the feeds of influencers, socialites, writers, models, actresses. She'd look to see what photos they'd been tagged in, what tweets they had liked, what was being written in their comments. She was an encyclopedia for women in their twenties and thirties in the public sphere.

Her brother was the one who sent her a link to Caroline's episode of Maddie Brooks's podcast. At first she wasn't sure she wanted to listen to it—in fact, she was furious at R.J. for sending it to her. (what makes you think I have any interest in this, she'd texted him back.) But there was still a disappointingly raw part of her that couldn't help herself.

She hadn't told her brother (or anyone) that she'd read Caroline's book. She read it in two sittings the week it came out. It was surprisingly easy for her to disassociate, to imagine that the book had nothing to do with her. And truthfully, the details of the book bore so little resemblance to reality—to her reality—that it really could feel like the book was not about her. But then she heard Caroline say on the podcast that Liv was the inspiration for *Sparkling Day*, and *that was it*—she felt feverish again. Sadly, there was something intoxicating about the feeling.

Liv looked around at the strangers sitting near her at the gate. No one ever looked happy at an airport, in her experience, but yet everyone around Liv at the moment appeared to be in cheerful spirits. A woman to her left, in a matching purple sweatsuit, was humming along to the faint Christmas carol emanating from the Starbucks. The couple across from her was holding hands. Holding hands while waiting for a flight.

Liv opened Safari on her phone and typed "Goodreads" into the browser—it autofilled to the page for Caroline's book.

She started typing, fingers gliding across her phone screen:

I happened to hear a few minutes of Caroline on Maddie Brooks's podcast, where she referred to me (not by name) as the central inspiration for Sparkling Day. *I never imagined I'd want to "weigh in" publicly on this book; I felt quite content to remain private, to keep my thoughts locked up within. But it's time for me to stop overthinking or censoring myself. I guess it's kind of odd that I am finally voicing my perspective in a comment on Goodreads—but why not, it's just as meaningful as anywhere else on the internet. Also I feel certain Caroline will see it this way. (Hi, Caroline!!!)*

I don't live in New York anymore. The inciting "incident" described in this book feels like it occurred in a different lifetime of mine. When I was living in New York, I learned quickly how easy it was to lure in someone like Caroline Stevens. Whether these sorts would admit it or not, their self-worth is predicated on being worshipped by people like me. I wasn't doing anything malicious. I wasn't extorting anyone. I didn't WANT anything. It was more like a hobby than anything else. A distraction.

I don't want to discuss Caroline herself, really. I was fascinated with her for a while. And then it all went away when I met her. I don't mean this in a rude way. It's just that the illusion shatters completely when you meet someone like her in person. The nervous tics, the small imperfections—it becomes all you can see. Maybe that is why I wanted to meet her, actually. Maybe I knew on some level that meeting her in person would "cure" me.

I am, truly, deeply and honestly flattered that she wrote an entire book that is "based" on me. However I am nothing like "Ella" (I feel like I can say this objectively) and I find it HYSTERICAL that a novel about a demented criminal mastermind who kills herself would be, per the author, triggered by an interaction with me. As Caroline noted on the podcast, I did call her after she left my apartment (she didn't mention this on the episode, but she ran into my brother in our building,

*which is how she found out about everything). We had what
I thought was a breezy and pleasant phone call. I am frankly
shocked that any of this had any sort of lasting impact on her. She
was probably in my apartment for eight minutes, max.*

*I would be remiss if I didn't say I was a bit hurt by the
characterization. I feel like, even back then, I had a fairly
accurate self-perception. I don't think I came off as menacing
to Caroline in person, and some of her descriptions of Ella
("her vacant expression," "her ratty bangs," etc.) struck me
as projections Caroline must have about anyone who doesn't
conform to some standard of beauty or "coolness" that Caroline
has developed, whether consciously or not, about the world and
people around her. Or maybe she was just revealing her own
insecurities without realizing it.*

Also, obviously I didn't kill myself IRL, either.

*(My brother btw is not a creep. He is a bit of a loner, but
really, what man isn't these days? I am not a book reviewer and
my opinion on the quality of her writing hardly matters, but I
thought the scenes in the book about the brother's sex life were
cringe and I feel like the story would have been better served
without them?)*

*What actually rankles about Caroline's book, what still
occasionally makes me laugh, is that I'm the only character in
it who comes off as "pathetic." Like, the upshot is that I am this
sad, sniveling weirdo who is just so desperate for approval and
validation that I trick COOL WOMEN into hanging out with
me. Well, I'll let you in on a secret: I have met a whole lot of
these so-called COOL WOMEN—who post the cropped selfies
in their sunglasses, and have the perfectly dewy skin and all the
right books on their bookshelves and the gorgeous sliver of sunlight
streaming down their breasts—and I will tell you, they are all*

starving (they don't eat), miserable (they have no actual friends), and most of them call themselves writers even though they haven't written anything in eight years (and even then it was a free-verse poem for their friend's newsletter). Caroline is extremely representative to me of this sort of New York character. So for her to write a book where she accuses a woman like ME of lacking an interior life, of stewing away and sharpening my knives for a kill . . . makes me want to scream.

Caroline, what do I want to say to you, in the end? Truly, despite everything I just wrote, I do not have hard feelings. You said on the podcast episode that, thanks to me, you felt like things had "worked out the way they should have" in your life. I feel like nothing in my own life has played out in the way I thought it would, so there was some sort of irony in hearing you say this. It also made me wonder, though, after meditating on what you said, if perhaps my life is progressing in the way it was meant to—if perhaps, in some screwed-up way, I owe you some thanks. I definitely feel much healthier where I'm living now, and, unexpectedly, reading your book helped provide me some closure on the frenzied, upsetting chapter of my life comprised of my years in New York. Maybe if I had stayed there longer I would have become a depraved and emptier person. Maybe, if I want to be overly generous and a touch dramatic, I can tell myself that you killed me in your book so that I could live in real life.

I still look at your Instagram from time to time. I will admit that. I don't think, no matter where I am living or how I feel about you, or, rather, how I feel about myself, that that will be something I ever stop doing.

Sincerely, Liv

Liv didn't even hesitate in pressing Submit.

She stared, beaming, at her published comment. It was thrilling—a major-key, full-body thrill. She wanted to print it out and frame it.

She looked up and realized they'd just finished boarding her flight. She grabbed her bag and ran up to the gate. She blew right past the attendant and out onto the walkway; he called out for her—"Ma'am!"—and Liv turned around, wondering what she'd done wrong, before realizing he just needed to see her boarding pass.

28

I was alone in Paris. It had seemed like a really smart idea when I booked the flight—and now that I was here, it still felt like a smart idea. There had been a promotion offering $199 round-trip flights, and I figured, *wasn't this the point of freelancing?* I could spend two weeks in Paris. I could even extend it to a third if I wanted.

I went right from the airport to the Musée de l'Orangerie, which I'd visited for the first time as a high schooler. I'd fallen in love then with the mural-sized impressionist paintings, comprising the entire curved walls. I liked the sense back then—and I really liked it now—that I was drowning within the painting. *Wrap me up and suffocate me, Paris!*

I was looking to drown right now—not the depression-fueled, *actual drowning* that I may have yearned for in previous eras of my life. But in the sense that I wanted to completely lose myself in the oil colors, to disengage from my thoughts.

After visiting the museum, I walked to my Airbnb in the Marais. Even though I was hauling a wheeling suitcase and an overstuffed duffel bag, walking the two miles felt romantic and sensible to me. In New York, I would have Ubered.

By the time I arrived at the building, the back of my T-shirt was affixed to my body. I stripped it off immediately upon entering the apartment, which was tidy and compact and filled with light and exactly what I wanted. There was a faint scent of lemon permeating the space.

I sat down, still shirtless, at the wooden table, and opened the binder resting next to a glass vase (the white label on the binder's front shouted "SIGHTS!" in block letters). I left it open on the first page of typed copy. There was a print of an orange cat on the wall. An intrusion of a potted plant brushed against my arm.

Given the recent events in my life and, really, more pertinently, given Zoey's understandable frustration with me, I had felt like I needed to separate myself physically from New York City. I'd been having a recurring dream where I watched Oliver dive into a swimming pool. In the dream, it was the Olympics or some other serious sporting event. I was in the stands with a bunch of people I'd gone to school with—we were all cheering and holding flags. I'd watch Oliver dive into the water, and everyone would be shouting in ecstasy, and then I'd wake up and my chest would be sweating and I'd want to scream. After enough of these dreams, I decided I needed to sleep in a different bedroom in a different city for a while.

I opened my suitcase and slipped on a green striped polo shirt. I had packed clothes that I rarely wore in New York, as if to give them an out-of-town tryout.

I left the apartment without showering and entered the first café I spotted. I enjoyed that all the cafés in Paris, to my eye at least, were more or less interchangeable. You could produce the same experience for yourself at any of them, and there was something comforting about that. I liked not having to worry about the choice.

I sat down at a small round table near a woman smoking a cigarette. She looked to be in her forties, but her hair was mostly gray, up in a bun. She smelled incredible, like a teaspoon of vanilla extract. She was wearing a beige trench coat, no jewelry. She didn't have a phone out, or a laptop, or a book. She was just staring straight ahead. It was hard to even imagine her using a phone.

She looked in my direction, as if aware of my train of thought. I waved. She didn't wave back, but she nodded slightly. Or at least I thought it was a nod.

I ordered a bottle of wine and a baguette.

My initial plan had been to delete all my social-media apps in Paris: a complete detox. I was going to write for a few hours every day—I had the outline for a script and I was going to finish it before returning. But now that I was actually here, the agenda I'd devised for myself felt totally unappealing. *Why come to Paris if I was going to sit in my Airbnb and stare at my laptop all day?* I took my phone out and opened Raya. I had a message from a guy named Henry who was visiting Paris from New York: hey

I wrote back hey yourself. I was really bringing my A game.

About twenty minutes later, the woman in the trench coat stood up and moved toward me, holding a paper bag that had been under her chair. "I have . . . a few pastries," she said, in thick accented English. "I'm not going to eat them. Do you want?"

"Oh, uh, sure," I said. She placed the bag down in front of me on the table. "Thank you so much. You're sure?"

"Yes. I was going to bring them to a friend's house," she said. "But I'm not going anymore."

She moved back to her chair. Our two tables were close enough that a stranger watching us chat might have assumed we were siblings, passing time between family engagements.

"How'd you know I was American?" I asked.

She laughed and didn't answer at first. "A hunch."

"Are you from here?"

She nodded.

"You don't have a—this is probably a weird question, but I noticed for the past, like, half hour . . . you don't have your phone out, nothing to read. You're just here."

"I'm sorry—I don't follow."

"I guess I'm curious what you're thinking about. If it's not totally bizarre for me to ask."

"I sense you want me to say something very profound," she said, smiling. "But I'm just thinking about what I'm going to make for dinner. I'm deciding between two recipes."

"Right, yeah," I said. "That makes sense."

A few minutes later, she got up to leave. "Well, good luck," she said. I didn't need to ask her what she meant, what she thought I might need luck for.

"Thank you so much," I said.

I took my phone out and opened Raya. It turned out Henry was staying at a hotel a few blocks from my Airbnb, so we made plans to get coffee in the morning. Paris Victor was a bit more spontaneous, it turned out. He was a bit less paranoid.

After another fifteen minutes, or maybe it was an hour, I left the café. I had a bag of pastries, half a bottle of wine, and a date in the morning.

The next day, sipping on my espresso at a different café near my Airbnb, I felt energized. I'd slept thirteen hours the night before.

Henry arrived at the café, and I was pleasantly surprised—for once, a guy from an app looked more or less like his pictures had suggested he might.

He was shorter than me by a few inches, and looked like he could be a relative of Tom Holland—compact with blond, wavy hair. What appeared to be an intricate dark tattoo on his bicep peeked out from his short-sleeved white button-down. He was wearing tight brown corduroys and loafers. As my eyes moved back up, I noticed his shirt was unbuttoned halfway down his torso. His skin was glowing, and he had a slight indentation on his right cheek that I found confusingly attractive.

Meanwhile, I was wearing an oversized blue sweater and hadn't shaved since landing in Paris.

He waved and sat down next to me as if we were old colleagues.

"It's happening," he said.

"It's happening."

We had exchanged a total of three messages each, but I felt very comfortable in his presence.

"What brings you to Paris, Henry?" I asked.

"I'm on a work trip. I'm a consultant. Don't stab me."

"Why would I stab you for being a consultant?"

"I don't know. People have been stabbed for less."

He looked around and hailed a waiter and ordered a coffee in perfect French. *Of course.* I was awed by the way he took up space while somehow maintaining a certain elegance.

"I went a little aggressive with the bare décolletage," he said, gesturing to the undone buttons. "When in Europe, right?"

"I do not mind at all," I said, straining to imbue my speech with an air of mystery.

"So what brings *you* here?"

"I—well, where do I start?" I wanted to be *good* for him. It was essential to not place so much import on every single glance or breath. "I left my full-time job recently and now I'm freelancing. So I decided to come to Paris."

He seemed to approve of this answer. There was a curl at the edge of his hairline I really wanted to hold on to.

"Were you named after Victor Hugo?" he asked.

"Sorry? Oh, uh, no, not that I know of. But I like that. That'd be more glamorous. I might start telling people that. No, my mom said there was a character on a TV show she liked who had the name Victor. I once tried to figure out the show, but when I asked her about it, she said she couldn't remember. It was disappointing." I paused. "I kind of feel like maybe there never actually was a TV character."

He grinned. "What if I just called you Hugo? As a pet name kind of thing?"

"I'm not a Hugo."

He laughed at this. His teeth were straight and shiny and—fuck—they reminded me of Oliver's. But I let that thought wash over and then drift by, and I watched it float off to the hazy horizon.

After coffee, Henry and I walked around the Marais for about thirty minutes before he had to get back to his hotel before a meeting.

After leaving him off, I decided to walk to the Seine. I'd find salvation there. I sat on a bench and watched a woman in a beanie and a long coat sketch our surroundings in her notepad. Her rendering was extremely realistic until she took out a colored pencil and made the sun purple.

When Henry and I had parted ways, he asked if I wanted to get dinner together later that night, and I'd said that sounded great. It all felt natural with him in a way it never usually did for me. He was a little intense, perhaps—the consultant energy, wanting to brand me with a pet name within minutes of meeting me—but I felt like I was due for a new experience, for the excitement of navigating fresh terrain.

I'd clearly felt restless for a while. And I could see now—it was so clear—that I had taken a lot of that frustration out on Zoey. I'd been a lunatic. I'd been completely immature.

She'd taken the reins of her life—*she actually left Tom; she started her own company*. And I wasn't sure why I had taken that as a personal affront. She was always present for me; maybe I felt ashamed that I didn't know if I could be the same in return? I knew she valued me in a way that was impossible to quantify. And I knew I felt that same love for her. I had so much to offer her. To offer everyone. I had completely failed her, and I felt guilty and morose.

I let these sensations linger. For the first time in a few months, I could see a path back for me and Zoey. I knew I had it in me to win back her trust.

I walked by the river and felt thrilled that no one here knew anything about me. I also felt like a cliché, having this moment of self-realization *in Paris by the fucking Seine*.

I wasn't sure if the instinct I suddenly had to call my dad was self-destructive, or if it was . . . whatever the opposite of self-destructive was, but I decided to *relax* and trust my gut—this approach had worked well for me since arriving in Paris. I hadn't talked to him on the phone in about a month.

I stopped and sat down on a bench in front of a vendor who was selling shiny ribbons and medallions.

"Hello?"

"Hey Dad."

"Oh, Victor, hello. I'm about to run out the door."

"That's okay. Just kind of wanted to hear your voice."

"Is everything okay?"

"Yeah, I'm fine."

"Is there anything you need?"

I was silent for a few moments.

"Nothing I need, no."

"Okay, that's good."

I watched an old man throw something into the river. It looked like it might have been a bottle.

"Dad, I was dating a guy for a few years. Oliver."

"I know. Your mother told me at one point."

"She did?"

"We do talk every now and then."

This felt surprisingly comforting. It was unnerving that it made me feel this good.

"He died last year. A car hit him while he was biking."

"I didn't know that. I'm sorry to hear that."

"Yeah, it's not ideal."

I was breathing deeply into the phone. I liked the idea that wherever my dad was right now, he was listening to me breathing—across the world from him, breathing.

"Do you remember Zoey? My best friend from college?"

"It sounds familiar."

"You've met her before." I smiled to myself. "Anyway, we're not really talking at the moment. And for some reason when I was thinking about how I've . . . messed things up with her recently, I had the thought to call you."

"And why is that?"

"I'm not totally sure. I feel like a trained professional would probably be able to put it together for me without too much trouble."

"Victor, I'm late to a breakfast with—I'm sorry to have to cut this short."

"Do you hate having to talk to me? I've always wanted to ask you that."

"What? No, of course not. What do you mean? I don't think I really know *how* to talk to you. But I love you."

"You could love me and hate having to talk to me."

"I guess that's true."

"All right. Have a nice breakfast, Dad."

"Goodbye, Victor."

I stared at my phone for a few seconds—I absentmindedly checked the weather—and then slipped it back in my pocket.

I stopped at an ice cream stand and bought a cup of strawberry ice cream—it came with a small plastic spoon. A mistake I used to make was assuming that there was an order to the world, that a linear narrative would always emerge, a pattern in the way life played out—now I understood that belief system was what led to continual disappointment.

The ice cream tasted really great. It was a simple takeaway, but it occurred to me I should eat foods that I liked more often.

When I met Henry later that evening for dinner, he was wearing a well-tailored black suit, matching jacket and pants. I was in the same blue sweater I'd been in all day.

"You're seeing the real Victor today, unvarnished," I said, upon his arrival.

He gave me a hug. "What do you mean?"

"You just look really nice, and I look . . ."

"You look great." He leaned in and kissed my cheek. Was he an AI creation? I felt concerned I'd hit my head on the plane and that this was all some kind of head-injury-related fantasy and I was actually lying in a coma in a Parisian hospital right now, IVs connected to my arm.

I snapped out of it. "Thank you," I said, forcing myself to hold eye contact. I refrained from adding any sort of patented self-deprecating remark.

When we sat down at the table, he ordered a glass of red wine; but when the waitress asked me what I wanted to drink, I shocked myself. "I'm good with water," I said. Henry didn't look up from the menu when I said it, but I felt like there should be fireworks.

I didn't bring up Oliver once during dinner. I didn't think about him, either.

Henry and I shared a tiramisu for dessert, and he asked me who the most intimidating celebrity I'd ever interviewed was, and I asked him about his family, and I liked that—meeting as we were on a different continent—we both were existing in this odd liminal passageway, suspended in space and time, divorced from our usual, everyday selves.

"You need to keep in mind that this is Paris Victor you're having dinner with," I said. The check was on our table but neither of us had reached for it.

"And that's different from New York Victor?" he asked.

I was about to answer this one way, but then stopped myself. "You know what? Maybe it's actually not different."

The waitress came to see if our bill was ready to be collected. "Oh, sorry, take your time. You two are very adorable. Together a long time?" she asked. Her English was pretty good.

Henry laughed, and I smiled. "Forever," I said.

As we walked back to his hotel, I felt an overwhelming desire to tell Zoey about my day, to tell her I hadn't had a drop of alcohol at dinner, to tell her about my phone call with my dad, to describe the indentation on Henry's cheek in extreme detail ("Is it crazy I want to *lick* it?"). And to say to her, to sing it, to scream—*I'm sorry.*

"For what *now*?" she'd say.

"For everything," I'd answer.

29

The Maddie Brooks Podcast—Transcript

Maddie: Well, well, well, sweet friends . . . Darren is out of town for the next month, as you know, so it's just your fave holding it down solo for the next few episodes. And we love it. *We love it*, right? Darren, if you're listening to this—which I know you are, creep—don't be offended. It's just nice sometimes to not have that leering male energy in the room. Even though, yeah, yeah, we all know Darren pretends to be more of a feminist than I am. And I give him a hard time, the hardest time. Darren's the best. But it also feels so good when he's not here. Ha! Anyway, we have a very fun guest today. I met her at a party a—I want to say a year ago? And I thought she was . . . I'm going to be honest: I thought she was kind of cold. I am cold, too! Obviously. Especially on first impression. We know I'm a frigid bitch. So I can say that. But now that this girl and I have become friendly, I can report that she is *actually* extremely interesting and funny and sharp and . . . very, very no-nonsense. And also maybe a little enigmatic!

Zoey: I'm dying that you think I'm enigmatic.

Maddie: You were dating that hot artist when we met!

Zoey: Oh my god. Thad. Yes. He's a graphic designer. I was. He's the coolest guy I've ever dated, I think.

Maddie: Plus, I found out when we met that you know Wiles Cooke, who was like . . . basically my weird fancy surrogate uncle growing up. He was always around the house when we lived in Europe.

Zoey: That is true, very true. I do know Wiles Cooke.

Maddie: Let's promptly move on from that topic, shall we? Though of course, we love you, Wiles. Anyway—Jesus, I haven't even introduced you yet: this is Zoey Prince. She just officially launched her new app, Terry, which—well—you may have heard about it, but you tell the app what you like, who you have a crush on, what band you're obsessed with— some of the questions it asks are really weird; I was getting into it—and then they mail you accessories and clothes and all kinds of stuff. And it works so well, you guys. It figures you out. Zoey gave me a free trial.

Zoey: Not just a trial. You're a member for a year, babe. *Then* you'll have to pay.

Maddie: Okay, wow, free year. And the clothes I got were incredible. I am wearing the plaid miniskirt now. You guys can't see it. But it's chic as fuck. I want to go out after this and, I don't know—what can I do in this outfit?

Zoey: You look so good. I could never wear that, but it's very . . . you're riding the pop-punk wave. You could go to a roller rink. Oh my god, I'm a loser. Roller rink!

Maddie: So tell me, who was your initial, when you were growing up, your *fashion icon*, your style muse? And you can't say Princess Diana. I feel like everyone says Princess Diana or—

Zoey: Or Carolyn Bessette?

Maddie: Ah no, oh my god—that's crazy. I haven't thought about her in so long.

Zoey: Yeah, I actually do usually say Carolyn Bessette. I also have a thing for Woody Harrelson and Mandy Patinkin, when they were younger—or even the way they dress now. I admire people who know who they are and understand themselves.

Maddie: I want to ask you—you're a recent divorcée.

Zoey: [*laughter*] Yep.

Maddie: And you also just started your own business.

Zoey: Also true. I feel like this is leading somewhere scary.

Maddie: What do you—I guess my question is, where do you get your drive?

Zoey: I'm trying to figure out how all of those things are . . . related to each other.

Maddie: It made sense in my head to string all of that together. That's so funny. The longer I have this podcast, the less I feel like I narrate how I get from one place to another—does that make sense?

Zoey: No, please, you can ask me anything. I do happen to be divorced. I did start my own company. Both true. I feel very, I guess, yeah, self-actualized right now. I'm about to freeze my eggs. I just bought an apartment in Brooklyn, which is crazy to me. I tend to be someone who—I think I am pretty present in my life. Or, I didn't used to be so much—but I am now. I know how I feel in any given moment about the situation.

Maddie: Interesting. I feel like I am the opposite. Even when I was starting this podcast, I remember it took me and—I was developing it with this girl Hannah for a while, but then she dropped off the face of the earth, and it was just me and dopey Darren . . . But it took us almost a year—more than a year—from coming up with the idea to actually starting it. It took me so long to decide I actually wanted to do it. And for a while I thought I was going to have a TV show, and that didn't work out like I thought it would, so . . . I guess, none of it feels like it was very thought through.

Zoey: A year to develop a podcast isn't very long, I feel like, for something like that. And you got *here*, to this point. Now you're killing it, Ms. Spotify Deal.

Maddie: Thank you very much. Okay, so how did you come up with the name "Terry"?

Zoey: It's sort of personal. But I—I was having trouble naming the app. I was calling it "Zoey Inc." forever. And I wanted it to be meaningful. At my old job, my boss hired some expensive branding agency that did all this research and tons of name generation. It was the opposite of personal.

Maddie: Selah?

Zoey: I wasn't going to say it. But I decided to name this venture after my uncle who passed away when I was in college. He was my mom's best friend and just a really special person.

Maddie: So I am going to pry now and ask about your former boss, Perri Patrick. She was—she was your mentor, right?

Zoey: She was an important figure in my career, yeah.

Maddie: She recently shut down Selah, her company, where you used to work.

Zoey: Yeah. Yes. It's unfortunate. I don't really want to say too much about the whole situation. But I have nothing negative to say about Perri. And I of course read all the statements made in the *Times* piece—

Maddie: And there were other Twitter threads, too.

Zoey: I didn't get caught up on all of that, but—you know, listen, this stuff is complicated. She is not an easy person to summarize succinctly in a sound bite. I cherish my relationships with everyone who worked at Selah, and I want everyone to end up where they should be, in the right place. No one should feel uncomfortable in his or her workplace. Goes without saying.

Maddie: You're good at this.

Zoey: I'm just being me.

Maddie: Do you think—do you think you have any responsibility to speak out more directly—or, you know, really *weigh in*? I assume you knew Kiki, who was the focus of that *Times* story? Presumably you could verify her claims? Or dispute them? You are one of the few people who probably knows what actually went down.

Zoey: Yeah . . . I'd rather not get into all of that.

Maddie: Right. Right. You were saying, before we started recording, that your good friend—you said he always makes fun of you when you do press?

Zoey: Oh, no. That's not how I meant it. No. He—all of a sudden I was doing a lot of interviews; I was on TV. And he's actually a journalist. Victor Harris. He works at *Corridor*; he's back there now after taking some time off. He interviews major, high-profile celebrities. So I think he just thought it was funny seeing me now . . . on this side of things.

Maddie: Oh my god. *Wait.* I think I met that guy! A while ago. At this bizarre junket for Ghirardelli chocolate. That was before I even started the podcast. How fucking funny! I totally know him. He was sweet. Quirky but sweet.

Zoey: The New York media scene. I always feel like there's only actually like fifteen people total.

Maddie: Do you—would Victor ever interview *you*?

Zoey: I don't think that would be a good idea. We don't—

Maddie: You don't what?

Zoey: We aren't in regular contact right now.

Maddie: I always say, you can't really keep friendships in this industry. Whenever I think someone is a real one, they end up . . . using me or fucking me over or doing something shady . . . You look like you're contemplating something, Zoey. Or lost in thought. If Darren were here, he would bang the keypad thing and blare that annoying siren to get you to spill.

Zoey: Oh, no . . . I'm just thinking about, this feels funny to say out loud, but . . . the strange . . . precariousness of friendship. As adults. Like, how often do you check in with your friends and really talk about how the friendship is going? About if you're meeting each other's needs? No one ever does that with their friends. It would be so bizarre. But I think maybe we all should? It's how we keep the peace—or try to keep the peace—with our romantic partners. But never with our friends. We let things fester and get annoyed at them about the smallest, most minor bullshit, and start acting passive-aggressively, and then talk shit about them to our boyfriends or our other friends. When is it worth it to be like, "Let's really get into it, bitch," like Carrie and Miranda at the end of *Sex and the City*? You know, *come out with it and let's solve this!* Or when is it easier to just let things drift apart?

Maddie: It sounds like you're really going through something.

Zoey: Sorry, I went off on such a tangent there. I can't believe I said all of that. Sorry. I am not used to podcasts! You forget you're being interviewed. I just—it's funny. In some ways, in my life right now, I am incredibly confident, and everyone sees me clearly, I think. And then . . . in other ways, I feel like I am still holding back. I'm still piecing things together.

30

I've never been able to sleep when someone else is in bed with me. I can barely sleep when there *isn't* someone else in bed with me.

It was 6:12 a.m., and I was deep in a Brooklyn comedian's Instagram feed, while Henry slept next to me. He was a silent sleeper, which made me self-conscious. Oliver used to tell me I'd make "whimpering" noises in the night ("It's like there's a spirit inside you yearning to get out"). I hadn't broached the topic with Henry yet, but, at least for now, I tried to make sure he fell asleep before I did and woke up after me. So in this one sense, I felt a semblance of control.

Now that we were spending a lot of time around each other naked, it had become impossible for me to ignore just how "toned" Henry was. He worked out most evenings, typically spending about two hours in the gym, which I found completely baffling. What could one *possibly* find to busy oneself with in a gym for two hours?! I managed to stay (relatively) skinny now by not eating as much as I should. Henry ate whatever he felt like, and I was deeply jealous. Once, a few weeks after we'd returned from Paris, he ordered cookies on Seamless at 11:30 p.m., which was to me an incomprehensible act, for multiple reasons. I wanted to text Zoey about it: "Henry just ordered chocolate-chip cookies on Seamless for $8.89. That was the whole order. They're coming here in a Lyft." She would have written back: "fucker."

At 7:10 a.m., Henry woke up. I was on my back, phone resting under my arm. He reached his cold hand onto my stomach, and I flinched.

"Hey."

I turned to look at him, as he let his hand travel just south of my belly button.

"Are you free next Thursday?" I said. "Do you want to come with me to a party?"

"What party?"

"It's the after-party for some premiere. I think *Interview* magazine is throwing it. It's at the Boom Boom Room."

"Sounds chic."

I hadn't invited him to any *events* yet, though I had come close a few times. Voicing the words now, though, I felt a little embarrassed.

He moved his hand off my stomach and rolled over to the other side of the bed, taking his phone off the end table.

"Did you really just say *chic*?" I asked, aiming to reclaim my footing.

"I should be free that night," he said, checking his calendar. I was now worried it might have been a bad idea to invite him. He rubbed his eyes. "Will famous people be there?"

"Depends on what your definition of famous is," I said.

———

I walked into Cafe Cluny and scanned the room for Caroline Stevens. Even though we had met before—I had smoked a cigarette in her presence! We followed each other on Instagram!—I had forgotten the command she held in person. Yes, she was unassuming and beautiful, but it was the fact that her thoughts always seemed to be elsewhere—even if she was looking right at you—that made it hard to not feel inadequate in her presence.

It was a busy Tuesday at Cluny, and our table was squeezed between two others, making it difficult for Caroline to swivel out to greet me. Instead she just raised her hand, as if to ask a question. "Victor!"

I sat down and took off my coat, fumbling to drape it on the back of my chair. She spoke, immediately, with a quiet determination: "It's really nice to see you again." She didn't have an accent, but she spoke as if she did.

"It's great to see you, too," I said, mustering enthusiasm. "That was a . . . funny day. At the panel. How was the rest of it?"

"God, that was like a year and a half ago, wasn't it? I only stayed in the auditorium for like five minutes. Otto and I did end up sleeping together that afternoon, though, and then he made us BLTs. So it was a bit of a funny day for me, too."

"He mostly lives in Europe, right?"

"Berlin. Yeah, he's back and forth. He was working on a book there. I guess he still is, technically. I don't know." She coughed daintily. "I'm sorry, again, for being so cryptic. In my note to you."

"No, no. Please. I enjoy a mystery." I noticed there was an unopened Diet Coke can on the table.

"I never really do stuff like this," she said. "I actually kind of can't even believe I emailed you. This is out of my comfort zone." I couldn't tell if she was being earnest, or if this was some sort of act. I'd recently listened to Caroline's episode of Maddie Brooks's podcast, released when *Sparkling Day* came out, and it made me feel . . . even more intimidated? She came off as confident, impenetrable. Even Maddie seemed a bit flummoxed by her. Across from her now, it wasn't so much that I felt actively nervous, but more like I was aware I was a means to an end for her, for some purpose I wasn't able to discern yet, and that anything I had to say hardly mattered. She'd already made up her mind, whatever it was.

"I was thinking about you and . . . the Valentina Lack situation. I know we only talked about it briefly. When we met."

I winced at her name. I really tried not to think much about Valentina these days, ever since my phone call to Erica. It felt like *history*, a
short paragraph in the Wikipedia entry of my life that would hopefully
not be edited further. Though every once in a while—lying in bed next
to a sound-asleep Henry, in a waiting room at a GI doctor's office—I'd
find my way back to the aggrieved tweets, the heated conversations
with Leon, the misguided phone call. One night I couldn't sleep and
I got out of bed and dashed off an op-ed about "what I learned" from
the experience, but I couldn't get myself to email it to my friend who
worked at the *Times* Opinion section.

The waitress came to take our orders—mixed green salads with
chicken for us both—and Caroline resumed: "I've been trying to
decide what I want to do for my next book—they've been hound-
ing me—and I was thinking, *maybe it's not fiction.* I mean, *Sparkling
Day* was basically nonfiction anyway, at its core. I'm just in this
moment where I want to write things that are *true.* You get it, you're
a journalist . . ."

Did I get it?

"Anyway, I know this is weird, since you're a writer too, and this
is clearly your story—it happened to you—but I want to write a book
about the dynamic between celebrities and journalists. Just the whole
interplay and give-and-take—and how social media plays a role in it. I
was thinking it could be exciting for me to write about *you,* and about
other people who have been through similar experiences." She looked
at me, right in the eyes. "I feel like your case is so interesting because her
fans didn't care about the truth, really—the actual fact of whether she
was mistreated or not. When she tweeted, you know, 'I'm pissed about
this story,' they all came after you. Blindly. It didn't matter whether
it was grounded in anything legitimate." She laughed, and it seemed
unnatural. "And of course, I just feel like we get along well and get each
other and it would be fun."

I was not yet clear if she was asking for my permission or blessing—she of course didn't need it if she were going to write a book about the broader topic. There was an uncomfortable dryness in my cheeks. I felt like she was encroaching on my territory. I had dealt with the fallout, had forced my friends and family to endure so many excruciating conversations—but now *she* was going to write the book and take ownership of my narrative and reap the potential rewards?

She continued, "My idea, which I thought of last week, is that I could structure it with you as my 'main character.' Since you have this firsthand experience, obviously. I would conduct a series of interviews with you, which—I still need to figure all of this out—but maybe I'd have bits and pieces of the transcript of our conversation interspersed throughout."

"Wouldn't it make more sense, in that case, for me to just . . . write my own book about it?" I felt like I needed to say this, that I shouldn't just immediately acquiesce.

Caroline finally snapped open her Diet Coke can. "You could." She took a long sip of the soda. "If that's something you feel like you could do. Or want to."

Caroline had essentially won me over at the college event, but now I saw her as a bit more of an untrustworthy figure. It didn't seem surprising to me that her and Zoey had lost touch.

"Well, let me think about it," I said. "It's a big—I have to process it. I'll get back to you." She now looked almost disinterested, as if mentally already on to a different conversation, a different person, in her head.

"It's funny you and Zoey went to camp together," I continued. "I can't really picture you guys hanging out."

"It wasn't really a camp," she said. "It was a four-week creative arts program. But yeah, we snuck out one night to go smoke hookah with a few boys. That was our real bonding moment. Neither of us vibed much with the other girls." She looked bothered by something. "The three of us should get together sometime. It's been forever since I've seen her."

I nodded vigorously, even though I knew we never would do this, and so did she. My early thirties seemed increasingly characterized by this stuff: empty offers, kind phony gestures, polite smiles. In the end, we all did what was best for ourselves and rationalized it later.

When the check came, Caroline offered to pay for our meal. "Please," she said, signing the check. "You're here because of my crazy idea." She struck me as someone who usually ended up getting what she wanted.

———

I decided to walk back to my apartment after lunch; I put my AirPods in and instinctively called my mom.

"What is it?" she said.

"What?"

"You just don't usually call me in the middle of the day like this."

"I'm a surprise a minute."

"Right."

"I'm walking back from lunch with this writer. I met her a while ago at that talk I did for the college kids. She actually knows Zoey from this program they did a long time ago."

"Sounds nice."

"She wants to write a book about me. About the Valentina Lack saga. She wants to interview me."

"There's enough on that topic to fill up a whole book?"

"I don't know."

"Why would you want her to write this?"

"I don't think I would. But she's kind of an interesting person. She wrote a novel about a scam artist that got a lot of buzz. Or I guess it's a novel. It's based on real people. I still have to read the actual book. She's very pretty."

"She sounds like she has trouble coming up with her own ideas."

"Hey, it's working for her."

"So she would write a book about your life and profit from it?"

"Well, I mean, who knows what *profit* there would be. But I don't know. I haven't really thought about any of that. This just happened."

"It seems like you could just write this book yourself, if you wanted. Haven't you always wanted to write a book?"

"Yeah, I—I mean, I guess she'd do research and frame my story in the larger context of celebrity journalism in the age of social media. Or whatever." I paused. "Also, I don't think this is the kind of story I'd want to write myself."

"This sounds ridiculous. It sounds like she's trying to manipulate you."

If I was being truthful, I'd had a similar initial reaction. But the impulse to defend Caroline—or rather, to argue against my mother—had fully taken hold of me.

"I don't know. I don't even know why I'm telling you about this. It probably won't turn into anything." I arrived at my block and circled a trash can. "I don't even think I could write a whole book if I—"

"Of course you could write a book. Anyone can write a book."

"That's definitely not true."

I hadn't seen my mother in about eight months. She was supposed to come visit me in New York with Warren, but they canceled the trip a few weeks prior. All the explanation she had given was an email that read: *It was going to cost $165 to check our two bags. That's ridiculous.*

"Are you going into the office?" she asked on the phone.

"No, I'm heading back to my apartment. I have to write up this interview I did with some 22-year-old furniture designer."

"Are people interested in that?"

"I don't know, Mom. I don't care if anyone reads it."

Shortly after I returned from Paris, I took back my job at *Corridor*. I had assumed that after a year removed from it, I'd have a new sense of serenity about the day-to-day. I thought the aggravations—the passive-aggressive emails, the harassment from publicists, the social-media "discourse"—would bother me less.

Naturally, that was not the case: it all still bothered me a lot. That I had thought it would be any different was comical to me now. But the benefits of reentering this world—the return of *structure*; that I could now, again, casually invite Henry to a premiere after-party—made it feel worth it. More and more, it seemed to me that the 53-year-old I went on the strained Hinge date with had actually been pretty percep-tive: the proximity to power and glamour drew you in and infected you and didn't let you out of its grip, particularly when the alternative—an existence out at sea, your phone out of range—made you feel like you had been locked out of your life.

"I'm almost back," I said to my mom, looking up at my apartment building. I'd moved to the East Village a few months ago, and the live-wire neighborhood didn't feel like "me" at all, but I liked the contrast. There was a woman in her sixties who lived on my floor whose schedule was unexpectedly aligned with mine. Whenever she saw me on the ele-vator, or walking into the lobby, she'd say, "Where's that smile?" It was so irritating, and like something out of a bad cartoon strip, but I felt somehow I deserved it, that she was meant to serve as a reminder for me: I might never be truly happy, but I had to do my best to approxi-mate it. Sometimes I even allowed myself to believe Oliver was speak-ing to me through this neighbor: *where's that smile?*

I met Henry on the street outside of The Standard. He was dressed up, and his hair was slicked back. He really was handsome, more handsome than I was. He was wearing a skinny crimson tie, which I took in my hand.

"Do I look ready?" he said.

I gave him a brief kiss that turned into a slightly longer one. I was, it turned out, happy he was there.

"You look great," I said.

"Now if I see Leonardo DiCaprio, I'm just letting you know, all bets are off. I am going to have to tell him that I brought a *Romeo + Juliet* poster with me to college. And I may have . . . let's just say I enjoyed waking up to him each morning."

"You are not going to see Leonardo DiCaprio," I said. I thought about taking his hand as we walked toward the hotel, but I didn't.

"Are you, like, covering this event?" he asked.

"No, no, I am long past my party reporting days. They just invite me to stuff like this."

Henry followed pop culture only casually. He was five years older than me, and had two sisters, three nephews, and a niece—he was close to them all, but not in that aggravating way where you feel like you're being shown a video of little kids falling into a pile of leaves every five minutes. Henry's mom and him cooked together whenever he went back home to Michigan. He played golf with his dad.

Henry and I entered the lobby of The Standard and were told to wait in a short line outside. "*I'm on the list*," I said, without even a trace of irony. Of course, on some level, I was reviving a favorite role for a new audience tonight.

Once Henry and I made it in, I felt calmer.

Henry immediately grabbed a glass of champagne. I'd drunk only a handful of times since I returned from Paris five months ago. I wasn't "sober"—there had been one or two semi-drunken nights out with Henry—but I was picking and choosing. I wasn't drinking as a default.

"I know I probably sound like a tourist or something, but I hadn't really thought about how it's just . . . an open bar at stuff like this."

"Yeah, you start to take it for granted," I said.

Henry had surprisingly good rhythm. Even standing against a wall with me, his torso and legs vibrated in sync with the electronic track. Henry and I were still at the stage where most everything was a surprise. Sometimes it was a nice surprise—*wow, he remembered that I told him on our second date that I dyed my hair pink for three weeks in college* (he really listens to what I say!). And other times, it was a letdown, like when I realized he takes an average of six hours to respond to a text, or when he told me he didn't like Natalie Portman's acting and I responded that I legitimately wasn't sure if I could date someone who felt that way (I was joking, but only kind of!).

All in all, I was really trying to live in the moment with him—to be *present*, as some irritating dating expert on TikTok would probably advise, and to not fast-forward in my head. I made a point of not giving a real voice or weight to any of my doubts and snark, which I might have texted Zoey about in the past ("He doesn't ask me as many questions as I ask him," "He's, like, freakishly obsessed with *Schitt's Creek* . . .").

I looked around the room and pointed out various B- and C-list celebrities to Henry. "Did you watch that British spy show on Amazon last year? She played the vixen, or the one who got killed, I think." He seemed genuinely impressed.

A few of my contacts had continued to invite me to parties and events during what I thought of now as my "sabbatical year." Though when they realized I wasn't writing full-time for *Corridor* anymore, that I wouldn't be able to guarantee them coverage for their brands or movies or celebrities, I stopped getting the invites. That's when I muted former colleagues on Instagram—it was easier to pretend these kinds of events weren't even happening anymore, that no one went to them.

Of course, now that I was going to them again—as I'd clearly wanted for myself—I was reminded that the parties themselves were not even fun. There was never any food. Everyone anxiously looked past the people they were talking to, trying to see if someone "more important" might be around the corner. The celebrities didn't want to be there, and they left as soon as they'd had their picture taken enough times. Still, every time I received a new invite now, I felt elated.

I spotted my old co-worker Maya across the room, and I grabbed Henry's wrist. "I know her."

Maya was dressed in a black turtleneck and dark pants, and she was holding a fancy camera. "Victor!" She gave me a hug. "I had no idea you'd be here. *Interview* is letting me photograph this for them."

"Oh, that's amazing." I turned to my date. "This is Henry. Maya used to work at *Corridor* with me. She was a photo assistant then. But this is great. I always said you should be taking photos yourself."

"Well, this isn't exactly a highly coveted assignment. I just, like, degraded myself to get a blurry shot of John Mayer talking to Don Cheadle at the bar. I think it was John Mayer? It may have just been some random white dude."

"Yeah, this is sort of a funny one."

"I'm having a good time," Henry said.

Maya was studying Henry. "How long have you two been—?"

"We're a—what?—solid five months in, I think," I said.

"Solid five months," Henry repeated, putting his arm around me. "You sound like a sports coach."

"That is definitely the first time I've been accused of that."

"I was just thinking about the day you called me when—" Maya stopped herself.

"It's okay. He knows." In the past, I would have needed to be drunk to be confident in this sort of situation; now, I just tried to channel a "Paris Victor" energy—*did any of this really matter? Just say what you want.* I swiveled to Henry. "She was going to say 'the day Oliver died.'"

Henry nodded. "*Right*."

Maya was fidgeting with her sleeve. "Sorry, I wasn't trying to bring the mood—we're at a party!"

"It's so fine," I said. "I'm so casual about everything, it's *crazy*."

"But it seems like—you're doing all right?"

"Oh yeah. I'm very great."

"I'm going to get a refill," Henry said suddenly, spinning off.

Maya smiled at me. "He's so cute."

"Yeah, going places with him makes me feel like I'm an ogre."

"Don't say that," she said, scanning the room. "I can't believe you went *back* to *Corridor*. You had escaped. You were free! I feel so good and, like, in control of my destiny now that I'm not there. I don't have to think about any of those freaks anymore."

"Yeah, I know. I had the thought the other day that I should be disqualified from complaining about work to anyone anymore. I willingly went back!" I did feel sheepish about returning to the magazine on some level. I had made such a show of quitting—farewell Instagram post, mass emails.

Henry returned with another glass of champagne. Maya moved in and gave me a kiss on the cheek. "It was so good to see you," she said. "And to meet you, Henry." She held up her camera. "I need to get back on the prowl."

She flashed a weary smile and made her way down the stairs to the bar.

Henry and I moved close to the floor-to-ceiling window, where it was less crowded. I squinted, looking out at the Hudson River.

"She seemed nice," he said.

"Yeah, she is." I grabbed his ass with my hand. I was feeling playful and restless and loose. He moved my hand off him. "Keep it together, cowboy," he said.

I felt like being dramatic, like being a C-lister myself. We were on my turf. I really did feel glad to have him here with me. My job was where my confidence came from—*what of it?* Why was that something I had to feel embarrassed about? Something I had to deny?

"Do you want to stay here? We could also go get food somewhere else."

He frowned. "Whatever you want. Though the drinks here are free . . . Also, don't you want to say hi to Zachary Quinto?"

"Oh, we're not actually . . . friends. I just interviewed him for a story once."

"More than most people can say."

"That's true, but also—" I stopped myself. I took a quick breath and looked around the room. Maybe it was a sign of maturity—I hesitate to call it growth—that I was able to repress the urge to contradict or clarify. That I felt—in the company of this handsome man, soundtracked by this loud generic music, the sheen of glamour around us—a sense of contentment.

We were up on the roof now. It was chilly, mid-forties. Usually the cold didn't bother me, but tonight I noticed I was shivering. Henry was talking to a model named Inez—they were nestled in a banquette, both nursing glasses of champagne. They looked gorgeous, and the whole tableau was ridiculous.

I had worked hard all night to not think about Zoey. I listened to her episode of *The Maddie Brooks Podcast* a few weeks ago and was genuinely shocked when I heard my name. "We let things fester and get annoyed at our friends about the smallest, most minor bullshit, and start acting passive-aggressively, and then talk shit about them," is what she had said. I had it committed to memory. She had actually told Maddie Brooks that the two of us weren't "in regular contact."

I thought about texting Zoey now, but I didn't know what exactly to say. It had been months.

Zoey was still the first person I wanted to talk to when I had a new revelation about Henry, after I argued with my mom, when I got an amusing assignment at work.

I had a bunch of regrets. I never tried—really tried—to be kind to Tom, to give him the benefit of the doubt. I truly regretted not trying to place the Selah story in *Corridor*—*that goddamn story*. I had distanced myself and let myself get caught up in work. I think I wanted to feel like my life at work was as *important* as her life with Tom—as though that would make me feel more fulfilled.

What she said to Maddie Brooks was probably right—we should have talked about all of this, talked about it all the time. Now it was too late.

Henry was the first person I had dated since Oliver. And I guess it was a good sign that I didn't think about Oliver when I was with him. Every now and then, when he would kiss me in an elevator, or when he would suggest a Hulu show with a certain inflection, it would conjure a brief flash of Oliver. But it never lasted long. And in a strange way it was welcome—it allowed me to remember elements of Oliver I had forgotten about, minor but lovely. Henry was less nimble than Oliver—there was not the same kinetic energy—but I liked that, too. Henry was grounded. He wasn't constantly in motion.

A sick part of me wondered on occasion if my distance from Zoey now had actually allowed for this semi-healthy relationship with Henry. Rationally, I knew it didn't have to be one of them or the other—that's not how this worked. I knew it wasn't that simple. Maybe the timing was just a coincidence. But I wasn't sure. When I heard her say on the podcast she was freezing her eggs—a disclosure she had not shared with me—I couldn't help but think of it as another point of divergence. We were on different paths.

My mom now sent me links to all of Zoey's media appearances, as if I wouldn't be seeing them myself, usually with "GOOD FOR ZOEY!"

written underneath (my mom didn't know we weren't talking now). I didn't feel professionally envious of Zoey, at least not in the way I was used to when I would watch "adversaries" of mine succeed. But I did feel like Zoey was evolving—and if I felt any anxiety, it was that Zoey's ascent cast into relief that it was not clear to me at all what *I* was evolving into.

At this point in the evening, the party was winding down. The celebrities—the few who had showed up—had left. I went back inside to get a reprieve from the cold, and I walked down the stairs, making my way to the bathroom. I turned down the hallway, looked up, and saw Valentina Lack strutting in the opposite direction.

I stood still. I inhaled. It wasn't a dream. She was wearing a short purple sequined dress, and her hair was up in a loose bun. For her, this was a casual look. Her skin was noticeably smooth and resplendent.

"Oh my god," I said, before I realized quite what I was doing, or saying, and that she could hear me. She did an immediate double take.

She appeared, in a strange way, both more assured and also more subdued, more hollow, maybe even sadder, than when I'd had lunch with her years ago.

In a flash, though, she came alive. "Darling!" she exclaimed. She kissed both my cheeks, holding on to my arm with her soft hand. "It's so nice to see you." I remembered something I'd read about how celebrities address everyone they meet with a generic "It's great to see you!" so as not to offend someone they may have encountered before but don't remember.

"It's Victor. Harris. I—I wrote the *Corridor* cover story on you." I felt instantly shameful and pathetic introducing myself to her like this, groveling.

"Of course I remember!"

Her cheeriness—while probably more welcome and easier to manage than the alternative—was annoying in its own right. *Did she not remember what she had tweeted about my story?*

"I—you—" I paused. "You weren't so happy with me back then, though!" My filters had been removed. Of all the ways to broach the topic, though, this was probably one of the least smooth approaches.

"Oh goodness . . . I hardly remember," she said. It was clear she did not want a confrontation. "I remember we had a great lunch. It was your first cover story. I remember that. You told me a story about a boyfriend."

"Yeah. I was really nervous. I was so scared I was going to mess it up," I said. I felt guilty now for having introduced tension. "But you put me at ease. At least, that day you did."

She was looking beyond me now. "Well it is *so* great seeing you." She reached out and clasped one of my hands.

"Hey," I said. "I also should—I feel like we probably deserve some blame, too. So, I'm sorry. We didn't—you know, we put your quote in the headline, without all the context."

There was nothing on her face that suggested she was registering what I was saying, or even knew what I was referring to. Anger was rising in my chest. "Of course," she said. "Stay well, Victor." She moved past me toward the stairs. It killed me that I still wanted something from her.

I turned around and shouted, "Hey, *Valentina*?"

She didn't turn around, but twisted her head back slightly, looking at me from the landing.

"Did *you* write that tweet about my story? About how disappointed you were by it?"

She smiled, as if I'd just asked for the name of the perfume she was wearing. "Oh. Hmm. You know, I'd have to ask my publicist."

And then just like that she was gone. Maybe I had dreamed the entire interaction.

I started up the stairs looking for her, but didn't see her anywhere. Had she evaporated?

The encounter would seem to call for a ridiculous performance of catharsis—my screaming to the invisible moon, or sprinting across a bridge. But I felt no need to scream. It was over. Relief. I'd spent so much time the past few years obsessing over Valentina Lack. And for what? *Why?* She wasn't a real person. She didn't exist on the same earth I inhabited. Our exchange by the stairs burned in my forehead—but it was the sort of burn that almost feels soothing, that you know is only temporary. The whole time, my angst was never really about *her*. I'd known on some level that she had moved on immediately, never to think about me again. Meanwhile I'd let it fester, and it became a virus. But I was free now. I wasn't sick anymore.

It was strange—I could feel a gleefulness bubbling up inside of me. It was close to joy. If anything, I felt something resembling pity for Valentina now—or, more than that, I didn't feel any emotion about her at all. When I tried to picture her in my head, her features looked a bit blurry.

I closed my eyes. I saw a flash—clear and detailed—of the sweating, furrowed-browed Victor, waiting to interview Valentina in the restaurant. I wanted to tell him to chill the fuck out.

I should call Zoey, I thought. I remembered I'd seen on her Instagram that she was in Milan now. But she wouldn't want to talk to me. Zoey had never really understood why the Valentina fallout affected me in the way it had, why I hadn't been able to move on.

When I was ten years old and publishing my family newsletter, I interviewed my mom once for an article about the Italian restaurant we would go to almost every Sunday.

"When is the first time you went to have dinner there?" I asked her. I had a yellow lined notepad on my lap, and was writing with a purple marker.

"I don't remember," she said. She was never a chatty interview subject.

"Why do you like it?"

"Because I go with you."

"What else?"

"Because I like the food."

"Is there anyone you wish you could invite to go there with us?"

At this, she had started crying. It was instantaneous. I remember watching her cry for a few seconds, stunned and terrified. I'd never seen her cry. And never did again.

That was the first moment I recognized I wielded a certain power. What exactly that power was wasn't clear to me then. Where did it leave me when my interview subject felt angry, sad, or betrayed? Others in my situation wouldn't let it get to them—they wouldn't let themselves get invested.

I walked back out onto the roof. I sat down on a metal chair, positioned around the corner from where Henry and Inez were perched. They were still in deep conversation. I didn't feel like joining them, but I took a picture of them with my phone. It came out blurry, and I posted it to my Stories with a black-heart emoji.

I stretched my legs out and tried, even just for a few moments, to think about nothing, to clear my head. I could hear the faint sounds of the music underneath us. You know what? It wasn't just a mantra I was repeating—I *did* feel free. Present and calm. I reached out and touched my toes. I thought about the conversation I'd just had with Valentina and smiled, and then smiled harder—it hurt my mouth. How quickly, in a flash, angst and self-loathing can morph into something so funny. "Stay well, Victor." I was full-on giggling, on a metal chair, alone, outside, sober, employed, a few yards away from a man who I liked and who I liked sleeping with. It could be worse!

I opened Instagram and deleted the Story I'd put up; I realized I didn't actually feel a desire to broadcast. For some reason, this impulse felt connected to how I felt about Henry. The waters were less volatile for me right now—and I felt like I had Henry to thank for that. I didn't need to be anything other than someone he wanted to hang out with. I felt like I could manage that.

I'd worked at *Corridor*; I'd not worked at *Corridor*; I'd worked at *Corridor* again. I'd blocked accounts and muted feeds, and then unblocked them. The whole time, throughout it all, I'd always felt that what everyone was saying about me was *right*. It was exhausting to live with. No matter what I said or how I acted, I couldn't help but believe everyone else was right about me. That I didn't want to hear what they had to say because they were right. Other people knew best. I had to feel everything.

I took out my phone and texted Caroline Stevens: Hey, I thought about it and you should totally write the book. Take my story! Interview me as much or as little as you want! I'm around. As much as her book was about me, it didn't have anything to do with me.

Sitting outside, in the cold, I felt an overwhelming stillness. Not still in the sense that time had stopped or someone had pressed pause. But *still*—my head really was clear. This stillness was streaming light. *You're fine.*

I picked up my phone and called Zoey.

31

Zoey

Zoey turned off Ludlow Street and entered Cervo's. She immediately spotted the back of Victor's head at the bar. She started to walk toward him; he still hadn't seen her.

Up until she got out of the Uber a minute prior, she'd felt uneasy, like maybe it had been good for them to have this time apart—maybe it wasn't the right moment to see each other again. But now that she was here, a few feet from his unkempt brown head of hair, she felt like she had made the right decision.

"Hey, stranger," she said a bit too loudly.

He turned around and smiled, scooting his chair to the right. "They only had seats at the bar."

"Your skin looks really good," she said, taking off her coat and sitting down.

"Yeah, I've lost six pounds since the last time I saw you. I don't really drink now."

Zoey's eyes widened. "That's interesting."

"Yeah. It *is* interesting. I don't know how long I'm gonna keep it up. But I like it. You know J.Lo doesn't drink? Blake Lively, too."

"Of course I know that."

"But I'm still . . . you know. I'm still Victor. I still have *catastrophic problems.*" He was talking quickly. "I'm still—what's the saying? The more you try to run away from yourself, you're still exactly where you are."

"I don't think that's it, but I follow."

Victor turned in his chair and he took his hand in hers.

"I'm really sorry, Zoey. I just need to say it right now. Before anything else. I lost sight of . . . I was placing value on the wrong things. I wasn't taking care of myself. And that wasn't fair to you. At all. As your best—as your person." He paused. "Okay, sorry, I just had to say all of that, right off the bat."

Zoey looked for the bartender. "*I'm* still going to drink," she whispered.

"I wouldn't want it any other way."

Zoey searched for the reason she still felt a tinge of hesitation, something holding her back. She loved him. She trusted him. She could tell he was trying, that things might be different. Or maybe they wouldn't ultimately be that different. But he was trying *something*. She could feel his effort, the love he had for her.

She knew that Victor might not be her closest friend, her *person*, for the rest of her life—maybe there would be a time, years from now, in a decade even, when she had a husband and a kid, and Victor and Zoey only saw each other a few times a year. And when they did, they'd catch up on their jobs, laugh about their old friends from New York (pulling up Instagram feeds, waiting impatiently for the photos to render). She'd show him some photos of her kids; maybe he'd hang out with her kids (maybe they'd even be close)—and then after a dinner and a few glasses of warm wine he'd head to the train, or get an Uber to the airport, and then they wouldn't talk again for another four months.

And maybe that would be just fine. They'd call each other on their birthdays. They'd text each other photos when they happened upon them. They'd reminisce about their time together in New York when their lives were intertwined, when the stakes felt impossibly high, when there was no evening that wasn't dissected ad infinitum the next morning—the decade where every day felt like a week, and every weekend a year. A decade of drinking and mistakes and jealousies and more mistakes.

Or maybe she was being overly pessimistic and Victor and Zoey would be inseparable forever, through their thirties, forties, and beyond. Perhaps they'd live in apartments ten blocks from each other and meet at The Odeon once a week for breakfast.

Either path was possible.

She hadn't cried in a long time, but she felt the beginnings of tears. "Hold on a second," she said. "And order me that vermouth I like."

She got up from her chair and walked outside.

Standing on Canal Street, near a few teenagers looking at one of their phones, she took a breath and tried to compose herself. Her relationship with Victor had at times felt like the most fulfilling one in her life—at others the most frustrating. It had been impossible to watch him at certain moments. But he always saw her in a way that no one else did. He saw her as the most beautiful version of herself.

In the end, it was his voice she heard in her head; it was there when she called for it.

Zoey turned around and opened the door to find her friend.

ACKNOWLEDGMENTS

I often skip ahead to peek at the acknowledgments section—it's usually when I'm about a third of the way through a novel and overcome with "what's this author's deal?!" curiosity. If that's you right now: *hey, we're the same.*

You would not be holding this book were it not for the belief, support, and commitment of my agent, Elias Altman. I am extremely grateful for his insight and guidance.

I feel immensely lucky to have found the incredible James Melia, who edited this book. James, you're a gem, and you've made this process an utterly joyful experience.

Everyone who has worked on this book at Simon & Schuster has been so exceedingly wonderful, thoughtful, and lovely. My sincerest thanks to Matt Attanasio, Jennifer Bergstrom, Sally Marvin, Mackenzie Hickey, Lucy Nalen, Sophie Normil, Caroline Pallotta, Jamie Selzer, Jaime Putorti, and John Vairo.

Thank you to the teachers from my childhood and young adulthood, in particular: Mary Beth Fletcher, Connemara Wadsworth, Liz Bedell, and Fred Strebeigh. When I was in second grade, Mrs. Fletcher "published" my *Tree House Kids* series (presumably at a Kinko's, in gorgeous laminate); I feel now that she saw something in me that I hadn't identified yet. Connemara, you emboldened me as a preteen to write what was in my heart (at the time, a very long story about a super-model who doubled as a spy). Liz, you made me the writer I am today. Prof. Strebeigh, I wrote your advice about endings down on a piece of paper and still have it on my desk to this day.

Thank you to Graydon Carter and Chris Rovzar, who both took a chance on me and believed in me and changed the direction of my life.

Aimée Bell, your office has been a safe haven for the past decade. I can't thank you enough for everything.

Thank you to Justin Bishop and Dan Watkins, for your time and expertise.

I feel absurdly blessed to have so many close friends in my life whom I consider family. Thank you to Alex Trow, Allison Battey, Amanda Meister, Amber Thrane, Amitha Raman, Amy Davis, Andrew Gomez, Andy Diez, Ben Abramowitz, Caity Weaver, Cari Tuna, Carrie Brody, Chiara Marinai, Dan Aron, Eli Hill, Emily Jane Fox, Greg Nortman, Jordan Rosenbloom, Julie Miller, Katie Allen, Kia Makarechi, Liz Zink, Louisa Strauss, Matt McIntyre, Patrick Barrett, Paul Needham, Rachel Geronemus, Rob Bruce, Steve Rabbitt, and Zach Story. This book is as much yours as it is mine.

Nathan, thank you for the wisdom and the levity. Janet, thank you for being my Dua Lipa. Andrea, it's like we're the same person—thank you for always knowing what to say. Marissa, thank you for picking me up time and time again.

Alyssa, let's be ten minutes late for the rest of our lives. Thank you for being the most generous reader, gut check, and ally through this journey. I'd follow you anywhere.

Thank you to my extended family for being in my corner. Linda, thank you for always encouraging my creative spirit. Grandma, I recalled memories of you often when writing.

Brett, your humor, good nature, and perspective are so appreciated—always, and especially when I was starting work on this book.

Sam, nothing I write here will be sufficient. Thank you for being my north star. There is no way I could have done this without you.

Dad, you're who I strive to be. I feel so proud to have your last name. Thank you for your belief in me.

Mom, I hardly know where one of us ends and the other starts.